GONE
BY
MORNING

Also available by Michele Weinstat Miller

Widows-in-Law
The Thirteenth Step: Zombie Recovery

GONE
BY
MORNING

A NOVEL

MICHELE WEINSTAT MILLER

CROOKED
LANE

NEW YORK

Published in the United States by Crooked Lane Books, an imprint of The Quick Brown Fox & Company LLC.

Crooked Lane Books and its logo are trademarks of The Quick Brown Fox & Company LLC.

Library of Congress Catalog-in-Publication data available upon request.

ISBN (hardcover): 978-1-64385-740-4
ISBN (ebook): 978-1-64385-741-1

Cover design by Meghan Diest

Printed in the United States.

www.crookedlanebooks.com

Crooked Lane Books
34 West 27th St., 10th Floor
New York, NY 10001

First Edition: August 2021

10 9 8 7 6 5 4 3 2 1

To my family

PART I

1

T HE TRAIN SQUATTED at Forty-Second Street/Times Square. Going nowhere. Tourists and commuters squeezed in the double doors, filling every inch of space. The scent of marijuana seeped in with an early-morning smoker, the smell repelling Kathleen. It was the smell of a troubled person, inebriated before ten AM, evidence of a problem.

Kathleen was grateful to have a seat instead of standing like a clove in a garlic press. She glanced around, observing a young lady who'd sidled through the crowd to perch in front of her. The bullring hanging from the girl's septum was entirely wrong for her. Bullrings weren't Kathleen's favorite fashion look in the best case, not that they lacked a place in the fantasies of men. But this girl's face was too long and skinny. The ring morphed her nose into a snout.

Kathleen cringed inwardly at her own harsh judgment—her mind had a mind of its own. It had once been her business to judge the beauty of women, and their stability, and sometimes Kathleen wanted to shake sense into random people.

Kathleen exchanged a momentary smile with the young woman before averting her eyes, imagining the girl's mother forcing herself to remain silent about her daughter's choices. One disapproving look could push a daughter toward twenty more piercings. At sixty-eight years old, with a longer runway of life behind than ahead of her, Kathleen wished more than anything that she'd been there for her own daughter's poor decisions. Kathleen brushed aside a moment of deep loneliness and regret. Self-pity was not a good look on her either. Better an old woman with a bullring than that.

"Stand clear of the closing doors, please." A disembodied voice spoke from above. "Thirty-Fourth Street/Pennsylvania Station next."

A latecomer slipped in, holding the door open for the person behind him.

Kathleen looked toward the laughter of a rosy-cheeked family in souvenir T-shirts and Yankees hats who were amused by their slow New York subway experience. They were hoping for stories to tell. She heard the hard edges of Dutch or German when they spoke to each other.

Kathleen's phone vibrated in her hand. The City's harsh emergency ring tone sounded. Akin to a World War II air raid siren, it echoed through the car, the alert going off on many phones. Someone's hand shot out, catching the closing door, keeping it open as if he realized he'd forgotten something at home and needed to get out.

Kathleen looked down to read her phone. Her heart pounded in her chest. Bullring girl peered up from her own phone at the same moment as Kathleen. Their eyes met. Fear.

Word-dominoes fell through the length of the car: "Getting off." "Excuse me." "Getting off!" An edge of hysteria in the voices.

The crowd moved toward the doors.

"What's going on?" asked the man sitting next to Kathleen as she began to rise.

Kathleen showed him the screen of her phone:

CNN Alert: There are initial reports of an explosion in the New York City Subway System.

Below it, the City's official emergency notice:

Notify NYC: Due to police activity at 34th Street, avoid subway travel in that vicinity. Expect mass transit delays.

Her muscles bunched for flight, Kathleen took her place among the people heading toward the doors. She tried to stay calm, telling herself there were hundreds of miles of subway. Odds were they were safe, even if the explosion was on Thirty-Fourth Street, one stop away. But no part of the subway system was as enticing as Times Square. She was stuck, waiting to move, at the heart of a terrorist bull's-eye. Aboveground was where they all needed to be.

"Move, move, move!" heavy-hipped police officers shouted, their handcuffs and keys clanging noisily against them as they ran down the stairs to the Times Square platform, trying to get through the crowd.

Seas parted for the cops, the commuters bunching together on the sides of the stairs to open a corridor. Kathleen held tight to the banister, making sure she kept her balance as the cops passed and the crowd jostled her. She was in good physical shape for her age but knew a fall would be worse for her than for a younger person. And more likely to happen.

She warily scanned her surroundings with each step upward. Explosions came in sets, like the one in London, where the bombs emptied out the trains before hitting a bus, or the one in Brussels that hit a train and an airport. Kathleen climbed, not really knowing if she was headed away from danger or toward it.

Just then, Kathleen heard a boom. Below. Displaced air hit the crowd. Screams from the platform. Screams around her. Kathleen cried out, too, startled into an upward lurch that threw her into the back of a man on the step above her. She grasped a handful of his back to balance herself. He didn't seem to notice. The throng sped upward, panic replacing the slow and steady evacuation. More police were running down, toward the noise, shouting louder at the civilians as the police aisle narrowed. "*Move it. Move! Move! Move!*"

The crowds lurched faster. A wisp of metallic black smoke above their heads raced them up the stairs. Kathleen ran, cradled by the crowd scuffling upward, stepping on each other's heels from the sheer closeness. Her muscles screeched as the mob sprinted and she thankfully kept pace.

She heard a young child cry, a woman calling to him shrilly, "Go, go."

The woman had a toddler in one of her arms while an overwhelmed boy of about four years old strained against her, nearly in temper-tantrum mode. The mother was struggling to keep the boy moving. He didn't understand the danger. He was tangling up and pulling back, becoming long armed and dead weight to keep his mom from dragging him.

Kathleen released the safety of her banister and took his hand. "I've got him," she said to the mother, then looked into the boy's wet eyes. "Don't worry. I've got you."

The boy held tight to Kathleen's hand, cooperative for some reason, and she climbed alongside the young woman who carried his younger sibling. Kathleen noticed now that a man in the crowd above them had a stroller held high as he climbed.

At the top of the stairs, the man who'd carried the stroller left it with an infant still sleeping inside. The boy stepped on the plastic runner at its back. With a quick thank-you, the woman was gone, two babies piled inside the stroller meant for one. Kathleen paused to catch her breath.

CHAPTER

2

IT WAS A warm summer morning, the light slanting brightly on
Forty-Second Street from the east. A six-story-tall male model
pranced on a building, selling underwear. Emergency vehicles
had blocked off Eighth Avenue in front of the Port Authority
Bus Terminal. Cops with assault rifles and revolvers in hand
were sprinting toward the subway entrances from all directions
and tracking alongside police cars. Civilians flowed out of office
buildings and the subway, milling and taking in the field of
ambulances, SWAT trucks, and police cars.

The crowd watched but seemed to reach consensus in unison:
they would head out on foot to their neighborhoods, where they
could lock their doors and be safe inside, no matter how long it
took to walk there. Living tendrils of tension and sorrow moved
from the high-risk tourist area along side streets. It was obvious
that some people wouldn't be getting home today, although no
one in the crowd knew the extent of it. Tens of thousands of
people trying to text, call, and check the internet had crashed
the cell signal.

More wailing ambulances arrived at the subway entrance
a block south of where Kathleen stood. She turned away and
walked north. She would only be in the way if she stayed.

Kathleen walked most of the way home, the subways shut
down until the NYPD and Homeland Security could ensure that

the threat was over. There were no cabs in midtown. Without usable internet, Uber must be spinning around like a malfunctioning robot.

Kathleen wanted to walk anyway, needing to burn off her nervous energy. She walked with various strangers along the way, hiking from Fiftieth Street to West Seventy-Second beside an Asian woman with a baby in a stroller. She strode ten blocks up Central Park West with an old man, stooped over and fast-walking in a warm-up suit befitting an Olympian. He told her where he'd been when the explosions happened and she told him where she'd been.

He gave forth a gravelly humph when he heard her story. "You walked with angels today."

After two hours, Kathleen stopped at a hot dog stand at 110th Street and Central Park West, but the food fell like a brick into her belly. She took a few bites, drank half an iced tea, and tossed it all in a corner garbage can. She resumed her hike north, downhill through the Harlem Valley and uphill in Washington Heights.

There was a hush over the city once Kathleen arrived in her neighborhood: Inwood. The northernmost tip of Manhattan. Upstate Manhattan, she sometimes told people. Her feet and legs ached from the seven miles of unyielding cement underfoot. She was as happy as she'd ever been to arrive at the cocoon of home.

She turned on NY1, the same station she'd watched non-stop on 9/11. In 2001, she'd lived in a Tribeca apartment, one flight up from her business in a doorman building where no one asked questions. All residents had to leave the area, which lacked breathable air. She'd walked with a scarf held to her mouth and nose through the dissipating cloud of pulverized buildings and people. She'd been lucky enough to snag a hotel room on West Seventy-Second Street that day because of her friendship with the hotel manager. Crowds camped out on sofas in the hotel's lobby, not so lucky. The bridges and tunnels were shut tight, barring anyone in or out on that first night.

Now, gazing as if hypnotized, Kathleen stood in front of the flat-screen TV in her ample living room. Two soft couches sat catty-corner to each other. Under a deeply grained oak coffee table, an area rug covered a shiny oak floor. Afternoon sun streamed through the windows, which were on a high enough floor to allow the privacy of treetops without blocking the light.

A ribbon of headlines ran at the bottom of the TV screen. Two explosions. Times Square and Penn Station. Dozens dead. When she saw the photos, her sadness deepened and her anxiety for her friends and family ramped up. From the moment she'd reached safety on Forty-Second Street, she'd wanted to see the Facebook safety check-ins. They were usually ridiculous in a place as big as New York City, where millions of people would check in even if they were nowhere near the site of an attack. But it wasn't ridiculous when there had been an attack with mass casualties, the one New Yorkers had feared since 2001.

In an alcove area meant to be a dining room, Kathleen had set up a home office with a computer station, bookshelves, and a plush reclining chair. Kathleen preferred the eat-in kitchen for meals, even if she had company, so she had no need for a dining room. She sat at her desk and clicked into Facebook. Her profile appeared on her PC monitor: a photograph of a woman in her twenties with freckles, full cheeks, and short auburn hair stared back at her with a wry smile. She bore no resemblance to Kathleen, whose own skin was luminous and lightly wrinkled, her cheekbones prominent, gray-white hair cut to just below the nape of her neck. Kathleen was attractive. But she was by no means a young woman who'd recently graduated with a master's degree from a Wisconsin university like the woman in her Facebook photo.

*   *   *

Kathleen entered Emily's name. A photo of Emily appeared, twenty-six, wearing jeans and sneakers. She was crouched next to a half-grown golden retriever with a little girl of two and a half between her knees.

Kathleen paused, appreciating Emily's ash-brown curls, a lighter version of her mother's hair. Emily had recently cut her hair short, haphazardly, in a cute, longer-in-front style. Kathleen knew she was being objective when she appreciated Emily's beauty. Emily had an inner glow and sparkling gray eyes that took Kathleen's breath away, creating a longing that she carefully hid when she was in Emily's presence. Kathleen more easily got away with her obvious adoration of Emily's daughter, Skye, with her wheat-colored curls and eyes and glorious laugh. Everybody loved babies.

Kathleen scanned Emily's page, seeing nothing about her whereabouts. She was probably working at crisis pace at City Hall, a job that Kathleen had greased the wheels for her to have. Not that Emily knew it. Emily thought Kathleen, named Sophie Monsey for Facebook and Instagram purposes, was a college friend she couldn't remember meeting. Emily thought Sophie had graduated with a bachelor's from NYU the same year as her and moved back to her home state of Wisconsin. Kathleen had grabbed an anonymous girl's Getty image two years ago and created a Facebook page with a Gmail address she'd set up for that purpose. Emily was too polite to ever acknowledge that she didn't remember meeting the young woman who'd friended her.

Kathleen had named herself Sophie after looking up the most popular girl's names twenty-six years ago. As Sophie, she'd reached out to Emily enough times, commenting, sharing, and messaging her about trivia, that Emily had likely forgotten she never knew her. They'd become good friends, although Emily thought they lived in distant states now. It was Sophie who'd told Emily to apply to a City Hall job she'd seen online, sending Emily the posting. Kathleen had made a few confidential telephone calls to old friends once Emily said she'd applied so she could at least get an interview.

Now Kathleen wrote Emily on Messenger. **Are you okay? Heard about the attack.**

Kathleen knew Emily pictured her in a house in the woods of Wisconsin. Emily had no idea her friend was typing in Manhattan, age spots on the back of her veined hands. Kathleen intended to keep it that way.

CHAPTER

3

Emily walked on the edge of a herd of staff and security that surrounded Mayor Derick Sullivan, who stood a head above even the tallest member of his dark-suited NYPD security detail. The temperature was perfect for a June day, upper seventies and sunny. The leaves of City Hall Park's huge old trees rustled in the cooling breeze, cicadas humming in rhythm. A whiff of salt floated in from the East River half a mile away.

On Broadway, a platoon of cops lined up outside the wrought-iron fence that encircled City Hall. Sirens and helicopter blades chopped the air. But stores were open and people were doing oddly regular things, walking their dogs, taking their kids to playgrounds, and lining up at Starbucks. Emily could hear the music from the break-dancers who entertained tourists at Brooklyn Bridge Plaza at the opposite side of City Hall. She found it hard to imagine that the tourists were in the mood.

The people Emily passed on the street had a darkness in their eyes, quiet, mournful, watchful. They were all starting to get the death toll on their phones. It was the children that ripped at Emily the most. There were some middle school kids missing from a school she herself had attended on West Seventy-Seventh Street. They'd been on a field trip, traveling to a Broadway showcase. She could imagine their anxious parents waiting for word now. She had to push away the thought of how she would feel if she were among them, waiting for Skye.

Emily entered a glass structure manned by two uniformed security officers. Her phone rang. Hector, Skye's father. She flashed her ID card and bypassed the X-ray conveyor belt that scanned visitor briefcases and pocketbooks. The metal detector buzzed repeatedly as Emily and the others walked through. She exited a second door, held open by the person in front of her, and entered a plaza at the foot of City Hall within the fenced-off perimeter.

"Is everyone okay?" she asked Hector, holding her phone to her ear as she climbed the sweeping City Hall stairs.

Hector worked nights as a chef at a boutique hotel in SoHo, so he would have been out of harm's way, just waking up. But his mother worked at a midtown office and he had three younger sisters, one a student at the CUNY Graduate Center not far from Times Square.

"My sisters were still home when it happened. My mother was at the office and walked home. What about yours?"

"My mom's fine. She was supposed to go to a doctor's appointment with Carl today and didn't come downtown."

"A friend from work is picking me up later and we're driving down. I'll get Skye from day care before I go. I can bring her to my mom's if you have to work late."

"I really appreciate that. Thank you."

Emily followed Mayor Sullivan and the rest of their group into the soaring, domed rotunda. Floating marble staircases led to a columned mezzanine overhead. She hung up, grateful she hadn't needed to ask Hector for help with Skye. She couldn't have hoped for a better partner to raise a kid with. On a day like today, she needed to be a part of the mayor's team, staying as late as needed. Everyone would have understood if she'd needed to leave work to pick up her kid, but she knew that was no match for being there during an emergency.

Mayor Sullivan paused to give quiet instructions to Martha. Dark-complexioned and skinny, Martha was the mayor's press secretary and Emily's boss. She virtually thrummed with energy all the time, but even more so today. Emily saw stress and determination on Martha's and all her coworkers' faces. It didn't take a rocket scientist to know this was the mayor's big test. His career was on the line. Maybe even his sense of purpose in life was at stake. He had probably imagined this scenario many times. Emily knew how important it was that he do a good job.

It was also close to presidential primary season. The mayor had needed to fly back to New York from New Hampshire when the explosions happened. He'd been campaigning and had a fair shot at winning the nomination. The terror attack would be either his campaign's viral miracle or its never-ending nightmare. No one knew when or if the laser beam of public scorn would end up pointing his way—if he made a mistake, if he missed a cue that cost lives, if he were perceived as insensitive. That had to be heavy on the mayor's mind. He was only human.

The press office was on the first floor, a desk-filled room where light streamed in through tall windows. TV monitors along one wall played multiple news stations. The phones were already ringing, reporters calling. Before coming to City Hall, Emily had worked at an online local news site, first as an intern and then as a reporter. When the site went bankrupt, she landed a job in public affairs at Con Edison. For two years, she'd spent much of her time explaining power outages to angry callers and standing under a sweltering tent, handing out logo swag at street fairs. She'd been lucky to eventually land a job as deputy press secretary at City Hall. It had been excellent timing for her—she'd been soul-searching about how she could use her journalism and communications degrees to do more good in the world.

Now, the worst kind of emergency had come, and she needed to behave like a leader. When terrible things happened, she had to consciously choose between taking responsibility and expecting someone else to take care of her. The latter was not an option if she wanted a career in politics.

"Emily," Martha said, "you have the mayor's schedule?"

Emily sat at her desk. "Everything's canceled. Decks cleared for the press conference."

Roger Merritt entered the room, grabbing a piece of candy from a bowl on the receptionist's desk before heading their way. He leaned back against the empty desk of a staffer who'd taken a leave of absence to work for the campaign. Roger looked more like a politician than the mayor. Tall, with a bronze golf tan, he had a full head of silver hair that gleamed preternaturally for a man in his fifties. Emily had googled him when she'd first come to City Hall. He was "old money," born rich. Based on Emily's observation, that seemed to bestow a full head of hair on men way past middle age, unless they were English royalty.

Roger was a powerful lobbyist, although he was mostly referred to as a "political strategist" if his name came up. He was with Mayor Sullivan as often as the most senior staff and wielded more power. He'd helped the mayor get elected to progressively more powerful positions since Sullivan began his career as a community board member in Queens. Roger made money from clients who used him to get access to the mayor. If Mayor Sullivan became president, all the people in this room, including Emily, would likely go with him to the White House. And Roger would know all of them, access worth millions instead of hundreds of thousands. It would also mean world-size power. If there was one thing Emily had learned in her stint as a reporter and now working at City Hall, it was that money and power went hand in hand.

"We're getting flack about the mayor being out of town when the attack happened," Roger said to Martha.

Martha looked askance at Roger. "So much for trying to build a relationship with the press corps."

She said it with snark, but then looked to one of the flat-screen TVs. Tears pooled in her eyes. Emily followed Martha's gaze to a video of stunned parents at the middle school.

Emily swallowed hard, wishing she could unsee the look on their faces. She spoke to Roger. "The mayor was back here in three hours. He never lost contact."

Martha looked from Emily to Roger, all business again. "We'll make sure the media knows that."

Emily turned to pick up her phone. "The mayor will speak at five PM Eastern," she told a reporter who had a thick French accent.

Reporters were calling from all over the world, and her job was to say nothing quotable at this point. People didn't realize how much of a press officer's job it was to make sure City Hall *wasn't* quoted . . . until they wanted to be. Martha spoke to Max, a deputy press secretary like Emily. "I need you to work with Operations to set up the press conference at NYU hospital."

"Got it," Max said from the desk next to Emily's.

"Emily, call the press officers for Transit, NYPD, and FDNY and tell them to refer all inquiries directly to City Hall. We need centralized messaging."

Emily normally covered the uniformed services, NYPD and FDNY, and Max covered transit and transportation issues. So, this meant they were working as a team on the subway attack. Max seemed enthusiastic about that. He was a nice-looking guy, a state senator's son with dark hair and long-lashed blue eyes, but Emily didn't want to mix business and pleasure. And he'd fallen squarely in the friend zone as she'd gotten to know him.

Martha looked down at her phone and then back up at them. "Meeting in the COW, five minutes."

At mezzanine level above the rotunda's floating staircases, the COW—short for Committee of the Whole—was where City Council committees had met in the nineteenth century. But it had been a mayoral conference room for as long as anyone could remember. A round table sat at its center, and dignitary portraits in gilt frames lined the walls. The mayor and Roger were in a heated discussion at the far side of the room next to a marble fireplace.

At six foot seven inches, Mayor Sullivan had the limbs of a daddy longlegs. He had a generous smile of bright white teeth and charisma that shaped his awkwardness into approachability. When he spoke to people, even for a moment, he made them feel they had one hundred and ten percent of his attention. None of that was on display now as he cursed at Roger, the governor's name threaded like pearls on a string of profanity.

"He's just afraid you'll do a Giuliani on him," Roger told the mayor, eyes flashing.

The mayor whisper-shouted, "This is a City issue, goddammit."

Emily sat in the second row of chairs surrounding the conference table, the deputy mayors and agency commissioners taking seats at the table. New York politics were tricky. She'd been in elementary school when Giuliani was mayor, but she'd later learned how he'd overshadowed Governor Pataki after 9/11. The governor had been left looking like he was photobombing in every shot, trying to get attention at the expense of the victims.

The FBI, Homeland Security, MTA, and the federal Department of Transportation began announcing themselves on a speakerphone as they came on the conference line.

"Okay, let's get started," the mayor said as he sat down at the table.

An NYPD chief in uniform stood and spoke from the second row near Emily. "For those of you who don't know me, I'm Chief Fred Reilly. I will be embedded at City Hall for the duration of this crisis."

Emily had worked with Chief Reilly before and found him competent and approachable.

"We've reviewed the video feed," he continued. "One man planted the bombs. It looks like he acted alone. He placed the first bomb in a subway garbage pail at Thirty-Fourth Street, and the other was in a suicide vest. The bomber is dead, pending identification."

Mayor Sullivan leaned forward. "So, the threat is over?"

"We believe so. We've inspected every subway station in Manhattan. We'll have the whole system done by the end of the afternoon."

A tinny voice spoke up from the speaker. "Mr. Mayor, this is ASAC Gendell from the FBI. There was no uptick in terror cell chatter prior to the attack. No one has claimed responsibility. ISIS generally waits to make sure the killer is dead before taking credit. So, it's too early to say definitively, but we believe he was a lone wolf, potentially ISIS inspired, of course. We'll remain on high alert, but we believe the danger is over."

"Is there any word on who he was?" Mayor Sullivan asked.

"Not yet," Chief Reilly said. "But I can guarantee you this. The NYPD has dozens of cameras in the subway stations and all over Herald Square and Times Square, plus private security cameras in the commercial establishments. By the end of the day, we'll not only know who he was but where he lived, where he went to school, and where he got his molars pulled."

4

Kathleen hadn't heard from Emily, but she guessed she'd been at work by the time of the first nine-thirty explosion. It spoke well of the young woman that she wasn't checking her social media at a time like this. Still, Kathleen would feel better when she knew for sure that everything was okay.

Kathleen drank Earl Grey tea as she watched the news, knowing her binge watching was a ridiculous compulsion. In times of greatest powerlessness and danger—meaning every time there was a major terrorist attack or mass shooting—Kathleen obsessed about learning everything she could: how things had unfolded, even how people had died or survived. It was as if knowing the details made her less powerless, preparing her to survive when it was her turn.

Deep down, she believed she was going to have a turn. It didn't matter that she lived a quiet life that minimized the risk of premature death. Given her life history, she sometimes felt as if she were a haunting spirit who mistakenly thought she was alive. Like Bruce Willis in *The Sixth Sense*, one day she would find out that her improbable life had all been a delusion. She'd really died or gone irreversibly insane a long time ago, at a time when any bookie would have placed odds on her life ending badly. Yet the reality was that she'd kept living, and living well, for many years now. It had been a close call for her today. But it was getting a little late for a premature death.

Still, when really bad things happened, she always found herself Velcroed to cable news. And in recent years, she'd added a computer to the mix, so she could check the latest unconfirmed information on Twitter and see bystander videos too.

Kathleen forced herself to get up and away from the TV. Her apartment was spacious for one within a nondescript building of thirty rent-stabilized apartments. She'd combined two apartments, taking down walls and opening up the space. When she'd retired, she hadn't abandoned comfort. She had enough money saved for moderate comforts for the rest of her life. But she'd never wanted the attention of wealth. Most of the tenants in the building didn't even know she owned the building.

She had once been a tenant in a run-down version of a building like this on the Lower East Side, one that had since been gut renovated, apartment by apartment, as the rent-stabilized tenants were forced out or died. She'd seen ads for apartments there, renting now for five thousand dollars or more, on a block that was once known for its open-air heroin and cocaine markets. When she'd lived there, addicts in Alphabet City used to joke that Avenue C stood for coke and Avenue D for dope. Her days as a tenant, always behind on the rent, felt like another life completely. She was grateful she'd been able to leave that life behind like the bad dream it was.

Unfortunately, she'd left her most cherished things behind too. She'd never completely forgiven herself for that. Or gotten over it.

Kathleen returned to the TV as the news anchor resumed talking after a commercial break. "This just in. We have some video of the bomber right before he placed one of the bombs into a garbage bin on the subway platform at Thirty-Fourth Street. The NYPD has not yet identified him. If you recognize him, you can call the number at the bottom of the screen: 212-555-8980. The NYPD asks that you *not* call 911; 911 must remain open for emergencies."

The video was grainy, but Kathleen stepped closer to the TV, as she knew a million people were doing right now. She studied the young man—a ten-second video loop played repeatedly. He strode from the bottom of the subway stairs onto a crowded platform. A group of preteens with blurred faces stood nearby among the commuters. The man walked to the garbage, looked around, put a backpack in the bin, and walked away. No one turned to look at him.

Kathleen wondered how soon afterward the explosion had happened. Was she seeing the dead on-screen too? The man looked toward the camera and she studied him; young, white, maybe still a teenager. He seemed fit and had a short haircut, but she didn't think he was military.

She didn't recognize him. Not that she'd expected she would.

* * *

The sun dipped behind the trees of Inwood Hill Park outside Kathleen's window, throwing the living room into shadow. Her doorbell rang. She asked who it was and heard Emily's name through the door. A weight of worry lifted off her. In the doorway, Emily's eyes were sunken in. Skye was fast asleep in her stroller, a thumb in her mouth.

Emily appeared exhausted. She smiled sadly at Kathleen, the way people did at funerals and after terror attacks. She seemed relieved, as if she'd worried about Kathleen too.

Emily put down her shopping bag from the fruit store on Broadway and hugged Kathleen. "I'm going to take your phone number," Emily said. "It's ridiculous that I couldn't check on you to make sure you were all right."

"I'm glad *you're* all right," Kathleen said. "You didn't have to worry about me."

"I just stopped by to make sure you got home okay. You mentioned you had an appointment downtown."

They talked, standing in Kathleen's doorway, not sitting-down, hanging-out friends. If they'd been the same age, that barrier would have broken down more easily.

"I was on the train. Too close," Kathleen said. "I had to walk home from Forty-Second Street."

"Wow, you *were* close. Were you there?"

"I heard it, but I didn't see anything, thank goodness."

"That's a long walk. How do you feel?"

"I feel like my gym workouts paid off. It wasn't a bad walk, physically. It took about five hours. Do you know anything about who he was?"

"Not yet," Emily said. "There's no match on his fingerprints, so that means he didn't have a criminal record. We think he might have been a boogaloo boi—you know, the ones in the Hawaiian shirts. It was over eighty degrees. He looked innocent enough, like he'd just come off a cruise ship. We don't know his motive."

"Those poor children who were killed . . . and their parents," Kathleen said, tearing up. She took a deep breath, steadying her voice. She wasn't on crying terms with Emily.

Emily took a breath too.

Kathleen asked, "How was the subway coming home?"

"They're running on a limited schedule. I had to take the One."

"You must be hungry," Kathleen said. "Do you want to come in? I was about to order."

"No, no. Thanks. I have to put the baby to bed. And dozens of emails came in while I was on the train."

*   *   *

Shortly after nine, Kathleen unloaded a plastic container of Chinese food and a cardboard box of rice at a tray table in the living room, where she already had a plate and silverware laid out. Lacking the patience for Rachel Maddow to get to the point, Kathleen switched the channel from MSNBC to CNN.

"We now know the bomber was named Jackson Mattingly," said the anchor. "He was twenty years old. The police still have no information about his motive. There was apparently no manifesto or social media posting to warn of the attack. We will bring you more information as it arrives."

Her phone buzzed. A photo of Sharon appeared, her name under it. It had been a long time since Kathleen had heard from her old friend, and she guessed Sharon was calling to check on her. Kathleen picked up.

"Hey. How are you? Are you okay?"

"I could be better, Kat," Sharon replied.

Only old friends called her Kat, a lifelong nickname she'd outgrown in recent years.

"You weren't there?" Kathleen asked, her voice hushing with concern.

"No, no. But I need to speak to you. In person. Can I come over now?"

"O-kay," Kathleen stretched out the word, mystified. But she had no job to wake up for in the morning. She didn't mind an unexpected visit. "I'll be here."

Keeping herself busy while waiting for Sharon, she sat at the computer in her office alcove, half listening to a panel of celebrity psychologists and ex-FBI agents on the TV in the living room.

"At this point," a former FBI agent said, "Homeland Security is trying to ascertain whether he had any accomplices. And, as always, they're looking for the flash and the boom." He motioned as if creating two silos for the flash and boom with the knife edge of his hands. "The agents are going to ask themselves whether there were signs of the killer's desire and capability to do this, and whether they failed to interdict it before the flash became a boom."

Kathleen looked back to watch him talk momentarily, then swiveled to her PC. It was the psychologist's turn now to say the same things shrinks said every time there was a mass killing. She listened while she opened her small-business program and began paying bills for the building electronically.

She finished up an hour later and wondered what was taking Sharon so long. She was never the type to be late. Even when she was young, Sharon had been dependable, never any trouble if she booked a job. She'd been one of Kathleen's favorites.

They'd met when Sharon was still in college. She was an international student from Eastern Europe, although she lacked even a hint of an accent. Sharon had started tricking to make ends meet. She was ripe to be picked off by a pimp, but she'd run into one of Kathleen's employees at a club. The woman who introduced Sharon to Kathleen hadn't stayed with Kathleen long, but Sharon had been a keeper. No drugs. No personality conflicts. A hard worker. Loyal.

She was a lot like Kathleen in those ways. Kathleen had found it impossible to get a regular job after prison. She'd tried to get office jobs. And retail. But she couldn't get past the box you checked on the employment application that asked whether you'd ever been convicted of a crime. And a female convicted felon was greeted with even more skepticism than a male felon. The idea of a female criminal was so far from the experience of most people that female ex-cons were as alien as a new gender. And hers wasn't just any crime. Homicide wasn't exactly on an employer's checklist of desired experience.

So, Kathleen's first job out of prison had been as a "spa" receptionist. Her boss was a friend from prison, and she covered for Kathleen with her parole officer, who never knew she worked at an escort service. Kathleen had used her time in prison to get clean, five years clean by the time she came out. That earned her some leeway with her PO, and it made her a trustworthy addition to her former cell mate's business. Thankfully, Kathleen's parole officer didn't ask too many questions about the job. He knew what an impossible bind a felony conviction put you in.

When Kathleen's boss was sidelined by breast cancer, Kathleen had taken over the business gradually, supporting her old friend financially as a matter of honor and loyalty until she died.

Kathleen had been in charge for a couple of years before she met Sharon. The young woman was smart and elegant. Kathleen would have sworn Sharon would eventually turn the page, find a rich husband or end up with a PhD or both, and move away, with no one the wiser about her youthful sex work. But it hadn't turned out that way for Sharon. Twenty years later and she was still hooking and dancing, last Kathleen had heard.

The Life left an indelible mark on some girls. Maybe that mark was scar tissue. Kathleen had never thought she was hurting anyone in her days as a madam. But she wasn't so sure anymore. She would have wished for a better life for Sharon.

Kathleen looked at the time on her phone. It didn't seem like Sharon was coming. They rarely saw each other and only occasionally caught up by phone. Maybe Sharon needed money. But that seemed out of character, even though Kathleen wouldn't have thought twice about trusting Sharon with a loan. She wondered whether the subway attack had triggered some inner terror for Sharon and she just needed somebody to talk to. But Sharon had never been the type to open up in that way, at least not to her.

She stared at the news for a couple of minutes, keeping it on mute. More of the same videos of the perpetrator, people taken away in ambulances, a burst of fire in a train station. Cable news had begun recycling videos, milking the story when there was nothing to add to it. She turned off the TV and headed to bed. She thought she wouldn't be able to sleep after the frightening day, but she fell into the blackness of sleep the moment her head hit the pillow.

5

CARL SAT IN his favorite recliner chair, up late. He was tired at all the wrong times. Even though the city was in an uproar, he'd been too tired by midafternoon to stay awake. Now he couldn't sleep because of the nap. His wife, Lauren, had gone to bed over an hour ago. The cable news was on mute, and Carl studied the video replay of the subway bombing that he'd seen several times already.

A fat black-and-white cat rested beneath his muscular arm, which had softened disconcertingly over the last two years. Carl had been okay today, all but his legs, which felt like they were encased in cement, waiting for Mafia hitmen to dump him in a body of water.

He'd had way worse days—trouble swallowing and talking. Tingling in his hands and legs. Poor balance. A couple of times he'd fallen. He wasn't feeling any of that now. Heavy legs he could live with. Any improvement meant he was headed in the right direction.

At six feet tall and fifty years old, Carl wasn't ready to say good-bye to the FBI yet, despite Lauren's reassurance that they had enough money and he could find a less physically demanding and stressful career. He'd scoffed at that. He'd been on medical leave for nearly three months, and he had every intention of returning to work when his FMLA leave expired. He'd be damned if he'd take disability retirement before he hit the twenty-year mark, and frankly, he didn't want to retire at all. He liked his job.

Multiple sclerosis was a disease of remission and relapse, a roller coaster of hope and brutal disappointment. Either scenario could come without warning. For Carl, his condition had badly worsened this year, two years after his diagnosis. But a remission could happen any day, which could mean complete or nearly complete relief from his symptoms for months or years, even decades. For the last several months, he'd woken up each day and taken inventory with his eyes still closed. Did he feel any different? Would he be able to pass the physical and go back to work? No surprise, most days he woke up in the same condition as before he fell asleep. Trapped in his body. *Groundhog Day*, MS style. But he was on a new drug trial now and the doctor had reassured him that it wasn't all in his mind that he'd begun feeling better, less tired, less heavy, better balance.

Carl stared out the window at the far end of their living room. The George Washington Bridge was a looping string of lights in the black distance. He pulled himself back from his thoughts, back into his living room. He couldn't allow himself to hope too high. He was afraid of the crash.

A banner at the bottom of the TV screen caught his attention: **The Associated Press confirms that the NYC Subway Bomber is a man named Jackson Mattingly, 20 years old, from Beacon, New York.**

Carl's frustration flooded back. Being out on medical leave after a terror attack was like being on the disabled list during the World Series.

The TV turned to live feed. In the glare of news van spotlights, a frenzy was going on outside the home where the killer had lived with his parents. Carl pitied the parents. When it came to young killers, it was generally true that the parents had played some part in making a monster or giving him access to weapons. But whatever they'd done wasn't necessarily worse than what a million parents had done, and they were doomed to a living hell as parents of a mass murderer. They would endure people spitting and cursing at them, vandalism, death threats, and worse, for the rest of their lives.

Carl called his partner and close friend, Rick, who was working late in the office, along with hundreds of other agents, tracking down every aspect of the killer's life, activities, and associates.

"Hey, Carl, what up?" Rick said.

Carl spoke softly, not wanting to wake Lauren. "I see they've found the parents."

"The media found them at the same time as us but beat us there. Beacon police haven't even arrived yet to put tape around the place to keep the reporters in check. Our team is on its way."

"What do you have?"

"He was white, homegrown." Carl heard the click of a mouse. Rick seemed to be reading from an email. "The parents have lived in the same place for almost twenty-one years." Rick paused. "Bought a house there shortly before their killer son was born in Newburgh General Hospital. We're starting to get his medical records, school records. We'll execute a search warrant with Beacon police at the parents' home. Hopefully, we can search before reporters get in there like tomb raiders, screwing everything up."

Carl watched the muted TV. A man he assumed was Mattingly's father came to the door of the small house. Squinting in the lights, he was waving the cameras away, apparently asking for privacy. *Good luck with that, buddy. Your days of privacy are over.*

A flicker of alarm crossed the man's face. A white flash, brighter than the klieg lights of the news vans. The father was torn off his feet, head over heels. A massive explosion whooshed the house into a fireball, the father igniting, becoming a human firebomb, hurtling toward the reporters. The CNN reporter's arms flew over her head from shock, exclaiming in pantomime. The reporter was running away, her cameraman filming the scene choppily as he sprinted backward.

"*Holy shit,*" Carl said.

"What is it?" Rick asked, but before Carl could answer, Rick said, "*Damn.* Gotta go." He hung up.

Carl unmuted the TV. The CNN reporter was recovering herself but crying and panting while she spoke. "Suddenly, a massive explosion engulfed this house. A man was *engulfed* in flames before our live cameras. Others appear to be hurt, Brett," she said to the news anchor. "You can hear the sirens approaching now. We don't know how many people were inside the house, but I cannot imagine anyone surviving the blast."

Carl watched the flames as the reporters moved aside to let firefighters run past, their hoses already spraying. He considered the unlikelihood of what he'd just seen. Who would have killed these people? Who would have known they were the killer's parents in time to set the explosives before the police arrived? And who would have the skills, supplies, and access to do it?

*   *   *

Kathleen didn't know where she was for a second. The phone was ringing, buzzing and flashing in her dark bedroom. The clock on her dresser said two AM in bright-red digital light, supersized for geriatric eyes. She rolled over to the nightstand next to her bed to pick up the phone, which was still attached to its charger. Sharon was calling.

"Hello," Kathleen mumbled.

A sob. "Kat." Crying, whispering: "Oh my god. Kat. They're going to—"

Kathleen shot up in bed. "Sharon?"

The voices were muffled now, distant, like a pocket call.

Kathleen strained to listen. Silence.

She looked at her phone, her heart pounding: Call Ended.

6

EMILY WOKE AT dawn. Skye had climbed out of the crib in her bedroom and crawled into Emily's bed, inserting herself under her mother's arm. Emily smelled Skye's sweet baby scent and kissed her pudgy face. Skye popped up in the bed smiling when she realized her mom was awake.

"Good morning, Firefighter Skye," Emily said.

Skye wore firefighter-themed pajamas. At two years old, she had passed quickly through the princess stage and was now firmly committed to her future career as a firefighter. Emily had needed to buy two pairs of the pj's, because Skye refused to sleep in anything else.

Skye had come upon her stubbornness honestly. Emily and her mother, Lauren, frequently accused each other of having insufferable stubborn streaks.

Emily sat on the side of the queen-sized bed in her compact bedroom and pulled out a dresser drawer to grab a bra and panties. Skye ran ahead to the bathroom with its claw-footed tub and just enough room for her fire truck potty.

Emily lived frugally on her modest City Hall salary and Hector's contributions to Skye's support. She usually appreciated how lucky she was, but on days like today, she had to make a conscious effort to be grateful. When she was a child, her mother had taught her to make gratitude lists to keep her daily upsets in perspective. Now, at the top of the list, she was grateful that she was alive, her baby was safe, and no one she knew had been hurt or killed. And she loved her little apartment in Inwood. Even though she lived far, far uptown, that meant she always got a seat on the subway. Her apartment was a straight shot, thirty-five minutes on the A train to work. And she was grateful she had a job she loved and excellent childcare.

But she was so tired, having worked for hours after Skye had gone to bed. Then she'd had trouble sleeping, her mind spinning with thoughts of her to-do list for the next day. Lack of sleep inevitably darkened her mood even on days when there hadn't been a terror attack.

She sighed and leaned against the bathroom doorframe, waiting for Skye and reading the latest news alerts on her phone. A man with mysterious motives had blown up forty-three people, injured a hundred more. Five kids from her old middle school had died. A pregnant woman too. And a tourist couple from Dallas, celebrating their twenty-fifth wedding anniversary in the Big Apple. She felt so sad, imagining the pain of those left behind.

And things like that made her take a hard look at her own life. She adored being Skye's mom and had great relationships with her friends and family. Hector too. He still referred to Emily as his best friend. But, despite her gratitude for all the people who loved her and that they were all safe, being single was challenging at times like this. She imagined how much easier it would have been last night if she'd been answering emails while cuddled up on the couch next to someone she loved. And when she'd been unable to sleep, she might have listened to his breathing instead of her own racing thoughts. But finding a partner wasn't easy when you worked nonstop and had rules against bringing dating-app guys into your child's orbit.

"Mommy, my lollipop?" Skye looked expectantly up at Lauren from her fire truck potty.

"Did you go?"

Skye nodded her head solemnly. Emily looked inside the potty, but no jackpot.

Emily had taken Skye to Coney Island last week, and the girl had pointed with glee at a huge carnival lollipop the size of her face. Emily had bought it, telling Skye that, when she pooped in the potty, the lollipop would be her reward. Emily reminded herself that everyone potty trained successfully—eventually. Skye would certainly know how to use a toilet before college. But even the coveted lollipop hadn't yet done the trick. It was that damn stubborn streak.

"Sit longer, baby."

"I'm not a baby," Skye said.

Emily sighed. "I know."

She looked down at her phone and clicked into the stunning video of Mattingly's father coming out of his house to wave away the cameras, then the smoldering remains of the home. It was bizarre. Anxious to hear what her coworkers knew about the Beacon explosion, she checked the time on her phone. She wanted to get to work as early as possible.

"Mommy!" Skye called, startling Emily from her thoughts. "My lollipop now!"

* * *

Carrying a plastic trash bag and pushing Skye in an umbrella stroller, Emily took the elevator to the basement. Glossy gray walls. Gray cement floors. A faint smell of old food emanated from garbage bins lined up against a wall. Kathleen was breaking down Amazon boxes. Emily often saw Kathleen doing odds and ends around the building, gardening, and hosing down the sidewalk when the super wasn't around. Emily wondered whether this might be a part-time gig for her, something to make ends meet in retirement. But from what she'd seen last night from the doorway, Kathleen had a very nice apartment and didn't need to do building chores.

The older woman nearly jumped when Emily said goodmorning from behind her.

"Sorry," Emily said.

Kathleen smiled at her. "I'm a little on edge. Good morning, Skye. You are very quiet!"

Skye looked up at Kathleen, assessing her.

"Yeah, so scary," Emily said, not in the mood to goad Skye into saying good-morning to their neighbor today. Emily threw the trash bag in a metal bin. "It's hard to believe anyone is that evil. Even after all the mass shootings," she said, considering whether to talk about it in front of Skye. Skye didn't seem to be listening, but Emily spoke carefully. "It feels different when it's our town, our train."

Emily waited with Kathleen for the elevator. "Did you see anything strange last night?" Emily asked.

"Strange?"

"There was a woman walking toward our building." Emily lightened her voice, trying not to communicate her irrational discomfort. "Probably nothing, but I happened to look out the window. I saw a woman. I thought it was one of your friends at first."

"Why did you think that?" Kathleen said, seeming anxious.

"She was tall and very pretty. Like she was one of your model friends." Noticing the dismay on Kathleen's face, Emily asked, "Is everything okay with her?"

"I was expecting a friend to stop by last night." Kathleen pulled her phone from the back pocket of her jeans and showed Emily a thumbnail photo for a contact named Sharon. She had shoulder-length auburn hair and high cheekbones. "Is this her?"

"That could be. I'm not a hundred percent sure, but I think so."

"What happened?"

"It was just a little weird. She was walking from the direction of Broadway. A car pulled up and double-parked. A man got out of the car and talked to her. She seemed surprised at first. There was something about it . . . she sort of flinched backward. Then she went with him. It didn't look like she was being forced to go, but it was strange that she would change her destination like that."

7

WHEN KATHLEEN RETURNED from the basement, she turned on the TV. She paused in front of the screen. Every few moments there was a new story about the subway bombing, someone spouting theories about the bomber's motive, or an anecdote about people helping victims. The stories about people saving others made Kathleen feel better at times like this, refreshing her sense of the goodness of humanity. She always looked for those stories after disasters. She'd read that the world was, statistically speaking, less violent than ever before; it was only technology that broadcast every atrocity into people's lives constantly, magnifying the world's awareness of the savagery of humans. It was hard to believe, but she hoped it was true.

"We are learning more every hour about Jackson Mattingly, everyone wanting to know why he committed mass murder in New York City," the CNN anchor said. "He lived in Beacon, New York, with his parents, Jason and Elyse Mattingly. Beacon is a small edge city of fifteen thousand people a little over an hour north of New York City."

The picture switched to a panorama of cookie-cutter homes in a virtually treeless lower-middle-class tract with green Mount Beacon rising in the background. As a child, Kathleen had gone to sleep-away camp there on scholarship, back when Beacon had been a tiny rural town. By the eighties, it had become a larger, depressed town with a raging crack epidemic, but over the last twenty-five years it had remade itself again as a cultural destination for Manhattan day-trippers. Its formerly blighted Main Street had filled with art galleries, quaint shops, and restaurants.

Kathleen sat in her office alcove and turned on her PC. She clicked on the desktop icon for the building's security cameras. She picked the camera that unobtrusively watched the front of the building and clicked into yesterday's date. She fast-forwarded, watching choppy images of people, dogs, cars parking and pulling out. The shadows lengthened in the video. She slowed down at nine PM, when she'd first heard from Sharon. Kathleen moved from minute to minute of the recording, the street becoming dark. Then she saw her.

Sharon was in frame for a second. She turned around. A maroon car pulled up, only a small slice of it visible. Emily had been right about Sharon seeming initially surprised, but not upset, by the person in the car. Sharon turned back to talk to someone. He was out of frame, a position Kathleen couldn't help but believe was intentional. Sharon left the frame. She and the maroon car never reappeared.

Kathleen considered what she could do. She'd wanted to call Sharon back immediately after their call disconnected last night. But she'd worried that, if Sharon was in trouble, the call would reveal her position or, if she was being held captive, that she had a phone hidden away. After waiting a few minutes, Kathleen had texted instead, reasoning that Sharon might not have sound notifications for texts and that if she was able to make a phone call, she'd be able to read a text. But Sharon never responded.

After waking up and seeing no message from Sharon this morning, Kathleen had called, hoping her friend would answer, maybe just waking up after a hangover, even though Sharon had never been a big drinker. She would tell Kathleen it had all been a mix-up. But Kathleen's call had gone straight to voice mail. She'd left a message but hadn't heard back.

Kathleen perused the contacts in her phone and began making calls. She dialed several of her and Sharon's mutual friends from the old days. No one had heard from her. It appeared she didn't run in the same circles as before. No one thought it strange that they hadn't heard from Sharon.

Kathleen hadn't called the police last night, but should she call them now? She didn't fool herself about how useless that would be. A call girl picked up in a car and not showing up at a friend's house was not exactly a case that would interest the police, especially not on the day after a terrorist attack. The cops weren't much interested in the safety of sex workers even on slow crime days. That was probably why Sharon had called Kathleen in the first place. It had once been Kathleen's job to protect her girls, and old habits like that died hard. Many of Kathleen's former employees still came to her for help from time to time, although nowadays the women usually just needed advice or a small loan.

Kathleen had no desire to step back into those old shoes. She'd gotten used to her quiet, normal life, and she liked it that way. But she couldn't do nothing. Dreading the sleezy advertisements that would bombard her computer as a result, a small price for helping her friend, she began Googling strip clubs.

CHAPTER

8

THE PRESS OFFICE was still buzzing with energy when Emily
arrived. She got on a Zoom call with FDNY executive staff,
then rolled her chair over to sit next to Thea, the new intern.
Thea had cream-colored skin and a sprinkling of freckles across
her nose, as if she'd made the trip to New York City from Kansas
on a spinning bed. But she was apparently from Iowa. Martha
had sat her at the empty desk of the staffer who'd left to work on
the mayor's presidential campaign.

Emily explained to Thea how to assemble digital press clippings to email to City Hall staff, agency leadership, and agency
press officers each day. Even the day after a terror attack, the City
continued to have its usual problems, and staff needed to know
about all of it.

Emily looked over the young woman's work, and her eye
caught on a story about attempts to clean up a spot known for
prostitution in the Bronx. She'd received a call about it from the
reporter last week. The article was one in a series about sex work,
this one focusing on the drama middle-class people witnessed
when living in a gentrifying neighborhood once famous for
street prostitution. There were stories of residents hearing couples having sex in their backyards. A man said he'd once heard
a woman shouting for help, but when the police finally arrived,
they'd been unable to find anyone in trouble. The article said

prostitutes sometimes shouted for help to attract embarrassing attention if a dishonest john refused to pay. Even the cheapest guy didn't want to be caught on a viral video fighting about his bill with a pissed-off streetwalker. But sometimes the violence was real.

The article included a quote from Emily about Mayor Sullivan's interest in providing more funding for programs for sex workers facing violence. The disdain for sex workers was so strong that they were often isolated, disconnected from family and friends, and had nowhere to turn for help. Emily was pleased with the quote, which illustrated how proactive the mayor was being. She knew Martha would like it.

Emily had become the go-to person on stories about addiction and the opioid crisis, especially when they intersected with policing issues. Her own mother had been a heroin addict. Sex work went hand in hand with addiction, although Emily's mother had gotten clean at seventeen years old, before she'd had to do anything like that. Still, Emily was interested in the issue of the vulnerability of female addicts, how high the murder rate was for them, especially those who sold their bodies for drugs. Most of those murders went unsolved.

"The clips are good to go," she said to the intern. "After you send them out, I have a project for you. I'd like to come up to speed on the issue of violence against sex workers, prostitution diversion programs, and the like. I'm thinking this reporter may have more questions soon. You can help by looking for news stories and research on violence against prostitutes and legislative responses."

*   *   *

In the COW, several people were already at the conference table waiting for the morning muster meeting. Mayor Sullivan was running late.

"After the Beacon explosion, reporters are asking whether Jackson Mattingly might have planted other bombs with timers around New York," Martha was saying to the others. "The dominant theory on social media is that Mattingly was an 'incel,' involuntary celibate. They're angry young white men motivated by a hatred of women for not dating them. Incels fall into a rat hole of negative thinking, egged on by anonymous jerks on the internet. If he'd been a white supremacist, he would have attacked mosques, synagogues, or shopping areas where mostly people of color would be found."

Chief Reilly was seated across from Emily at the table. "Mattingly was wearing a Hawaiian shirt, but we don't think he was a boogaloo boi. He wasn't involved with them on the internet, from what we can tell."

Deputy Mayor Garcia, a tiny Ecuadorian American man, walked in. "Good morning, everyone."

He sat beside Emily and opened his laptop. When he logged in, she could see that the last thing he'd watched was video of the explosion at the Mattingly house.

Roger, sitting across from the mayor's customary chair, was looking down at his phone.

"So, it looks like Mattingly had no connection to New York City," said Marlo, the mayor's chief of staff, a thirtysomething Latinx of fluid gender. Marlo draped an arm over an empty chair. They wore a pencil skirt, silk blouse, and spike-heeled size twelves but had a large Adam's apple and a trimmed beard.

"Thank god," Garcia said. "I was waiting for the media to blame every teacher he ever had. The only thing worse than being his parent is being his teacher or principal. Even I want to know why they didn't notice he was crazy." He turned to Emily. "Am I a bad person to be happy that this problem landed in the lap of the Beacon school district?"

Garcia oversaw the City's Department of Education. Emily snickered and replied, "Yes, you are a horrible person."

"The Beacon news media can't possibly be as cruel and unusual as New York," Marlo said. "Any *New York Post* reporter would, without a doubt, throw educators under the bus for a chance to be an expert panelist on Fox."

"When do you expect the mayor to return?" Roger asked Marlo.

"Any minute. He's visiting Columbia Presbyterian," Marlo said, scratching their beard. "At least a dozen people there have lost one or both of their legs. Spinal cord injuries, damage to internal organs too."

Chief Reilly took a call on his cell, listened, then hung up. "Well, Mattingly's phone is missing and his PC was incinerated."

"I was on a conference call this morning with the fire commissioner," Emily said. "He said, and I quote, 'It was one hell of a timed explosion for a twenty-year-old kid to pull off.' "

Martha turned to Deputy Mayor Garcia with a smirk. "Maybe you would look good if he went to New York City public school. He was apparently quite the genius."

As Garcia chuckled, Roger banged the tip of his pen against a legal pad. "Is this a joking matter to you, Martha?"

They all turned toward Roger, the smirks wiped off their faces. He usually had the demeanor of everyone's favorite uncle, other than the whisper-shouting match with the mayor the day before and an argument with Marlo once after the mayor was late for a memorial service for a firefighter. Roger had been right about how the *Post* would respond to that. The next day, the headline had read Can't Wake for Hero Wake.

Emily looked down, chastened for laughing at the banter in the room. But she was also salty about Martha bearing the brunt of Roger's anger. The joking in the room had been like the chatting at a wake. Nervous chatter. The undercurrent in the room was dark and tense. No amount of snark could bury it.

"Let's get started, and we'll circle back when the mayor comes," Martha said, pissed, her words clipped. "Press avail is at noon in the Blue Room. He needs to talk about current public safety first. People are nervous after the Beacon explosion, worried that Mattingly left other bombs around. The mayor needed to reassure them."

9

Two days after the subway attack, Kathleen had reached her saturation point with the news. MSNBC had found Jackson Mattingly's first-grade teacher and a former classmate. Watching cable news after a crisis was like being a chain smoker, lighting up the next one even though you were already sick of smoking. Kathleen had quit smoking over twenty years ago but still remembered the feeling. She picked up the remote and shut off the TV.

She left her apartment and retrieved her Honda Accord from a garage under a neighboring building, where she rented a monthly parking space. The last time Kathleen had spoken to Sharon, she had been dancing at a club in Queens. After Kathleen closed her business and Sharon went out on her own, she'd begun dancing in an upscale Manhattan strip joint. But by the time dancers hit forty, they tended to work in the lesser clubs in Queens or New Jersey. Sharon had once mentioned to Kathleen where she'd been working. Kathleen had easily remembered the name—Easy Street Gentleman's Club—once she'd Googled a list of Queens strip clubs.

On a normal day, Sharon would be getting to work around now for the blue-collar, after-work shift. Outer-borough dancing shifts started by four PM. Kathleen braved the typically heavy weekday traffic on the Cross Bronx Expressway, crossed the Whitestone Bridge over a wide gray bay, and arrived in Queens.

Neon lights and a sign with a yellow brick road announced her arrival at Easy Street. Kathleen pulled into a small parking lot between a Burger King and the side of the club. There were only three cars in the parking area.

As Kathleen headed for the door, she saw a young woman walking ahead of her. Kathleen's breath hitched. "Sharon?"

The woman turned around. Not Sharon. She looked a bit like Sharon from behind, but she was a lithe version of the other woman, ten years younger. She peered back at Kathleen inquisitively, her features pinched and her lips scrawny, not resembling Sharon at all now. "Hi?"

"Oh, I'm sorry, I thought you were Sharon."

The woman's face slowly dawned with a thought. She didn't have Sharon's sharp intellect either. "Oh, gosh, I haven't seen her for days. You can ask Sal inside what's up with her."

Kathleen found Sal standing beside a dimly lit bar that smelled of old booze and sawdust. Sal's beer belly hung over his jeans, a black mariachi shirt smoothing the bulk. An Asian woman in a G-string danced on a U-shaped stage over the upturned face of a man of about thirty. The place was otherwise empty.

Kathleen put out her hand to shake Sal's. She liked to establish with a handshake that she was a businessperson, an equal, in a world dominated by men. Sal's hand was thick and chafed dry.

"She hasn't showed up for a couple of days, didn't give me notice. It wasn't like her," Sal told Kathleen after she asked about Sharon. "I've called her to find out whether she still wanted to be on the schedule, but no callback. She caught me flat-footed. I could normally depend on her, unlike a lot of the others."

"She is the dependable type," Kathleen said, keeping the conversation going. "That's why it's been weird that she hasn't been answering her phone."

"Yeah, no drugs or booze. She's all business. I'm telling you, she's the best girl I've had in the last couple of years."

"Was anything bothering her?"

"Nah. Not that she'd tell me. In my experience, there's two types of dancers. The talkative type that tell you everything, even the details of their girly infections, if you so much as ask how they're doing. And then there's the ones who keep shit to themselves. Sharon is of the latter variety. Good day, bad day, no way I'd ever know."

"Do you have an emergency contact for her?"

"You mean like on a human resources form?"

"Yes, like that."

"Come on. Get the fuck outa here." He shook his head, smirking. "All the girls are independent contractors. We don't want to know."

Kathleen thanked him, ready to leave.

"Wait a second. One thing that may help," Sal said, and Kathleen turned back to listen. "She has a chick she's been dating who comes to pick her up sometimes. Dressed like she was coming from construction work or some shit like that. I haven't seen her around for a while, so I don't know if she's Sharon's current girl. But maybe she'd know Sharon's whereabouts."

"Do you know her name?"

"Angel, Angela, something like that."

"Do you have any idea how to contact her?" Kathleen asked, although she knew it was unlikely.

Sal shrugged. "Nah. But, listen, if you see Sharon, you can tell her from me, no hard feelings. She can come back anytime. She was always a good example for the other girls."

CHAPTER

10

BY THE END of the workweek, the city had nearly returned to normal, at least for those who didn't know anyone killed or maimed. As she often did on Saturday mornings, Emily ran, pushing Skye's jogging stroller, from Inwood to Washington Heights. A balmy wind blew Emily's hair back from her face. Sweat trickled down her spine beneath her tank top and running shorts. The mile-long path along the Henry Hudson Parkway was wooded on one side, the Hudson River peeking through tree branches. On the far side of the three-lane highway—lightly trafficked on a Saturday morning—stood the forested cliffs of Fort Tryon Park. Emily breathed in the scent of jasmine.

Skye was laughing, shouting, "Run, Rusty."

Rusty, a copper-colored golden retriever, ran in step with Emily, wearing a mesh Puppies-in-Prison service vest. Rusty lived in Bedford State Correctional Facility, where female inmates trained service dogs. He was eighteen months old now and would soon be donated to a veteran with PTSD or become an explosives-detection dog.

Emily hadn't planned to take on the responsibility of training a dog with Skye still so young. Usually two weekends a month, volunteers acclimated the puppies to an outside world of cars, crowds, and smells they couldn't experience in the rural prison, and it was a lot of work. But Emily had previously trained several dogs for Puppies-in-Prison, starting when she was in college. The director had called three months ago, needing an emergency placement for Rusty after a volunteer bailed. Emily had hoped it would be a good experience for Skye, and it had been so far.

Carl's son, Alex, greeted Emily with a hug at the door to her mother's apartment on Cabrini Boulevard. Twenty-one and six feet two inches tall, her stepbrother had dark Caribbean-Latino eyes like his dad and a scraggly black goatee. He attended City College and lived with roommates in the Bronx, but he was at Lauren and Carl's apartment a lot.

A fat black-and-white cat observed Emily's arrival from where she sat on a shoe bench in the vestibule. The cat leaned down to sniff Rusty, less perturbed by the dog's visit than by Skye's awkward petting, which swiftly sent the cat to higher ground.

Emily smelled brewing coffee. In the sunny eat-in kitchen, she kissed Carl's cheek. He grasped her hand, a hand hug that didn't require him to get up. Emily's mother, Lauren, was making pancakes next to a window that overlooked the tall oak trees of the gardens behind the Castle Village apartments, the Hudson River beyond that. Forty-eight and fit, Lauren wore jean shorts and a Puppies-in-Prison T-shirt Emily had given her, her thick, long curls tied up only half successfully. Lauren was lean and strong. She could probably still beat Emily in an arm wrestle, even though Emily was in reasonably good shape.

Spatula in hand, Lauren gave Emily a half hug and Skye a kiss on the head. Alex placed a booster seat on the chair next to Emily and sat at the round wooden table. Rusty settled himself between Alex and Emily, lying with his chin on the floor. Emily poured herself coffee from a carafe.

"Are they saying anything interesting about Mattingly at City Hall?" Carl asked.

"His parents were normal people, quiet," Emily said. "Not a lot of friends. They think he made the bombs there, in the house. They found traces of the chemicals he used."

"He must have used a timer for the house . . . to set it off."

Carl's words slurred slightly, Emily noted with a wrenching in her gut. She'd studied up on MS on the web and knew slurred speech was a symptom. It wasn't clear yet whether Carl had relapsing MS or the more serious progressive type, which kept getting worse until the person was totally incapacitated. They were all praying that the new drug trial would work. Some days were better than others, today apparently being on the worse end of the spectrum.

"Yeah, FDNY thinks it was a timer," Emily said.

"Mass murderers sometimes kill their parents before their rampage, like Adam Lanza in Sandy Hook," Carl said, his voice clearer now. "It was two in the morning when the bomb went off." Carl took a pancake from a plate Lauren put on the table. "He would expect his parents to be home."

Alex reached for the plate after Carl. "Dibs on the chocolate chip."

"Dude, split 'em," Emily said. She could lose her mind over chocolate. She knew her mother had probably been thinking of her as much as Alex and Skye when she added chocolate chips to half the batch. "For Skye," Emily added, although she wasn't fooling anyone.

"Adam Lanza wasn't even stable enough to go to school, and his mother still let him have guns," Alex said. "It's hard to feel sorry for her."

"But"—Carl pointed his fork for emphasis—"I've never heard of a killer setting a timer to kill his par—" He stopped himself, noticing that Skye might be hearing too much.

Emily looked at Skye, who was totally focused on digging for a chocolate chip.

"Anyway, that was devious stuff, if Mattingly did it," Carl went on. "It gave the parents a chance to know they created a monster, that he was dead, and that their lives were basically destroyed. If a killer hated his parents, that would be a powerful 'eff you' before they died."

Carl seemed lit up from inside, relishing the crime puzzle. "It couldn't have been vigilantes because they would have needed to have a bomb handy, place it in the house, and beat the police there once they found out about Mattingly. It could be coconspirators covering up something. But my money's on Jackson Mattingly and a timer."

Emily met her mother's eyes for a moment, seeing the pain that so often lurked there lately. Lauren was worried about Carl losing the law enforcement career he loved. She had told Emily how anxious he was to get back to work, which was no surprise. Emily had all her fingers crossed about that too.

After breakfast, Emily got up and Alex joined her, making quick work of the cleanup so Lauren could enjoy her coffee. Lauren took Skye onto her lap and wiped the girl's hands with a wet washcloth.

Emily adored Carl, and she had since her mother started dating him ten years earlier. Still, she worried about her mother doing too much—maintaining her own law practice and looking after him. Carl was distressed by his medical condition and how it was impacting both his career and family, since Lauren had to go with him to all his appointments. She wanted to be there, she'd told Emily, to keep Carl from hearing only what he wanted to, going into denial about negative news, minimizing his symptoms when he talked to the doctor, or even hiding something from her to spare her.

Emily only hoped her mother wasn't repeating an old pattern of taking care of everyone and not herself. Lauren's parents had been addicts, so she'd basically become the parent in her house when she was still a kid. When Emily's grandfather had tried to get clean, Lauren had gone with him to Narcotics Anonymous meetings, serving as armor to help him resist doing drugs. Unfortunately, she hadn't been able to keep her father clean, and he'd died of an overdose when she was only fifteen.

Meanwhile, Lauren's mother, Emily's grandmother, had been useless, a crack addict. When Lauren's father died, it had been Lauren, not her mother, who cleared the drugs and illegal gun out of the house before the police arrived. Lauren had eventually ended up homeless on the streets, without so much as a word from her mother.

Lauren had told Emily that she'd seen her grandmother once when Emily was Skye's age and her grandmother approached them on the street. Emily didn't remember it. Lauren hadn't seen her mother in nearly twenty-five years.

Alex dried his hands at the sink and turned to Rusty. "So, dog, you got any skills?"

"Rusty." Emily signaled toward the kitchen light switch.

Tail wagging furiously, Rusty ran to the wall. He stood on his hind legs, leaned his front paws against the wall, hopped to steady himself, and nosed the light switch. He left all of them in shadow, laughing, Skye clapping with delight.

11

A T SIXTY-EIGHTH STREET, between Broadway and Amsterdam, Kathleen pulled into a circular driveway with a round garden at its center. Sharon lived in a white-brick condo building in the Lincoln Center neighborhood. It took up an entire square block and stood catty-corner to the Sony multiplex theater. Coming to Sharon's home was a last resort; Kathleen had exhausted all other options. Barging in at a working woman's home base was generally frowned upon, but Kathleen believed she was innocuous enough—a privilege of age—to avoid attracting unwanted attention. If she were wearing hot pants and thigh-high boots, it would be another story.

The doorman came out and bent toward Kathleen's passenger-side window. "May I help you?"

"Yes, my cousin, Sharon Williams, lives here. She called me a few days ago and said she was coming to visit me. I haven't heard anything from her since, and she's not picking up the phone."

His eyes narrowed in thought. "I haven't seen her for a few days either."

"Could I go up and check on her? I'm her only family."

"I'll call upstairs and see whether she answers. If not, I need to talk to my supervisor. Give me a minute."

"I'll park and be right back."

Kathleen pulled her car out of the driveway and made a quick turn down a ramp that led to a parking lot under the building.

When she returned on foot up the steep garage drive and walked around to the entrance, the doorman greeted her, key in hand. "I'm on break. I'll take you up. She didn't answer, but I'm sure she's okay . . . although you got me worried too. She's a nice lady, Sharon. Always has a kind word in the morning. She would usually leave her mail key with me if she were going away."

He held the glass door open, and Kathleen entered a large, carpeted lobby. A long reception desk like a hotel's stretched along one side of the lobby. An array of couches and chairs clustered on the other side under a chandelier.

"When did you see her last?" Kathleen asked.

"It's been a few days. I usually see her jogging at about ten thirty in the morning. She runs in Central Park. Maybe she's sleeping off a cold." He talked like he was trying to reassure himself, but he was making Kathleen more nervous.

They took one of three carpeted elevators with etched-mirror walls. Outside apartment 19C, Kathleen sniffed the air, grateful not to smell the sickly scent of a dead body. She hadn't expected to find a body, but she'd seen too much in her life to be surprised by the worst-case scenario. She became more edgy as the doorman rang the bell. He waited. Rang again. Knocked. He inserted the key, opening it a foot.

"Ms. Williams? Sharon? Are you here? This is Dunbar. Here to check on you."

An elevator opened behind them. Kathleen looked back to see two figures walking from the elevator.

They flashed badges.

Kathleen took in a husky male cop, over six feet tall with a football-player build. His partner was a woman. Latina. Short. Pretty, like an actress playing a cop on *Law and Order*, except for a roll of fat at her belt. Both rested their hands on their holsters as if evaluating the threat level of a uniformed doorman and an elderly woman—although Kathleen didn't think of herself as elderly.

"NYPD, Detective Banks," the husky male cop said. "What are you doing here?"

Dunbar held up his key. "The tenant hasn't been seen for a while, and her cousin was concerned about her. We came up to check on her."

"Cousin? Are you her next of kin?" Banks asked Kathleen gruffly.

His words fell on Kathleen like dead weight. "By affinity, not blood."

Dunbar gave Kathleen a look. She'd lied to him, and now he could be in a mess.

"Sharon has no one. I've been family to her for nearly twenty years," Kathleen continued. "I called in a missing-persons report but didn't hear anything back."

"I'm Detective Luna." The Latina officer handed Kathleen a card. "I'm sorry to tell you that she's dead."

Air blew out of Kathleen's lips as if she'd been drop-kicked in the solar plexus. Dunbar exclaimed beside her.

Kathleen couldn't breathe. She'd known in her gut that something bad had happened. But no, no, no . . . she didn't want it to be true.

She didn't cry, though she might have if she'd been alone. Instead, her face went hard. This hallway was not a safe space. She shifted mentally into the woman who had once played life as if she were always under threat of attack. She'd washed with too many bars of prison-issued lye soap to feel safe with cops.

"How?" Kathleen asked.

"Her body was found near the Gateway Recreation Area in Queens. A place they call North Beach, although it's mostly reeds out there," Detective Banks said, studying her as he spoke. "It's a dumping ground for dead hookers."

"*Excuse me?*" Kathleen asked, furious at the cop's tone.

He recited without expression, as if he were a bad actor cold-reading a script, "A serial killer's been dumping women out there for decades. We've seen her criminal record." He looked at Dunbar, whose eyes had reddened. "We'll take your statement."

Luna turned to Kathleen and spoke sharply. "You'll need to come to the precinct to talk to us."

PART II

PART II

12

Before

BEFORE HE'D BLOWN himself up along with forty-three other people, Jackson Mattingly had been a handsome boy. At first glance, people gravitated to him. None of them knew him, not really, although some recognized intuitively that danger lurked beneath his skin. Women with honed survival instincts could see in the depths of his blue eyes a future domestic abuser, poised to pounce. Boys and young men had sometimes sensed a bully lurking there, someone who would dynamite the neighbor's wandering cat if he felt the hankering, someone who felt no compunction about taking you down a notch if you were fat, skinny, or thin-skinned. They didn't see it consciously, but healthy people gave him wide berth.

He liked it like that. Most of all, he didn't want anyone to get close enough to truly scope him out. He didn't want them to see how any kind word he spoke morphed into calculation and how rage boiled beneath his calm surface. He was a natural for the high school football team, so he wasn't viewed as an outcast like the Columbine shooters. But he wasn't like other people. At all. That was his secret.

A year before Jackson Mattingly's simmering rage morphed into a road map, he walked along Main Street in Beacon, alone as usual. Twilight cast purple shadows over the stores that lined the street, mostly tiny art galleries, plus a bake shop. The best berry pies he couldn't afford. It was his last year of high school, and he didn't have any plans he intended to follow. But one thing that had made him deeply angry, as he peered at his reflection rather than the artwork in a gallery window, was his eyes—or more accurately, *their* eyes.

His parents'. Jason and Elyse Mattingly's. Brown eyes. Both of them.

It had never occurred to him that this was a problem. Not until he'd learned about genetics in high school and realized his parents were probably not his parents. He'd asked the question in class, trying to make it sound casual, about whether brown-eyed parents ever had blue-eyed kids. The teacher, a young dude with a denim shirt and jeans, had looked at him curiously, maybe wondering himself how an Adonis like Jackson could have come from parents like his. His dumpy parents—clearly graduates of the slow-reading class—regularly showed up for parent-teacher conferences, a mortifying exercise during which the teachers always said Jackson was smart but never, ever said he was a pleasure to have in their class. He'd never done anything much to get the teachers mad—at least nothing they were sure he'd done. Jackson attributed their discomfort mostly to his energy, which overwhelmed weak people, namely 99.9% of the population.

The teacher explained that if both parents had the recessive gene for blue eyes, it *could* be passed down, skip a generation, and create a blue-eyed kid, even if the parents had brown eyes. It wasn't the norm, but it happened.

Jackson had given some thought to that. He rarely saw his grandparents, aunts, uncles, or cousins. He and his parents had taken the four-hour car ride for the first time when he was five. Poor white trash, both sides of the family. They had weak chins, sallow skin, and lank hair, none above six feet tall like him. None a good athlete. Not an intelligent conversation from a one of them, other than a skinny cousin who'd become damn near a chemist from cooking methamphetamine in a shed behind his house. No wonder Jackson's parents had moved far away from that flock of losers. And none of them had blue eyes. That was some fucking recessive gene, hidden away for generations, just to come calling on tall, athletic, blue-eyed Jackson. Total bullshit. He knew the real deal.

He'd confronted his parents. But they'd refused to talk about it. He couldn't figure out their reaction. His mother wept and his father stormed around the house. Most of all, they seemed scared, which ate at Jackson and made his need to know even stronger. He didn't mind all that much about being adopted. It would answer a lot of questions about why he didn't fit in with the family. But the fear on their faces and refusal to acknowledge his questions drove him crazy. Anger swirled with his pumped-up teenage testosterone, fondling his eerie intelligence, which he was now sure he hadn't gotten from *them*.

He hadn't thought about it before, but genetics might also answer why he shared no interests with his parents, and why they were so nice to everyone while all he thought about was blowing shit apart. He'd been fascinated with explosions, fire, the force of a tsunami, every kind of mass disaster, for as long as he could remember. Violence filled and soothed a grating emptiness inside him. Violence made him feel something other than the fury that blistered his insides unless he did something to calm it.

Luckily, he was a guy who knew how to keep a secret. He wasn't a *sharer*, needy for people to recognize his accomplishments. He wasn't a *joiner* either, didn't need a group that required sharing secrets as the price of entry. No one person knew more than a small slice of his behavior, and no one knew his thoughts. From his earliest memory, every feeling other than anger that he'd ever shared with anyone had been a lie. He pretended to be happy, or loving, or excited, even as a child, and even then, only when it helped him get something he wanted. Most importantly, he hid the homicidal rage that spoke to him every moment of his life. And he hid his lurking fear, barely known even to himself, that it meant there was something *wrong* inside him.

Jackson turned a corner several blocks before he reached home. The houses here were 1960s ranches surrounded by squares of lawn. Several houses were dark. One belonged to his hip science teacher and his pregnant wife. They'd gone to visit her family during summer break. It took Jackson little effort to quietly break in with a gloved fist though a back window. Once inside, he walked the dark house to the bedroom, smelling the remnants of their last meal, the room deodorizer, the empty kitty litter that still left an ammonia mist. It was a pity they'd taken the cat with them. He pulled out dresser drawers until he found the wife's panties.

* * *

When Jackson returned home, his anger quelled by his little detour, his parents were in the living room. Worn recliners and a couch were arranged around a flat-screen TV. Jackson joined them, eating a plate of flank steak and potatoes on a tray table. They all watched a show about the one-year anniversary of a high school shooting. They didn't watch it together, exactly. They were all in one room, each of them on an electronic device, looking up periodically at the television screen as the announcers went through the blow-by-blow of the school massacre. Jackson caught the undercurrent of elation among the round table of guests reminiscing about their big-news payday a year ago.

Jackson's dad clucked when the announcer talked about the shooter aiming under desks at kids hiding there. "I don't know about this world."

"Terrible, terrible," his mother clucked back, her upper arms jiggling when she put her fingers over her mouth with a horrified gesture.

Jackson became more attentive when the TV flashed on the pockmarked face of the loser kid who'd done it. The boy had a dumpy, half-witted mother who reminded Jackson of his own mother. The kid's father was a dentist—far better than Jackson's own dad's line of work as a prison guard. Thirty years doing that and his dad had never even gotten a promotion. The announcer was saying that the kid's mass shooting had ruined the father's dental practice and that the mother couldn't leave the house without people following and shouting at her. Jackson laughed gleefully at the thought of it.

His parents looked over at him, startled, with worry in their eyes. It was a look he'd seen many times before. He lit a cigarette and flicked ashes onto his half-eaten steak, taking a long look back at them. His parents had gotten more than they bargained for when they found Jackson's baby basket on their doorstep, or however the fuck that whole arrangement had gone down.

He decided. He needed to find out the truth about that. It was clear that his real parents were special people, unlike the homely dimwits who'd raised him. His real parents were the missing link that would make sense of his life. He needed to reunite with his makers like a magnet drawn to metal.

CHAPTER

13

Aſter brunch at Lauren's and a much-needed nap for all,
Emily took Skye and Rusty to meet a group of Emily's
friends for dinner. Although most of her friends lived downtown, they were happy to come to the palm-lined outdoor
restaurants of Dyckman Street. The food was good and less
expensive than downtown. Plus, they doted on Skye and wanted
to meet Rusty.

After dinner, Emily waited for a traffic light a few blocks from
home. Skye slept in her stroller now. Happily, that meant Emily
would be able to transfer her to her crib without the drawn-out
routines of bedtime. Emily checked her phone. She'd missed a
call from Kathleen. It was the first time Kathleen had called
since Emily gave her the number.

Rusty growled. She looked down, startled. He was staring at
a man with a bucket and fishing pole who stood nearby, waiting
for the light. People fished in the Hudson nowadays, which was
supposedly clean if it hadn't rained a lot.

"Rusty, what's wrong?" she asked.

Rusty whined and let out a short bark in the direction of the
man's fishing pole. The fisherman looked over, raising an eyebrow but not saying anything.

"Rusty, sit," Emily commanded, troubled by his break in
training. Rusty sat but still seemed anxious, his hackles up. She

smiled sheepishly at the man. "I think he's afraid of the fishing pole."

The man amiably waved his hand good-bye and walked ahead, the light green now. Emily gave the fisherman a head start before walking.

She approached her building, the sun dipping behind the trees of Inwood Hill Park at the end of the block. The birds had begun singing. She always loved how there were so many birds roosting in the trees of her block, particularly at twilight. It wasn't something you thought about when you apartment-hunted. You looked at the commute, good elementary schools, and whether there was evidence of mice or roaches in the apartments. A bird-filled block was something wonderful she'd had no thought of making happen in her life.

Frankly, she marveled at having found her apartment at all. It had fallen into her lap. Last year, Emily had posted that she was looking to move from her studio apartment to a larger place better suited for her and Skye. Her Facebook friend Sophie had heard about an affordable two-bedroom apartment from a friend of hers who was finishing up graduate school at Columbia. Emily had jumped at it.

A man and a woman approached her from the entrance to her building. The man asked, "Emily Silverman?"

Emily felt Rusty standing at attention, his fur against the side of her bare leg below the hem of her sundress. "Yes?"

They flashed badges. "NYPD. Homicide."

Emily automatically glanced down at Skye, who was still sleeping. "Homicide?"

"I'm Detective Banks." The cop signaled toward his partner. "This is Detective Luna. We're investigating the death of Sharon Williams. We understand you saw her a few nights ago."

"Sharon . . . Kathleen's friend?"

"Yes."

"Oh my god."

Detective Luna repeated, "We understand you saw her earlier this week?"

Emily felt disoriented. Déjà vu. It was the feeling of life suddenly upended. The way it had been when she was sixteen. Emily had been looking out the schoolroom window one morning, daydreaming. Orange leaves floated down from the trees outside her classroom.

The teacher leaned over her desk, startling her. "Emily, you can finish the work sheet later. They want you in the office."

By nightfall, Emily was on a flight to Miami. There had been a hotel fire during her father's business trip. Emily traveled with her mother and stepmother, Jessica, to the hospital. But Emily's father, Brian, died that night, without them getting to see him. If Emily had learned anything from that experience, it was that nobody gave you a two-minute warning when your life was about to change completely.

Emily refocused on Detective Luna, reminding herself that whatever was going on now wasn't like that. At least not for her. But Kathleen would be devastated. "Yes. My neighbor, Kathleen, showed me her photo, and the woman I saw looked like her." Emily told the detectives what she'd seen that night.

"Can you describe the man she left with?" Detective Luna asked.

"I didn't see much of his face, but he had short dark hair. He was thick . . . not fat, maybe muscular, but it was hard to tell under his clothes. He had on a polo shirt. Maybe khakis. He was dressed . . . I wanna say"—she thought aloud—"corporate casual, as if he was maybe going out to dinner or he was working." She took in the plainclothes cops. "The way you two are dressed, pretty much."

Detective Luna cracked a wry smile, as if acknowledging that their "plain clothes" weren't a good disguise.

"What happened to her?" Emily asked.

Detective Banks spoke. "We're still waiting for the medical examiner's report, but the body was found in marshland near Jamaica Bay. It's a location where we've found numerous murder victims. Mostly prostitutes."

Emily tried to grasp what he was saying as if she were grabbing a wet branch in rapids. "She was a prostitute?"

"Yes."

"I thought she was a model."

"No. Is that what you were told?"

CHAPTER

14

Back home, Emily put Skye in her crib, removed her shorts, and left her sleeping in a T-shirt and Pull-Ups in the warm apartment. Emily lay in bed, replaying in her mind what she'd seen, ruminating about whether there'd been any sign of a problem that could have led her to do something to stop Sharon from getting into the car. Or that might have made her call the police. She gave up on sleep and ended up sitting cross-legged in bed for hours with her laptop, reading articles the intern, Thea, had sent her about violence against prostitutes. Then she did her own search about the North Beach killings and browsed through online bulletin boards, where amateurs traded clues, trying to solve crimes. The material wasn't exactly conducive to sleep.

When she finally slept, she dreamt of being attacked by a husky man in a polo shirt. She was running away from him on a beach. He was gaining on her. Then he was in her apartment. *Where's Skye? Skye!*

Emily must have groaned or thrashed. The next thing she knew, Rusty had pulled her blanket off her, startling her with the cool air of the room. The dog ran to the light switch and pushed it on with his nose, flooding the bedroom with light.

"Good doggy," she said, bleary-eyed but glad he'd woken her up from her dream.

* * *

When Emily woke again, it was just after dawn and Skye was raring to go. Skye ate her breakfast of fruit, scrambled eggs, and toast in their small kitchen, a space that allowed just enough room for a table for two. Emily put her laptop on the table and wrote in the online Puppies-in-Prison journal about Rusty's success at waking her up, which was exactly what he was supposed to do for veterans with night terrors. She was happy to have something excellent to say beyond the problem with the fisherman. She texted Kathleen to ask if she could come by for coffee.

Kathleen arrived ten minutes later. She bent down to pet Rusty as Skye peered at her from the doorway between the living room and kitchen.

"Good morning, Skye," the older woman said.

"Say good-morning to Kathleen, Skye," Emily said.

"Good morning, Kat-leen."

Kathleen put out her hands. "Can I get a hug?"

Skye came to her and allowed the hug.

Emily picked up the TV remote. "Skye, come watch *Dinostory*." She turned to Kathleen as the little girl ran to sit cross-legged in front of the TV. "I don't usually let her watch TV this early, but I wanted to talk to you."

Emily led Kathleen to the kitchen. "The police were here," she said, and held up a pot of coffee. "Do you want any? It's jet fuel, but good."

"Sure, thanks." Kathleen sat. "I gave them your name. I'm sorry to involve you."

"That was totally fine. What else could you do?" Emily poured coffee into a mug. "Are you okay?"

"Yes."

But when Emily sat, she noticed that Kathleen's eyes were puffy.

"Sharon was a prostitute?"

Kathleen looked at Emily, surprise flickering across her face at the mention. "Yes."

Emily placed a milk carton and sugar bowl on the table. "I was a little blindsided."

"Is her being a sex worker an issue? She's dead."

Emily was startled by Kathleen's tone. Emily had never seen any hint of anger in Kathleen. And besides, Emily was the one who should be pissed.

"Well, considering that sex work probably led to Sharon getting killed, I guess it was a problem," she said. "And honestly, I thought she was a model."

"Why did you think Sharon was a model?" Kathleen asked.

Emily's face heated with embarrassment. "You didn't say she was a model?"

"Well, no, Emily," Kathleen said. "Full disclosure, I do recall you mentioning my 'model friends' on occasion. I didn't correct you because it's not my habit to 'out' people. I can see from your reaction that it was wise of me not to overdisclose. It usually is."

"I just really don't understand it. All of your friends are call girls?"

"The oldest and most dangerous profession. Why are you so offended, Emily?"

"Look, things haven't always been easy for me. My father died in a hotel fire when I was a teenager. If that shock hadn't been bad enough, he left a mess for my mother and stepmother, who was pregnant at the time. There were problems with money. There were other women. It was a rough time for my family, and hard for me to face that my father hadn't been the dad I thought he was. So, long story short, I don't like being pulled into things without knowing what I'm getting into. I didn't have a choice when I was a kid, but I do now."

"I'm sorry about your father. But you understand that all your assumptions were *your* assumptions," Kathleen said in a kind but maybe condescending manner.

Emily couldn't decide if she should be annoyed by it. She was mostly embarrassed. She *had* made assumptions about Kathleen's friends. It had been a rookie mistake. As a former reporter, she deserved Kathleen's condescension.

Kathleen continued, "And, besides anything else, if I thought it was dangerous to be around me, I would have stayed away from you." She looked down, as if that statement were heavy with emotion she didn't want Emily to read. It was a little weird.

Hard to say what was going on with Kathleen, but she seemed sincere.

Emily asked, "Are you in some kind of trouble?"

"Me? No, I don't think so. Definitely no trouble with the police." Kathleen chuckled. "The statute of limitations has long run out on anything I ever did. I'm even an AARP member."

Emily couldn't help but crack a smile. "Are you saying without really saying that you were a hooker before, so I can assume it, and you can tell me later that I jumped to conclusions? Jeez, I'm glad I'm not interviewing you."

Kathleen smiled wryly. "No, I wasn't a hooker. I was a madam."

"Oh." Emily processed it. That made sense.

"Sharon is dead," Kathleen said somberly, changing the subject. "I knew her for a very long time. I feel as if I failed her. I tell myself she was an adult and made her own choice to do sex work. But maybe if she'd never met me, the Life wouldn't have been so easy, maybe it wouldn't have been so respectable and safe. It's difficult to get out of the profession once you're in it, even when things stop being so easy. It's hard for the women to avoid the shame that's laid on them. Self-hatred can weigh them down, get them stuck. Of course, for others, it's all about the money, more than they could imagine making in nine-to-five jobs. I thought that was Sharon's story.

"For me, I was becoming too old for the risk of running the operation. Women with my kind of business were going to jail. Kristin Davis, Governor Spitzer's madam. The woman from Westchester they called the 'Soccer Mom Madam.' Society takes deep vengeance against women who've been successful outside its laws. Maybe especially when they profit off what might be looked at as male weakness. When I left the business and bought this building, some of my employees didn't have a plan. I didn't have a part in getting Sharon into the game, and I hope I prevented her from falling into a pimp's trap, but I also made the Life easy for her. Maybe that helped her get deeper into it, stay in it. The sadness of Sharon's life and death, and what it says about me, my life, and my rationalizations about it, is damn near overwhelming."

"I'm sorry for the judgment. This whole thing has taken me by surprise."

"I understand."

"Did you say you own this building?"

"It allows for a moderate profit. The tenants don't know anything about my past, so please don't repeat what I've told you. I just want a quiet life and to be a good neighbor."

* * *

Emily took a peek into the living room to check on Skye, who hadn't budged from her spot in front of the TV. She returned to the table. "I guess what's freaking me out is that I was probably the last person to see Sharon alive. And I may be the only one who saw the killer."

"That concerns me too."

"The good thing is that the killer, if he was the killer, has no way of knowing I saw him."

"What did the police say?"

"Nothing, really. They said they may have me come in to look at photos. I was surprised they didn't want me to look at pictures right away or do a composite drawing. Last night, after they left, I searched for stories on the web about Sharon's murder. There was nothing."

"Hooker lives don't matter," Kathleen said. "Men can hook up with a thousand women, but it doesn't devalue their lives. Sex workers are like irregulars on a discount rack. The media doesn't care, the public doesn't care, and to cops, hookers are criminals, so the cops don't care. It isn't only serial killers who dehumanize them."

"I was reading last night," Emily said, "when a murdered sex worker disappears, more times than not, nobody calls in a missing-person report. And if there's a warrant because the woman didn't show up at court after an arrest, the police categorize her as a fugitive, not a missing person, even if somebody reports her missing. It gives serial killers a head start, because the police don't investigate it as a possible crime the way they would if any other woman went missing."

"You're right," Kathleen said. "And when they find a body, since there's no missing-person report to match the body against, it's hard to retrace the victim's steps to investigate. The body can go unidentified for years, if not forever, which makes it that much harder to catch the killer."

"So there is one thing that's bothering me about that," Emily said. "Sharon was beautiful and really put together. I thought she was a model. A serial killer wouldn't think she'd disappear without someone missing her. Why would he pick her? And Sharon knew the guy in the maroon car, or he said something that made her comfortable going with him. It didn't seem to be a long enough conversation for a business negotiation."

"It wasn't a random pickup by someone stalking the 'ho stroll,' which surely isn't this neighborhood, in any event," Kathleen said. "Sharon didn't work the street, and I'm sure she hadn't arranged a date with him. She was coming to my house. She would have called if she'd changed her plans."

Emily rolled her questions around in her mind, a thought jelling. "Victims of the North Beach Killer advertised on Craigslist, and the police believe they met the killer while working. But Sharon wasn't working. So, what if her murder had nothing to do with her profession? What if the killer left Sharon's body at North Beach just so the police would *assume* the North Beach Killer did it, to steer the cops in the wrong direction? That would mean he carefully researched and planned the killing and cover-up ahead of time."

Kathleen leaned forward. "If you're right, the cops are looking for the wrong killer with a completely irrelevant profile."

"If they continue down that path"—Emily looked Kathleen in the eyes—"we'll never know what happened to Sharon, a lunatic psychopath will stay out on the street, and he'll probably kill again."

CHAPTER

15

SIX DAYS AFTER the subway attack, Kathleen busied herself wiping down the television screen, which was tuned to CNN once again. She wiped at the morning anchor, who was reporting on the recovery of the injured still in the hospital. The subway attack stories had taken a back seat to floods, the first hurricane of the season forming in the Gulf of Mexico, and political scandal. But there were still intermittent updates.

Kathleen had given the cops the security video of Sharon and had called the detectives earlier today to get an update, but they hadn't returned her calls. By now, the cops had checked Kathleen's own criminal record. Convicted felons were right up there with prostitutes in the lives-that-do-not-matter category, even decades after their last run-in with the law. She didn't expect a call back.

Still, she owed Sharon, and she wouldn't abandon her with no one caring why she had died or what happened to her remains. If nothing else, she needed to claim Sharon's body and arrange for a funeral, although she had no idea whom to invite from Sharon's recent life. She would just cremate Sharon and spread the ashes on her own, if necessary. She wished she had some way to find the possible girlfriend, Angel or Angela, before making decisions. More importantly, Angel might have information about who would want to kill Sharon. Kathleen refused to sit back and let the police sweep Sharon's death under the carpet as if it didn't matter.

Thinking about how alone Sharon had been, Kathleen felt a pang of her own deepest loneliness and the decades-old pain and guilt over the loss of her daughter: Lauren. The guilt always flowed in once the loss-spigot opened. Kathleen had left Lauren alone at an age when no one should be.

Kathleen concentrated on swiping the television screen with her rag, feeling soothed by the cleaning. It took the edge off emotions that had haunted her for over thirty years. Keeping a clean home was the one good habit she'd acquired in prison. Before that, the apartment she'd shared with her husband and daughter on the Lower East Side had been a chronic mess. Boxes, black garbage bags, and old skates and clothes Lauren had outgrown gathered in high piles lining the hallway. Unlike the treasures of a hoarder, the items weren't saved because she and Michael were attached to them. The problem was that neither Kathleen nor her husband had the energy to do any sort of physical labor, no matter how minor. Plus, toward the end of her drug use, Kathleen had become too afraid to dump the trash in the basement. She'd thought people were waiting for her there. And Lauren had been trapped in the mess of her parents' addiction, chaos far worse than the physical trash.

Kathleen's phone shivered in the back pocket of her jeans, interrupting her housecleaning: Emily had posted on Facebook. Kathleen had meant to terminate the Sophie social media accounts once Emily moved into the building, but she hadn't brought herself to do it. Even though she didn't need to use a fake account to have contact with Emily anymore, she couldn't exactly open a Facebook account with a real profile photo and stay tuned in to Emily's life. Lauren might see it. Kathleen had taken a similar risk of running into Lauren, though, when she rented an apartment to Emily. But Kathleen had easily avoided Lauren the day she helped Emily move in, and Emily mostly gravitated toward the family home downtown when she wasn't working.

Emily's post was a video of Rusty. She was telling her friends that he'd woken her up from a nightmare yesterday. She wasn't sharing on Facebook what had caused her to have a nightmare.

Wise girl. She didn't need to broadcast that she might be a witness in a future murder prosecution, especially not when the killer was still out there.

Kathleen's phone buzzed again, this time a phone call from a number that wasn't in her contacts. She answered, expecting a robocall.

"Ms. Harris?"

"Yes, who is this?"

"Dunbar, at Sharon Williams's building."

"Oh, hello." He was the last person she'd expected to hear from.

"Sorry to bother you, but you're listed as an emergency contact for Sharon here at the building. I guess you did tell the truth about your relationship to her."

"I did," Kathleen said, although she was a bit surprised by this news.

"You know she only rented the apartment? From the condo owner. He wants to start cleaning out the place so he can rent it again."

"He's not wasting any time."

"I guess he needs the rent money." Dunbar lowered his voice. "He's not my favorite."

"I'll come over and start packing her things. Did the police do a lot of damage in there?"

"Not really. I stayed with them. It's building policy that we stay whenever we let anyone into the apartment, even the cops. They took her laptop, looked through some papers. I don't think they really put on their Sherlock Holmes caps."

"I can imagine. I'll be over later. Will you be on duty?"

"Until four."

Kathleen wasn't looking forward to emptying out Sharon's apartment. She thought she'd store the furniture until she could make sure no one was entitled to it. She could look for a will in the apartment, and maybe she'd find contact information for friends, business cards or event invitations. She could poke around and see if Sharon had left anything else around indicating that she planned to meet someone, perhaps after seeing Kathleen, on the night she died.

She doubted she'd find something like that, especially after the police had been at the apartment, but she hoped she'd at least find a lead on Angel. If she found a full name, she could look for her on social media. Sharon had no social media accounts, at least not under any name Kathleen knew, so Kathleen couldn't even peruse a list of Facebook friends. It was a pity no one kept real-life phone books and calendars anymore.

16

SHARON'S APARTMENT WAS as clean as Kathleen's. It was a one-bedroom with a view of a high-rise building across the street and the huge multifloor SONY movie theater. An apartment like this in a prime doorman building was by no means cheap. Sharon had plenty of cash for rent but no on-the-books job to qualify her for a mortgage. That would be why she'd sublet rather than bought.

Dunbar stayed close, watchful, while Kathleen looked around. The living room flowed into a small dining area and a compact kitchen that was separated from the rest of the room by a granite breakfast bar. Kathleen went to the kitchen first. Coffeemaker. Microwave. Shiny toaster. Nothing out of place. The counters were so clear of personal effects that the place could have been a vacation villa. Kathleen opened the refrigerator, looking for any sign of Sharon's life. She pulled out a box of garbage bags from her oversize shoulder bag. She could throw away the milk and cheese, which were already old.

"If I were you, I'd leave that for the owner to clean out," Dunbar said, his full lips pursed tight, dark eyes pained. "You don't owe him."

Kathleen shut the refrigerator. "You're right."

She opened drawers under the counters, hoping for a junk drawer full of clues about Sharon's life—whom she shared her life with, and who she would willingly accompany in the maroon car just when she was about to reach Kathleen's home. But there was nothing personal. Silverware, utensils, lighters, a couple of pens, but not a single notepad or discarded item. Even Kathleen's inner neat freak allowed for personal items, just stored away in an organized manner. Sharon had apparently taken out the garbage with her when she left her home for the last time. The garbage pail under the sink was empty.

The living room looked like a high-end doctor's waiting room. Leather Holiday Inn furniture. Neutral colors. There were even a few magazines on the end tables.

Kathleen turned back to Dunbar, who stood by awkwardly. "Did she bring tricks here?"

Dunbar looked scared. He wiped his palm over his close-cropped hair. "No, no. They don't allow that kind of thing here."

Okay, Kathleen thought, *she definitely brought tricks here, and Dunbar covered for her. Maybe he got a cut.* Kathleen would have told Sharon not to do that. One needed personal, untainted space. She didn't hold the lying against Dunbar. Sharon was dead, and he was alive and needed his job. End of story.

Kathleen looked at Dunbar, who appeared distraught. "You were pretty close to her, huh?"

He nodded, his large shoulders rounded. "I'm all messed up about it."

"Could you tell me about the last time you saw her?"

"It was the day of the subway attack. We talked about the attack for a couple of minutes."

"Did she seem upset or worried about anything else?"

"She was upset, just like everyone. She didn't mention anything else. We were standing out in the driveway, watching the crowds walking uptown, before she went out for her morning run in the Park. The sidewalks were packed with people going back home from work, since the subways were down. A lot of them were hiking ten miles and more, could probably have gotten home faster if they'd waited for the subway to come back on. She said a terrorist attack does that to you, makes you want to keep moving. She said she remembered that from Nine-Eleven."

"You're right. I walked up Central Park West from Forty-Second Street. I passed two blocks from here. It didn't even occur to me to stop here instead of walking home." The thought hit Kathleen now, a kick in the gut. "I might have seen you and her standing there if I'd walked on Broadway."

Kathleen's regret deepened. If she'd stopped here, she would have been with Sharon that day. Sharon might not have come to see her that night. Sharon might be alive now. The smallest change in a minute of Kathleen's day might have meant forty more years of life for her friend.

Kathleen inhaled, trying to clear her head of the sadness and frustration. She reminded herself that there was no way Sharon's death had resulted from random bad luck. She hadn't just been in the wrong place at the wrong time. The killer had likely known her and, as Emily had said, was probably someone who planned things out, including the cover-up.

Kathleen looked around the sterile room. There must have been more to Sharon's life than she was seeing. There had to be some answers here. "Did you know her friend—Angel, or Angela?"

"Yeah, Angela. But I haven't seen her for a while. I think Sharon used to stay at Angela's a lot. Angela would come pick her up in an old Toyota. But I haven't seen her for at least six months. Maybe they broke up."

They must not have been in regular contact if Angela hadn't come here to try to find Sharon as Kathleen had. "I'll start in the bedroom now," she said, mulling it over.

17

THE BLINDS WERE at half-mast in Sharon's bedroom, and the room lay in shadow. Kathleen turned on the light and homed in on the books piled on the night table next to the bed. She felt a surprising sense of relief. It was the first real sign that Sharon had lived here, or lived at all.

Kathleen picked up the top book: an Al-Anon meditation book with inspiring thoughts for each day of the year. Below it was an Al-Anon step book. Sharon had been attending Al-Anon, the twelve-step program for people who had relatives or friends who were alcoholics or addicts. Kathleen didn't think Sharon's parents were alcoholics, so maybe it was Angela who'd motivated Sharon to go. Long ago, Kathleen had tried Al-Anon herself. For a few weeks. She'd attended meetings at a building on Saint Marks Place where AA, NA, and Al-Anon meetings ran twenty-four hours a day. It had been a few blocks from the home she shared with her husband and then-twelve-year-old Lauren.

A speaker at one of the meetings, a graying elementary schoolteacher, had said, "Have you tried everything to stop him? Have you tried being extra nice to him, thinking—or maybe he told you—that if you only treated him better, he wouldn't drink or use drugs? Have you tried being a royal bitch? Have you tried drinking or drugging with him, thinking that maybe, if you drank with him, he wouldn't think of you as the square who's always nagging? And maybe if you got high with him, you could convince him to drink or drug *less*?"

For a fleeting moment a few months later, Kathleen remembered that woman's words when Michael came home with cocaine to smoke for the first time. Lauren was at a friend's house for a birthday sleepover. Michael was already high, rocking from foot to foot, hyped up. "Kat, come on, let's try something new . . . together."

He'd given her that irresistibly broad smile, teeth still white back then. The same smile that had coaxed her into her first consensual sex at seventeen. Kathleen had smiled back at him, nervously. "Okay, pass it here."

Until that day, Kathleen had been the stable one, a wife and mother who stuck with her troubled husband through thick and thin, unable to bear the thought of abandoning him or depriving Lauren of the father she loved. Maybe if Kathleen had gotten more Al-Anon under her belt, maybe if she'd really listened to the message of the graying schoolteacher—that it didn't help anything when you got high with them—she would have known better than to try crack even once.

After that day, they talked about it many times, passing a pipe back and forth to each other during long days and nights in their smoky bedroom as they discussed how they'd gotten hooked on crack the very first time. Neither Kathleen nor Michael had thought the drug would tilt their life off its already fragile axis after only one hit of a pipe. Sometimes Michael would weep, saying, "I know I got you into this, baby. I'm sorry."

But she'd ended up worse than Michael. Within just a few days of first smoking, Kathleen started to hear a secret transistor radio broadcasting in her head and saw terrifying images. She learned later that she had cocaine-induced psychosis. Each day, her belly and chest clenched with craving. The addiction was a drill sergeant that demanded she get high, but she'd had no idea that the drill sergeant was making her insane too.

It would be a long time before she knew the voices in her head weren't real and stopped doing drugs long enough for them to disappear. She'd been lucky in that regard. Some people lived with drug-induced mental illness for the rest of their lives, needing psychotropic medications to dull it even after they got clean. For her, she'd only needed prison and a counselor there, who helped her see that drugs were the cause of her problems. She'd stopped using completely in prison and the hallucinations had stopped too. Unfortunately, by then she'd already lost everything that meant anything to her.

And Lauren had lost infinitely more. Her childhood ended the day Kathleen began smoking crack. The guilt walked with Kathleen every day of her life.

Inside the pages of the Al-Anon book, Kathleen looked to see if Sharon had underlined anything. She yearned to feel some sign of her friend here, the old warmth of their relationship. As if in answer to her wish, the book opened to a photo that Sharon must have used as a bookmark: Sharon and a woman. The tawny-complexioned woman—African American or maybe Latina—had a buzz-cut mullet, hiking boots, and a thick belly and breasts. She and Sharon were holding a parrot between them, a turquoise body of water in the background. It was one of those overpriced photos you could buy when you visited an eco-park in Mexico. They were both smiling, happy. Kathleen kept her tears inside.

She turned to Dunbar. "Is this Angela?"

He leaned in. "Yes. That's her."

Kathleen placed the photo back in the pages of the book and put the book into her shoulder bag. She found a few earrings and a gold necklace in the night table and took them too.

"Dunbar, can I ask you something?"

"Sure."

"Did anyone ever visit Sharon who drove a maroon car, a husky guy? He might have looked like a bouncer, or military?"

He paused, thinking. "I don't remember that. People usually don't drive their cars into the front driveway unless they're picking up or dropping off. He doesn't sound like anyone I've seen. I'm sorry."

CHAPTER

18

A WEEK AFTER THE subway attack, Emily entered the glittering basement of a landmark Tribeca restaurant for a fund-raising breakfast. Round tables for ten draped in white tablecloths were set with crystal and china. Carved tin ceilings. Romanesque columns at the room's edges. The restaurant was in a building that had once been a wharf warehouse, back when merchant sailing ships used to dock on the Lower West Side of Manhattan. A podium and microphone stood front and center, up a step from the rest of the room.

"Get some breakfast and we'll sit down at a table in the back," Emily told Thea, who wore a pink cotton dress and bright lipstick for the occasion. "You're not here to work. You can introduce yourself to the other people who end up sitting at your table. They'll be grateful for the icebreaker."

When City Hall staff did campaign work for the mayor, it was strictly on their own time. If interns came to campaign events, it was for the learning experience, and Emily was there in case something official needed doing. But aside from the flood of emails on her phone that needed monitoring, weekday fund raisers were usually a break for Emily too. And the food was always good.

Emily guided Thea toward the back of the room, where plates of pastries and fruit as well as coffee and tea urns covered a white-tableclothed buffet. Behind the long table, chefs in tall hats cooked omelets. Emily filled a plate with fruit and ordered a veggie omelet. While they waited for their eggs, Thea talked about a prostitution diversion program in Oakland she'd learned about. Max rolled up on them, wearing a suit and tie. He stared a bit too long at Emily's fitted sky-blue dress. There was a long beat before his eyes left her breasts.

"See the guy over there?" Max said to Thea as they carried their plates toward an empty table at the back of the room, farthest from the podium. He chucked his chin toward the side of the room at a short guy with curly hair that formed an awkward crown around his otherwise bald head.

Emily could tell what was coming next: Big Staff Member gonna lay some knowledge on the intern.

"He's the City's number-one lobbyist—or that's what he tells anyone who'll listen," Max said. "He's a bundler too. He puts together political donations from all his clients, who put together donations from all their friends and families. He hands politicians checks for hundreds of thousands of dollars. Even though politicians aren't allowed to accept individual donations above a few thousand dollars, they can accept unlimited bundles of them." Max smirked. "So the guys with money and connections still have the power, screw campaign finance laws."

Emily wondered why Max sounded so gleeful about that. Probably because his father was a politician. Personally, it always made her uncomfortable that the mayor was basically indebted to the donors. The biggest bundlers had the mayor's personal cell phone number.

Emily read her emails on her phone as she ate, while Max talked to Thea nonstop and she displayed appropriate fascination. Someone else joined the table and began chatting with Thea.

Max leaned toward Emily.

"So, we've never talked about it, but who do *you* know?"

Emily looked up from her phone. "What do you mean?"

"You know, who got you the job? Who's your rabbi? I've never been able to figure that out. We can assume our intern is the daughter of a fund raiser, from Iowa, no less. But you, I don't know." He threw his tie over his shoulder and picked up a fork, sawing into a plate of huevos rancheros. "You're as white and middle class as they come, so you're not here because some wise person decided City Hall needed diversity."

Emily scoffed, covering her rising anger. "Look me up on LinkedIn, Max. I got my job based on merit. Through a posting."

"Ha. Good joke."

Emily whispered, her face going hot, "You're so used to privilege, you think *nobody* who gets what you have could possibly have *earned* it."

Max put down his fork. "Whoa, a little harsh, Emily."

The lobbyist with the curly crown blew into a microphone at the podium at the front of the room. "Good morning. Good morning, everyone. Thank you for coming. We are going to have a stimulating discussion about city and national policy with the greatest-ever mayor of the City of New York, Derick Sullivan! The next president of the United States!"

The attendees, who now filled almost all the tables, applauded and smiled as the mayor halfway stood and took a small bow from his seat at one of the front tables, his hands in a humble namaste pose. One middle-aged man in a corner pumped his fists awkwardly, calling out, "Woohoo."

The curly-crowned lobbyist gave the woohoo guy a humorous royal wave. "Without further ado, to introduce the most important politician in America today is a man far more eloquent than me, who has known the mayor longer than any of us: Roger Merritt."

Roger stepped up to the podium, where he looked down at curly crown, shaking his hand, then turned to the audience. "I won't keep you too long, because I know you've come for the main event." He paused, letting the audience focus fully on him. "Derick has been hailed as an overnight success story, catapulted onto the national scene. But really, my friends, I can attest that he has been a long time in the making. And the learning. This is a man who has shown himself ready for the biggest job in the greatest nation, a man who will bring back the prestige of the Office of the President after, I'm sure we would all agree, some rocky years."

A spattering of pained chuckles. Roger listened to the laughter, smiling.

"I've known Derick and have worked with him since he was an earnest volunteer for my ill-fated run for Congress representing the Upper East Side. As many of you know, it became clear to me at that time that I was a better mentor than a politician. And I am proud to say that I found this guy." Roger swept his hand toward the mayor. "He has the rare combination of smarts and an innate ability to connect with people. But I will tell you a secret: he is also a huge policy wonk. And I am sure you will appreciate his discussion today of affordable housing, infrastructure, and immigration.

"I thank you all for coming out and contributing to make it possible to hear his thoughts on the challenging issues that face our nation and to help him move forward in his quest to do something about them. Ladies and gentlemen, I give you Derick Sullivan."

The house broke into applause. The mayor kissed his wife on the cheek and rose to shake Roger's hand at the podium.

"Just over a week since the second-worst mass killing in New York City history," Mayor Sullivan began, on a somber note, "I continue to work closely with the NYPD and all the federal agencies to figure out why it happened and how they would prevent it happening again. As a small aside, while we all know that the NYPD patrols the subways, the subway system is itself the responsibility of the governor."

Emily groaned inside. The governor was also "exploring" whether he would run for president, and she was sure the mayor was about to steer the wheels of the bus over him.

"We have gone on record in the past that we want the MTA to remove garbage bins on subway platforms. Studies have shown they merely attract trash and do nothing to prevent it. Worse still, they are the perfect receptacle for an improvised explosive. Exactly what happened here. We know the terrorist had no real connection to New York City and was from upstate New York. As the greatest city in the world, we will inevitably attract sick people looking to do maximum damage, whether they are affiliated officially with a terrorist organization or not. That's why, if I am elected president, I will make sure that the cities of this great nation—most especially this great city—receive the funding necessary to deal with our terrorism risk. We will not be shortchanged by Homeland Security anymore."

The room exploded with applause.

Carrying a bowl of yogurt and a cup of tea, Roger sat next to Emily as the mayor began to speak at length about health care. Hers was one of the few half-empty tables, probably because there were no movers and shakers sitting there, just two staffers, an intern, and an old man.

Roger wiped off his spoon with his napkin before putting the napkin neatly on his lap and spooning yogurt and fresh fruit into his mouth.

"So, Emily, you've been with us for about a year now?" Roger asked, after the mayor finished his speech and took a question from a man at the far side of the room.

"Yes, just over."

"How are you liking us?"

"I'm very happy. I love it."

"Where did you go to school? I confess," he said in a conspiratorial manner, "I've heard Derick's Q and A at least a hundred times, and it gets boring."

Emily saw Max out of the corner of her eye, looking dubiously at Roger as if wondering whether Roger was moving into Max's imagined territory, even though Roger was old enough to be her father.

"NYU, undergraduate and graduate."

Roger leaned in to be heard over the noise of another round of applause. "Is your family from New York?" Emily noticed the pores of his skin, rolling along light wrinkles that had probably been chemically smoothed. No frown lines. "You have a born-and-bred New York accent," he continued, "not that young people have much of an accent nowadays. When I was young, New York sounded like New York. Boston sounded like Boston. Nowadays, even southerners sound virtually indistinguishable from northerners."

Emily gave that some thought. Her mother had the thickest New York accent of anyone she knew, and even that wasn't like the Brooklyn accents in old movies.

"What do your parents do?" Roger asked.

"My mother is an attorney. A divorce lawyer. My stepfather is an FBI agent."

He raised an eyebrow. "Interesting."

Emily didn't say anything about her real father. Her father dying young in a fire was too dark for breakfast conversation.

"Family is everything, in my opinion," Roger said. "Work hard, play hard, but family is the most important thing. Don't ever let work become more important than that. Although this man here"—he signaled to the mayor—"he's as close to me as family. I'm a true believer. Honored to be along for the ride with him."

After the Q and A, Mayor Sullivan began stopping at tables to personally greet the donors. Roger also worked the room, schmoozing with the people Emily figured he'd invited—and whose checks he bundled. Emily spotted Chief Reilly standing near a wall, watching the goings-on. She wondered if he was off duty, working campaign security. A thought jelled in her mind.

She went over to stand beside Reilly. "Good morning."

"Hey, Emily, how are you?"

"I'm great, thanks. You?"

"Can't complain. Nobody likes a complainer," the chief said dryly, still looking out at the room.

"Listen, I wanted to get information on a case. Could I call later?"

"What's the case?"

"Sharon Williams, a prostitute murdered last week."

"Pretty far out of your wheelhouse, isn't it?"

"There's a reporter doing a series of articles about prostitution." For some reason, Emily hadn't thought about what she'd say if he asked why she was interested in the case. She hadn't thought through her impulsive ask at all, and now she certainly didn't want to talk about her friendship with Sharon's former madam. "I thought we might get ahead of it."

"Oh, yeah, I saw the story about Hunts Point in the clips. Nice quote in there. What do you need?"

"Mostly I was wondering if I could get the results from the medical examiner's report. I'm wondering how she died. The North Beach Killer has been on the loose in the city for a long time . . ."

"That's easy enough." Chief Reilly took out a small notepad from his inside jacket pocket and jotted down a note. "I'll give you a call."

CHAPTER

19

THE NEXT DAY, Lauren lay next to her beautiful, perfect husband in their king-sized bed. Golden late-day light seeped around the edges of the venetian blinds. Thank god Carl could still have sex. For his sake more than hers, although Lauren could admit to herself that she might not feel as sanguine about it if she wasn't getting any.

Carl kissed the top of Lauren's head, which rested on his shoulder. He wasn't as strong as he'd been, but her heart still inflated every time she saw his bottomless chocolate eyes and generous smile. His love showed plain on his face when he saw his special people, not just her and Alex, but Emily and Jessica and Rick too. Plus, his sisters, aunts, and cousins. Carl loved freely and deeply.

That pretty much guaranteed a houseful of visitors a lot of the time, and Lauren embraced it. It was so different from the isolation and paranoia of her childhood home. Carl's family, Emily, and Skye were her only family now, and she was grateful to have them.

She thought, *Why him? Why me?* Why did a man like Carl have to draw such a rough hand?

Of course, the answer was: Why not him? Why not her? Life was gnarly and complicated, if you risked having one. After the trauma of her childhood, she'd battened down the hatches against every possible storm. Unsuccessfully. She'd married safe, keeping her life small, only to have it upended by Brian, her irresponsible, philandering first husband. Then she'd met Carl. Despite how shaken Lauren had been by her failed marriage and her ex-husband's sudden death, she had taken a chance on loving Carl. Her life had become full and joyous. She had no regrets. Even if Carl's current drug trial didn't pan out, even if he ended up with the worst sort of MS, she wouldn't change a single thing about her being in that battle with him.

She drifted off to sleep in the crook of Carl's arm, imagining the drug trial working and picturing Carl back to his old self. She heard Alex's voice from the front door, "Anybody here? I brought company."

Lauren opened her eyes. No time for a nap.

Lauren heard the chatter and yelps of young children first and Jessica shushing them. Jessica was her best friend, Brian's second wife. They were an unlikely duo. Widows-in-law, they called each other jokingly, if anyone asked how they'd met. They'd pretty much raised Emily together—Jessica never writing off her teenage stepdaughter—after Brian's death. Lauren could hear Jessica's nine-year-old twins darting ahead of their mother to come look for Lauren and Carl. Type A boys like their father, who'd died before they were born. Gray eyes like Emily, their half sister. Lauren rushed to get dressed before they barged in.

Jessica greeted Lauren in the hallway. She gave Lauren a knowing look and smile, taking in Lauren's bedhead. "Are we interrupting? We could go to the playground for a while."

"Don't be silly." Lauren released the boys, who had run into her arms to greet her. She smoothed down her hair and walked Jessica to the living room. "Just napping." Lauren took in the circles under Jessica's eyes and added, "It looks like you could use one."

"What's a nap?" Jessica said as she sat heavily in an armchair.

At forty-three, gorgeous even when exhausted, Jessica was always stretched too thin. It wasn't easy going through medical school and now the twenty-four-hour shifts of a resident, especially without a partner to help raise her twins. Lauren and Emily had tried to do what they could to help with the kids, although Lauren felt stretched thin as well now, dealing with Carl's medical appointments and challenges and her own fear about that.

Carl came out to the living room, walking more steadily than he had only a few days ago. Lauren's eyes met Jessica's and they smiled.

Carl sat and surfed channels on the muted TV. "How are the subway victims doing? Do you still have a lot of them?"

"It's starting to calm down," Jessica said. "We had a dozen emergency surgeries last week."

Alex brought the boys to the kitchen to get cookies. The uproar of their chatter trailed behind them, fading to a hum.

"I've been having trouble sleeping," Jessica continued. "We had to amputate the leg of a thirteen-year-old yesterday, below the knee." She lowered her voice so her sons couldn't hear, even though Lauren would bet they were thoroughly focused on Alex, their hero. "It took a lot of energy to tamp down my emotions so I could show up fully for her, although all I did was stitch her up after the surgeon finished. The emotional blowback is bad afterward. For me, at least. The girl's alive and her parents are grateful, but her life will never be normal again. It sucks that we couldn't save her leg. We really tried."

"Mattingly wasn't even an outcast like the school shooters," Lauren said. "I just don't understand it."

Carl put out his hand so Lauren would sit on the arm of his chair next to him, which she did. "He was more like the Las Vegas shooter," he said. "He kept his distance from people, not the other way around. He didn't seem to be an attention seeker. He had that one very young girl who says he was her boyfriend, although it sounds like sex was the extent of their relationship. No one ever saw him with her or even talking to her. Based on what she said about their encounters, he was probably a misogynist, but he was a handsome guy, having sex. Not an incel.

"The Bureau's starting to find some of Mattingly's more obscure social media posts. He had several online identities. He never spouted off an ideological point of view. He just followed, liked, sometimes posted laughing emojis on photos relating to mass killings. He followed ISIS types. He was a fan of Jihad John's beheading videos."

Jessica groaned.

"And he was a total fanboy of the New Zealand mosque massacre too. It doesn't look like it was political or religious."

"In other words," Lauren said, "the kid was even less principled than a narcissistic ISIS executioner."

"Yup, if you can imagine that."

*　　*　　*

At dusk, Kathleen wrote on a pad on her desk as she listened to the person on the phone. "Okay, and the hourly rate? Yes, okay, tomorrow will be good."

She turned on wall light switches in the darkening apartment and walked to the door while she talked. She looked out the peephole before opening the door.

Wearing cutoff denim shorts and a spaghetti-strap shirt, Emily kissed her on the cheek. Despite the recent tension when they'd talked about Sharon's profession, they were becoming friends.

Kathleen waved her into the living room, where the TV played on mute. "I'll pay the deposit on Venmo and see you tomorrow at ten AM. Thank you." Kathleen put her phone down on the thick arm of a couch and spoke to Emily. "I have a storage company coming to pick up Sharon's things."

Emily sat on the couch. "That's a big job. Can you manage it yourself?"

"It's a surprisingly small job. The furniture belongs to the condo owner. It was a furnished rental, it turns out. She had clothes that need to be boxed up, very little else. It was an impersonal place. It makes me feel like she had somewhere else where she really lived. But the doorman said she was there regularly. She had her routines, running in the Park, grocery shopping. Not that there was much in the fridge. I wish I had been a better friend to her. I didn't stay in touch in ways that count. I didn't know anything important about her life."

Emily gave her a long look. "She knew who to come to when she was in trouble. I think that shows that you were a friend in the ways that count. It's not like she committed suicide and you missed the signs. She was killed, and you didn't do it."

Kathleen felt warmed by Emily's words. Emily had grown up into a compassionate and insightful person. "Thank you. I needed to hear that. So, where's my favorite baby?"

"With Hector. He works Saturday and Sunday and gets two weeknights off. He keeps her then."

"You have a good relationship?"

"We've been friends since middle school. He was my high school boyfriend. We broke up in college but stayed friends. I guess you'd say friends with occasional benefits. When I got pregnant, he wanted to get back together. But in my mind, we weren't together before, so why would it work if a baby pushed us together? Plus, from what I've read, the outcomes are better for kids who have parents who never lived together than for kids who have parents who break up. It avoids trauma."

"You've read studies on it?" Kathleen asked, raising her eyebrows.

Emily smiled. "Evidence-backed child-rearing. It can't hurt to be informed."

"I see your point," Kathleen said, but she wondered whether Emily's stance on Hector was based on evidence or, more likely, on Emily's disappointment in her father. It was one thing to have a high school or college boyfriend. It was another to risk becoming a family together. Kathleen wondered if Emily's fear of that risk had caused their breakup in the first place.

"Hector is very traditional," Emily went on. "He doesn't entirely see things my way. Beside that little point of contention, I couldn't be luckier. He's an amazing father and a great partner to raise Skye with."

On TV, a news anchor was saying something about the subway attack. Video of the ambulances racing away from the scene played in the background, the hundredth time Kathleen had seen it. She turned up the sound.

"Today, the MTA announced it would remove all the garbage containers from the subway system. After the commercial break, we will have an interview with the parents of Jackson Mattingly's secret fifteen-year-old girlfriend. We are learning that Homeland

Security took her in for extensive questioning this week. We will find out more from her parents about whether she is suspected of helping Mattingly in the attack and whether he gave her any hints about it beforehand."

"*Oy.*" Kathleen muted it. "I'd lay odds they won't report any new information from exploiting the teenage girlfriend." She pulled Sharon's Al-Anon book from her shoulder bag. "Let me show you a photo I found at the apartment."

"Why was Sharon going to Al-Anon? My mother went there," Emily said offhandedly.

"Really?" Kathleen sat next to Emily, trying to hide her interest. It wasn't surprising, but the thought triggered her familiar vortex of painful memories, mixed with hope that Lauren had gotten the help she needed.

Kathleen fished the photo out from between the pages of the book and handed it to Emily.

Emily studied it. "They look happy together. Her girlfriend?"

"Yes. The manager at the Easy Street said Sharon had a girlfriend named Angel or Angela. Sharon's doorman says it's her. But he didn't know her last name."

Emily took out her phone. "Do you mind if I take a picture of it?"

Kathleen shrugged. "That's fine."

Emily laid the photo of Sharon and Angela on the coffee table and snapped the picture. "I have an app that does reverse lookups of photos. It will tell us whether the picture has been posted anywhere."

Kathleen looked over Emily's shoulder as she uploaded the photograph of Angela and Sharon. They watched the rotating circle for a few seconds before the app reported that it had found no match for the image. A paragraph explained that it had searched over 40 billion images but that personal photos often lacked matches.

Emily sighed. "Well, we tried."

CHAPTER

20

KATHLEEN UNLOADED PLASTIC containers of rotisserie chicken, rice, and beans from Casa del Mofongo, a local Dominican restaurant that delivered. Green trees brushed the screens of her kitchen's double-wide window. The room was old-fashioned, with distressed wood cabinets and shiny appliances that winked at the rustic style of the room. The squawking of twilight birds gave Kathleen's kitchen a country-cabin vibe, which was why this was her favorite room in her home.

On her iPad, Emily searched for social media pages of people who had known Sharon. Kathleen had thought of several old employees whose phone numbers she didn't have. But Emily had found few of them on social media and none had photos of Angela among their friends.

"Eat," Kathleen said as she sat. "It wasn't as if I checked social security cards to make sure new employees used their real names. If they're living square lives now, they're probably using names I never knew. And if they're using social media professionally, they'd use stage names I can't even guess at."

"Do you have pictures of any of them? We could try reverse lookup of your friends like we did with Angela, maybe get stage names and work our way back from there."

"I'm not the selfie type and didn't advertise. Sorry."

Serving the food onto blue ceramic plates, Kathleen felt nearly blissful sitting across from Emily. She'd have to resolve her secret soon but hadn't figured out how to do it. The problem with deception was that it created a loop that trapped you in even more lies. She needed the truth to come out, but Emily might want nothing to do with her if she knew who Kathleen was. And Kathleen had no doubt that, once the secret was out, Emily would hear things from her mother that would make the situation even worse. Deservedly so. But she couldn't bear to lose Emily now.

Kathleen's phone buzzed against the wood of a cookbook shelf. She reached behind her to see who was calling. Dunbar. She answered, mystified. Emily began reading work emails on her phone as Kathleen took the call. Emily was always on call, perusing emails every spare minute.

"Miss Harris."

"Kathleen, please."

"Kathleen, I'm calling because, when the owner inspected the apartment, he packed up a box of stuff that he said wasn't his. I had to change the mailbox lock too. We never found Sharon's key to open it, and a new tenant is coming in. I took out Sharon's old mail. It's mostly junk, but there's what looks like a credit card bill and a phone bill. The owner told me to just take the box and the mail and do what I want with it. That would be fine, but it's not his to say that. I know you already sent her clothes to storage, but can you take the rest of her things?"

"Of course. I'll come. Are you still on duty?"

"Until midnight. I'm working a double."

When Kathleen hung up, she turned to Emily, who looked at her with open curiosity.

"Want to take a ride? Dunbar has Sharon's credit card and phone bills. Maybe we can find out more about what she was doing over the last few weeks. It could give us more leads to find Angela too."

* * *

Emily rode shotgun in the fast-moving traffic of the Henry Hudson Parkway. Across the blood-orange Hudson River, the sun morphed into fiery trails behind tall buildings stacked on New Jersey cliffs.

"I've been thinking about the North Beach Killer," Emily said. "It's unusual that they found Sharon so quickly. A lot of the bodies on North Beach were hidden there for years before anyone found them."

"I think they're keeping an eye out for bodies left there," Kathleen said. "You don't see much about it in the media anymore, but the family of one of the women was raising hell at one time, saying the investigation's been shoddy."

Emily thought about it. "Maybe you could do that too."

Kathleen glanced at Emily. "Do what?"

"Raise hell in the media. It can help."

Kathleen exited on West Seventy-Ninth Street and waited in a bottleneck at a traffic light at Riverside Drive, where cars fed in from the uptown and downtown exits off the highway.

"If I revealed publicly how I knew Sharon, I'd be dismissed just like the sex workers," she said. "The family of the prostitute that's been complaining about the North Beach investigation is just a square family with a troubled, addicted daughter. But having a sex worker for a daughter throws shade on them as far as law enforcement and the media are concerned. The sense I get from the news reporting is that the family is viewed as one step up from being prostitutes and addicts themselves. You can imagine how the media would look at me, basically Sharon's pimp—even though that's not true at all and never was. I'd hate to open myself up to the public scrutiny."

"I can understand that."

Kathleen turned into a sparkling circular driveway surrounding a lush garden. Emily took in her surroundings. A circular driveway in Manhattan was a sign of wealth. Any use of real estate was, especially in this part of town. A man in a maroon door attendant uniform, apparently Dunbar, approached the car. Emily rolled down her window. He bent to look in and held out a batch of mail in a rubber band.

"This is all of it. Even the junk mail."

Kathleen exited the car. She opened the back door, and Dunbar placed an open cardboard box on the back seat. After he closed the door, Kathleen stood next to Emily's window to talk to Dunbar. A warm evening breeze carried the scent of flowers, trees, and summer car exhaust, something soothing about the combination. It brought Emily back to summer evenings of childhood innocence, going to the Bennett Park playground with her father after he came home from work.

"Have the police come by or contacted anyone?" Kathleen asked Dunbar.

"Not that I know of. No one on the building's staff has been interviewed. It's a damn shame."

Through the sideview mirror, Emily saw Kathleen touch his arm. "Thanks for helping me. I'll let you know when we're having a service. No worries, though, if you can't come."

"I'll come if I'm not working."

As they drove away, Emily's phone rang. An unidentified number.

"Emily, this is Chief Reilly."

"Oh, hello. You're working late." Emily noted it, but there was nothing unusual about nighttime calls and emails. He was on twenty-four-hour call, like her.

"The day got away from me and I wanted to get back to you. I received the ME's report on Sharon Williams. Her throat was cut. That was the cause of death. She suffered a massive loss of blood."

"Did she die on the beach?"

Kathleen's face snapped to Emily with surprise before her eyes returned to the road.

"Dumped," the chief said. "The North Beach Killer has been using that location for years. He doesn't kill the women there. We've added the case to the other open cases. We don't close them when the serial killer is still at large."

After the call, Emily turned in her seat toward Kathleen. "The investigation was moving so slowly, I asked a friend from the NYPD."

"I wish you hadn't done that," Kathleen said, seeming startled.

Emily got the point: for all her air of respectability, Kathleen still distrusted cops. She'd told Emily that the cops had been brusque and uncaring when she'd spoken with them, as if they viewed her as a potential suspect. Emily hadn't consulted with Kathleen before asking the chief. She'd overstepped her bounds.

"What did he say?" Kathleen asked quietly.

Emily took a deep breath. "Her throat was cut. Her body was left on the beach afterward."

Kathleen accelerated the car onto the highway, heading home, her eyes glittering with moisture. "Did he tell you when she died?"

"Yes, the same night she disappeared."

Kathleen nodded. "Okay. At least that."

Emily knew what Kathleen was thinking: at least her delay in calling the police after Sharon called her hadn't contributed to her death.

* * *

Emily carried the uncovered box of Sharon's things from the car to Kathleen's apartment. Kathleen had seen that it held a French coffee press, a landline phone, and some soaps and lotions. Kathleen sat on the couch in the living room and began thumbing through the mail, Emily sitting beside her. Most of it was junk, but finally Kathleen tore open a Visa bill. She and Emily scanned the purchases: Amazon, a clothing store, a restaurant dinner the night before Sharon died, and Whole Foods.

Kathleen raised her eyebrows and pointed to an entry. "This is interesting. A fifty-dollar bill from Securus."

Emily frowned. "What's that?"

"It means she had a friend in prison. People buy calling cards for prisoners. Securus is the company that sells them. It used to be that inmates in upstate prisons could only make collect calls. Now there are calling cards."

"The cops will subpoena the company if they think it's important," Emily said. "But the company won't tell us anything."

"Sharon must have been close to the inmate, or she wouldn't be paying for the calls," Kathleen said. "The person must be going crazy trying to reach her. Calls to the outside can be the only light in an inmate's life. Believe me, I know."

"Really?" Emily always seemed surprised, as if she'd forgotten Kathleen's background, but she wasn't outright shocked anymore. Kathleen felt a deep need for Emily to know.

"Long before I was a madam, my husband died of an overdose. They charged me with murder because I bought the drugs for him."

"You're kidding. They do that?"

"Yes. He'd been dope-sick that morning and asked me to call his connection to come over. Begged me. The cops got a record of my call. Calls were on landlines back in those days. Dealers weren't using throwaway phones like they do now. I even left a message on the guy's answering machine, not that I said much on it. When they busted him, he turned state's evidence *on me*. I wasn't even a heroin user, and I wasn't a dealer like him. But they gave him a reduced sentence for agreeing to testify against me. I think he ratted out a lot of people to get the no-jail deal. I didn't have anyone to offer to get a deal.

"I pled guilty to manslaughter. They had proof that I bought my husband the drugs that killed him. I did five years in prison, but it could have been fifteen if I hadn't pled guilty."

"It's crazy that they charged you for that."

"I try not to dwell on my regret for every step I took that day that led to my husband dying and me going to prison. Some regrets are too big to fade away, although a tornado wouldn't have kept my husband from copping that morning, whether I'd helped him or not. In the final analysis, prison probably saved my life. I got clean there and stayed clean. I never did heroin like my husband, but we both smoked crack and I developed cocaine psychosis from it. I heard voices, saw things. It cleared up after I got clean, thank god. I haven't touched a mood-altering substance in over thirty years."

"Wow. I thought my mother's story was extreme. She was an addict too. She's been clean almost as long. You know, you guys have a lot in common. I would love to introduce you. Maybe we could have brunch?"

Kathleen shook off her reverie, wanting to avoid that meeting. "Sure, maybe." She turned her attention to Sharon's telephone bill, opening it. "Nothing much here. All local calls. They don't give the phone numbers for local calls."

"The police would have to subpoena that too. They may have done that already and it's just a matter of time." Emily looked toward the open cardboard box she'd carried upstairs. "Wait a sec. Can't we get the list of recent calls on a landline?"

Emily rose and pulled the black landline phone from the box. She plugged it into an outlet near the couch and brought the base and receiver back to Kathleen.

Kathleen took the phone from her and pressed the LIST button. "There's me, my number." Kathleen pressed again and the next number showed up. "She called this other number right before she called me."

"Let's Google the phone number first. If that doesn't work, there are apps for reverse phone lookup. They work better than the reverse photo ones."

After a moment, Emily showed her iPad screen to Kathleen. "There's a bunch of hits for the number. It's for this law firm." A sleek web page opened to a sky-blue background and white lettering. "Does the firm mean anything to you?"

"Sharon could have kept a lawyer on retainer," Kathleen said. "There had to be a connection between her calling a law firm and calling me right after them. Maybe she was in legal trouble and wanted to talk to me about it."

"Let's scroll through the staff listing," Emily said, clicking into a link called *Our Attorneys*. "Most firms have a page for each attorney with their picture and bio, and their specialties. Jeez. They've got hundreds of lawyers at this firm. And how do we know the person she called was a lawyer? It could be anyone who worked there. They could be IT or a clerical worker."

"True. But let's look."

Kathleen scanned the list of names on the first page. Nothing. Emily clicked into the second page. Kathleen ran down the names starting with B, then C, and then she saw it: *Carrier, Wayne*. All the synapses in her brain lit up. Kathleen knew him. So did Sharon.

Emily looked at her. "Any ideas? Are any of them familiar?"

Kathleen paused, pretending she was still reading. She shook her head. "Let's look at the next page."

After they'd read all the names on all the pages, Kathleen said, "I'll call the firm tomorrow to see if they have a record of her as a client. I can tell them she died and we found the firm's number in her apartment. Maybe they drafted a will for her."

CHAPTER

21

THE NEXT MORNING, Emily called Marlo, checking on the status of negotiations with the State Department and Nigerian embassy. Nine days since the attack and Marlo was still trying to smooth the way for the mother of a critically ill subway victim to come to New York from Nigeria. So far, it hadn't been easy. Emily had received a voice mail from a reporter at the *New York Times* and needed to give him information, at least somebody in the State Department to talk to . . . and blame, if need be. City Hall was doing all it could.

"This is the thing," Marlo said. "The victim, Rachel Ajiboye, was a Dreamer, born in New York, but her mother has a ten-year bar on entry after she was deported several years ago."

"Why was she deported?"

"Overstayed her visa. Not because of a criminal conviction, thank god. The State Department just has to issue a waiver for her to return. We've been pushing, but it takes a lot to move the federal bureaucracy."

"Do you have a name and number at State?"

Emily called the reporter from the *Times* to tell him that they were working on it. She gave him their contact at the State Department.

Then she pulled up the day's news clips that Thea had worked on with Max. The *Post* had written a scathing editorial about

Sullivan not canceling his fund raiser, which had taken place a week after the terror attack. The story was picking up steam. Other news outlets were starting to hype it.

Emily looked over at Max's desk. She let out a breath, surprised: a photo of Sharon was on his screen. It was a story about the police finding her body and the medical examiner's report about her cause of death. It was only a short story, but it had rated a mention in the *Daily News*.

Emily rolled over to Max, two feet of navy carpet separating their desks. "Is that going in the clips? What's that have to do with the mayor?"

"It just came in. The woman was last seen in Inwood. The mayor was asked about it when he was visiting a senior center near there. He said he didn't know about it. Now the *News* is accusing him of being too busy campaigning across the country to know what's going on at home."

"I didn't think the newspapers were going to cover it."

"His being away a lot?"

"The murder."

"You knew about it?"

"I saw her." Emily said. "I live in Inwood."

"You've gotta be kidding. You have streetwalkers in your neighborhood?"

"No! Jeez, why would you even say that? She wasn't a streetwalker, anyway. That's why they call them call girls. People *call* them."

He put up his hand in surrender. "Sorry. You really knew her?"

"No, but I saw her the night she was killed. I was questioned by the police. I think I'm the last one who saw her. A man pulled up in a car and she went with him. But she wasn't turning tricks. She was just walking to my building."

"Wow . . . so you're, like, a murder witness now?"

"Not really."

"I'm impressed. I'll put a notation on this that you're involved."

"Please, don't," Emily said, more intensely than she'd meant to. She modulated her voice. "It's not positive attention, or relevant."

Max shrugged. "Okay."

Emily returned to her work, regretting that she'd told Max. There was a gossipy quality to his interest in the clips and in her. She was starting to get the feeling that maybe she should have just kept what she'd witnessed to herself.

*　　*　　*

Carl and Rick walked together on Cabrini Boulevard, alongside the complex of buildings where Carl and Lauren lived. Rick was tall and fit, wearing a leather backpack on one shoulder. His brown skin had turned a deep russet after a recent Caribbean vacation. Rick was probably visiting him out of pity, although Carl tried to push that thought away.

They stopped at Café Bruuni, a tiny Ethiopian coffee shop on Pinehurst near 187th Street. Carrying cardboard cups, they doubled back to sit in the shade on a bench in Bennett Park. The sound of children playing in playground sprinklers mixed with raucous birdsong from within the park's tall trees. Dogs barked, several of them meeting up on the path that circumnavigated the small park's perimeter—two blocks in length and a block wide.

Carl felt a twinge, thinking Rick had suggested they sit down to save Carl from walking much farther. He could have told Rick that was unnecessary now. But Carl wanted Rick to notice for himself. It would look like Carl was fishing for reassurance if he brought the improvement up himself.

"So, have they got any new theories about Mattingly's motive?" Carl asked.

"We're still ruling out possible accomplices."

"Did they run his DNA?"

"No family on CODIS."

There was nothing surprising about the lack of a match on CODIS, the FBI's national database of DNA. A person had to have been arrested, and in some states convicted, to be forced to give up DNA. The Bureau would always run a mass murderer's DNA in its quest to track down accomplices, sometimes finding a family relationship to known terrorists who might have helped. But Mattingly came from an American prison guard family. Families like that needed to keep their records clean. Although

Carl might have expected at least one DWI conviction among them.

"Do you have an iPad with you?" Carl asked.

"Yeah." Rick pulled one from his backpack, punched in his password, and passed it to Carl.

Carl Googled Mattingly and chose the image page. "You've seen the family photo. The Christmas one with the whole family." A statement, not a question.

"Who could miss it?"

"Have you noticed anything strange about it?" Carl passed the iPad back to Rick. "Just tell me your impressions."

"He's tall. A lot taller than his parents and his cousins. But there's nothing strange about that. He's also way better looking than his parents, even when they were young. I've seen some of their old photos."

"Look at their eyes."

Rick enlarged the photo with two fingers on the touchscreen. "The parents' eye colors. Yes, we've seen that. It happens."

"Right. But what are the odds of having blue eyes if both your parents *and* grandparents have brown?" Carl raised his hand, answering his own question. "Not impossible, but when you consider his eye color, his height, his intelligence—I find it intriguing."

"He's not adopted," Rick said. "There's no family court records in Orange County where the family lived, and he was born there at Newburgh General. Per the hospital records, the mother had a normal delivery. The parents were together when he was born; both their names are on the original birth certificate and the hospital records. So he wasn't a stepchild to one of them. If anything, maybe he was a love child that Jason Mattingly raised as his own, either knowingly or unknowingly."

"The real baby daddy isn't going to step forward and claim that mistake now," Carl said. "The infamy of being the parent of a mass murderer lasts long after the thrill of fame wears off."

"We've talked about a sperm donor too."

"Don't couples who use sperm donors usually pick ones who look like the husband?"

"I guess, but a lot of the times, the sperm donor isn't the donor the parents chose. Some of the fertility doctors have been unethical, even used their own sperm if they thought they'd have better success. There's a doctor in Texas with hundreds of kids."

"If a doctor were Mattingly's biological father, it would at least explain his IQ," Carl said.

Rick shrugged. "It doesn't matter where his genes came from. We're not focusing on it. When it comes to nature or nurture, nurture is what we care about. We need to give the public an explanation about how this guy came to the point of bombing a subway. We need to learn everything we can so the Behavioral Science Unit can create a profile that can help us prevent future attacks. It won't add much to the story if they used a sperm donor."

"Yeah, but maybe there's more to this story . . ."

"That's cool, yeah," Rick said, more dismissively than Carl would have liked. "But there *is* something much more intriguing."

Carl smiled. "What?"

"He was interested in our mayor."

"Really? Interested how?"

"He showed up for his reelection inauguration. He had to stand outside. We have a photo of him. It was twenty degrees that day. It takes a high level of interest to travel two-plus hours and stand in the cold like that when you don't even have a ticket to get in for the ceremony."

"He's not from the city," Carl said, thinking it through. "That was before the mayor started campaigning nationally too."

"Right," Rick said. "It's a very weird man-crush for a teenager."

Carl agreed. "Derick Sullivan doesn't even have much youth appeal."

"It's given us new angles to look at."

22

A WOMAN SITTING BEHIND a long reception desk asked Kathleen to have a seat. Kathleen took in the expansive Big Law reception area with its muted colors, overpriced paintings, and wall of windows overlooking Rockefeller Center. It was a new firm for Wayne Carrier, but nothing much had changed since the last time she'd visited him. Wayne had never been as respectable as his surroundings. He was a fixer—a guy who got things done and brought in billable hours. Any real legal work was done by others at the firm.

In her business, Kathleen saw a side of people that others didn't. Some people were good at heart, like her late husband, even when he was hopelessly addicted. Others were sleazy and a natural fit for the underworld, even when they dressed up nicely and only went underground as tourists to visit whorehouses or drug dealers. Wayne was in the latter category, a chameleon who fit perfectly in both worlds. That changeability was probably his greatest asset, at least from a financial point of view. She imagined he had his fair share of Russian oligarchs for clients now. But you dealt with him at your own risk.

That was only one of the reasons Kathleen couldn't include Emily in this. She hated lying to Emily again, but she needed to talk to Wayne privately and couldn't tell Emily about it. Kathleen and Wayne were bound by a vow of secrecy.

Sitting on a leather couch in the firm's reception area, she thought back to meeting Wayne. One of her best clients, code-named Client 13 in her proverbial black book, had referred her to Wayne to form an LLC for her business. That was one of the ironic things about being a madam: the men wanted no emotional connection with their sex partners, but a good madam was like a work-wife. The clients sought a relationship of trust with the madam, and everyone knew the madam had the black book to make that trust important. So it was natural for Client 13 to seek to ingratiate himself with her by sending her to one of his personal lawyers for help with her business needs.

Wayne had also been the one to draft her eventual contract with their mutual client, an NDA that handed her fifty thousand dollars and called for a million-dollar penalty if she ever told anyone the things she knew about the client. She didn't mind signing an NDA, since she had no intention of talking about him. In her mind, it was free money.

"Ms. Harris."

Wearing high-heeled pumps and a Jackie Kennedy red dress, a woman who must be Wayne's secretary came to get Kathleen. The gender roles were as familiar as the decor. Kathleen had dressed for the occasion herself. If being in the Life had taught her one thing, it was how to compensate for people's prejudices. Kathleen had dressed as a well-heeled client—confidently casual, linen slacks, a short blazer, and pumps. She carried a Coach shoulder bag large enough to transport an iPad and her personal effects.

Wayne stood when Kathleen and the secretary entered his office.

"Kathleen," he said, coming around his desk to kiss her cheek. "Good to see you!"

"Wayne, how are you?"

He wore a black suit, tailored to fit a build that he'd kept up well for a man of close to sixty. His hair had begun to silver, which conveyed gravitas, not frailty.

"The years have treated you well. You look good," she said.

He spread his hands, smiling. "I'm good. The kids are done with college. Once we had an empty nest, my wife, Linda, launched a travel blog. Despite my naysaying, Linda's done well. Sold it last year. The stars have aligned for us."

"That's good to hear." Kathleen sat in the chair in front of his desk, and he returned to his seat.

"Best of all, I've been staying out of trouble, which has been no easy feat over the last few years," Wayne went on. "Politicians have been arrested with more frequency than drug dealers. It's made me quite the rainmaker here. I've pulled many of them in as clients for the firm, and I've managed to keep myself from becoming a target of investigation. Don't get enmeshed with your clients. Stay the lawyer. That's my motto."

"Staying out of trouble is always a good thing."

"I hope you're not here for that. Trouble, I mean. I thought you'd retired. I was surprised to hear from you."

"I'm happily retired, you're right." She watched Wayne's eyes. "I'm here about Sharon. Sharon Williams."

"Really?"

A tightening of his mouth. The slightest twitch, but Kathleen caught it.

"She's dead," she said.

"No! Jesus. I'm sorry," he said somberly. "That's terrible news."

Kathleen made a mental note. He hadn't seemed to *know* she was dead, but he wasn't surprised either.

"What happened?"

"Murdered. Her throat was cut."

He grimaced, a nauseous look. "I didn't know you two were still close."

"We were. Always." Kathleen paused.

Wayne nodded and steepled his hands, talking as if he were reminiscing at a funeral. "Sharon always lived up to her agreement. Our friend was a smart one."

"I always thought the nondisclosure agreements were overkill. Him burning money."

For the most part, Client 13 had been standard fare. The girls never complained about roughness or him wanting to wear their underwear. What he did want, which was counterintuitive for a guy seeking a hooker, was exclusivity. He'd been a germaphobe, afraid of what he might catch if he shared a woman who'd recently had sex with others. Even in the age of AIDS, Kathleen had thought his predilection was more fastidiousness than rational caution.

His proclivities had resulted in a profitable financial arrangement for Kathleen. He'd bankrolled an apartment in Kathleen's name for one woman each month, a pied-à-terre that would never be traceable to him. He paid a retainer for a woman to stay in the place and meet with him there on demand, a month at a time. Kathleen chose women for him who didn't have personal lovers, since they needed to be monogamous for the month. Like her, they each signed an NDA with a penalty of a million dollars if they ever talked.

"The women liked the gig," Kathleen said. "It was lucrative. Basically a monthlong vacation—one man, not even every day, and he would call first so they wouldn't be tied to the apartment day and night. I used to give the job out as a reward to the most solid workers. They only needed to be stunningly beautiful with a clean medical report."

"Sharon was certainly stunning," Wayne said.

"Sharon was nearly the last girl." Kathleen looked into Wayne's eyes. "She called you the night she died."

"Oh?" he asked warily.

"Were you representing her?"

"No." He seemed to shift mental gears. "I wondered why she called. I wasn't even sure it was her. I hadn't spoken to her in years. I thought maybe she drunk-dialed my line, but my phone number has changed since the last time I spoke with her. She must have tracked me down here, so it seems unlikely she randomly drunk-dialed me. Maybe cocaine too? That would account for it. Cocaine and Google—a wicked combination."

"She wasn't a drunk or an addict," Kathleen said. Why was it that people were trying to make Sharon out to be something she wasn't? First, the police, assuming she was a streetwalker. Well, she didn't seriously expect them to distinguish between a call girl and a streetwalker. They didn't recognize the difference between survival sex for a desperate woman and a career choice either. But now Wayne was making Sharon out to be an addict in a spasm of irrational cocaine hyperactivity.

"I couldn't get what she was talking about on the voice mail," Wayne said. "She was incoherent."

"She didn't seem incoherent to me. I spoke with her moments after she called you."

He shrugged. "Maybe it was a bad signal."

"Do you have the message? I'd like to hear it."

"I deleted it. There was no reason to think it was important."

Kathleen folded her hands in her lap, letting Wayne see her impatience. "She called you and me the night she died. There was only one connection between the three of us."

Wayne leaned forward, his voice edgy. "Just remember, Kat, you signed an NDA."

"I know that."

"It's okay for you to talk to me, get it out of your system, but that's it." He stared at her meanly. "I expect this to be the last time you talk about it."

Kathleen spoke with a severe tone she had once reserved for poorly behaved customers. "Of course. I don't need to be schooled on the Life by a *john*, Wayne."

Anger flashed across Wayne's features, his lips pressed shut.

Kathleen rose to leave. "I think we're done here."

She strode out of the office without looking at Wayne. It was ironic that men thought they were superior to sex workers when they were the ones who had to pay for it. She felt some catharsis from sticking a pin in Wayne's puffed-up testosterone bubble.

But she also knew there was often a cost to getting the last word, and she wished their meeting had been more productive. She paused in front of the building and took a deep breath of fresh air—a cleansing breath, as they called it in yoga—before she headed to the subway.

23

Before

JACKSON SAT AT a weather-worn picnic table in his backyard, laptop open. Pink sky. Crabgrass and dust underfoot. The picnic table and a pockmarked charcoal grill were the only backyard accoutrements. He could barely stand to be inside the house, listening to his father hacking away, smoker's lungs scarred and wheezing. Luckily, the Wi-Fi reached the backyard.

Jackson reread the DNA report from XFactor.com. There were eleven probable cousins, three of them supposedly close cousins. And there was one common thread among them: they were complete strangers to Jackson. Not a single Mattingly. Not even one familiar name. The list confirmed it. He was trapped in somebody else's life.

He'd Googled each of the possible cousins but hadn't been able to find out much. They had last names like Johnson and Roberts matched with first names like John, Sara, and Leslie. Dozens of Facebook pages came up for each name. Some were actors with IMDb pages. Others had LinkedIn pages and seemed accomplished. Some were nobodies. There was no way to tell which ones were the relatives and whether they were worth knowing, except by emailing the addresses XFactor had provided.

He copied and pasted to create eleven identical emails. He told each cousin that he was adopted and looking for his biological parents. He used the same alias he'd used when he signed up with XFactor. Privacy was power, either in his own hands or in someone else's. Privacy was even more vital now, because he didn't understand why his parents had seemed so scared when he questioned them about his birth. He didn't know where the threat lay, so he had to guard himself. Plus, he didn't want to end up like the Golden State Killer, caught through DNA on a commercial website. Jackson had no idea where his own life would lead him and wanted as small a traceable footprint as possible. That was ultimately why he'd chosen XFactor for his genetic testing—they accepted Bitcoin, which he'd had no trouble buying on the web.

Jackson hit send on each email, lit a cigarette, and looked out at green Mount Beacon beyond the graying picket fence that surrounded his yard.

An email appeared in his in-box before his cigarette had burned halfway down. Excitement shot through him, but the response had been at stalker speed, worrying him. The last thing he wanted was crazy knuckleheads entering his life and never leaving. Another good reason to use an alias: perfect for ghosting.

He read the email: Welcome to the family. I live in Charleston, South Carolina.

The distant cousin wrote that their common ancestor had been a founding father of Charleston hundreds of years ago and that the family had a hospital named after them. *She's gotta be shitting me.* He grinned, feeling a fizzy glee like a soda can shaken up inside his skull. She was saying that he was a descendent of an important family. He called the phone number.

* * *

The woman was bubbly, a big talker with a southern accent. She sounded as old as his mother, with the scratchy voice quality of a person whose larynx was nearing its expiration date.

"We have an ancestor that goes back over eight hundred years to England, before the family moved to Charleston," she said. "I've traced the family tree pretty far, using news clips and public records to supplement the DNA. There's a branch of the family that ended up in New York, where you are, about two hundred years ago. Another group moved up there too, after World War II, during Jim Crow."

Jackson thought that through, not really getting the Jim Crow reference. "But how do I narrow things down further?" he asked. "I'm trying to find my birth family."

She paused. "Are you Black?"

That confused him. "Uh, no."

"Okay, so you haven't hit pay dirt here. I'm from the Black side. Descendants of the same white man as you and a Black woman on his plantation."

"Yeah?" Jackson's excitement plummeted.

"We've found a large group of us on the Black side, but it probably won't help you much. Never know, though. Some of us are pretty light skinned and have ancestors who passed for white who could have married white. Their descendants would be as white as Ivanka Trump. So, you *could* be one of us."

"My DNA profile doesn't include any African American," Jackson said, trying to keep the huffiness out of his voice, wondering whether this call would be a total waste of his time.

"Well, we've had contact with the white side. Not that they're much interested in us. Don't believe everything you see on CNN about the Black and white sides living happily ever after as one big extended family once they find each other. Most of them are like Thomas Jefferson's white family, trying to fend off the kin of Sally Hemings. Maybe the white side will be more open to you. Most of them treat us like gold diggers . . . even though some of us are doing quite well financially.

"Truthfully, it should be us who wants nothing to do with them. We've got family stories passed down from slave times. We've all heard them from our parents and grandparents. Our ancestors were the worst kind of slave owners. Punished hard, raped the women in the most sadistic way, didn't have even a semblance of decency when it came to separating families.

"Still, they're your kin, and I'm sure there's some good ones in the bunch. A couple of the white ones come to our reunions. They seem okay, even if they think their presence provides healing . . . and it's so *nice for us*. Don't make that mistake. *We* always knew we had white relatives. It's only them that needs to heal from the surprise of finding us." She laughed. "They tend to be the poor relations who come, though, not the hoity-toity ones."

"There are some who still have money?"

"Boy, not just money. I'm talking about *a lot of money*. There's a branch of the family that came to this country rich and has milked it successfully for four hundred years. Each baby is born with millions. They all go to Yale. That's a legacy school for them. Affirmative action is alive and well for rich white people." He heard her exhale, now talking low. "They've got a lot of power. More than people know. In both political parties. But don't get me started. I'm sure you didn't contact me to hear my political views."

She was right about that. Jackson didn't want any more involvement with her than was necessary to get to the rich white side. He didn't want to know anyone who couldn't help him.

"If you don't mind, I'll give your information to a couple of my cousins. They can give you some names and phone numbers. You're going to need to narrow things down a lot more if you're looking for your parents. Didn't XFactor give you names for closer cousins?"

"I emailed, but no answers yet."

"What are their names?"

He told her.

"Oh, yeah, that's the snooty white side, for sure. Some of the younger generation took it upon themselves to get tested for school projects or for fun. I'm sure their parents would never have allowed it if they'd known. They know they have skeletons in their closets. They certainly don't want to learn the identities of all the people they still owe forty acres and a mule to." She sighed wearily. "Well, anyway, once my cousins and I get you all the information we've gathered, you'll have a good start—at least to fill in your family tree some more. I'll send you over my file of news clippings too. I bet you'll find your parents."

24

ON SATURDAY MORNING, Emily and Lauren walked a lesser-known path that led from the back of the Dancing Crane Café to Congo Village, the Bronx Zoo's gorilla house. They'd come early to beat the worst of the weekend crowds. At ten AM, it was quiet enough to hear birds singing—the calls of local Bronx finches laced with the chatter of exotic zoo birds up ahead.

Lauren looked happier than Emily had seen her in a long time. "Carl's doing so well," she told Emily. "The doctor thinks the next round of tests will confirm that the study drug is working."

"He seemed better last time I saw him. I noticed."

"Fingers crossed that he'll be going back to work soon. Before he drives himself—and me—crazy."

Emily pushed an empty stroller while Skye ran ahead, past a flock of flamingos standing in a pond. Emily kept her sights trained on the little girl, who paused slightly now as she approached brightly colored exotic birds as tall as her in cages along the path.

Emily knew every path in the zoo, the map tattooed on her mind from her own childhood. Lauren had kept an unlimited membership to the zoo when Emily was young and brought her there several times a month, even in the dead of winter. Emily had heart-level memories of those days that made her feel a deep sense of comfort here. When Skye turned two, Lauren had surprised Emily with a membership.

"How's it been going with the dog?" Lauren asked.

"It's been good. My main concern was that Skye would get too attached. But she only sees Rusty a couple of weekends a month and I always tell her Rusty is a guest, not ours. I'm thinking that, when he goes to a veteran—a few weeks from now—a new puppy will arrive to replace him and she'll be excited to meet him."

As Emily and Lauren reached the exotic-bird cages, Skye was off running again. She shouted with excitement and pointed, launching onto an empty lawn. Emily and Lauren double-timed up the path after her.

"What is she looking at?" Lauren asked.

Skye shouted, her little legs picking up speed. "Fire hydrant!"

In the middle of the stretch of lawn, a green fire hydrant stood about a foot taller than typical street hydrants.

"Oh lord," Emily said, laughing. "Lions, tigers, and bears, take a number."

The women watched from the path while Skye climbed and examined the hydrant closely, clearly imagining herself as a firefighter.

Lauren spoke after watching for a while. "Hector dropped by the house yesterday. He was in the neighborhood."

Emily sighed, knowing where the conversation was going. "Do you know how much this sounds like a sitcom? My ex-boyfriend hanging around my mother's house. My mother advocating for him."

"Art imitates life, my child."

"I began dating Hector when I was sixteen. He's a great guy and an even better father. but I don't know anyone who ends up life partners with their high school boyfriend."

Lauren ran her fingers across her lips, zipping them.

"Oh, you are so exasperating." Emily laughed. "Sometimes it amazes me how traditional you are. You and Hector are peas in a pod. You both really thought we should have gotten married because I was pregnant."

"I will spare you the lecture about it being better for Skye to grow up in a two-parent household."

Emily looked askance at Lauren. "That right there was the lecture."

Although she wouldn't admit it, Emily had given her mother's point a lot of thought. She believed she'd made the right decision. Skye was flourishing. But she also had to admit to herself that she missed the comfort of Hector as a boyfriend. She couldn't even date him anymore because that would be a slippery slope, confusing now that they had Skye together.

Emily and Lauren watched Skye step up onto a metal lip near the bottom of the hydrant and grab the top as if she were riding it. It must have morphed into an entire fire truck in her mind. Watching Skye, Lauren gave Emily a hug around her shoulders. Her mother was known for random hugs, and Emily leaned the side of her head against Lauren's shoulder.

Emily changed the subject as they parted. "I didn't have a chance to tell you . . . it's terrible—a friend of my neighbor was killed."

"Killed? How?"

Emily told Lauren about Sharon and the apparently lackluster murder investigation. "It turns out that Sharon was a call girl. And my neighbor was her madam."

Lauren's face hardened. Emily could see the gears clicking in her mother's head, drawing all the wrong conclusions about Kathleen. Emily wished she hadn't said so much. She talked too much, sometimes without thinking, especially when it came to her mother.

Lauren exhaled. "You've gotta be kidding."

"She's retired. She really is just a nice old woman."

Lauren scoffed, her silence speaking volumes.

"Mom, she's not trying to recruit me. She's *retired*. Anyway, my theory is that the killing had nothing to do with Sharon's sex work."

Lauren spoke tensely. "You may be the only person who can identify a murderer and you mention it more casually than telling me you lost your iPhone. Plus, you're hanging out with a pimp like that's okay."

"She is not a pimp! You're overreacting."

"I'm going to talk to Carl. Maybe he can find something out and make sure you're not in any jeopardy."

"Mom, I'm an adult. And a journalist. I can handle this myself," Emily said, remembering how upset Kathleen had been about her going to Chief Reilly to ask about Sharon. "And Kathleen wouldn't want me to involve Carl. It might piss off the local cops."

"An overage criminal wouldn't want you to tell your cop stepfather about you being the only person who can identify a murderer? You're crediting that?"

"We don't know he was the murderer. He could have been Sharon's friend. He could just be a material witness."

"I see you've been watching *Law and Order*," Lauren said in the most annoyingly sarcastic manner. Then she blew air through her lips, her features softening gradually.

Emily was glad. She hated fighting with her mother, although they seemed to have these squabbles a lot. Skye wasn't the only stubborn one. Emily wasn't looking forward to Skye's teenage years. She could only imagine the three of them.

"Okay. But please stay out of it," Lauren said. "You don't know anything about the Life or the Street. You have too much to lose to get involved with shady people."

Knowing it would be better to end the conversation before it took another bad turn, Emily called out, "Let's go, Skye."

Skye looked toward Emily from her perch atop the hydrant.

"Come on. Let's go to the gorillas."

"Okay!" Skye took off in the direction of the Congo Village, already knowing where it was.

CHAPTER

25

THE PHONE RANG, cutting short a Mariah Carey song, just as Kathleen was getting ready to head out for a morning power walk in Inwood Hill Park. She always tried to get outside before the midday sun superheated the sidewalks. "Hello," she answered.

"Ms. Harris? This is Mr. Lee from Riverdale Funeral Home. Ms. Williams's remains have been released from the morgue."

Kathleen talked with the funeral director, confirming her choice to cremate Sharon, given that there was no one to express a preference.

"I'll email you forms," he said. "I need your electronic signature to attest that there's no next of kin and that you're taking responsibility for disposal of the remains."

"Okay. I can do that."

Kathleen hadn't found anything among Sharon's belongings to give her a clue about her family. Sharon had emigrated from Europe on an education visa as a teenager. She'd never gotten a green card, so she wasn't permitted to work on the books, and there'd never been any reason for Kathleen to know her birth name, which was surely not Sharon Williams. For whatever reason, Sharon had never mentioned her family, and Kathleen honestly believed there was no one Sharon viewed in that way.

Kathleen supposed that must be what her own daughter felt too. Lauren had lived most of her life without Kathleen. It appeared she'd done just fine without a mother. Kathleen was glad for that, even though she wished Lauren had been even a little needy, just to provide *any* opening that would have given Kathleen a chance to enter her life again.

The other women in prison understood what it was to lose their children. They'd told her, *Don't worry. She knows who her mama is. She'll come back to you.* But it hadn't happened that way.

*   *   *

Kathleen took a path through Inwood Hill Park, where ancient caves peeked out from the hilly woods above. She thought about how she had hoped to be a better mother than her own mother had been. Kathleen was sure her mother had suffered from undiagnosed bipolar or a severe personality disorder or both. At best, Kathleen's mother had not been known for kindness.

Kathleen remembered one June day, a beautiful day like today. She had been seventeen years old, quietly eating a bowl of cereal in the kitchen of the Columbus Avenue brownstone apartment where she lived with her mother. Dressed for work in a dress and pumps, her mother turned to Kathleen out of the blue and said, "I've never known whether you're the child of my husband or my father."

Memories of Kathleen's grandfather, long dead, streamed into her mind at that moment. Was her grandfather also her father? He'd had sex with Kathleen's mother. He'd had sex with Kathleen too. Her emotions ricocheted within her that day as the memory came back, his heavy weight on her, the physical pain that had pulsed through her when it happened. He'd been dead since she was seven years old, so it had happened before seven.

Kathleen stared at her mother with unadulterated hatred.

"Well, I've got to go to work." Kathleen's mother drained her coffee cup and placed it in the sink. "Good luck on your Regents today."

Kathleen's life at that point was like two sticks rubbing together. Sparks were inevitable. Shortly after graduation, she moved in with Michael, wild and handsome even when he'd been up drinking the night before.

But the sparks became flames when Michael was hurt in a car accident while their daughter was in elementary school. He'd been a good dad until then. Even though he had been barely twenty when Lauren was born, his love for Kathleen and the baby had stabilized him, other than his occasional binge drinking. But his use of prescribed pain medication after the accident morphed into heroin addiction. Kathleen tried to hold the family together, although her nagging and yelling at Michael had surely made their daughter think she was the bad parent. Being high on heroin made Michael playful and affectionate, while Kathleen became an anxious shrew.

On their last day together, after three years of crack and heroin addiction, Michael lay sprawled in the bathroom with a needle jutting from his arm. Lauren cleared the apartment of drugs and weapons like a child soldier clearing a minefield, rushing to finish before the police arrived. Was there something Kathleen could have done instead of shrieking about the worms and snakes she saw coming out of her dead husband toward her? She remembered knowing that her husband was dead, and she remembered the reptile invaders just as clearly. It had been as if fifteen-year-old Lauren were a specter passing through the room, busy at her own task, unaware of the creatures launching themselves at her mother. And the invaders seemed just as unaware of the young girl. Kathleen had screamed and screamed.

When Kathleen finally came to her senses, she'd found herself on Rikers Island, awaiting trial for the murder of her husband. After her plea bargain, she spent most of her five-year sentence in Bedford Hills Correctional Facility for Women. She'd known Lauren had gone to residential drug treatment. The caseworkers had come to Bedford to get Kathleen to sign the consent papers. But when she tried to contact her daughter again, the caseworkers told her that the drug program had helped Lauren become an emancipated minor. Kathleen didn't even have the right to know the name of the program. From the disdainful way the caseworker spoke to Kathleen—treatment she richly deserved—Kathleen knew the caseworker and the program had done everything they could to make sure she didn't cause Lauren any more harm than she already had. After that, it was as if her daughter had vanished from the face of the earth. There wasn't even an address where Kathleen could write to her.

Kathleen had never forgotten that she was accountable for the nightmare Lauren's childhood had turned into. In prison, Kathleen had joined a twelve-step program that called for her to make amends to those she'd harmed. Lauren was at the top of the list. Kathleen wanted to explain, apologize, make up for what she'd done, even though she could never undo it. But when Kathleen finally located Lauren after prison, she'd wanted nothing to do with her mother. Who could blame her? After two angry rejections, Kathleen's sponsor had finally suggested that the best amends Kathleen could make to her daughter was to honor her wishes: stay away from her and stay out of her life.

Kathleen had mothered dozens of women instead, filling the painful chasm inside her with their challenges and affection. Some would think her promoting sex work was predatory, but she'd never turned out a girl who wasn't already hooking. Instead, she treated them fairly, rescued some of them from abusive pimps, and tried to keep them healthy and safe. For some of them, she was the closest thing to a mother they'd ever known.

Now, Kathleen wished she knew more about Sharon, wished Sharon had been more open about her past so that Kathleen could find her family. Sharon's ability to keep information to herself was an asset in their business. Kathleen could keep a secret, but she wasn't cut from the same cloth as Sharon. Her secrets burned fiercely in her, leading to a constant sense of inner discomfort, even now—especially her new secret, her snowballing deception of Emily.

Ultimately, staying out of Lauren's life had become more difficult as time passed. Kathleen's yearning for her child had led to the very kinds of deception that had likely motivated Lauren to reject Kathleen's amends in the first place. Instead of respecting her daughter's wishes, Kathleen now owed additional amends for worming her way into every facet of Emily's life.

Kathleen felt a flash of self-hatred. That was why she'd started to unravel her deceptions, the easiest one first: Sophie. She'd taken down her Facebook, Instagram, and Twitter accounts, though she still yearned to check in and see what Emily was posting today.

Kathleen walked along a lake now, Columbia University's sports arena on the far side. She looked toward the sound of squealing children in birthday hats playing tug-of-war on a field nearby. She watched them, turning her mind away from the negative thoughts that were keeping her from enjoying the day. She completed her circuit on the path around the field and headed home, thinking about the calls she needed to make. Absent any information about Sharon's current friends or family, Kathleen would reach out to their mutual friends, Kathleen's former employees, and invite them to come to a memorial.

26

I N THE CITY Hall press office on Monday, Emily checked her personal Twitter account during a rare idle moment. She noticed a post from Sophie. Sophie said she was taking a social media break to avoid the politics and snark. It wasn't unusual for one of her friends to announce a break. It was stressful to see constant political vitriol, plus social media could eat up your life if you let it. But Sophie had helped her so much in the last year. It was amazing how important Sophie had ended up being to Emily, considering she hadn't even remembered her from school. She didn't have Sophie's email address to keep in touch, and Emily felt a moment of loss.

Martha rolled her chair over and sat next to her. "You should tell us when something newsworthy is going on in your life that the press can get hold of," she said firmly. "You know that."

"Max told you?"

"What did you think? Gossip is his stock-in-trade. Don't tell him anything you don't want others to know. So that's two take-aways: tell me when there may be press about you, and choose your confidants more carefully. Of course, there are times when you want information to get out through gossip." Martha cracked a smile, relieving Emily's tension. "That's what people like Max are for."

"So everybody knows?"

"Probably. Doesn't it make you nervous?"

"That everyone knows?"

"That you're the only person who saw a possible murderer?"

"I just think of him as a person of interest," Emily said. "That helps me sleep at night."

"Good idea." Martha winked. "Come on, we're having a prep session for the mayor's afternoon avail."

Emily and Martha entered the Bullpen on the second floor. The Bullpen was a massive open space. Huge windows. Carved ceiling. Chandeliers overhead. The deputy mayors, the chief of staff, and the senior staff worked at desks surrounded by low cubicles. Mayor Sullivan walked by, wearing a gray suit and red tie, heading toward the balcony conference room overlooking the Bullpen. He paused. "I heard, Emily," he said. "If you need anything, please let me know."

"Thank you. Nothing is really going on. They don't even have a suspect."

"That's too bad. Well, anything you need . . ."

Emily walked alongside Martha, the mayor loping ahead by several strides.

Martha offered, "Marlo must have run him down about your involvement with that case."

Emily cringed at the thought of the unwanted attention, imagining the mayor sitting in his office talking about her. Now he shook hands with Roger, and Roger glanced back at her too. *Jesus, everyone knows.*

"Don't worry," Martha said. "It's not a major story. No one's worried about it. And he's happy about the *Times* mentioning the State Department's delay in getting a visa for Rachel Ajiboye's mother."

At the bottom of the stairs to the balcony, the security details for the NYPD commissioner and mayor sat at empty desks and chatted while they waited for their bosses. They were all police detectives who drove for the mayor and the police commissioner, securing the area at each stop before they got out of their cars. Emily noticed one of the detectives giving her a once-over, studying her. Same old shit: leering men, twenty years older than her.

She met his eyes defiantly. But she saw something she hadn't expected: meanness, not lust, behind his stare. She felt startled by it, tried to shrug it off, and looked away. He must be one of those guys who thought a woman was a bitch if she didn't smile politely when he showed his admiration for her body parts.

On the balcony, the deputy mayors, Marlo, and a few others were already there, bringing plates of sandwiches and chips from a side table to the conference table. There was always a spread of food for staff up there, which was why it was the favored spot for lunch hour meetings. Chief Reilly was chatting with the police commissioner, the chief's uniform contrasting with his boss's tailored suit. The chief left the commissioner and headed Emily off before she sat. "Let me speak to you a minute."

With five minutes left until the meeting officially started, Emily followed the chief out an exit door to an empty marble-floored corridor.

She noticed the chief's face reddening from jowl to forehead as he leaned closer to her. "What the fuck did you think you were doing?"

"What?"

"Asking me for information on a murder case you're personally involved with?"

Emily froze.

"Don't you know that's an ethics violation? Using your position to get personal information?" he continued, enraged.

"No, I didn't think—"

"Stuff like that can ruin your career!" He threw up his hands. "And about a *homicide*? You've gotta be fucking kidding me. And now we know you're a fucking liar. Jesus fucking Christ."

Her eyes hot, Emily tried to keep the quiver out of her voice. She had made a huge mistake. There was nothing she could say. What *could* she say? "There *was* an inquiry from a reporter . . . about violence against prostitutes. But you're right. I'm so sorry. I didn't think."

Chief Reilly's red face began fading. He paced a moment, long enough for Emily to imagine Martha's disappointment when she found out what Emily had done. And if Emily lost her job, Lauren's disappointment. She was about to lose everything. How could she be so stupid?

The chief took Emily's measure, probably noting the tears in her eyes. "Look, I'm going to keep this between you and me. You're a good kid, and I've always liked working with you. But don't *ever* do fucking shit like this again. Getting confidential information like that was some career-blowing shit, and it would have fucked me up too. If you want to be reckless with your career, at least think of the other guy."

*   *   *

Emily couldn't look anyone in the eye as Martha ran down the topics of discussion for the press conference, calling on people to brief Mayor Sullivan on each subject. Max reported on talking points and questions that had been bubbling up on social media. Barely able to make out their words, Emily's mind roiled with residual fear and embarrassment. She felt like crawling under the conference table and hiding. She hated to make even mundane mistakes, and this one was huge.

"So, last item," Marlo said, "*not* for public consumption. We now have IT searching to see if Mattingly sent emails to the mayor or staff relating to the inauguration or anything else. The search will try to rope the emails in through rolling key word searches and Mattingly's IP address. They believe Mattingly used aliases and multiple email accounts. The FBI will be feeding us information about any known accounts Mattingly had so we can expand our search. Emily will ride herd on that project, interfacing with IT, reviewing the emails and reporting to us on content, and updating the FBI as needed. She'll be our point person."

Emily perked up. She hadn't expected that assignment, but it was a good one. All heads turned to her, and Martha smiled encouragingly, obviously having known about it. Max gave Emily a thumbs-up, which was nice of him, since he probably wanted the assignment. The chief nodded slightly at Emily, a sign that all was forgiven if not forgotten. Emily breathed a little easier.

27

IN A WAITING room at Mount Sinai Hospital, the sun shone through the windows, which overlooked a railroad trestle and East Harlem housing projects. Lauren was doing everything she could to hide her nervousness. They'd been waiting a long time. They always did. But Lauren wasn't complaining—not aloud, at least. Carl had a great doctor at a great hospital. They were lucky to live in the city, where the hospitals and doctors participated in cutting-edge studies that benefited patients who suffered from an insidious disease without any known cure. Besides, if she let Carl go to his doctor's appointments alone, he came home either beaming with hope or miserably depressed, offering an incomplete story of what was going on. She needed to know.

Carl had a love/hate relationship with Lauren's new rule about attending every appointment with him. He still enjoyed her company and support, but it was just one more chink in his self-image as a strong, independent man. And it interfered with Carl's ability to act as if nothing were happening. He didn't have to pretend for her, but it was second nature for him to try to protect her. Even today, when his doctor would evaluate how the study drug was working, the most important appointment in the last two years, he was trying to act like it was nothing.

But Lauren wasn't in denial about how important today was. Carl's recent improvement could be the regular MS roller coaster, or Carl might be one of the lucky ones who ended up with long-standing recovery because of the new drug. Lauren dreaded news that might crush Carl, and she didn't dare hope too high herself.

Carl picked up a copy of *Sports Illustrated* from a low table in front of the couch where they sat. He thumbed through it.

On her iPad, Lauren logged in to a real estate website. She told herself it was just curiosity, but doing this had been on her mind since her conversation with Emily at the zoo. Lauren often used the website when a new client came to her and she wanted a quick read on the property involved in a potential divorce proceeding. Now she typed in the address of Emily's building. She was concerned that a criminal had wormed her way into her daughter's confidence. *Former criminal*, she reminded herself. And Lauren was the last person to judge someone for that. Still, she worried that Emily wasn't streetwise enough to discern between a former and current criminal. It wasn't as if the woman would tell Emily the truth about it.

Lauren knew she was overprotective of Emily, who had grown into a self-sufficient, intelligent woman. She was a great mother and had an amazing career. When Emily lost Brian as a teenager, Lauren had been terrified that Emily would end up self-medicating with drugs or alcohol like Lauren and her parents had. Emily had shown her rebellious streak early in adolescence, and there had been rough patches when she'd cut school and hung out with a worrisome crowd. But luckily, Emily must lack the gene that made a person dive headlong into the rabbit hole of addiction. By the time Emily emerged from the bleak period of mourning for her father, she'd corrected her own course, focusing on school and swearing off self-destructive behaviors. Lauren hadn't needed to worry about her for a moment since. But nothing in Emily's life had prepared her for manipulation by criminals. Besides, no harm could come of Lauren poking around a bit.

She pulled up the listing for Emily's building and its vital statistics. Thirty rental units. Built in 1920. The page linked to public documents: filings for fixture replacements, an old Department of Buildings work permit, and a mortgage filing. The building had a twelve-year-old mortgage for just over a million dollars, although it was worth four times as much. The building could have been bought during the recession at a discount, or the owner could have paid mostly cash for it. She looked for the owner's name: Inwood Associates, LLC.

She next went to the home page for the state Division of Corporations and entered the corporate name in a search box. A page appeared that listed a contact person for the corporation: Kathleen Harris. The famous Kathleen. Lauren switched to Google and typed the name. She sighed when two hundred thousand results came up. LinkedIn said there were over two thousand profiles with that name. Lack of privacy on social media was one of Lauren's pet peeves. But, ironically, you could hide in plain sight if you had a common name.

Carl put down *Sports Illustrated* with an air of boredom and glanced over at Lauren's screen. "Work?"

Lauren wouldn't lie to Carl, but she'd promised Emily. So, a half-truth: "Just idle curiosity. Nothing too interesting." She closed the iPad.

"Rick is coming back from Lake Placid tomorrow," Carl said. "They're almost done interviewing Mattingly's family members. The media is camped out at the grandparents' house."

Lauren put the iPad in her leather shoulder bag. "They all work at Clinton-Dannemora, right? By the Canadian border?"

"Rick said the interviews were basically a bust. They're a prison guard family with generations of Mattinglys working in the state's prison complexes. Mattingly's parents worked at the prison near Beacon, and yeah, his cousins and grandparents work at Clinton-Dannemora. There's nothing particularly weird about them. The grandparents say they never felt close with Jackson and they never liked him much. It looks like he had a higher IQ than all their other grandkids combined. They'd hoped he'd become a movie star, or just be the one to get rich."

"They must be devastated."

"Yeah, they're especially pissed off that he used his talents to ruin their lives rather than making sure they all lived happily ever after. But I don't think the family was completely blameless."

Lauren turned to him. "No?"

"There were warning signs. Missing pets, a decade ago in Beacon," Carl said. "It got bad enough that people began keeping their pets inside. The local newspaper reported at the time that the coyote population had grown in upstate New York and, with the forests shrinking, they'd begun wandering into towns."

Lauren was pretty sure Carl had been doing independent research online and that Rick hadn't told him that. Still, she was glad Carl had that outlet. "When I lived upstate for the first couple of years after college," she said, "there were reports of coyotes, bobcats too, in residential areas. We stopped letting our cat go outside."

"Yeah, but there were similar news reports up north one summer, when Jackson spent the school vacation with his grandparents. And in Beacon, one of the reporters noticed that the pets were mainly missing from within a small section of town, about four square blocks. Not just cats, either."

Lauren's eyebrows lifted. "What does that mean?"

"There were some who questioned the coyote theory back then. Some of the missing dogs were unusually big for coyote prey, and there would have been bones if a coyote took a big animal. It's not too important now. I'm just connecting the dots in Mattingly's biography. But Mattingly's house was dead center of the four-block radius where animals went missing. He couldn't have been more than eight years old when it started happening. And there was a string of break-ins at homes in that area a few years later. Nobody hurt, just items randomly broken, as if the burglar went in and took a baseball bat to people's prized possessions."

"So they missed all the signs that he was a psychopath. Even as a child."

"Mr. Cintron," a nurse called from the door to the inner sanctum of the medical office.

Carl and Lauren rose, holding hands as they walked toward the door. Lauren didn't feel like she was helping Carl maintain his balance. It was better. Her heart pumped hard with hope. She said a silent prayer that his tests would confirm that the study drug was truly working and the doctor would give Carl his back-to-work note.

CHAPTER

28

HISTORIC TOMBS AND mausoleums shaded by ancient trees occupied several square blocks between West 153rd and West 155th Streets from Riverside Drive to Amsterdam. Broadway separated the west and east halves of the pastoral cemetery, but the wide roadway hushed as it passed through the twin graveyards, barely noticed. Just over two weeks since Sharon's death, Emily walked with Kathleen on a winding path bordered by imposing oaks to a small single-story building.

Inside was an elegant room. Tall glass vases filled with long-stemmed purple flowers graced its front corners. A framed photo of Sharon, the one Kathleen had saved from her phone contacts, stood on a grand piano at the back corner of the room. A floor-to-ceiling window looked out on the cemetery forest from the far side of the piano. The room was small but could fit seventy-five people in rows of upholstered folding chairs facing a podium.

Over Kathleen's protestations, Emily had insisted on attending. She knew how hard it would be for Kathleen if no one showed up.

Emily had chosen a playlist of mellow jazz to play as people arrived, if any did. Since Kathleen didn't know what music Sharon would have liked and had warned that there was a good chance no one would come, Emily had done her best at picking music she thought Kathleen would find soothing.

The allotted time came. The music played. Sun and shade dappled the room in rhythm with a breeze that swayed the trees beyond the glass wall. Kathleen's former employees began to arrive. At first a trickle, then dozens of them, mostly women. A couple of young men, muscular like bouncers, came from the Easy Street Gentleman's Club. Sharon's doorman, Dunbar, entered and sat in the back row. Three heavyset men who had the look of plump, retired weight lifters kissed Kathleen on the cheek when they entered.

"They used to provide security for us," Kathleen told Emily.

Emily found herself studying the face of each man who arrived to see whether he might be the person who'd taken Sharon away in his car. But no.

The women, who outnumbered the men five to one, were all in their thirties and forties, most tall, all of them attractive. Although some had become comfortably middle-aged and probably plainer with the years, Emily could see that they'd all been beautiful in the way of an actress or model. The women greeted each other with long-lost kisses and shook hands with Emily when Kathleen introduced them. Emily guessed they might have come to the memorial more for Kathleen than for Sharon.

Emily saw the mix of melancholy and joy in Kathleen's face when she saw her former employees and fawned over a woman carrying a sleeping infant in a sling. Emily couldn't help but be impressed by the love the women evidently felt for Kathleen, although it shouldn't have been a surprise, given how attached she herself had become to her.

Kathleen had prepared some words about Sharon and spoke to the crowd for a few minutes. Then a woman named Brittany, who said she'd originally introduced Sharon and Kathleen, took a turn at the podium. In her late forties, built like Dolly Parton, the caramel-skinned woman told of meeting Sharon at an after-hours club in Chelsea when Sharon was in college and tricking part-time. Emily listened, fascinated, hearing of a glittering but gritty world she'd barely known existed.

Brittany said she'd swooped in to grab Sharon just as a pimp was eying her. If a pimp got hold of you, you could count on ending up broke, beaten, and saddled with a dose of posttraumatic stress or addiction. "I brought Sharon to Kathleen . . . where I knew she'd be safe. It became a lifelong career for Sharon." She wiped away a tear. "But I think you've got to know when your time is up."

After the speakers were done, everyone filed outside and down a flower-lined path. Tombs the size of safe-deposit boxes, meant for ash urns, filled the outer walls of the building. Sharon's box was fronted by curtain-covered wood. Emily figured the door would be engraved like a tombstone to mark the resting place later.

One of the women began to sing "Amazing Grace," a cappella. Emily looked over in surprise at the beauty of the woman's voice. Kathleen was weeping.

An attendant placed the urn in the box, and the women took turns saying a few words to Kathleen, who held Emily's hand. Emily felt comfortable and honored by the way Kathleen claimed her. She brushed away the memory of all the negative things her mother had said.

Brittany approached Kathleen. "It was a beautiful service, Kat, really nice. You did a good thing here."

"Thanks. She deserved it," Kathleen said. "Tell me, do you know anything about her girlfriend, Angela?"

"No. The last time I saw Sharon was—jeez, must have been twenty years ago. In the East Village."

Kathleen nodded sadly.

"I was going to an AA meeting on Saint Marks Place. I remember it clear as day. It was hot as hell out there that day. One of those fry-an-egg-on-the-sidewalk days. And who did I see? Waddling down the block? At first, I couldn't believe it. Sharon. She was pregnant as all be. She told me she was nine months. Glowing. She was so beautiful. She said she'd stopped working and was back in school."

Kathleen's face froze. "She was pregnant?" Emily could see Kathleen's mind going from surprise to trying to figure something out.

"I'd hoped to see her baby here, all grown up," Brittany said. "But I guess not. Untoward stuff has a way of happening to us. I hate to ask what happened to that baby. This thing here is sad enough."

CHAPTER

29

KATHLEEN NOTICED THE beauty of the summer afternoon. A breeze rustled through the leaves of the trees. The temperature was comfortable in the shadow of the apartment buildings that stood between her and the western sun. Emily had gone to work for the afternoon, and Kathleen marveled that she had shown up for a memorial for someone she didn't know. Kathleen knew she had no right to feel proud of Emily, but she did.

Kathleen's thoughts turned to Sharon's pregnancy. Sharon had never told her. There had been a gap year in their relationship. Sharon had quit hooking and returned to school, or so Kathleen thought. Then she'd returned to Kathleen, saying she'd given up on school and wanted to come back to work. Kathleen had to revise her whole understanding of Sharon's life. Sharon had been pregnant while she was away. They'd worked together for a decade after the pregnancy and had remained friends after that, but Sharon had never said a word.

Kathleen imagined her friend walking on Saint Marks Place in the East Village. Kathleen had waddled on that very sidewalk when she was pregnant, glowing and hopped up on mommy hormones. Kathleen remembered passing the hippie stores selling records and handcrafted items in displays set up out in front of the tiny shops there. Michael drank too much sometimes, but they were relatively happy in their modest lives. Michael worked as a sound engineer at an East Village recording studio, and she worked clerical jobs in the Garment District while going to Hunter College part time. She remembered walking from the subway stop at Astor Place toward their home a few blocks east. The cement's heat bathed her swollen legs and she was short of breath because the baby took up so much of her breathing room. But she hadn't cared at all about the discomfort. She'd never been more content.

She'd needed a C-section when Lauren was born, because Lauren had never turned head-down—always an independent-minded child, even before birth. The obstetrician had given the baby to Michael after cutting the umbilical cord and Michael had grinned, the tiny baby cradled in his long hands.

Now, as Kathleen approached her home, she knew immediately that something was amiss. She sensed it before she saw her apartment door ajar. It was the breeze in the hallway. She stopped and took a step back, her heart thumping, then proceeded cautiously toward the door. Was it possible she'd left it open?

She heard voices. They didn't sound as if they were hiding their presence. She took another couple of steps closer, almost near enough to push the door inward. She heard a female voice. She recognized it, grasped the doorknob, and walked in.

Detective Luna turned from the vestibule of Kathleen's apartment and met her eyes.

"What are you doing here?" Kathleen asked.

Luna pushed a piece of paper toward Kathleen. "Search warrant. I assume you know the drill."

Kathleen walked farther inside, edging past the cop, furious. Her living room was a shambles. The cops hadn't even tried to minimize the damage. She felt a burning behind her eyes and a familiarity, too, almost a déjà vu to her old life, when cops and corrections officers had complete power over her. But she was clean now, of sound mind, not doing anything against the law. She hadn't been prepared for this.

Kathleen tried to keep her cool. "What are you looking for?"

Detective Luna signaled to her partner, who moved forward.

"As it turns out," Luna said, "we only recently learned that you were Sharon Williams's madam. We think there's a whole world of stuff we don't know about your . . . business. A lot of information relevant to the murder. You haven't exactly been forthcoming."

Fear gripped Kathleen. She didn't know what they could accuse her of doing. There was, of course, no evidence that she'd been involved in Sharon's murder. They'd interviewed her at length that first day when they'd asked her to come to the precinct. She'd told them the truth about Sharon dancing and working as a call girl and about Sharon being her friend. There had been no reason to tell them about her own former profession. But she had zero faith in the justice system after doing five years for supposedly killing her husband. "I'm not a madam. I'm a retired old woman, and you've destroyed my apartment."

Detective Banks shoved his way closer. "You don't even qualify for social security, not a year of legal earnings on the books. So enough with the retired-old-lady bullshit."

Detective Luna added, "She was here. We want to know who she was meeting and everything about the date. We don't care how you went from ex-con to real estate magnate, but—"

"Oh, you really are a piece of work, the both of you," Kathleen spat, her anger drowning out her drumbeat of fear. "Sharon wasn't here for a date. She was coming to visit. Do your *jobs*. I've been in this neighborhood for years. I own this building. The building's small profit supports me. You will never find a witness to say I'm running prostitutes. This is ridiculous."

"We'd like your consent to check your telephone records."

"You'll have to deal with my lawyer," Kathleen said. "You're headed down the wrong path. Don't ask me to help you on it."

*　　*　　*

Even after the trauma of the police searching her place, Kathleen couldn't get the question out of her mind: where was the baby? As she assessed the damage and started returning books to shelves, she counted back the decades in her head. Twenty-one years ago, before Sharon left for the year, Kathleen had already been well established in her business. She had a long client list of wealthy and often powerful men. Sharon was nearly the last girl in Client 13's pied-à-terre. A couple of months after Sharon's stint, he told Kathleen he wasn't going to need the apartment anymore, and Sharon stopped working for Kathleen. The two events hadn't seemed related, but maybe Sharon's pregnancy had scared Client 13 away from what had, until then, seemed a low-risk activity.

When Sharon returned a year later, saying she missed the money, Kathleen had assumed she'd met someone and tried to leave the business but the relationship simply hadn't worked out. Kathleen had wondered at the time whether it was Client 13. Women as beautiful and smart as Sharon sometimes found wealthy clients who pulled them out of the Life. Some even married them. Of course, Client 13 was already married.

He was not only married; he'd also started to have an interest in politics. In those days, a sex scandal would have doused his political ambitions. She imagined he wouldn't have been too happy if Sharon refused to get rid of the baby. And that much Kathleen knew about Sharon—she would not have had an abortion. She might have been a hooker, but she was also Catholic. She'd told Kathleen that she thought abortion was a mortal sin.

There had been a sadness to Sharon's return to Kathleen. Kathleen hadn't asked any questions at the time. Women in the business didn't have to explain their choice to do sex work, nor the disappointments, heartbreaks, or hopes that had led to their choices. If they wanted to talk about it, Kathleen was there, but she would never push it. Her business model was all about respect. As Kathleen thought back on it, though, she wished she'd pressed Sharon to tell her about what had made her leave and return. Sharon had been young when she'd come to Kathleen. Not a minor, but young enough for Kathleen to feel a maternal duty to make sure she was okay.

So, where was the child? Kathleen imagined that Sharon had given the baby up for adoption. She clearly hadn't raised the child. And Kathleen doubted Sharon would have had her family raise her baby if she refused to have anything to do with them herself. It hit Kathleen: who would have been the attorney on a very private adoption of Client 13's love child?

*   *   *

"I was surprised to hear from you today," Wayne said to Kathleen when his secretary had left and closed the office door behind her. His manor was bedside-mild, as if their last interaction hadn't been dicey.

"The police searched my apartment this morning," she said. "I don't think I need an attorney on that yet."

He smiled slightly. "Well, you know I'm always here for you, if it comes to that."

Kathleen had no intention of hiring Wayne if she was charged with anything criminal regarding Sharon, but she wasn't going to tell him that. The prospect of a payday would buy her quite a bit of loyalty from a guy like him. She didn't mind playing that card for what it was worth.

"Sharon's baby would be grown up now," she said.

Wayne looked surprised. "Baby?"

"Sharon must have had an NDA about that too. Our client never left things like that undone. He didn't mind spending money for peace of mind." Her voice hardened. "It was his baby, wasn't it?"

"Kathleen." Wayne said her name reproachfully, as if she should know better than to ask. She assumed it was the gangster code of ethics, not the attorney one, that silenced him.

"Let's go over this again. Why did she call you on the night she died?" Kathleen waited as Wayne took in the question.

"You're cross-examining me?" He laughed, leaning back in his seat. "I don't know anything about a baby. I don't know why she called me. And I don't see what a baby has to do with what happened to her."

"I wonder whether they have any suspects in her murder," Kathleen said. "I could think of one. She called you and me, and we both know who's the only nexus between the three of us. Next thing, she winds up dead."

"You've been reading too many crime novels, Kathleen. If it were even true that our guy had a kid with Sharon, do you think rich men, political guys, would kill to keep a love child quiet? In the age of philanderers like Trump? Decades after the supposed child's birth?" He leaned forward, and his tone grew cold. "You ask whether there are any suspects? I'll tell you. Only every horny dude in the city."

Kathleen's jaw clenched. She measured her words. "Sharon's dead. Do you think now is the time to insult her for doing sex work?"

"Since when are you so sensitive about the topic of sex work? The lifestyle is a killer. She was over forty. Way past the expiration date for a hooker."

"Wayne, I—" Kathleen took a breath, forcing herself to pause before she said more. He was trying to shift the tables after her jab the last time about him being a john. Or maybe his belligerence was something more.

His expression softened with false sympathy. "There is one thing I know: some people don't like being messed with. I also know that there are risks beyond violating your NDA . . . even after one's life of illegally promoting prostitution is long over. Lifelong risks. For you. Besides the million-dollar penalty."

Kathleen's spine pressed back against her chair.

"For instance, did you know there's no statute of limitations on tax evasion?" Wayne went on. "You failed to file your taxes during several of your *spa's* best years. The income you reported for taxes pales in comparison to all the assets you possess."

Electricity rolled up Kathleen's vertebrae to the base of her skull. Her feet were planted firmly on the carpet, but she felt as if the floor were rolling under her.

"Tax evasion is always low-hanging fruit for prosecutors. But you know that." He smiled smugly. "My suggestion, Kathleen, is that you continue to do what you've been doing the last few years. Mind your business and go quietly into the night until you die of old age. I like you, Kathleen. I always have. I don't want to become your defense attorney, or see something happen to you."

Her face burned. "Are you saying you'd drop a dime to the IRS? Need I remind you of attorney-client privilege?"

"I wouldn't be the one dropping the name." He leaned back in his chair. "And that might only be the beginning. You're screwing with the wrong people, Kat."

CHAPTER

30

EMILY LEFT THE subway at the last stop on the A. The sky was gray with clouds and tinged amber by the setting sun. The pavement was wet, rain puddling on the concrete. It had rained while she was underground. She walked west, inhaling deeply, taking in the scent of the damp trees and meadows of the park two blocks away. At a green light, she crossed the street in front of a car that had paused to make a turn. A second car pulled out of a bus stop on Broadway where it had been idling. It made the turn as well. It was a black SUV, like the ones the mayor used with his security detail. She wondered whether a City official was riding in there, but it was more likely an Uber.

She walked past a church. Children on three-wheeled scooters whizzed by. Their mother carried a pizza box. The mother called out to remind them to stop at the corner and wait for her before crossing the street. Seeing them, Emily missed Skye. She appreciated having free time but often felt a tug of yearning on Hector's nights.

When Emily turned onto Seaman Avenue, she noticed the black car was still with her. It didn't take much for a woman to feel vulnerable on a darkening street, and the street was empty now except for her and the car.

Emily's mind flashed back to Sharon, the moment she turned back to speak to a man who approached from a car. It struck her that this might be the exact route Sharon had walked that night.

With a force of will, Emily coached herself not to look for the suspicious car to see if it was *him*, the stocky man with dark hair who had taken Sharon.

The black car passed her, and she exhaled. Nothing to worry about. She took a couple of easy breaths before she noticed a gray SUV now traveling slowly up the block, seeming to keep pace with her. *Damn.*

She knew law enforcement used multiple cars if they wanted to remain incognito when following you. So, it wasn't out of the question that more than one car was following her. On the other hand, they weren't making much of an effort to remain incognito, if she'd spotted them so easily.

She chided herself for her paranoia. The driver of the gray car was probably looking for parking. Her fear had to be a delayed reaction from seeing the man pick up Sharon. Maybe she'd been more affected by what happened than she'd realized.

Emily tended to stuff down her feelings about traumatic events, forcing herself to keep her focus on the next tasks that needed doing. She was always busy, even overscheduled. After her father died, she'd made up for her bad GPA that semester by maintaining perfect grades and tons of after-school activities. It had helped her get into a good college, but more than anything, it had kept her from dwelling on her father's death. Her propensity to drown her feelings in work and extracurriculars had never lifted completely.

Emily could still sense the gray car following. *Calm down,* she ordered herself. There was no reason for a team of people to follow her. Whatever trauma she'd experienced was mushrooming into irrational anxiety.

But Emily made a snap decision. She turned down a one-way street, where cars flowed toward her. If the gray car was following her, it couldn't turn onto the street going the wrong way. If it wasn't, no one had to know how neurotic she was being.

Emily found herself finally alone, no cars, no pedestrians. She turned another corner and saw her building ahead. No one was following, but she couldn't get home soon enough. She keyed the lock to her building and walked into the vestibule. She paused, her lungs an untied balloon.

*   *   *

"What happened?" Kathleen said with alarm when she answered Emily's knock at her front door. Emily knew she must look shaken. Kathleen didn't look much better.

"I don't know. I swear to god, Kathleen, I felt as if I was being followed. From the subway. I know it sounds farfetched . . ."

Kathleen brought her inside and locked the door.

Emily looked around. "Oh my god, what happened here?"

The place was ransacked. Papers were strewn around, drawers still open, furniture askew.

"The police searched it," Kathleen replied. "They thought I might have booked the date for Sharon the night she was killed. The date with the killer."

"Get out of here. That's ridiculous." Emily pushed a love seat back to its old place, perpendicular to the sofa. She unfolded an area rug, struggling to pull it to its spot in the center of the floor in front of the couch.

"You don't have to do that. I'm going to hire someone to come in and help me."

"Don't be silly." Emily began picking up books from the floor to reshelve. "Could it have been the police, following me? Would they think I'm involved in some weird way too?"

"I don't think so. You work at City Hall, for god's sake." Kathleen put a hand on her arm as Emily bent to pick up a second pile of books. Emily straightened up to look back at her. "Who did you tell about seeing Sharon?" Kathleen asked.

Emily frowned. "Everyone at work knows. And all my friends." Seeing the look in Kathleen's eyes, Emily put up her palm. "The friends I talk to, not Facebook and Instagram friends."

Kathleen raised her eyebrows, saying dryly, "That's something, at least."

"I didn't think it was a big deal to tell my friends. I mean, I don't know anyone who would know anyone that could be involved. Should we call the detectives about someone maybe following me?"

"We don't have anything to tell them. It could have been nothing. And I don't think they're on our side, at least not mine or Sharon's."

31

Before

A T THE APPOINTED time, Jackson approached a brownstone in Greenwich Village. He had spent hours drafting an email to the man in a decades-old *New York Times* wedding announcement that his distant cousin had sent him. Jackson's spitting image had stared back at him. Same eyes, same jaw, same chin. His doppelgänger. And the man was not only rich, he was important. The patriarch of twenty-eight heirs to a family fortune of over fifty billion dollars.

Within a day, Jackson had received a response to his email: a call from a lawyer. "My client will meet you at 436 West Tenth Street. Tomorrow."

The lawyer hadn't said directly that the groom in the photo was Jackson's father, but Jackson had fought not to hyperventilate.

"The matter requires discretion. You're a young man. Can you handle that? Keep it quiet?"

"Of course I can," Jackson said, trying not to take offense.

During the call, Jackson had kept his voice calm, asking no questions. He'd seen a viral video once of a guy who misread a lotto ticket. The dude had a damn fit of joy about it for a full minute, screaming and rolling on the floor, thinking he'd won a million dollars, before he realized he'd misread the number.

Jackson had no intention of humiliating himself like that. But still, after he hung up, he'd literally jumped for joy. Everything he'd dreamed of was coming true. *Pay-fucking-dirt.*

A door at street level led to a garden apartment. It was unlocked, as promised. Jackson walked in and looked around; no one there yet. There was no clutter like in the homes of his family in Beacon and upstate, which were filled with decades of junk. He didn't think anyone lived here, at least not full-time. He sat on a couch and put his feet on the coffee table, trying to get comfortable.

Jackson had dressed nicely, new Old Navy jeans and a clean indigo-blue T-shirt. He had found his *father.* He hoped there would be a night out on the town for the two of them. Fancy places Jackson's parents couldn't afford or even imagine. It was almost too much to believe that, after nineteen years of feeling like he'd been parachuted into a family where he didn't belong, he'd solved the Rubik's Cube that was his life.

The man who was meeting him was a hotshot, obviously skilled at meeting people surreptitiously at places like this—including women, Jackson guessed. Jackson figured the dude had given him up for adoption when he got a woman pregnant. It wasn't excusable, but based on Jackson's research, his dad had already had other kids to worry about back then. The shit would have hit the fan if the wife found out about him. Jackson posed the question to himself: what would he have done if he were in his father's shoes? He smirked, thinking of it. Give the kid up, no doubt. He totally got it. The past was past. Now was what counted.

A knock sounded at the front door, the way doctors warned you they were coming into an examining room. A man entered the room, and Jackson stood. The man's eyes took Jackson in as Jackson did the same, both noting each other's resemblance as if looking into a funhouse mirror.

Jackson's father put out his hand to shake. Jackson felt the smooth, soft skin, so unlike that of the men Jackson knew. He felt a deep discomfort, not knowing what to do with his body after they shook. He wanted to hug the stranger, but his father's grip made clear that their hands would be the only contact.

"Well, it's good to meet you, son," his father said.

"It's good to meet you too."

"Was your trip okay?"

"Yeah. Yes"—he corrected his working-class speech—"it was fine."

"I wanted you to be raised without any knowledge of me, but I see that hasn't worked out."

"I understand, sir. But it was unnatural."

"Naturally," his father replied with a wry smile.

"Leaving me with strangers who were nothing like me . . . I couldn't help but wonder. Not that they told me. They denied everything." Jackson surprised himself by protecting his parents from unknown consequences. He felt uncertain, not knowing the rules of engagement with this man.

"You do understand that I have a wife and family who don't know about you? There are many other considerations at stake."

"I could meet my brother and sister." Jackson's tone took on a disconcerting whine. The way his father was speaking, Jackson could see the rejection coming like a tsunami against a gray sky. "You are my father."

"Not legally, no. And there's no basis for you having that issue tested and proved. You're an adult and the legal child of your parents, the Mattinglys. There will be no paternity test, just your suppositions."

"I wasn't stolen, then."

The man chuckled, his expression darkening. "Of course not. People don't steal from me."

Was that a warning? As if Jackson, his own son, was some sort of gold digger?

Jackson found himself pacing, feeling reduced by the look in the dude's eyes. His deeply buried feeling that he was an alien being, an abomination belonging nowhere, nearly bubbled to the surface, stomped down only by his razor-sharp rage. "What the fuck? You don't even want to know me? You'd deny your own blood?"

"I have already denied you. For nineteen years."

Jackson recognized the meanness in the man's facial expression. Jackson had used that same disdainful expression himself with the weak: nerds, girls, stray dogs. He'd never seen that look in anyone before, the depth and poison to it. Directed at him. Jackson seethed. *This motherfucker has no idea who he's fucking with.*

His father went on. "You understand you have no legal claim to my money or estate. You are the legal son of the Mattinglys, and our connection, assuming a connection, is an illusion. All my money will go to my wife and children. You may not understand the legal basis, but I have a will, and you can't make a successful claim. I have no obligation to you whatsoever."

Jackson's eyes burned. "You fucker."

"I gave you a life where you would be properly cared for." The man must have seen the killer look in Jackson's eyes, because he talked more softly, ingratiatingly. Jackson knew it was bullshit. "I'd like to claim you, but I can't. What I will do for you, though, is help you. Once. Now."

All righty then, here comes the con job. Jackson listened.

"Do you know what Bitcoin is?"

"Of course."

His father opened a small leather portfolio he'd brought with him, pulled documents out, and placed them on the coffee table. "I'm going to give you the account number for a Bitcoin wallet with two hundred thousand dollars in it. Please spend it slowly. This is a one-time deal. I have a document for you to sign. It's called a nondisclosure agreement."

"I know what they are," Jackson said bitterly. "Everybody knows what they are."

"If you talk about me or your theory about our relationship, or contact anyone else in my family, you will owe ten million dollars in penalties for each violation. If you don't have that much money, my attorneys will make sure you lose everything I've paid you, anything you've bought, and will even garnish your wages if you so much as utter a word about me. So spend the Bitcoin wisely. I don't want to hear anything more about your paternity theories, or anything from you, again, at all, ever. This is the last time we'll speak."

The man pulled out a pen and turned the agreement toward Jackson for him to sign.

Jackson sat on the edge of the couch and pulled it toward himself. "What about my mother? I want to meet my mother."

"She has no interest in you, and if you met her, you'd have no interest in her. There's no more to be said on that point."

"I'd like to be the judge of that."

The man looked hard at Jackson. There was a glint in his eyes. He was enjoying himself. "Impossible."

Jackson took the pen, assessing the man who, unbeknownst to him, had landed firmly in enemy territory. Payback would be a bitch. Jackson didn't know how, but he would get his father back. If needed, he'd use every penny of the guy's own money to do that, to destroy him—it would be worth it. The thought of retribution was the only thing that soothed the burning in his gut and throat. He looked up after signing the agreement that would give him more money than he'd ever seen, feeling no joy in it.

He stared at his father's eyes, identical to his own, not only in their blue color but in their ruthlessness. "You're just like me, aren't you?"

His father offered a bare flicker of acknowledgment, turned, and left.

PART III

CHAPTER

32

ALONE IN HER kitchen after a quiet Sunday with Skye at the playground, Emily eyed a neon video game tournament on a propped-up iPad. She hardly played anymore but still enjoyed watching a good game of *Fortnite*. A pearl-white fish fillet sizzled in a frying pan on an old-fashioned four-burner stove. The olive oil crackled, the scent of browning garlic cloves giving her hunger pangs. She wore a pair of drawstring shorts and a frayed, faded tank top.

A pasta pot gave off warm steam in contretemps to the cooling air coming from a window AC unit. Emily picked at a bowl of loose spinach she'd rinsed, chewing a leaf as she dumped the rest in the frying pan, planning to keep it on the flame only long enough to soften it. Thankfully, Skye still ate spinach. Skye's "terrible twos" had brought along daily rejections of foods she used to eat. Skye had opinions now. Endless opinions.

Smoke.

The instant Emily thought it, the smoke alarm over the kitchen doorway blared, painfully loud.

"Damn." She looked at the frying pan, annoyed that the smoke detector was going off for such a miniscule amount of smoke. But it wasn't the fish.

She breathed acrid air now: wood, plaster . . . metal burning?

Her chest constricting, Emily heard fire rushing up the stairs like a train outside her apartment.

Skye. Where's Skye?

Her daughter's paper and crayons lay on the kitchen table. She'd said she was going to the living room to get pencils.

Time seemed to crawl. Between alarm wails, Emily heard crashing and popping outside her apartment. She thought she heard a scream through the walls, but it was hard to tell over the alarm.

Emily ran. "Skye!"

In the living room, she grabbed her daughter, who'd come running, crying, startled by the alarm. Skye clutched her neck.

Stay calm, Emily told herself. *You've rehearsed this in your mind.*

In the first few years after her father's death, Emily had often found herself imagining him waking up in his burning hotel room and escaping. Staying low, under the toxic cloud, running for his life. Emily did that now, running through the living room with Skye tight in her arms.

Gray smoke roiled at the ceiling, moving into Emily's apartment. The smoke was thicker in the living room than the kitchen, but the apartment door and fire escape were both that way. Smoke flowed through the frame of the front door and under it. No need to feel the door for heat. A sound, nearly an explosion, crashed beyond the door. Emily yelped and jumped at the sound. *The staircase had collapsed.*

Skye began shrieking.

"Mommy's here, it's okay," Emily told her. Skye's fingers clawed into her neck.

Emily could hear a distant yelling from the street, the booming bass voice of a man below, warning people: *"Fire, fire, fire."*

Her heart rippling with fear, Emily ran toward the window. She could feel the smoke scratching her throat with each breath. Skye began coughing. Emily felt a terror for her baby beyond anything she'd ever experienced.

She reached the gated window at the far end of the living room. The apartment lights went out. Blackness. Blindness.

Her eyes adjusted. She could see shadow. The lights from neighboring buildings provided wavering illumination through the window. Skye was coughing, crying, Emily's neck wet with her tears.

Black smoke outside the window streamed upward beyond the glass. There was an orange glow outside, coming from below. The front door was burning, impassable. They might not be able to escape through the window, not if the smoke and fire were coming from somewhere below, out there. The living room was getting hotter. Emily imagined the apartment below as a furnace heating her floor. Her apartment was a death trap. The window was her only choice.

Emily held tight to Skye, balanced on a hip. She reached with one hand inside the window gate's metal casing and grappled with the latch, crouching as much as she could below the lowering smoke. She and Skye were coughing, sweating, the room stifling, pressured with heat.

Skye's crying was a steady drumbeat as Emily tugged manically on the gate. "Goddammit, open!"

It creaked and, finally, opened, thank god.

She pulled upward at the window. Nothing. It didn't budge. *Jesus.* She felt for the window lock above the bottom window frame. It was highlighted by a strobe light of smoke that obliterated the streetlight with each breeze. She flipped the latch.

Emily's back bunched with tension before she tried the window again, afraid new oxygen flowing into her apartment might feed the flames beyond the apartment door. The fire could explode toward them when she opened the window. Ready to launch herself and Skye out, Emily pulled upward on the window with all the strength of her free hand. A gust of fresh air rushed in.

She climbed quickly onto the metal fire escape, feeling steam coming off her body. She took a breath of air just as flames shot upward from the apartment below. Inches from her feet. She screamed to the people gathered below, "Help us, please!"

A gust of wind blew the flames and smoke away from Emily's feet. Skye had gone quiet, dead weight, maybe unconscious. Emily looked down. Skye's eyes were open. She could feel Skye's breath on her neck. She was like a trapped animal hoping for invisibility.

People were shouting from the street. The same booming male voice she'd heard before shouted, "Go up, go up!"

The fire was burning the building from the bottom up. Emily scampered up the metal stairs, her heart galloping. Kathleen would be on the fourth floor, two flights up.

Emily peered through the glass of Kathleen's darkened window just as a frightened face emerged from the darkness on the other side of the glass. Startled, Emily's head jolted back. Kathleen was grappling with the window lock as Emily had just done. Smoke streamed out when Kathleen opened it a few inches with obvious exertion.

"*Hurry, hurry,*" Emily said, sticking her fingers in the open crack.

Together, Emily and Kathleen yanked the heavy window up, pushing it fully open.

Hugging the ceiling within Kathleen's apartment, a ball of fire sped their way, toward the outdoor oxygen. Kathleen threw herself out the window. Holding Skye tight, Emily launched herself sideways, out of Kathleen's way. Emily's bones crashed into the hardness of the fire escape, but she cushioned Skye's fall. Kathleen fell to the metal slats too.

"You all right? Come on. Come on!" Emily yelled. "We've got to go up!"

Kathleen scrambled to her feet. She steadied herself and ran up the metal stairs behind Emily and Skye. They'd run a dozen steps upward before the fire exploded from Kathleen's window. Sparks flew at them, pricking Emily's skin. Skye whimpered when sparks hit her.

When they reached the next landing, Emily took in the sight above, horrified: the roof was on fire too. Flames towered upward from there, a huge torch.

They had nowhere to go. Emily's terrified eyes met Kathleen's. They were trapped between the flames above and the flames below.

Over the roar of the fire, Emily could hear the crowd yelling and screaming below, fearing for them. She heard a woman's despairing cry: "*La niña!*" It had to be one of their neighbors, realizing that Skye was trapped with them.

Men were running, dragging mattresses and full garbage bags to the sidewalk below the fire escape. Emily knew what those men saw: death. Were the men hoping to catch her baby? Could she be expected to *drop* her baby to them? A groan rose from Emily's belly.

The wind ripped the flames toward them from below. Emily teetered and slammed her back against the brick wall to steady herself, attempting to cover Skye's back and head with her forearms and hands. The makeshift cushion the neighbors were constructing wouldn't be enough. She could not throw her baby over.

"Where are the firemen?" Kathleen yelled above the noise of the fire and exploding glass. She was holding on to the fire escape railing, the fire only a few feet below them.

The metal of the fire escape was heating Emily's bare feet. Panic enveloped her that she would *need* to trust her baby to the four flights of air and the hands of strangers. *No!*

Finally, Emily heard the sirens. Through the smoke, she glimpsed a flash of red. A fire truck. Even before the truck stopped, a ladder with a bucket swung around and up, toward them. The bucket bumped against the railing of the fire escape. A firefighter in a mask scrambled up the ladder.

Emily cowered against the brick wall as a new shot of flames burst from the window below. Emily could see the reflected red glow in the firefighter's face mask. The firefighter reached out to take Skye.

Emily extricated Skye from her neck. Skye looked at the man and loosened her grip on Emily. She put out her arms. "Firefighter!"

The firefighter quickly passed Skye along to a second fireman who stood below him. The first firefighter turned back to the women.

His voice was muffled as he spoke to Kathleen. "Can you climb over?"

Kathleen had always seemed strong, but she was off-balance now. "I don't know."

The fireman left the bucket, climbed over, and picked Kathleen up. Emily climbed over the banister after them, the rough metal catching her gym shorts and scraping her already-raw legs. She landed off-kilter inside the bucket, her feet on cool metal. The firefighter steadied her with his body, still balancing Kathleen. "Hang on."

The crowded bucket swooped through the air in a moment of vertigo, down and away from the building. It lowered to the street. People were clapping and cheering.

The second firefighter handed Skye back to Emily.

"Take her to the ambulance to get checked out. Watch for glass," the first firefighter warned Emily.

When Emily's bare feet landed on the ground and she tried to walk, her legs trembled with adrenaline, nearly giving out. A female EMS worker grabbed Emily's arm to steady her.

A woman who worked at the corner bodega approached and handed flip-flops to Emily and Kathleen. The ground Emily and Kathleen walked on had become a minefield of broken glass from the windows above. The sounds of axes, breaking glass, sirens, and sobbing survivors had created a sound bubble. The whirring of helicopter blades approached. None of it felt real.

Unable to think, Emily followed instructions. She and Kathleen went with the EMS attendant. Emily sat in the ambulance with Skye on her lap. The paramedic checked Skye's vital signs and looked at her throat with a flashlight. "She's fine. Good job, mama."

Emily found herself weeping.

The EMS attendant put ointment on a few specks of pink on Skye's arms. She had fallen asleep in Emily's arms. "Young kids sleep a lot after a trauma," the EMS worker said. "It's normal. There's no sign of serious smoke inhalation. The burns are no worse than sunburn. Keep them clean. Now let's take a look at your legs."

"I'm okay. I'm not hurt. You should look at her," Emily said, turning back toward Kathleen, whose legs were streaked with red where the sparks had hit them. Emily's legs looked the same.

From the back of the ambulance, Emily saw another ambulance pull away, siren blasting. Kathleen signaled the departing ambulance. "How bad?"

The EMS worker replied, "Some burns, but nothing life threatening. We don't know for sure yet whether others didn't get out. The firefighters will go door to door."

33

SITTING IN THE glare of the ambulance, Kathleen let the EMS worker look at her legs. She didn't need to go to the doctor. Her burns were minor. Red streaks ran down her legs, only a few blisters coming up, no worse than a minor kitchen accident, just more widespread. Emily was in similar shape. The baby was fine, thank god, asleep with a thumb in her mouth and an arm draped around Emily's neck.

The EMS worker shined a light down Kathleen's throat. "You're red. If you develop shortness of breath or the coughing gets bad later, seek medical attention. The damage from smoke inhalation can take time to show up."

"Okay," Kathleen said, but she was only half listening. With Emily and Skye safe, her mind was on her tenants. She just wanted to make sure the others were okay.

Kathleen joined Emily outside the ambulance. The tenants gathered in the cordoned-off street, staying out of the path of the firefighters entering and exiting the building. The group watched and waited for lack of anything else to do or anywhere to go. It was clear that none of them would be returning to their homes tonight, or anytime soon. Kathleen felt such sorrow for them. She'd lost her home too, but she hadn't raised children, shared a life with long-gone parents, or slept beside the love of her life for decades here. Her losses could be replaced.

A fireman came out of the building holding a small dog with a white coat turned mostly gray with soot.

A man exclaimed joyfully, "Coco, Coco, *mijo*."

"The Red Cross will be coming with a bus soon," Kathleen heard a cop say. "They'll put you up."

Kathleen considered that for the first time. Where would she stay? She didn't want to go to a Red Cross hotel.

"Thank you for helping me," she said to Emily. "For saving my life."

Emily let out a long, shuddering breath, unconsciously rocking the baby on her hip. "You had me worried."

"Do you want to come with me? To a hotel?" Kathleen asked.

"I'm going home. There's space for us." Emily's eyes were watery. "Truthfully, I really want my mother. I know it sounds stupid."

"Not at all." Kathleen felt a deep melancholy, wishing she could be a part of that. Times like this drove home the truth of how alone she was. "I'm going to stay here until the firefighters are done, in case I'm needed. You go on and put Skye to bed."

Kathleen kissed Skye on the head and hugged Emily around her shoulders. Emily gave her a strange look.

A man with a freckled face and an Afro approached Kathleen. He wore an FDNY uniform. "May I speak to you privately?"

They walked a few yards away from the tenants and Emily.

"I'm told you're the landlady?" he said.

"Yes."

"It will take a few days to get a preliminary report on the cause of this fire, but the way it burned, the speed it burned at, I'd lay odds on unnatural causes."

Kathleen's stomach tightened. "Arson?"

"I'm sorry to say."

"Who would do that? Why?"

Of course, he couldn't answer.

*   *   *

A drizzle began to fall, coating the ash on Emily's clothes and the ground. She stared at the building from the middle of the street. The sky spun with rotating red police lights. The windows at the front of the building had become charred black tunnels. The memory of Kathleen came back to her: Kathleen looking out at her from behind her window, terrified, trapped, as the room filled with smoke. The fireball coming toward them. The mattresses under the fire escape, four flights below. Emily's heart galloped again, her chest tight as she put her face against Skye's hair and forced herself to breathe.

"Does anyone have a phone I could use?" Emily asked her neighbors.

Coco's owner tapped in his passcode and handed Emily his phone, and an older woman reached for Skye to free up Emily's hands. "*Dejame.*"

"Thank you." Skye didn't stir when the woman took her. Emily dialed her mother's number, and her voice shook as she greeted her. "Mom. There was a fire in my building. We're okay, but I need to come home. I don't have money or my phone."

"Oh my god, okay. I'll get you an Uber."

Fifteen minutes later, Emily's Uber pulled up to the entrance to her mother's building. The rain had turned to a fine mist.

Lauren was outside waiting for them. She hugged Emily, Skye between them. "God, you smell like fire. I didn't realize you were *in* the fire." She kissed the limp toddler and held Emily at arm's length, examining them for injuries. "You're both okay?"

Emily collapsed into the nape of her mother's neck, sobbing. She just needed to get it out. All the fear and shock. "If anything had happened to Skye . . ."

"Okay, okay. You're all right. You're both fine," Lauren said soothingly.

Emily felt better within a moment and wiped away stray tears under her eyes. She and Skye were alive, amazingly unharmed. Nobody had died.

Carl met Emily inside the apartment door and hugged her. He stood aside to let her and Lauren in. She looked back before she followed her mother to her bedroom to borrow a change of clothes. Carl was walking better, no hesitation in his steps.

Seeing Emily's reaction, Lauren said, "He's already scheduled to return to work. He just needs to get final clearance from the FBI doctor. His appointment is this week at Federal Plaza."

Emily felt a deep joy and gratitude for that bright spot.

The black-and-white cat rubbed Emily's legs when she sat down to eat a meal of leftover baked chicken and rice. Emily was still damp from her shower, wearing a pair of her mother's sweats and a T-shirt without underwear or a bra. She'd washed her underwear in the sink and hung them up, but she doubted the smell of smoke would come out. Skye was fast asleep in the crib her mother had added to Emily's old room when Skye was born, for sleepovers.

"I have to buy clothes and a new stroller tomorrow," Emily told Lauren and Carl, who kept her company at the table.

"I have no cases scheduled," Lauren said. "We'll go to the Department of Health first to get you a birth certificate. They'll give it to me with my identification. Then we can go across the street to the Federal Building to get you a new social security card. I think, after that, you can get a new driver's license, if you want to get it in person. But you could order it online."

The stress knotted in Emily's chest again, and she put down her fork. "This is so overwhelming. Every minute, something new comes to mind that I need to replace or that I lost, and things that I have to do." She picked up the cat to pet him, a thought occurring to her. "And there's a cat here. They won't let me take Rusty next weekend if I stay here with you guys. The volunteers can have other dogs in the house but not cats. *Damn*. Rusty's already had a switch in weekend trainers. He's so close to graduation. It's the worst time for an upheaval."

"We'll figure something out," Lauren said.

"Call the puppy people tomorrow," Carl suggested.

Emily felt a welling in her chest. Gratitude for her mother and Carl. "Okay. After I call Skye's pediatrician. I want to make sure I do whatever I'm supposed to do to deal with the trauma. I can't believe she's had to go through something like this." Emily sniffed back tears. "All I wanted was to give her a normal, safe childhood . . . and now this."

CHAPTER

34

AFTER MIDNIGHT, KATHLEEN walked into the frigid air of a hotel lobby on West Seventy-Fifth Street and Broadway. Marble floors and gold banisters contrasted richly with the lobby's cherry-paneled walls. Without a watch or phone or home, she felt as if she were floating without time or place: brain fog. It must be the shock.

The hotel manager, barrel chested with a widow's peak like Eddie Munster, opened his mouth in an O and closed it primly. "Kat, my god. You're covered in soot."

She swallowed, close to choking up for the first time since the fire. "Stan . . . a fire . . . my building. I grabbed my keys, but the fire traveled so quickly, there was no time to take anything else."

Stan ushered her to the reception desk and handed the person on duty his credit card. "I'm booking her a room on my card. She'll bring hers tomorrow when she replaces it. She's a friend."

The receptionist smiled and gave Kathleen a key card. "I'm so sorry. Let me know if there's anything we can do for you."

"Put your clothes in a laundry bag," Stan said as he walked Kathleen toward the elevator. "We have bathrobes upstairs. I'll have your clothes washed and dried, so you'll have something to wear in the morning until you can buy something. Do you need any money to tide you over?"

"No, I'll be okay. Thank you for making things so easy for me."

"It's going to be hard enough."

*   *   *

The next morning, just before nine, the sun topped the apartment buildings on Central Park West. Kathleen squinted as she walked toward the park on a brownstone-lined side street. The sun bored into her eyes, aggravating a headache she'd treated with a couple of Tylenols that hadn't kicked in yet. She had a sore throat, too, and her legs felt as if she'd spent a July day at the beach without sunscreen.

Once inside the park, Kathleen took in the hush of the car-free zone and the cool shade scented with blossoms. The masses of tourists hadn't yet converged on Strawberry Fields, with its Beatles lyrics etched into the ground. Jovial groups of tourists had still filled the hotel restaurant when she left. She was grateful for the relative solitude: just her, the dog walkers, joggers, and speeding cyclists.

Twenty-five minutes later, she walked into a glass-walled establishment off the lobby of an office building on Lexington Avenue. She greeted the receptionist at the black lacquer desk. Kathleen gave her the box number and entered her password on a tablet the woman turned to her.

A deeply tanned security guard who looked like a CIA retiree—at least the way they looked in the movies—escorted Kathleen down a black-carpeted hallway. They reached a room with walls lined with safe-deposit boxes. She unlocked the box with a key she'd kept on her key ring, the only key on her ring that would fit any lock now. The guard unlocked a second lock on the box and left her.

Inside a small privacy room with a table, two chairs, and unadorned walls, she took her birth certificate and an expired passport from the box. She could use the passport for photo identification to get her credit cards and passport replaced. She next took out a rubber-banded packet of one-hundred-dollar bills and a second packet of twenties, wondering what Lauren would think about the contents of the box. She might be coming here sooner rather than later. Kathleen had left an extra key with her attorney and given him Lauren's contact information in case anything ever happened to her.

Kathleen had never forgotten her child, not for a single day. And now Kathleen's life felt precarious, riskier than it had felt for many years.

*   *   *

At the Apple store on Fifth Avenue, across from the Plaza Hotel, a sweet young man—pimples and short hair except for a bun on top of his head—helped Kathleen download all her information from the cloud. She breathed a small sigh of relief. Her life was housed online as much as in her building.

Next, she sat in a Starbucks to order a Windows laptop. She looked around, hoping no one in the store was waiting for a chance to hack anyone stupid enough to do payment transactions on an unsecured network. There was a mom with a toddler. A tourist family, rosy cheeked and blond haired. She guessed they were from Idaho or Indiana. A couple of college kids studied in a corner. It was early in the day for nefarious hackers.

One thing she couldn't get out of her mind, though, was the fire inspector telling her the fire hadn't been an accident. From what she'd seen on the news over the years, mental illness or domestic violence revenge was often the precipitating factor when it came to arson in occupied buildings. She didn't think any of her tenants were in that sort of fix, but one never knew.

Her mind returned to her visit with Wayne and his veiled threat. *I don't want to see something bad happen to you*, he'd said. *You're screwing with the wrong people, Kat.*

She felt a tightness in her chest as she brought the thought to full consciousness. Could Wayne have told someone she was asking about Sharon? Someone dangerous? Emily had thought cars were following her. Could Emily have told the wrong person that she was the only witness in Sharon's murder investigation? Was there a connection between the cars and Wayne's warning? And were both those things connected to the fire?

She chided herself for her fantastic imagination. If there were people who wanted to kill her or Emily, there were more efficient ways to do it than setting a fire.

She breathed in, filling her belly. She tried to breathe out her anxiety. She looked around, centering herself. She had to deal with insurance, police reports, finding a place to live, and buying clothes. It was odd how her mind could make an overwhelming situation worse by spinning conspiracy theories in her head, probably to avoid facing the real situation. No matter how unpleasant reality was, she refused to make it worse by entertaining paranoid suspicions. She scoffed at her musings: silly season.

She called her building manager, Greg, a sweet young man who seemed to know far more about building management than anyone could have learned during so few years of adult life. He'd once talked about a fire in another building he'd managed that had spread at lightning speed because the apartment doors didn't automatically shut behind the residents when they fled. At his suggestion, Kathleen had agreed to install automatic latches on every apartment door, which meant they'd slammed shut when people fled the fire. So why had the fire spread so fast? She wanted to hear what he thought about that and touch base with him about all that needed to be done, but he didn't pick up the phone. She left him a voice mail.

Next, she began searching for an Airbnb. By the time she'd finished her coffee, she'd booked a two-bedroom apartment in Washington Heights for two weeks. She'd propose a longer, cheaper rental period if she ended up liking the place.

Last on her to-do list, she called Emily as she walked back to the hotel and left a message when the call went to voice mail. Kathleen wasn't surprised about that. Emily must be out trying to reconstruct her life, as Kathleen was, and probably didn't have a phone yet.

A couple of hours later, Emily called back. Kathleen sat on her hotel bed while Emily filled her in on how Skye had slept for eighteen hours. "My mother went out and got me a new phone, some new clothes for Skye and me, and a stroller. We're waiting until tomorrow to get my new documents. But most importantly, she found firefighter pajamas."

They both got a chuckle out of that.

"Thank god," Kathleen said.

"Skye just woke up. The doctor said not to worry about her sleeping so long. But since she woke up, she's been fixated on Rusty." Kathleen could hear the distress in Emily's voice. "She's crying and asking for him. I keep telling her Rusty is fine, that he's at his regular home. But she's inconsolable. I'm pretty sure she thinks Rusty was in the fire. She won't be all right until she sees that dog. But when I called Puppies-in-Prison, they said I can't have Rusty here because of my mother's cat. We won't get our last weekend with him, and I'm afraid of how Skye will process that."

Kathleen didn't have to think twice about what she said next. "I've rented an Airbnb on One Hundred Eighty-Sixth Street. Come take a look. It's two bedrooms. You and Skye can stay with me if you want, and Rusty too."

"Really?"

"Of course. I love Skye. And besides anything else, I owe you my life."

"You won't have a moment of quiet."

"That sounds just fine."

35

CARL REPORTED TO the FBI doctor at Federal Plaza. He could tell that the doctor had already reviewed the medical records Carl's MS physician had emailed over. The examination was perfunctory. The "back-to-work, desk duty" letter was signed and ready for emailing to human resources before Carl walked out of the office a half hour after he'd arrived.

Carl had never imagined being happy to sit at a desk. But he was ecstatic, and the rush hour commute had been no problem for him today. Six weeks ago, he'd been afraid of falling on the subway, imagining himself unable to get up without help. Now he was pretty sure he'd be fit for full duty soon. He'd read blog posts by cops who had MS and stayed on active duty. He was determined to be one of them.

Carl went to the eighteenth floor of the Federal Building, which took up the equivalent of several square blocks in Tribeca. He checked in with the assistant special agent in charge, Patrick Gendell, who sat in his sunny corner office overlooking Worth Street and Broadway.

"Carl, it's good to have you back. It's good timing," ASAC Gendell said. He was tall and slim with chalk-white skin and wisps of gray hair that used to be red. "We've got a lot of forensic work to be done. We've been working with City Hall, looking for emails Jackson Mattingly might have sent to Sullivan or his staff."

"Is it possible he bombed the subway just to get back at Sullivan? You have to wonder for what."

"It would be bizarre. But a guy who kills a bunch of people without any gripe, much less an ideological justification, isn't exactly rational—even using the broadest definition of the term. Like Stephen Paddock, the Las Vegas shooter. That one flummoxed us." The ASAC sighed. "Look at Mattingly's social media activity and see what you think. You'll give us a fresh set of eyes. Mattingly followed the mayor on Facebook, Instagram, and Twitter, using several fake avatars. We're still finding new email addresses and social media accounts associated with him. This work will be good for you . . . while you're getting back to full strength."

As he noted the ASAC's cautious tone, a shadow of anxiety edged into Carl's optimism. "Okay, boss."

Carl left the office, trying not to ruminate on what Gendell might have left unsaid about Carl's status. They wouldn't let him resume full duty until he'd been symptom-free for six months. But, if he had a relapse during that waiting period, they might make him take disability retirement instead of keeping him on light duty. He tried to maintain a positive attitude, but living with uncertainty was not his strong suit. Still, he was thrilled to be working on the Mattingly case, and work would mean a full paycheck coming in. In his mind, failing to contribute to the household he shared with Lauren was not an option. And Alex had a couple of years left of college, so Carl needed his savings.

Toward the end of the afternoon, Rick arrived at the four-person office he shared with Carl and two other agents, including Rick's new temporary partner. Sunlight streamed in through a window overlooking Broadway, but the room was cool. It was always sweater weather inside the FBI building.

Rick gave Carl a hug and a huge grin. "Good to see you, buddy."

"Living the dream," Carl replied glibly.

Rick chucked his chin toward Carl's computer screen. "What are you doing?"

"I just got off the phone with City Hall. They're still searching for emails sent to the mayor or his staff from Mattingly's home IP address. And guess who's on the City Hall team handling it, our liaison?"

Rick paused. "Not a clue."

"Emily."

"Get out. Baby girl has arrived." Rick sat at his desk, smiling proudly. He'd known Emily since she was sixteen. "Does she have any thoughts on issues Mattingly would have contacted the mayor about?"

"She's off today. She had a house fire last night."

"What? Is everyone okay?"

"Yeah, she and Skye are fine. But her building was gutted. They're at my house."

"Crazy how life happens."

"City Hall IT hasn't finished their search for the emails yet anyway. They're hoping they can find new email addresses from Jackson's home IP address. That will give us new leads to track down communications with a handler. The more email addresses, the better."

Rick smirked. "No subpoena needed to get a hold of emails from this mayor. It's a lot easier to get cooperation when a mayor's not the target of the investigation. And with Emily the one we talk to, very promising."

"Sullivan has been on the scandal-free program, trying to get promoted." Carl leaned back in his chair, enjoying being in the office, talking about cases and their politics. "If I have to be on desk duty, there's no better time for it. But Gendell totally dismissed my idea that Mattingly wasn't the biological child of his parents. You two are on a mind meld there."

"It's a red herring, not a priority." Rick swiveled in his chair to boot up his computer. "If his mother conceived him through an extramarital affair and his father raised him as his own, the tabloids would care, but it wouldn't mean much for us."

"Yeah, but it irks, and I'm not so sure it's irrelevant. What if the father abused him his whole life because of it? That would be formative."

"Dude was not abused," Rick said impatiently. "We already know that. My partner, the dog with a bone."

Carl's stubbornness when it came to his hunches and Rick's impatience with him was an old dance. "Some welcome," he complained.

Rick shook his head and smiled as if he were putting up with a pesky toddler. "You got that right."

Carl chuckled to himself, feeling ironically soothed by the familiar quibbling.

36

A T DUSK, EMILY descended a long staircase from a building-lined cliff that connected the eastern and western halves of Washington Heights. At the bottom of the stairs was a modest residential area that lacked the gourmet stores and cute restaurants of the western half of the neighborhood, which real estate agents liked to call Hudson Heights. Emily approached Kathleen's temporary building on a shady street of mostly six-story apartment buildings, between Overlook Terrace and Bennett Avenue.

An Orthodox Jewish woman of about Emily's age used her back to push open the glass door to the building from inside. She held it open as she swung a stroller around to exit. Two preschool-aged children followed and picked up their pace to walk on either side of the stroller. Wearing a wig, long sleeves, and a long skirt, the woman must have been boiling. Emily was wearing a sundress and flip-flops, but sweat dampened her armpits and chest. A child, his white prayer fringe hanging below his shirt and black vest, held the door for Emily. She thanked him.

Emily reveled in the small lobby's air conditioning. A sign outside the elevator said it stopped automatically on each floor on the Sabbath. Bennett Avenue had a sizable Orthodox population. She wasn't surprised at the Sabbath accommodations, so residents wouldn't have to personally use electricity from sundown Friday to sundown Saturday. It was a little cheat, like the Amish using van drivers.

Kathleen greeted her at the door to the Airbnb. Kathleen's clothes had a freshly bought scent when Emily hugged her, and Emily recognized the color scheme of Kathleen's striped T-shirt. "The Gap?"

"Yeah."

"Me too." Emily looked down at her own sundress—which her mother had bought for her that day—in the same royal blue. "It's my mother's go-to store for some reason."

"Really?" There was a faint smile on Kathleen's face.

Emily looked around as she stepped inside. "Nice," she said. There were freshly buffed parquet floors and simple furnishings. Trees diffused the sunlight outside the living room window, which faced another building across a courtyard.

"Let me show you the rest." Kathleen led Emily down a hallway. "Two bedrooms, one with a bath. There's another bath here in the hallway." Kathleen opened the bathroom door. "You and Skye could have this bathroom, and I could use the one in the bedroom . . . if you want to stay, that is."

"I'd love to," Emily said without hesitation.

Kathleen smiled broadly. Emily guessed Kathleen was still shaken from the fire and needed the company. Her staying with Kathleen was a win-win.

Emily left to retrieve Skye and their few belongings from her mother's house. She walked back to Kathleen's an hour later. While Kathleen cooked dinner, Emily put Skye to sleep in the king-size bed they would share.

"It's hard to believe it's only been twenty-four hours," Kathleen said, putting out plates of pasta with seafood sauce on the dining room table. "I can still smell the fire if I breathe in through my nose."

Emily served herself salad. "Me too. Do they know whether we'll be able to go back to the building?"

"There will be inspections to make sure the building can be repaired, then major renovations, but only after the fire investigation is over."

"Fire investigation?"

Kathleen's phone vibrated on the table, a call from someone named *Greg–Building* with a man's photo. Kathleen put up her finger, signaling a pause in conversation before she answered the phone. "Greg. Hello. Yes, I'm fine, in an Airbnb."

Emily scrolled through the *New York Times* on her phone while Kathleen talked with Greg.

"Insurance inspectors?" Kathleen said, drawing Emily's attention. "Sure, I want to be there. What time?" When Kathleen hung up, she told Emily, "The insurance inspectors come tomorrow. The police have opened an arson investigation, and the insurance company will be investigating too."

"Arson? That's insane. Who would want to do that?"

"I don't know," Kathleen said.

Emily glanced down at her phone before setting it aside. "Isn't Ward and Hughes the law firm Sharon called the night she died?"

Kathleen looked over.

"One of their attorneys died," Emily said. "I just read about it in the *Times*."

"*What?*"

"They're saying the cause is unknown."

"What's his name?"

"Wayne Carrier." Emily saw Kathleen's face freeze. "I thought you didn't know anyone there."

* * *

Kathleen turned away from Emily. Wayne had been healthy, not a bit worried about his health when she spoke to him. Now he was dead, and Sharon was dead. Was Kathleen the only one alive who knew about Client 13's relationship with Sharon?

It had to be a coincidence, Wayne and Sharon dying—didn't it? And the fire?

But what if it wasn't?

That led her to her next set of questions. Should she tell the police? Would a judge enforce a nondisclosure agreement if she reported a crime? She doubted it. But would a judge enforce an NDA if her concerns were just wild speculation?

Wayne was probably sixty. People that age died from natural causes all the time. Heart attacks. Diabetes. There was no crime to report. Plus, she still had a hard time believing Client 13 was a killer, not to mention a serial killer. She didn't want to involve him in a police investigation when there was no reason to suspect him of a crime. As Wayne had said, Client 13 had no motive.

She had to try to find out how Wayne had died before she could even consider breaking her NDA. And if his death wasn't natural, she'd call Client 13. It might be taboo for her to call and ask him about a murdered prostitute he'd once dated, but calling to commiserate about the death of an old mutual friend, his lawyer, was a good excuse. Then she could feel him out, get a better sense of what he knew. Maybe he was as freaked out as her.

"Kathleen."

She heard Emily as if from a distance.

"There's someone at the door."

"Oh, jeez, I'm sorry. I was totally in my head. I'll explain . . ." Kathleen rose, not sure how she'd explain. She called through the door, "Who is it?"

A male voice. "Police."

Police? She looked back at Emily, shrugging, mystified. She peered through the peephole, speaking to Emily. "The detectives from Sharon's case. And others."

When she opened the door, the cops scowled at her. The two detectives were accompanied by a large-bellied man, so front-loaded Kathleen hoped for his sake he never had to run to save anyone. He was followed inside by a second, willowy cop, as concaved as his partner was front-loaded. None wore uniforms.

Detective Luna spoke. "Ms. Harris, this is Sergeant Johnson and Detective Gatti from the Arson Squad. Can we come in?"

Kathleen stood to the side as they crowded in. "As long as you don't ransack the place. This is an Airbnb. I don't want to lose my security deposit."

The cops looked around, taking in their surroundings from where they stood in the foyer.

Luna continued talking for her team. "You seem to have fallen on your feet."

"What can I do for you?"

Emily stood back, almost against the wall, and watched the cops interacting with Kathleen. Kathleen caught the flash of anger on Emily's face. Emily was seeing firsthand how disdainfully the cops treated an ex-con.

Sergeant Johnson stepped forward, pulling his belt up, a fool's mission—it immediately resettled below his belly. "You're having some money problems," he said.

Kathleen frowned. "No. I mean, I don't know what the fire will cost me, but I have insurance."

"It looks like this month's mortgage would have been a wing and a prayer."

"What are you talking about?"

"Motive for arson. The oldest motive in the book. Burn it down for insurance money."

Kathleen's chest tightened. He was accusing her of burning down an occupied building? An image of prison bloomed in her mind's eye, despite the ridiculousness of the accusation. "I always pay my mortgage and have funds to cover it. I don't know what you're talking about."

Detective Gatti, the wispy one, said, "Why don't we log into your bank account, if you don't mind?"

Kathleen didn't like the idea. She didn't want to consent. But she walked to a glass desk in the living room where she'd put her laptop, catching sight of Emily, who was visibly taken aback. This whole fiasco was so far outside the younger woman's reality.

Kathleen logged in, facing the laptop away from the curious cops. "It's going to take a couple of minutes. I've never logged onto my bank account from this computer. They'll probably send me an email with a security code."

"We've got plenty of time," Detective Luna said.

* * *

By the time Kathleen reached her accounts, she was prepared for what she'd see. The cops were too confident not to have seen it already. They must have gotten a warrant to look at her accounts—which meant they had to have evidence to support their theory that she'd committed arson. She coached herself not to show any emotion. She wasn't the woman she'd been when she was in the Life, engulfed in a risky lifestyle. She was less armored now to deal with this level of fear. But she couldn't show her weakness. Not to them. It wouldn't get her any sympathy, and she'd lose any power she had.

Her jowls fell when she took in the reality of her overdrawn checking account. Her money, over fifty thousand dollars in her business account, was gone. She clicked into her savings account. Zero. The investment account she kept with the bank contained only a few hundred dollars, not even enough for a month's mortgage payment. She looked up into the steely faces of the cops, their eyes betraying how self-satisfied they were in this moment.

"It had to be identity theft," she said.

"Sure you're right," Sergeant Johnson said. "You'll have to come with us."

Emily lurched forward. "Wait a second! What are you doing?"

Detective Luna strong-armed Emily back. "You should pick your friends more carefully. Or you could end up in jail with her. We don't care where you work."

37

L AST IN THE chained line of women exiting the paddy wagon, Kathleen braced herself. The corrections officer's keys jangled, a familiar sound even more than twenty-five years after the last time she'd heard it. She was back, 100 Center Street, downtown. Kathleen was trapped and afraid. This possible future had long ago presented an unacceptable risk in her mind. It was the chief reason she'd retired. It had only been desperation that motivated her to *ever* take the risk.

After walking a sepia corridor under the criminal courthouse, the women were divvied up among three large bullpens. The corrections officer took a massive key ring off her belt and opened the door for Kathleen's group. Before entering, Kathleen set her face into a stolid expression. She knew how a mature woman who could no longer physically fight had to carry herself. She'd done time with lifers who were in their later years. She could handle herself in a state prison, if that happened to her. In many ways, it would be easier than last time. She still knew women there who'd never gotten out, who would be happy to see her. She'd sent holiday cards with cash to some of them, repaying their kindnesses at various times during her last prison stay.

The ones she worried about were the new girls. The trifling and violent ones. She remembered from her last stint on Rikers Island that it was the boosters, streetwalkers, and petty larcenists who posed the biggest threat, not the murderers or wholesale drug dealers facing major time. The petty offenders had nothing to lose if they let their worst instincts run free and made a few enemies inside. Rikers was like evil sleep-away camp for them.

She sat on a hard bench where a woman, well over six feet tall, slept on her side with her legs halfway to a fetal position. Kathleen felt a small moment of gratitude that at least she wasn't detoxing or hallucinating like the first time they'd brought her here. That time she'd immediately started a ruckus, talking to herself and screaming about snakes and her dead husband, until the other detainees began yelling at the CO to "get the crazy bitch outa here, we can't sleep." Kathleen had ended up at Bellevue Hospital, where they'd drugged her enough for her to return to the bullpens for arraignment. Unfortunately, being crazy hadn't helped her as a defense against the murder charges.

She wondered how her bail application would be greeted by a judge. She had a felony conviction for manslaughter and a history of mental illness. Would they think that made her likely to set fire to an occupied building, even though she'd never done anything to intentionally harm anyone? Would they charge it as attempted murder of each of the residents in the building? Whatever it was, the sentence would be higher because she was a predicate felon. A two-time loser received almost double the sentence of a first-time felon.

She hadn't seen a lawyer yet, so she didn't know the exact charges or the basis for them. It was the middle of the night now, and she had no way to reach her own lawyer. She would have a free legal aid attorney for now, who would review her case for only a few minutes before the arraignment.

Keeping her eye on her surroundings, appraising the dozen women in the bullpen for the level of threat they posed and feeling relatively safe for now, Kathleen mulled over the case against her. She couldn't imagine how her bank accounts had been emptied, or why the police thought she'd committed arson in her own building while she was inside it. Like the police, she had to assume the draining of her bank account and the fire were connected—but of course not in the way the police had connected them. Somebody else had emptied out her bank accounts and burned down her building. And if she came to that conclusion, what were the odds of Sharon's murder and Wayne's death being a coincidence? Kathleen wasn't dead, but all three of them were now certainly out of the way. Not that the cops, or even a jury, would believe her if she started sharing conspiracy theories that tied all of it together.

Kathleen thought back to the question that seemed to be the key to everything: why had Sharon called her and Wayne?

A male inmate, housed in the jail upstairs known as the Tombs, pushed a metal cart filled with sandwiches and Styrofoam cups to the bullpen door. The sandwiches would be hard and inedible, made of soup-kitchen bologna and welfare cheese. The CO unlocked the door, and the inmate handed sandwiches to the women nearest the door, who passed them down to the others. Bullpen fare and the routines hadn't changed. The women passed the cups of tepid tea hand to hand until it reached those in the back of the barred pen. Kathleen took hers, placing it beside her on the bench. She took a pack of sugar from the plastic sandwich packet and poured it into the cup.

The big woman who'd slept on the bench rolled to sit upright and grabbed a sandwich a woman had left beside her. She took a bite and pointed to Kathleen's sandwich. "You gonna eat that?"

"No." She handed it to the woman.

"What you here for, *abuela*?"

"Arson."

"Oooh," she exclaimed. "That's gonna be a bitch-load of time."

Kathleen nodded.

The woman appraised her. "I can see you OG. Done time before?"

Original gangster. An old-timer. A first-timer, especially a first-timer of her age, would have smelled of fear.

Kathleen nodded, staring off. "Five years, Bedford."

The woman shook her head and grimaced. "Man, I hope I ain't still coming here when I'm old. *Shit*."

38

Emily called Lauren, asking her to come to the Airbnb. Skye was sleeping, so she couldn't walk over to her mother's. Pacing in the living room, Emily quickly told Lauren the story of Kathleen's arrest. She knew how Lauren would react. That was why Emily had insisted on talking to her in person. It was too easy to say no on the phone.

"Forgive me for saying I told you so, but I told you she was bad news," Lauren said.

Emily stopped short. "She's *not* bad news. She didn't do anything."

"And how do you know that?"

"I escaped the fire *with* her, remember? I saw how shocked and scared she was."

"Maybe it got out of hand and she didn't expect to be running for her life."

"Mom, that is ridiculous. She would *never* risk the lives of all the neighbors, or mine, or Skye's. She loved her apartment too, but that's a minor issue compared to the people. Only a psychopath would intentionally burn down a building full of people. For insurance money? Come on. It's the stupidest thing I ever heard. This is only happening to her because she has a criminal record. You should see how the cops treated her from the very beginning."

"If that's the case, I'm sure she'll be okay. She knows the system."

"She wasn't okay when she ended up in prison last time. She didn't deserve prison then either."

"First off, from what you've told me, she was an addict last time and she's not now, so she'll be better able to deal with this. She seems to know how to take care of herself. Second, about her being a psychopath, you don't even know whether anything she told you is true. Psychopaths can be charming, and compulsive liars too—no guilt about it. By definition. I don't like you mixed up with this."

Emily sat across from her mother, who sipped Earl Grey tea Emily had found in the kitchen. The scent of bergamot reminded Emily of countless times she'd smelled it in her mother's kitchen and, lately, Kathleen's. Maybe that was why she'd taken such an immediate liking to Kathleen. She reminded Emily so much of her own mother—without the needling and prying.

A small inner voice nagged at Emily, though, suggesting that maybe there was a seed of truth in what Lauren said. When Emily and Kathleen had looked at the website for the law firm Sharon had called, Kathleen had said she didn't recognize any of the firm's lawyers. Now one of those attorneys was dead, and Emily had seen Kathleen's reaction when Emily told her his name. Kathleen knew him. The police had interrupted before Kathleen had a chance to explain, but Emily had since checked and seen that Wayne Carrier's name was on the firm's list. There was no way Kathleen had missed it.

What if Emily's mother was right that Kathleen was lying about everything? What if Kathleen *was* involved in some way with Sharon's and Wayne Carrier's deaths, deaths that Emily couldn't help but think were related?

Emily brushed the thought away. She was connecting dots that weren't there. She hated when she did that. She needed to stick with facts.

Kathleen must have known the lawyer who died. But that was a far cry from Kathleen setting a building on fire with neighbors and friends inside. Kathleen had said she'd explain, before the cops arrived. Emily still wanted to hear it.

Lauren asked, "Did you ever think that being involved with Kathleen could put your career at risk?"

"Because I believe in my landlady's innocence and don't want an ex-con railroaded? I took the job at City Hall so I could have a positive impact on the world. Until I learn something that makes me think Kathleen isn't worth helping, I can't sit by and watch an innocent woman go to prison. I feel sick to my stomach just thinking she's in jail right now." Emily turned to the reason she'd asked her mother to come over: "And I want you to represent her."

Lauren's mug hit the table, sloshing tea over the side. "What?"

"For the arraignment."

"You've gotta be kidding."

"*Please.* I need your help, Mom. It's too late to find her another attorney for tonight. I wouldn't know where to begin. Please trust my judgment. I've earned that much."

Lauren's face softened. She blew air out. "Okay . . . but just for the arraignment."

*   *   *

Hector arrived at two AM, after he finished his shift at the hotel. At first, when Emily looked through the peephole, she didn't recognize him. Hector had grown a beard. She hadn't realized it had been that long since she'd last seen him. They talked by phone a lot, but their custody arrangement worked like clockwork: he picked Skye up from day care on Wednesday and kept her until Friday for his "weekend." He left her with his mother on Friday afternoons until Emily got off from work, where Emily picked her up on Friday night.

Emily took in Hector's golden skin and dark eyes, his beard trimmed to accent his strong jaw. He'd been shorter than her when they first met in middle school, a nerdy kid. He still had a nerdy streak, but he stood nearly a foot taller than her now, with broad shoulders and a slim waist. She felt a hitch in her chest, the feeling of affection and attraction she always got when she saw him after a long time. He grinned, happy to see her.

"Emily." He reached out to hug her.

She inhaled the scent of his coconut oil shampoo, which had graced her pillow nearly every college weekend. Feeling the warm familiarity of his lanky frame and a disconcerting need for his comfort, she stepped back quickly from the hug. "I like the beard. It's nice," she said, bringing him to the living room.

"Are you okay?"

"I'm okay. But Skye is still so clingy. On top of that, she's worried about Rusty. She keeps asking for him. I thought, if she woke up next to you in bed, it would be best."

A look passed between them. Hector thought it would be best if Emily woke up in bed next to him, too, every day. Hector dated other women, but Emily knew where he stood when it came to their relationship.

The silence hung for a moment before Emily turned the conversation to Kathleen. She told Hector everything, grateful to have someone to talk to.

"It sounds like your friend is getting a bad break," Hector said.

Emily felt relieved that he hadn't questioned her judgment about supporting Kathleen the way Lauren had. Hector's cousin, Tabu, had done a year in federal prison for computer hacking. But Hector's family had stood by him.

As Emily readied herself to leave, Hector looked up at her from where he sat on the couch. He picked up the remote control. "Do they have Netflix here?"

39

I N THE DEEPEST blue-black before dawn, Emily and Lauren approached 100 Center Street, a grim art deco building befitting Batman's Gotham. Lauren wore a charcoal pantsuit. Emily wore slacks and a blouse, as if she were going to work. Lauren said she'd take Emily into the attorney consultation room as her paralegal, if the court officers let her. Lauren checked the court calendar, a printed list of case names taped to the wall outside the arraignment part.

"She'll be called soon," Lauren said. "Must be a slow night. I thought it would take longer."

"Are we too late?"

"I doubt it. Come on."

Emily and Lauren entered through the double doors of the courtroom. It was a large room with twenty rows of benches separated from the working part of the busy courtroom. Up front were not only defense and prosecution tables before a tall judge's bench but desks where legal aid and assistant district attorneys worked on their cases between rounds in front of the judge.

Emily followed Lauren down the aisle. Kathleen was already standing at the scuffed defense table. Emily recognized her hair and erect, narrow back, even though any normal person would stoop with exhaustion after a night in the bullpens.

Emily pulled on Lauren's sleeve. "That's her."

"Okay. Stay here."

Emily sat in the first row, wanting to get as close as possible. The row was reserved for lawyers, but she was there as her mother's paralegal and figured the court officer wouldn't tell her to move.

She watched Lauren nod, acknowledging the court officers who sat at their scratched table next to the low wooden wall that separated the observers from the officers of the court. Lauren unlatched the wooden gate to enter. A legal aid attorney gathered up her files at a desk and walked toward the defense table. The assistant district attorney stood at the table on the left, a bony guy with a bow tie and loose suit.

Lauren met the legal aid attorney before she reached the defense table. The attorney was a heavyset woman in her late twenties, her hair highlighted in smoky blue. Lauren spoke with her in whispers. Kathleen turned to look at them. Emily tried to get Kathleen's attention to let her know she was there. Kathleen blinked with surprise, taking in Lauren and then glancing back at Emily.

Emily waved. Kathleen didn't look exactly happy to see her. It wasn't the way Emily had imagined she'd react, though she supposed Kathleen had more important things to think about. And maybe she didn't want Emily to see her like this: a prisoner.

Lauren walked with the legal aid attorney toward the defense table. Lauren had told Emily that if the attorney seemed to have a good head on her shoulders, Lauren wouldn't take over. She'd just second-seat her, in case Lauren needed to add any argument to the bail application.

Lauren stood to Kathleen's right, the legal aid attorney on Kathleen's other side. Kathleen cringed—Emily was sure of it—when Lauren stood next to her. Emily frowned.

What happened next seemed to happen in slow motion. While the judge read the charging papers, Lauren turned to shake hands with Kathleen, obviously planning to introduce herself. Kathleen halfway turned toward Lauren.

Lauren peered at Kathleen and reared back. *"Mom?"*

Emily sat back hard against the bench. Kathleen was her grandmother? Her addicted, screwed-up grandmother? Kat Davis had become Kathleen Harris?

Emily stopped breathing. Her mind spun, unable to put things together. Her reality refused to assemble into coherent pieces.

Kathleen slumped as if she were folding into herself. Emily saw Lauren take a deep breath.

*   *   *

The judge banged the gavel, oblivious to what was going on. "Appearances, counsel."

"Assistant district attorney Joshua Hunter for the prosecution."

"Carmen Benanti for the defendant, Kathleen Harris."

"Lauren Davis Cintron for the defendant."

Emily noticed that her mother's voice shook a little, something that never happened to her.

"Your Honor, the State has charged Ms. Harris with arson in the first degree. She started a fire in an occupied building in order to collect insurance proceeds. She is the owner of the building through Inwood Associates, LLC. It is a residential building. Dozens of people were in their homes at the time. She was financially insolvent and unable to make her next mortgage payment. The FDNY investigators have determined that the fire was started by an incendiary device comprised of a cigarette and a book of matches wrapped in gasoline-soaked clothing. The defendant's DNA was found on the clothing used to wrap the device. Defendant is a predicate felon, having a prior conviction for manslaughter under the name Kat Davis. The State is asking for one million dollars bail."

Lauren waited a beat for the legal aid attorney to speak, then cut in. "Excuse me, Your Honor, DNA on clothing . . . after a fire that completely gutted a building?"

ADA Hunter looked down at his notes. "Your Honor, this is an issue for trial . . . but there were multiple incendiary points with accelerant leading away from them. At one of them, fire investigators were able to sweep the ash and lift the evidence underneath."

"The prosecution is correct," the judge said. "It will be an issue for trial. Let's get to the bail application."

The legal aid attorney replied, "The defense requests that Ms. Harris be released on her own recognizance. She legally changed her name after her release from parole, and she is not a flight risk. She is sixty-eight years old with no history of violence. The manslaughter conviction, over thirty years ago, related to the accidental overdose death of her husband when the defendant was herself addicted and bought the drugs for him. It was not a violent crime."

Emily saw her mother's shoulders stiffen even more. Emily knew the story of Kathleen's imprisonment, but it was different from what Lauren had told Emily about their family history. After her father died, Lauren had lived on the street, then entered a drug treatment program. Lauren had told Emily the caseworkers had had to track down her mother, "interrupting her crack party," to consent to Lauren's treatment, and that her mother hadn't even wanted to show up at court. Had the caseworkers found Emily's grandmother in prison and not told Lauren the truth? A few months after that, while Lauren was in drug treatment, the program had helped her become an emancipated minor. That meant she wouldn't have to depend on an addict for medical consent or college financial aid applications. Lauren had been living on her own for over a year, so she didn't need her mother's consent to become emancipated.

"She did her time," the legal aid attorney continued. "She's been clean for thirty years and is an upstanding member of the community. Pretrial detention would pose an extraordinary health risk for her at her age."

"She is a risk to the community, Your Honor," ADA Hunter protested.

The judge nodded. "These are very serious charges."

"Your Honor, this was her building, and from what I understand, she did a lot of the building maintenance and cleanup herself," Lauren added. "It's likely that her DNA would be found all over the building. These charges are farfetched, and she should have the opportunity to prepare her defense without pretrial detention. Further, it is my understanding that there was an identity theft that emptied out her bank accounts in the last several days. There is no evidence that the defendant was behind in her mortgage payments. It defies reason that an upstanding member of the community would burn down her own building, her own home, and risk her friends and neighbors because of, at most, one late mortgage payment."

ADA Hunter raised his voice. "Your Honor, we simply cannot let this *woman* out to commit this crime again. She is *dangerous*."

The judge looked Kathleen over, probably seeing the frailty that Emily was seeing now, as Emily had seen it on the fire escape. The judge was processing the difference between Kathleen's demeanor and the charges, the same way Emily was trying to process that the wonderful woman Emily had known for months was also a compulsive liar. Kathleen was the ogre Lauren had been telling Emily about her entire life.

The judge banged the gavel. "Bail is set at one hundred thousand dollars, cash or bond. Plus, a GPS-monitoring device and house arrest, with the typical allowances for shopping, laundry, and appointments."

Lauren turned away without saying anything to Kathleen. One of the court officers approached to snap on the cuffs for Kathleen's journey back to the bullpen. Lauren shook the legal aid attorney's hand, then turned. Her furious eyes rested on Emily like a red laser beam before a bullet. She unlatched the gate and passed Emily. "Come on."

Emily scurried behind her mother, who power-walked up the aisle without looking back.

CHAPTER

40

THE UNDERSIDES OF low clouds glowed pink as the sun rose from the east behind the criminal court. The sidewalks were still in deep shadow. Lauren hiked on fast-forward past nineteenth-century warehouse buildings containing anonymous multimillion-dollar lofts.

"Shit, shit, shit. I can't believe it," Lauren said a few times as she walked.

Emily race-walked beside her. Lauren stopped short and turned to Emily at the corner of Church and Leonard Streets, three blocks from the courthouse. The sidewalks were empty, and Tribeca was quiet except for the rattles of delivery trucks speeding over the bumps and valleys of Church Street.

"How did you meet her?" Lauren asked.

"You know, through Sophie on Facebook. Sophie heard about an apartment."

"*Sophie*? Do you even *know* a Sophie?"

Emily paused, then shook her head. She'd never remembered knowing Sophie.

"So, I'm only guessing here," Lauren said with angry sarcasm, "but my criminal mother stalks you on Facebook with a bogus avatar and gets you to move into her building, which god knows how she bought—probably a front for the mob or money laundering. She knew I wouldn't let you get involved with her, and clearly for good reason. Since you've known her, you've been a witness in a murder investigation, had to escape a burning building, lost everything you owned, and moved in with a woman charged with trying to kill dozens of people, including you and your child."

"She did *not* burn down her building. That is bullshit!" Emily argued.

"Oh, you've had your bullshit detector on? You're obviously the last person to recognize bullshit when you see it."

"That's not fair. And I'm not a child, Mom. Jesus Christ."

"First off, we're getting your things from her apartment before she puts up her shell of a building for bail."

"I'm *not* leaving the apartment. Rusty's coming this weekend. Skye needs to see him again."

"For a *puppy*, Emily? You've gotta be kidding."

Emily could feel her own anger heating her jaw, spreading up her cheeks. "Kathleen was lying about a lot of things. You're right. I don't know what to think about that. But what was she supposed to do if she wanted to know me? You just said you'd never let her know me. She knew you'd poisoned my mind against her. And check your own bullshit detector. Did you know she *wasn't* bullshit? Did you even know she was clean? Did you give her a chance to show you she'd changed? You kept me away from my grandmother and kept yourself from your own mother without knowing anything about her, based on events that happened thirty years ago."

"*Events*? Like leaving me homeless on the streets at fifteen years old? Events!" Lauren resumed walking furiously on Church Street toward the subway, past tiny storefronts with garish signs for cheap takeout and lotto tickets. "I knew all I needed to know."

"You said your mother was too busy partying to come to family court when you signed yourself into drug treatment."

Lauren's gaze snapped to Emily, and she stopped walking. Emily could see the confusion in her mother's eyes.

"She said she was hallucinating when her husband died," Emily pressed on. "She had cocaine psychosis. She thought snakes were coming out of the walls and out of him when he died. She was terrified. They arrested her and took her to Bellevue. They had proof she picked up the drugs for your father from his dealer. She wasn't even a heroin addict, but he was in withdrawal and begged her to do it. They charged her with murder because she bought the drugs that killed him."

"*No.*"

"Yes. Then she pled to manslaughter and went to prison for five years."

"Why didn't the caseworkers tell me that?" Lauren asked, as much to herself as to Emily.

"Maybe they thought it was better to keep you away from your crazy addict mother. Maybe they were afraid you'd change your mind about treatment if you thought she needed help."

Lauren's eyes were distant, looking toward the World Trade Center to the south but staring a thousand miles away, probably seeing the early days of her drug treatment as a teenager. "At first, they needed her signature to consent to my treatment. They got it and showed it to the judge. Children's Services didn't need to work with her to help her get me back home if I was in residential treatment . . . and I would be an adult by the time she came home from prison." Emily could tell Lauren was tapping into her knowledge of family law, fitting it in with her teenage memories. "The program helped me file emancipation papers once I was there. They did that as a matter of course for teens who'd been living on their own, whose parents were dysfunctional . . . addicts. They didn't want unstable parents to interfere and throw their kids off course. But she was in jail."

Lauren teared up. She spoke almost to herself. "It's true, she wasn't a heroin addict. I remember the day my father died. That morning, I think he was dope-sick, sweating but shivering under blankets. She was scared, but she always seemed scared. I couldn't focus on that. I hated her too much."

The two began walking again, silently.

"Look, Mom, I don't know what to think of her," Emily said gently. "I don't trust her. She has a lot of explaining to do. But one thing I'm sure about is that she did *not* start the fire. Believe it or not, I do have a working bullshit detector—working imperfectly, maybe. But the only thing I have no doubt about is that she wouldn't burn down a building filled with her neighbors and me, and Skye. And the thing that bothers me is that it doesn't feel like a coincidence that so much has happened since her friend Sharon died."

41

O N RIKERS, EACH cell on Kathleen's floor had a rolling metal door that was left open for a ten-minute window each hour until lockdown at night. During that ten minutes, each woman could freely walk in and out of her cell and choose whether to stay in, reading, writing, or sleeping, for the remainder of the hour. If a woman stayed out, she could spend her fifty minutes in a dayroom with a TV, tables, and the other inmates, or she could hope to make a phone call. For the current hour, ten hours after her arrival on Rikers, Kathleen waited in line for a chance to use the phone.

Several feet above them, the corrections officers looked out from what was known as "the bubble," a fortified glass guard station with a view of the corridor of cells and the dayroom. From there, they could also keep an eye on the phone, a frequent cause of fights.

Wearing a green hospital gown that exposed legs that oozed with abscesses from shooting up, a young heroin addict stood in front of Kathleen in line. They hadn't distributed clothing to the newcomers yet, so Kathleen had washed her clothes in the sink and also wore a hospital gown while her street clothes dried, draped over a bed rail. After ten hours on Rikers, Kathleen's panties and bra were drying on her body, where they stuck to her uncomfortably like a wet bathing suit during a drive home from the beach. It was luckily a warm day, so the incessant breeze penetrating the roomy armholes of her gown didn't cause goose bumps to rise on her skin the way it had when she'd first been on Rikers in late October, decades ago.

Nothing had changed about the phone routine. At an appointed hour, the CO opened a slot in the bubble, placing the phone on a shelf outside it. The women lined up, waiting for twenty minutes, a half hour, or more to make a call that clicked off automatically after five minutes. The COs put the phone out for inmate use once or twice a day. The women waited, chatting with the person next to them in line or silently inside their own heads, all of them having plenty of angst about their criminal cases and upended lives to keep them mentally busy.

The whole process was so familiar that Kathleen expected to see a dial on the phone when the CO placed it on a ledge outside the bubble, but they'd switched to touch-tone phones since her last incarceration. She suspected she was the only inmate here old enough to know how to dial a phone.

Kathleen had been lucky that a CO had let her copy down a few contacts from her cell phone before locking up her property. So far, Kathleen's ability to cope with jail and the strip searches—squat on command and let them look between her legs—had come back to her like riding a bike. She thought the COs were taking it easy on her, looking away, handling her gently when they snapped the cuffs on and off, because of her age. And the large, masculine woman, Doris, who'd talked to Kathleen in the bullpen, had made clear to everyone on the floor that Kathleen was OG, facing big time. There was a certain respect that came with that, and many of the women were looking for someone older to play mom for them, so Kathleen's stay had been uneventful so far.

Of course, that didn't mean Kathleen could let down her guard for even a moment. She'd have no ready-made allies in jail based on neighborhood or common friends or gang affiliation. And the old prison adage remained generally true anyway: there are no friends in jail. At her age, it would be only her wits and the sympathy the inmates naturally felt for someone they viewed as a suffering old woman that would keep her safe.

The worst thing was the return of her fear, the desolation, the darkness that was settling within her. And seeing Lauren, standing right next to her for the first time in decades, had yanked open old wounds. She was sitting in jail, again feeling all the pain of losing her child, and now she feared losing her grandchild and her great-grandchild too. Like before, she was caught in something entirely unexpected, and it was going in a terrible direction.

She kept coming back to Client 13. He was the common thread. Yet Kathleen had never found him threatening. He had so much to lose by engaging in this kind of crazy conspiracy. She could no longer dismiss that as impossible, but why would he do it? It had to be something other than an affair that produced a love child twenty years ago.

"Bitch, you better step off." A squeaky voice spoke behind Kathleen. "I'll wreck your fucking ass."

Kathleen looked toward the commotion. A tiny woman with South American features, who stood under five feet tall, moved to stop a stocky woman ten inches taller and seventy pounds heavier than her from jumping the line in front of her. Kathleen took the stocky aggressor for a mugger by vocation. Muggers had a certain vibe to them. The little one had to speak up to defend her place in line and fight if she needed to, even if she lost, or she'd be victimized for the rest of her stay on the Island. Plus, if she got a bad reputation here, it could follow her to state prison if she had to do more than a year.

Kathleen knew she might have to fight too. Her muscles and joints felt every moment of the decades she'd aged since she'd last been behind bars, and she imagined her bones were even worse. She'd fallen on ice a couple of years back, and her wrist had snapped as if it were hollow. She'd worn a cast for the rest of the winter. That experience had given her the caution of an almost old person when she walked Manhattan's icy sidewalks, and she had no denial about the implications of using her old bones and tendons to defend herself against a young person. But for now, she just hoped the two women wouldn't fight and the CO wouldn't remove the phone as punishment.

Doris stepped from the line. She'd been standing a few places behind the South American woman. She moved toward the line-jumper, looking down on her. "Get. The. Fuck. Out. The. Line. We ain't having that shit here."

The line-jumper seemed ready to hash it out with Doris, but, jaw jutting, she looked the tall woman up and down and thought better of it.

Kathleen reflected on Doris. You could find good souls in jails, maybe the best of them—people who kept their humanity in the most dehumanizing circumstances.

A woman sitting on a schoolroom chair next to the bubble hung up the phone. Kathleen moved to take her turn. She dialed Greg, her building manager. She needed to know why her application for bail had been denied. She knew her bank account was empty, but why weren't they accepting her building as collateral? The building was a burnt shell, but it was still valuable Manhattan real estate. She'd expected to be out of jail already. Disappointment washed over her when Greg's phone went to voice mail. She'd get no answers today. There were no return calls to jail.

She pushed down her distress and forced words out. "I'll call you tomorrow, Greg. I want to know what's wrong with the building's title." She hung up and spoke through a grating in the bubble. "Officer, I got a voice mail. Could I have another call?"

She heard profane grumbling from the line of women behind her, but luckily nobody objected.

"Okay. Just one more," the CO said.

Kathleen dialed.

CHAPTER

42

HECTOR TOOK SKYE to the playground before he headed to work in the afternoon. Emily needed to get through dozens of emails for work after taking off the morning to sleep. She set up her laptop in the kitchen and felt a shot of excitement when she saw an email from the director of IT. They'd forwarded a batch of potential Mattingly emails.

The FBI had provided IT with a preliminary word search list that their behavioral science team had put together. Each email contained words a person who committed mass violence might use. This batch of emails mentioned conspiracies. They were mostly from mentally ill people whose minds had woven tentacles of plots against them.

Hector dropped off Skye, and Emily set her up to eat an early dinner in her booster seat. Red sauce and spaghetti quickly splotched her cheeks and the floor. Emily called Carl at his office while Skye ate.

"Hey, Dad," Emily said when she heard his voice.

"Ms. Silverman," he said with affectionate formality. "Do I take it this is our first official call?"

Emily chuckled. "It is, indeed, Agent Cintron. I've got a batch of emails for you from the conspiracy theory search. Hundreds."

"Excellent."

"A surprising number of people think there are government plots brewing against them. They're all at the center of their own pizza pedophilia ring, and the mayor delivered the pizza. I hope the emails help."

"Most won't," Carl said. "But we're approaching the forensics problem from as many angles as possible. Besides searching for emails from Mattingly's known IP and email addresses, we're looking at the conspiracy theory emails to see if there was anything connected to Beacon, the New York City subways, that sort of thing. Mattingly could have emailed with a disguised IP address and an email address we don't know about."

"I didn't see anything like that," Emily said. "There's one from a guy who thinks zombies are breeding giant rats in the subway. Anyway, Mattingly seems like he was more of a psychopath than delusional, don't you think?"

"You're right, no one has reported him talking about any delusions," Carl said. "But conspiracy theories have become almost mainstream. If he shared a conspiracy theory, a lot of people would probably agree with him."

After she hung up with Carl, Emily wiped sauce from Skye's hands and face. She changed Skye's spattered T-shirt, and they took the subway to the Upper West Side. She was glad Carl had stuck to business and hadn't questioned her about staying in Kathleen's Airbnb. By now, Lauren must have told him everything.

"I guess there's no harm," Lauren had finally said about Emily staying at the rental. They'd talked more about it while riding the train uptown together after court. "Especially with Kathleen in jail."

"Nobody knows where the apartment is, so it's safe, even if she's being targeted by somebody."

Lauren had looked sideways at her. "You bought that whole story?"

"What do you mean?"

"Her being a victim? Someone emptied her bank accounts?"

"Yes, I was there when she saw her accounts. She was surprised."

"You don't know her like I do," Lauren said bitterly.

Emily shrugged. "Maybe neither of us knows her."

Now, Emily exited the subway at Ninety-Sixty Street and Central Park West, carrying Skye in her stroller up the stairs. Emily put down the stroller on the sidewalk and followed behind a stream of commuters headed home to the tall apartment buildings in the area. Emily saw a voice mail notification on her phone that had come in while she was underground. A 718 area code.

"Emily, I was hoping to speak with you," Kathleen said in her voice mail. "I'm on Rikers now. Thank you for coming to court. I probably won't get another call until tomorrow. I hope you can forgive me . . . and understand."

Emily hung up, sad, but angry too. She didn't know whether she could forgive Kathleen or understand. Her mind kept going in circles, trying to sort Kathleen's lies from the truth. Kathleen had told Emily a lot of truth about herself. The DA said she'd been convicted of manslaughter. Kathleen had said she had a daughter whom she'd neglected and lost. But Kathleen had lied constantly. She was sure Kathleen had catfished her. It had to be Kathleen, not a woman named Sophie, who had lied about going to NYU, who'd posted about parties she'd never been to, who'd heard about an apartment and a job at City Hall from friends who didn't exist.

Emily hadn't conceded any doubt to her mother, but she wasn't so sure that Lauren was wrong about Kathleen. Normal people weren't that stealthy. Emily didn't know if she would ever trust Kathleen again.

Of course, arguably, the most important thing Kathleen had done as Sophie was make opportunities available to Emily— great opportunities. Which lent credibility to the idea that Kathleen had been doing her best in a bad situation, making contact secretly when she knew Lauren wouldn't approve.

Emily felt a weird loyalty to Kathleen, despite all her lies. Maybe, as Lauren said, Kathleen wasn't Emily's battle, but Emily didn't believe she could walk away and not look back. Kathleen was her grandmother, her only grandparent. Emily had to help her if she was truly innocent.

So she decided to do her own fact-checking. If she was going to keep putting her neck out for Kathleen, Kathleen had to be worth it.

With that conclusion, her next step was clear. She'd already been warned not to turn to her contacts at City Hall or NYPD for information. She couldn't talk to the FDNY either. That left one person. And if there was anyone who could tell her whether Kathleen's story made any sense, it would be Hector's cousin, Tabu.

*   *   *

On West Ninety-Seventh Street, Emily entered an enclave of three large residential buildings surrounding lawns, a small playground, and a dog run, all hidden behind Whole Foods and the big-box stores of Columbus Avenue. She walked down an unnamed street that was little more than an alley leading to the buildings. The yapping and barking of dogs replaced the heavy truck noise on Columbus.

Skye began arching her back in the stroller, pointing at the dog run. "Out. I want to get out! I want to see Rusty!"

"Skye, Rusty will be back this weekend. Rusty isn't there."

Skye began hiccupping in tears. *Oh, lord, a tantrum coming.* Even Hector had noticed that Skye was far less placid than usual. Emily only hoped that Skye's fixation on Rusty would relax when she saw him this weekend, and that Skye would relax overall.

Skye's crying became louder. Emily bent down to unstrap Skye and picked her up. She stopped near the dog park and let her look over the fence at a labradoodle playing with a pit mix. Skye sniffled in her tears.

"Look, see, Rusty isn't here. He'll come to our house this weekend." Emily put up three fingers. "In three days. Show me three fingers."

Skye held up three fingers.

"Good girl. Now let's go see Uncle Tabu."

Emily returned to the path to one of the thirty-story buildings, Skye holding her hand. A giant sign running vertically up its side marketed the apartments as no-fee luxury rentals. Emily knew they had originally been built as middle-class housing, back when middle-class families could afford the area. Now, unless you'd been there for decades and had one of the few rent-regulated apartments, you paid luxury prices.

Tabu had lived there only a couple of years. Emily was glad that he was apparently doing better than before.

On the ninth floor, Tabu gave Emily a bear hug. Heavy-set with a beige complexion, Tabu wore thick, chocolate-brown glasses, a new addition since she'd known him—probably the computer work screwing up his eyes.

"Skye. My baby!" he exclaimed.

"Uncle Tabu," she said, and raised her arms for him to take her. Skye often saw Tabu when she was at Hector's mother's house. Thankfully, Skye wasn't so clingy that she'd refuse to go to family members. It gave Emily hope that Skye would bounce back to normal, despite the trauma of the fire.

In Tabu's arms, Skye launched into a monologue about Rusty. She held up three fingers. "Three days," she said triumphantly.

"Good. I'd like to meet Rusty."

Tabu led them into his modern living room. There was no sign of computer equipment, even though his parole restrictions had expired years ago. Through the living room window, Emily saw that his apartment overlooked the brown brick of the Dou-glass projects, where Tabu had lived with Hector and his family. Hector's mother had raised Tabu after both his parents died of AIDS when he was twelve. He'd been a big brother to Hector and his sisters.

Tabu followed Emily's gaze. "You can see Auntie's apartment from here. Right there, ninth floor. The apple don't fall far from the tree. But in this apartment, I've got my own bathroom, con-sistent AC, no roaches, no mice, no mold. I never have to walk up nine flights because the elevator is broken, and believe it or not, the gangs stay on their side of the street. They appreciate living in a housing project in a good part of town. They're not looking to screw that up."

It was one of the ironies of how Manhattan had changed since Emily was a kid. People felt safe enough to pay high prices for luxury apartments across the street from public housing projects. And the Douglass projects—smack in the center of a

neighborhood where apartments sold for over a million dollars—
was one of the safest projects in the city.

Emily looked around the living room, with its leather couch
and low coffee table. A breakfast bar separated the living room
from a small kitchen off to one side. "I like this place."

Tabu gave a grudging nod. "It's a step up from a room in
Auntie's house, now that I can work again." He chuckled to himself. "And I can still keep an eye on the family. A win-win."

Family was the most important thing for Tabu. He'd been
a member of Anonymous until he'd gotten busted. He'd plea-
bargained because he needed to help his aunt support her kids
when she was having medical problems. After jail, he was barred
from the internet for the term of his parole. After that, he'd
joined a security consulting firm, all transgressions forgiven.

"So, Loli, what brings you?" Tabu sat, Skye sitting between
them on the couch. "If you're here for advice about Hector, my
vote is you give my young cousin another chance. You guys are
meant for each other."

Emily grimaced, feigning annoyance. "I'm not Loli anymore." *Loli* was hacker slang for an underage girl. He'd been
calling her that since she was sixteen, clearly to annoy her when
she was young. But now it had become a nostalgic routine.

"You will always be Loli to me," Tabu said affectionately.
"But come on, what gives?"

Emily took a deep breath. "Something weird is going on with
my grandmother. I need help."

He frowned. "I didn't know you had a grandmother."

"I only met her recently."

He asked, deadpan, "She need help setting up her computer?"

"Come on."

Tabu laughed. "Okay, I'm all ears."

"Skye, come draw at the table," Emily said as she pulled a pad
of paper and a box of crayons from the stroller pocket. The other
day, Skye's head had popped up when Emily said the word *kill* to
Lauren. Skye was starting to understand too much and needed
a distraction.

"*No,*" Skye said, grabbing her. Emily could see the tears welling, Skye's chest expanding before a crying jag.

"Wait a second." Tabu pulled an iPad and headphones from a drawer in the coffee table. "Here you go." He instantly thumbed on a preschool video game and slipped oversized headphones on Skye's ears. Her eyes opened wide, and she poked at a cartoon character.

"So, what's going on?" he asked.

Emily told Tabu about the fire and the withdrawals from Kathleen's accounts. "Is there a way to find out if she was telling the truth about being hacked? The cops aren't going to help. They just want her in jail because it solves their arson case. Plus, she has a criminal record, so it's killing two birds for them."

"I hear that." Tabu thought it over. "If the key to proving motive in a major felony case is that she had no money and burned down the building for insurance, the cops would have checked the IP address and confirmed she was the one who withdrew the funds before they busted her." He shook his head. "I don't know, Em."

Emily bit her lip, thinking it through. "But is there a way that it could be made to look like it came from her computer? I know that's farfetched, but could someone take all the money out of her accounts and make it look like she did it? Not just by hacking her bank password, but by making it look like the transactions were done from her home computer?"

Tabu leaned back and crossed his legs, his ankle resting on his thigh. "There's guys who can penetrate the Pentagon, so of course it could be done. There's a process, opening her portal, taking her IP address, posing as her. Anyone doing that is a real player."

Emily inhaled, feeling the weight of that idea.

"But here's the problem with that theory. It's easy to disguise your IP address when you hack someone's account. Hackers could hide their identity if they wanted to steal from her and never get caught. They don't need to go to all that trouble, making it look like the victim was withdrawing her own money, if their goal is to avoid getting caught. So, why would a hacker with those skills waste his time doing that to your grandmother? Sorry, Loli, but if the withdrawals were from her IP address, which odds are they were, she probably did it. I can't see anyone going to that much effort. For what?"

Emily thought back to how surprised Kathleen had been when the police said her accounts were empty. "I don't know. I would swear she didn't know."

"Bottom line, Em, it would need to be an exceedingly nefarious enemy for them to have the ways, means, and desire to do it." Tabu pulled his glasses down his nose to look at Emily over the rim. "She's not an enemy of Putin, is she?"

CHAPTER

43

THE MAN SAT in a leather swivel chair in the back of his Mercedes van. The interior of the van resembled a private jet. High ceilings. A bar with crystal glassware. Thick carpeting. The leather seats could recline into a bed as if he were flying cross-country. He watched York Avenue through smoked-glass windows that provided an excellent one-way view. One-way was how he liked things. The most powerful figures maintained their anonymity, keeping track of others without being seen while they moved their chess pieces around the board.

It was ironic that his own blood had nearly deep-sixed that. It was also ironic that Jackson had managed to take the hush money and do the proverbial double cross. *Chutzpah*, the Jews called it. *Cajones* in Spanish. He wondered how many languages had a word for that kind of crazy balls. His family could have coined their own term for it, the trait was so common for them.

Clearly, anger had fueled Jackson in a way that greed never could. He'd had a score to settle.

The moment Jackson pulled the stunt of the century, the man had known the answer to "nature or nurture." The need for control. The complexity of their minds. The knowledge that no one and nothing mattered more than making sure they got what they wanted. Jackson had the gene.

The nurture part that Jackson lacked was the sense of righteousness of a born-and-*bred* aristocrat. Jackson had been self-righteous in the whiny way of someone who lacked a complete certainty of his right to the things he demanded. Jackson had also killed himself for revenge. That was absurd; it would not have happened had he been raised to lead. Even Osama bin Laden, born to Saudi wealth, had made sure he sent *other* people on the suicide missions. No martyr-in-heaven bullshit for Osama, at least not on purpose. That was the memo Jackson missed.

Jackson clearly had a deep-seated inferiority complex that the man supposed resulted from the lack of a support system of others like him. Jackson hadn't had anyone to tell him he was not only okay but superior, born to lead.

The man toggled between an all-consuming rage at what Jackson had done and a grudging respect for his ability to send a royal "fuck you." Jackson couldn't be part of the family, so he'd tried to blow the whole family up, figuratively speaking. The man could imagine how Jackson must have gotten stuck on the siblings and cousins he couldn't meet once he signed the NDA and the prominent name he would never have. Of course, he could never have been allowed to stake a claim. The men of the family had a long history of rejecting love children. Paying them off was a newish phenomenon. There'd been a time when they'd *sold* them off. Throughout history, the bastard children had known their place.

The man was sure nothing less than a prince's throne would have satisfied Jackson anyway. That was also a family trait. Marital problems were only one of many things that would have resulted from the secret of Jackson coming out. His siblings would have launched an internecine war. Lacking his gene, Jackson's sister and brother were far too close to their mother, and the family's tax evasion strategies—putting assets in the children's names to avoid inheritance tax—would have boomeranged unacceptably on the family. But more than that, Jackson hadn't received the proper training. He hadn't been raised to make good use of his gift, and he hadn't internalized the golden rule that went with it: always put the family first. There was just no guarantee he'd toe the line in times of trouble.

But now the entire family was on the line. If their connection to him ever came out, Jackson's generation—his siblings and cousins—would be unwelcome at the drunken parties of their friends in the Hamptons. Even their Adderall dealers would cut them loose if they were the family of a terrorist. Worse still, the next generation up could kiss all their board memberships good-bye, those high-paying corporate positions bestowed upon them fresh out of school due to their family wealth and power. The family trust would keep them all fed and clothed, but not nearly in the style to which they were accustomed—especially not the children and grandchildren who came after wealth creation ceased. And for those who'd entered politics, or hoped to, which had a key role in the family's power, that path would be as dead as Jackson's victims. No politician would be able to accept their donations. They wouldn't be welcome to lick envelopes for a campaign. And they certainly wouldn't be able to run for office themselves.

The family could trace its ancestors back to twelfth-century England. Since that time, public relations specialists—at first, monks in robes—had kept the lurid details of their embarrassing family chapters from coming to light. But in the age of the internet, Jackson's stain on the family's reputation would make its brutal, slave-owning history pale in comparison. And, no doubt, that dark history would also be pulled into the public spotlight. They lived in an era when the lowliest members of society could send a viral tweet. That created incentive for any random asshole to dig deeper into their family history, a bread crumb trail of buried scandals spanning nine hundred years.

Still, he wasn't overly concerned. If there was one piece of wisdom to take away from *Game of Thrones*, it was that you weren't truly rich unless you were rich with an army. And he had an army.

He saw the lawn and outline of Gracie Mansion ahead and rested his eye on the security officer who rode alongside him. Burly, moustached, an ex-cop. There were few retired cops or former military too proud to receive a generous pension supplement. Add to them mercenaries on sabbatical from private wars and the family's hackers. And the family didn't accept just anyone on its payroll. Full background checks on those recruited ensured they'd have something more than money on the line if they ever strayed from the path. That had been the key mistake made with Jackson—thinking money would be enough to control him. Jackson's veins ran with pure ruthlessness, without anyone to rein him in.

A half block from Gracie Mansion, waiting for a traffic light to change, the man gave the ex-cop a slow smile. He noted the other man's faraway eyes, probably counting Bitcoin in his head, imagining the piles of it accumulating in his dark-web account.

"So, how'd it go in court?"

The ex-cop straightened from a slouch. "A hundred grand and an ankle bracelet."

"And if she gets out?"

"We're already in the computers at Probation. What Probation sees, we'll see. We'll handle it. I doubt she'll be getting out, though. Yesterday, a contractor who was doing work in her building hit it with a mechanic's lien. So the title's not free and clear for collateral." The ex-cop smiled slyly. "A *coincidence*. It will take her a while to get past that. She has no other assets."

The man looked the ex-cop in the eyes, getting a charge out of imagining Kathleen Harris's face when she learned that she lacked assets to bail herself out. Rikers was a hellhole. Like a cat with catnip, he rolled around in the thought of her suffering there.

Kathleen Harris had lit his self-protective flame. Hatred heated and rose in his gorge whenever anyone had even a scintilla of power to hurt him. And, once lit, there was only one way to put the flame out. Kathleen Harris had become his newest project. His obsession. He would destroy her. He could barely keep from doing it himself. Yet there were rules: on U.S. soil, the army had to do the work. The most he could do was call the shots, a rousing game of high-stakes fantasy football.

"I wouldn't underestimate her," the ex-cop said. "She's a hardy bitch."

The man cut his eyes at the ex-cop. "I would never do that."

The van stopped. The driver came around to slide open the door.

Before the man moved toward the door, the ex-cop leaned in and spoke to him again. "We can't underestimate Emily Silverman either. She's been doing research, asking her friends questions—brass at the Department."

"I know that," the man said curtly.

"She's on the wrong track, for now, but she made a call to a hacker. She didn't say much to him on the phone, but . . . she could be getting warmer."

The man gave the ex-cop a tepid smile, betraying only a fraction of the rage that roiled his insides. Another uncontrolled player could unspool him if he didn't get a grip on the situation.

He bounded out of the van without answering, intent on not revealing to his subordinate the intensity of his emotion. He talked himself down. Despite her near miss in the fire, Emily Silverman had no clue that she was in jeopardy. She was just helping out a friend and seeking "justice." A nauseating thought, both motivations unimaginable to him. But he was consoled by her delusion that she had no skin in the game. It would make her a less ruthless adversary.

He walked the path to Gracie Mansion, pushing Emily Silverman out of his mind to the extent that he could. He approached the security booth, his mild-mannered game face in place.

44

KATHLEEN SAT ON the plastic chair outside the bubble, relief washing over her when her attorney answered her call. He was the first familiar voice she'd heard beyond voice mail since she'd been on Rikers. There was no feeling worse than having no one outside to look out for you—or even to talk to you. She'd been in that situation before. But this time she had an attorney. Although she'd left the Life long ago, she'd never asked Bob Green to return the few thousand dollars she'd given him to keep him on retainer, more out of superstition than any concern she'd be arrested.

She'd left Bob several messages since she'd arrived on Rikers, thirty hours ago: one-sided telephone tag. She'd kept him on retainer when she was a madam to avoid this very situation. It was a down payment in case trouble came. She would have thought he'd come to see her after getting her message. Or sent an associate, if he wasn't available. She was angry about that, but her relief at reaching him swept that away in the moment.

"Kathleen. I'm glad you finally got me," Bob said after saying hello.

Kathleen smiled, needing the succor of friendly words. "It's good to hear your voice. I'm worried about my bail application. Do you know what's wrong?"

"I talked to your building manager. He said there's a lien on the building. The equity's not free and clear. You have to use something else for collateral."

"How could that be?"

"It's a mechanic's lien. An electrician claims you didn't pay for work he did on the building."

Kathleen felt a tendril of fear running through her at yet another inexplicable bad turn. "I've always paid the bills. There were no disputes."

"Look, Kathleen, let's put that to the side for a moment. You've got a big problem with this case. As a predicate felon, you're facing a minimum of twelve years in prison, probably a lot more. Are you thinking about pleading it out?"

"I didn't do anything! You know me. How could you even think that?"

"I'm sorry, but you have to be realistic. Jail is no place for a woman your age. A case like this could be a life sentence if you don't plead it out."

"You haven't even looked at the evidence."

"Right, I haven't filed a notice of appearance yet. I've only talked to the ADA briefly."

"Okay," she said warily.

"The DNA evidence is strong."

Kathleen had to remind herself to breathe. "What about the security cameras?"

"I asked. All destroyed in the fire. I hate to talk about this, Kathleen. It's the worst part of my job. But I need seventy-five thousand dollars to begin work on this case and another hundred thousand or more if the case goes to trial. Do you have that?"

A whoosh of fury flushed Kathleen's face. She knew the deal. The defendant wasn't going to get *more* money as time went on in a case. People accused of crimes were generally unemployable, and unless they were wealthy, they lost everything before they even got to trial. So criminal lawyers set a price at the beginning and wanted to be paid in full up front. And the DA was saying she was broke. That was the crux of the case against her. Bob wasn't treating her with the care due a long-term client because he was worried that she was broke. And he wouldn't be able to count on her building as collateral for his fee either. Besides the mechanic's lien, if she were convicted of arson, there would be a line of victims suing her—her tenants, their insurance companies, even the City, which had spent money putting out the fire.

She took a long breath. That was why he hadn't taken the trip to Rikers to see her.

She didn't let on that their attorney-client relationship was coming to an end. She deserved better than his complete lack of faith in her. But for now, she would keep him hoping for a big payday so he could complete one more task. "We need to get me out first. I'm going to send someone to see you. You know what to do when she gets there."

"Okay. I know."

"I'll call you tomorrow. We'll talk more about your fee then."

Kathleen hung up, the conversation replaying in her head. The anxiety came in electric waves. She was too old for this. But plea bargaining would not be an option, not that she could imagine pleading guilty to arson.

She walked back to her cell and lay on her cot under a window made of translucent material that let in diffuse light, allowing her to see a glimmer of the outdoors: razor wire, weeds, and dark water. The cell door rumbled closed.

She'd long imagined that her days of worrying about imprisonment were over. The business she'd run for nearly twenty years had prevented her from entirely letting go of the idea that she might end up back here. It had caused her a constant thrum of anxiety under her calm businessperson's surface. She'd truly relaxed into her life only after she'd retired.

She might have fought harder to have a relationship with Lauren years ago if she hadn't been living a risky lifestyle. She'd known her work could mean arrest and renewed trauma for Lauren. Because of that, she'd accepted that it might be better to spare her daughter by honoring her wish not to have a relationship. But it seemed Kathleen hadn't avoided that result after all, and now she'd drawn her granddaughter into her life too. She couldn't whistle back what she'd done to insinuate herself into Emily's life. But now she had to consider whether she would get

Emily and Lauren even more involved. Unless the two walked away from her without looking back, Kathleen's situation might bring them still more pain. Right now, with a dark hopelessness settling into her, Kathleen doubted she was worth it.

Yet, when she reviewed her list of friends and acquaintances, there was no one else she could trust with the next task that needed to be done. Her entire life was at stake. It had to be Lauren and Emily. If she was lucky, she'd get another chance to make a call tonight.

45

LAUREN HEARD THE front door open, someone entering her apartment. She hadn't looked up from her computer screen for hours. Focusing on her clients' problems, solving their legal puzzles with an artful phrase or deft argument, was a relief from thinking about her own life.

Emily entered, and Lauren rose from her desk in a corner of the living room, happy to see her daughter. "Hi, honey. Where's Skye?"

"Hector's night." Emily hugged her. "Mom, we need to do something about this situation."

"What if I want to forget there *is* a situation?"

"I heard from Kathleen. I finally talked to her." Emily spoke quickly, ignoring what Lauren had said. "They're not accepting her building as collateral. She's been on Rikers for three days. We cannot leave her in jail. She's too old."

Lauren's back stiffened. She took in the strain on her daughter's face and knew Emily's concern came from a good place. She'd brought her daughter up to care about others and about fairness, but she'd be damned if she'd allow her own mother to take advantage of that and break Emily's heart the way she'd broken Lauren's.

Emily went on, "Somebody put a lien on her building, and she needs a hundred thousand dollars."

Kathleen asking Emily for that kind of money hit Lauren like an errant pitch. She choked out the words. "She asked you for *a hundred thousand dollars?*"

"No!"

"Oh, so she wants you to ask me for it, I get it." Lauren began to pace, furious.

"Ooh, you are *so* infuriating." Emily threw up her arms. "I didn't ask you for the money, and she didn't ask me. She just wants us to go see her lawyer."

Lauren paused, taking that in. "No way. I don't want to be involved. If there's anything I've learned in my life, it's to be careful about who you let into your orbit. It will be one drama after the next with her. The camel's nose under the tent."

"Bad things happen to good people, Mom. You of all people should know that."

Lauren turned away. She was completely out of sorts over the reappearance of her mother in her life. She would have made an emergency appointment with her therapist if she had one. Instead, she'd called Jessica and listened to her calm assurances. She'd of course told Carl too. He wasn't happy about her criminal mother showing up, even though he wouldn't outright tell Lauren what she should do. Family was family in Carl's mind, not so easy to write off. He'd bailed a nephew out of jail a couple of years ago, and he had an uncle who'd done time. Even though Carl was a cop, he didn't disown family for their mistakes.

Emily spoke slowly, overenunciating. "She has a safe-deposit box. She gave me the code name and box number. She said to pick up the extra key from her lawyer. What harm could it do? I don't agree with you about Kathleen. She's not a person who causes chaos in other people's lives. But two heads are better than one here, and I'd really appreciate you coming with me. I hate to admit it, but you may be right that I've been naïve. As annoying as it can be, your skepticism is kind of helpful."

* * *

An hour later, an administrative assistant in a small law office handed Lauren a sealed envelope containing a key. Once again, Emily had struck at Lauren's Achilles'. It was hard to turn down the rare request for support from her typically self-sufficient daughter. And beyond that, she really was curious about what they'd find in the safe-deposit box.

Lauren tried not to read too much into Kathleen's lawyer not coming out to see them in the firm's reception area. Maybe he'd already left for the day.

Lauren and Emily walked twelve blocks from the lawyer's office to the address Kathleen had given Emily, an office building on Lexington Avenue. While they walked, Emily talked about sex worker blogs and internet bulletin boards where people tried to catch serial killers.

Lauren sighed. "I wish you weren't getting in so deep. Sometimes the killers are actually members of the internet groups investigating them."

"I'm just lurking. No one even knows I'm there. I've been doing some research into arson investigations too. It's true that DNA can be found under ash. But in a fire this intense, the arsonist must have started the fire so the accelerant led *away* from the flash point. It feels similar to Kathleen's bank accounts being drained. A setup. Who would have the ways and means and knowledge to do that? Or the motive?"

Reverting to an old habit from her days as an addict, Lauren looked around before they entered the building. Her eyes met a man's gaze for an intense second before he looked down the block at an approaching bus. Anxiety tightened Lauren's chest until she glanced back to see him get on the bus.

To the right of the building's lobby were double glass doors without a name on them. A receptionist behind the expansive curved lacquer desk in the carpeted entry area turned a cash-register-style iPad toward Lauren. Emily showed Lauren her phone, open to the numbers Kathleen had given her that Emily had typed into her notes. Lauren typed Kathleen's username and password into the iPad login screen. Halfway through typing, Lauren realized she was entering her own initials and birth date. She drew back her hand as if shocked by an electric current.

What if Kathleen had, decades ago, resumed being the normal person she'd been when Lauren was a child, before crack and apparently psychosis? What if she'd resumed being the woman who'd helped Lauren with her first-grade homework every weeknight and who'd taken her to the playground on dewy weekend mornings? Although Lauren had always blamed her mother for everything, fuzzy memories came back to her now of waking up in the morning and her father not being there. His side of the bed hadn't been slept in. She remembered the worry in her mother's eyes—and a fake smile that failed to hide her sadness.

"What do you want to do today?" Lauren's mother would ask, pulling Lauren into bed to cuddle.

If that was the woman who'd been walking around in the world for the last thirty-three years, how had she felt, alone and without her daughter? How would Lauren have felt if she'd lost Emily for decades? Would she be using Emily's birthday for passwords? Would she be stalking Emily's children on Facebook? She felt tears coming: *Hell yes.*

"Ma'am?"

"Mom."

Lauren looked at Emily. The woman smiled at Lauren politely.

"You have to press enter," Emily said.

"Oh, sorry." Lauren smiled sheepishly at the receptionist.

The woman said, "No worries," and picked up her phone.

A moment later, a man with a military bearing opened a door at the back of the reception area. He appraised Lauren and Emily. "This way."

Lauren wondered momentarily why Kathleen trusted her after decades apart, after barely having a conversation with her since Lauren was fifteen. But Lauren now knew that Kathleen had been keeping track of her. Lauren was sure Kathleen would have friended her on Facebook, too, if Lauren had been on Facebook. This whole incident was the best I-told-you-so to those who said people like Lauren were unduly paranoid about their privacy. But what harm had Kathleen really done?

Lauren and Emily followed the security guard to a room full of safe-deposit boxes. It was clearly a safe place, but Lauren didn't feel safe taking this step toward helping her mother.

The man turned a key, and Lauren turned hers. He lifted the box and took it to a small room with a couple of chairs and a table. It was a large box, about two square feet.

"I'll be out here." He pointed to a button on the wall next to the door. "Signal when you're done." He closed the door behind himself.

Emily didn't wait for Lauren. She opened the box.

CHAPTER

46

A CALL ON THE PA system interrupted the steady flow of R and B and hip-hop that was piped into the cells of Rikers Island from dawn until lights-out. A female CO spoke over the PA system from the bubble: "Kathleen Harris. On the visit."

Kathleen sat up in her cot with a start. She wasn't expecting anyone. She slipped on her sneakers. The cell door rolled open in time for her to walk out.

"I'm Kathleen Harris." She said through the speak-hole at the bubble.

"Go on. To the gate." The CO handed Kathleen a pass through a slot under the speak-hole. She pointed Kathleen toward a barred gate that led to a wide outer corridor that ran the length of the jail.

Kathleen walked the corridor, allowing herself a moment of fantasy about who could be visiting. She hoped for Emily, or even Lauren, although she knew it was highly unlikely.

In a changing room near the visiting area, Kathleen took off her jail greens and put on an orange jumpsuit that left a layer of cold air between her narrow frame and its stiff cloth. The bright jumpsuits prevented inmates from walking out unnoticed among the visitors. And when wearing jumpsuits, the women couldn't easily place a drug-packed balloon into an orifice.

Kathleen sat in the grim waiting room filled with orange-garbed women. It was jail-style hurry-up-and-wait. A corrections officer sat at a desk next to the door that led to the visiting room. Nearly an hour after Kathleen arrived, he called a list of names: "Jones, Mack, Tavares, Morrison, Harris."

Kathleen lined up and filed through the door to the visiting room. Rows of school desks stretched the length of the room. Inmates sat on one side of each row of desks and visitors sat on the other side, which allowed the COs to see up the rows. The place echoed with dozens of conversations amplified by poor acoustics.

Kathleen scanned the room for a possible visitor. Her eyes rested on a young inmate kissing her baby, tears in her eyes, while an older woman, a grandmother or caseworker, watched grimly from across the desk. Kathleen remembered that as the most painful sight in prison, the mothers separated from their babies. Yet those women had been more fortunate than Kathleen, who had few visits during her five years in prison and never one with Lauren. Kathleen's mother had made one visit on Kathleen's first birthday inside, which had only served as a reminder of what their relationship lacked. They hadn't repeated the uncomfortable event, which had been punctuated by her mother's nervous distraction and awkward silences. Kathleen had been glad. She'd been relieved to avoid the visiting area completely. The sight of women with their visiting children had wrecked her. It took her days to get back on an even keel after that.

Kathleen kept looking around until a CO checked her clipboard and pointed Kathleen toward the right side of the room. Kathleen focused. A woman waved. She was around forty years old, with dark, shoulder-length hair and black-lined eyes. She wore slim jeans and suede loafers. Kathleen recognized her. She lived with one of Kathleen's tenants. They'd said hello if they crossed paths, asking each other politely how they were doing or commenting on the weather, nothing more. Kathleen couldn't have been more surprised.

Kathleen slid onto a wooden chair across from her. "Antonia. Hi."

"Hello," Antonia said in measured and heavily accented English.

"Thank you for coming. I'm surprised."

"I'm sorry you're here," Antonia said sadly. "None of us believe you set fire to the building."

"Thank you." Kathleen felt a physical brightening, relieved that her neighbors didn't think she'd done something so horrible to them. "I could never do something like that."

"Most of us are staying in the same hotel. For now."

"I hope it's comfortable."

"Luckily, it's just Javier and me in one room. It's worse for the families."

"I'm not going to sell. When I get out, I will rebuild so everyone can move back in. It will be even better than before. Everything new. You can tell them that."

"They will be happy to hear that, but that's not why I'm here—we know you got your own troubles. I'm here because Javier asked me to come."

"Oh?" Javier was Antonia's live-in partner. He'd been a tenant in the building for decades.

"He couldn't come here." Antonia looked embarrassed. "You know, he does not have papers." Undocumented.

"No, I didn't know."

"But he said we have to tell you . . ."

"Tell me what?"

"He saw a van near the building before the fire. An elevator-repair truck. Javier noticed it because there was nothing wrong with the elevator to need a repairman in the night. A man came out of the van. He was wearing"—she motioned with her hand toward her head, searching for her next word—"a hoodie. He went inside."

Kathleen leaned forward. "What happened?"

"Javier said he was not a homeless guy or somebody *loco* who did it. That's what we all thought at first. We would *never* think it was you. But Javier said no, he was a big man." She raised her palms beside her shoulders. "Big here. In good shape, like he goes to the gym. A serious man. Javier saw him right before the fire started."

"You're kidding." Kathleen had also imagined the arsonist was someone who was mentally ill, *loco*, as Antonia had said, somebody sickly fascinated with fire. She couldn't imagine anyone intentionally risking so many lives otherwise. She wasn't a big believer in evil. But maybe she'd underestimated the idea of evil.

She felt a glimmer of hope that she could prove herself innocent, now that there was a witness.

"You know, Javier cannot tell the police or testify what he saw," Antonia went on. "He could never take the chance."

Kathleen's hope plummeted. "I thought they didn't arrest witnesses for immigration status."

Antonia shook her head. "None of us trust that anymore since Trump. But it's worse than that." She chewed her lip, pausing, scared. "Javier said the guy who went in the building *was* police. He said he doesn't know what kind of cop. But you don't live without papers for twenty years without knowing a cop when you see one. Javier said he knows by the way he walked. By the way he moved. He said he's sure."

47

Emily's eyes widened at the stacks of hundred-dollar bills inside the safe-deposit box. She picked one up. "I guess we should count them?"

Lauren's facial expression was all business. "Thumb through and make sure they're all hundreds throughout the stacks."

While Emily did that, Lauren dug into her shoulder bag and pulled out a thin metal digital scale and placed it on the table. Emily frowned. "What—?"

"Are they all hundreds?"

Lauren picked up a pack Emily hadn't checked yet. The only sound was the quiet shuffling as they fanned through the money.

"This one is hundreds." Emily picked up another stack. "This one's twenties."

Lauren pressed a button to turn on the scale. "Separate the stacks of twenties from the hundreds."

"Is that Jessica's?" Emily asked, mystified.

"She left it at our house when she stayed with us while her bathroom was being remodeled. I thought it might be useful." Lauren considered the money. "Each bill weighs a gram."

"How do you know that?"

"I learned it from your grandfather when he was selling drugs." Lauren raised her hand in a don't-ask gesture and added under her breath, "Some things you don't forget. Your grandmother said we'd find money here, so it stood to reason we'd need to count it."

Lauren pressed a button to switch from ounces to grams. She put the first packet of hundreds on the scale. "Exactly a hundred grams. Ten thousand dollars. I'm getting the feeling your grandmother became quite the businessperson." Emily noticed how Lauren was referring to Kathleen as her grandmother, as though the relationship had skipped a generation.

Emily pushed the packs toward her mother and quickly pulled each pack toward her side of the table. She counted to twenty-eight.

"Two hundred eighty thousand dollars. Plus ten thousand in twenties."

"How are we going to carry it?" Emily asked. The money took up too much space to fit in her mother's shoulder bag and her own mini backpack. "We should have brought a suitcase. You didn't think of that when you brought the scale?"

Lauren smirked at her. "Actually, I did. But there's no way we can pay the bail in cash without raising questions," she said. "I'm not putting myself in that position. And I have no intention of walking the streets with a hundred thousand dollars."

In the box, a blank envelope caught Emily's eye. She opened it. The document folded inside said LAST WILL AND TESTAMENT. Emily skimmed the first page, feeling queasy about invading Kathleen's privacy. But, on the other hand, she felt as if she had a right to know everything about Kathleen, whose life had somehow wrapped around hers without her permission.

Lauren also rummaged through the paperwork in the box. Always the lawyer, Lauren picked up some legal papers and perused them, not seeming to notice what Emily was reading.

"She has property on an island called Bequia," Lauren said. "There's a deed. They probably wouldn't accept it to guarantee her bail. I've never even heard of the place."

"It's in the Grenadines," Emily said, "It's a small island. I heard it's beautiful." Emily scanned the will's captions and wherefores until her eyes rested on a paragraph that mentioned her mother. She looked up. "She left you everything."

"What?" Lauren's face dropped. "That's her will?"

Emily handed it to her, and Lauren took it and glanced through the document.

"Her building. A house. Hundreds of thousands in cash." Lauren paused. "I imagined she was living in some homeless-person nursing home by now, or dead. It hurt less to put her out of my mind entirely, as if she never existed."

"A lot must have changed."

"This is all so hard to believe." Lauren put the will back into its envelope. "When the ADA said she did five years for your grandfather dying. . . ." Lauren shook her head, as if trying to clear her mind. "I don't think she deserved to go to jail for that. And the idea that she would suddenly burn down a building with people—you, Skye, and herself—in it, that makes no sense, especially since she obviously had plenty of money to pay the mortgage. Not that she can say she has all this money, or she'll be charged with tax evasion."

Emily pulled a notebook from the box and looked through the pages. "There's names and phone numbers here. First names, and some look like code names. It must be the so-called black book."

They put everything back in the box except the one hundred thousand dollars they needed.

"You stay here," Lauren said. "I'll be back in five minutes."

"What are you doing?"

"I'm going to rent another box and put this money in my own box for collateral. If I put up the apartment, it won't raise questions."

Emily gave her a look of grudging respect. "You should have been a criminal."

Lauren returned a half smile that told Emily she'd hit on a truth.

Emily didn't know as much about her mother as she'd thought. Emily spoke under her breath as Lauren turned to leave: "I guess Kathleen's not the only one who's changed."

CHAPTER

48

CARL HUNCHED OVER a computer screen, his back tired and aching. All morning he'd been going over emails that Emily had sent. He felt a shot of anxiety that his fatigue was related to the MS but then reminded himself that he just needed to take a break and walk the stiffness off. It was Friday. He had gotten through his first week back at work and felt good about that. He arched his back, stretching his hands over his head, and resumed reading. He would focus on the City Hall emails for a few more minutes, then go get coffee.

An agent from the IT team, Charlotte, entered the room. "Hey, Carl, did you see the email I sent you?" She sat in the chair next to his desk.

Carl was glad for the break. "Oh, sorry, I was looking at the PDFs from City Hall. I didn't have a chance yet."

"Open my email. Let me show you."

"Sure." Carl closed the file he'd been looking at and opened her email.

"You know we subpoenaed Amazon's records of purchases. We've been looking for three things: purchases with Mattingly's known Amazon account, purchases made from his home IP address from any email account, and purchases delivered to Mattingly's home address. The deliveries could be purchases by him on IP addresses other than the one at his house, or he could have disguised his IP address by purchasing through the dark web. We also subpoenaed Walmart, Home Depot, and Lowe's.

"We've received some information. No nefarious orders from the home IP addresses or Jackson's known email addresses, but there was quite an uptick in deliveries to the home. Computers, iPads, a TV. The spending at the Mattingly residence appears to have increased threefold, starting about a year before the attack. But here's the kicker: even though he used Bitcoin, which is pretty much untraceable and highly suspect, the kid screwed up."

Carl leaned forward, looking at the document he'd opened on his computer screen, unable to decipher from the line of figures on the screen a conclusion that seemed so obvious to her.

"He got sloppy." Charlotte pointed to an entry in the spreadsheet. "He received a laptop at his home from Amazon. It was bought with a gift card, purchased with Bitcoin, from an email address we hadn't known. There's no identifying information associated with the email address, and the buyer used a disguised IP address to buy the gift card. We've found two other purchases at Home Depot from the same dark-web IP address using two more email addresses we had never seen before."

Carl grinned. "So he outed multiple email addresses. We can trace all his purchases associated with those email addresses now and probably come up with new IP addresses and maybe more email addresses. That will give us more to search for in the City Hall emails too."

"Exactly. And, most importantly, the two purchases from Home Depot were delivered to a Fifth Avenue address, not Mattingly's home. So now we can trace all the purchases shipped to *that* address and find other emails he used for those purchases. My bet is that eventually we'll find some communication with whoever gave him the Bitcoin." She raised her palms in a sweeping gesture and said victoriously, "Pay dirt."

"What do we know about the Fifth Avenue address?"

"It's a commercial mail-drop place. That's where he sent the more suspicious bomb-making components from Home Depot. The orders were delivered to a Yuri Ziskina there."

"A Russian connection?" Carl said. "Wow. Do we have anything on the guy?"

Charlotte swiveled her chair around to look at Carl. "I don't think there *is* a guy named Yuri Ziskina. It doesn't look like there's a real person by that name in New York. People rent a mailbox and have their stuff delivered to a chichi address. They don't require ID, so the renter can use any name."

Carl thought aloud. "We'll get a warrant, find out what we can about the rental and whether there's anything in the box. We'll have to send in the bomb squad and the dogs first to make sure the box isn't booby-trapped."

"They're sending a team as we speak."

Carl felt a twinge: they hadn't included him. They were only filling him in after the fact. He sighed inwardly. His boss had built in redundancies to the investigation, so they wouldn't lose a step if Carl woke up in bad shape on any given morning. It made sense. But it felt like a no-confidence vote. He was *totally* expendable. The MS was nothing if not humbling.

"Great job," he told Charlotte, putting aside his personal feelings about the way things had been done. He couldn't afford to feel sorry for himself, and this was great news.

Charlotte's earnest expression spread into a smile of accomplishment.

CHAPTER

49

After work, Emily stopped at the Airbnb to change, a slapdash race to replace her office clothes with shorts and a T-shirt. She'd needed to work late, then been stuck on the subway for nearly an hour.

The elevator stopped at each floor when Emily left the apartment, automatic stops for the Sabbath. A wave of anxiety surged in her every time the door opened and she had to wait for it to close, nobody entering. The stress of the whole week weighed heavier on her each time. Too much had been going on—the fire, Kathleen's arrest, the tectonic shift within her family—and she was late to pick up Rusty at the Puppies-in-Prison van on 125th Street. Her nerves were shot.

Thankfully, it had been a quiet week. She and Skye had settled into something close to their normal life. Skye had new toys and clothes. They'd slept comfortably together in their room. Skye would return tonight after her normal two days with Hector. Emily only wished she could turn off her own brain. A slow elevator ride down, a little bit late, and her brain was roiling with worry.

At the first floor, she rushed from the elevator. In the vestibule outside the building's locked inner glass door, a man was examining the directory and standing there, not going in. She paused. Her anxiety ramped up. Was she taking enough precautions?

The man turned toward her, and she took in his beard and hat. He was Orthodox. She exhaled, realizing he couldn't ring an electric intercom buzzer on the Sabbath. He was waiting for someone to let him in.

Emily opened the door.

"Thank you. I'm going to the second floor, the Meltzers."

"Oh, okay, sure." Emily held the door open so he could pass.

Emily laughed inwardly at her own nervousness. But when she turned onto Overlook Terrace to walk to the subway, she had a strange feeling, almost a physical shiver at the back of her neck. She turned around.

A black van passed.

She knew those vans: they were the "discreet" limos mega-rich people used nowadays. From what she'd seen at a show-room on Park Avenue, they had more space inside than a limo but were less obvious to the "little people," who could be hostile toward them. It was maybe the only concession rich people made in New York to the huge income gap between them and most everyone else.

For a second, she saw the outline of the driver. He looked at her. A bouncer type. It seemed that large, fit men were every-where lately. It gave her a moment's pause. But then the car sped up and pulled away. She talked herself down: one more sleazy creep checking her out, nothing new about that. But everything had been so sketchy lately. She picked up her pace to the subway.

*   *   *

Rusty's mouth-breathing in the back seat was the only sound as Lauren drove over the RFK Bridge onto the Grand Central Parkway in Queens. They passed the limestone Bulova Watch building with its giant clock. Modest single-family homes lined residential side streets once they exited the highway. The GPS directed them to a parking area near a bus stop, where dark water lapped the rocks at its perimeter. Private vehicles weren't allowed to park on Rikers. Emily and Lauren waited a long time for a bus.

Emily took in the oldest, creakiest bus she'd ever seen as it approached. She imagined mostly Rikers visitors used it. The driver waved them on. Long after visiting hours, the bus was empty except for one corrections officer who sat near the driver, chatting with him.

In a reception area, they sat for hours on bolted-down plastic seats while the paperwork was processed for Kathleen's release on bail.

"They must be making copies with carbon paper," Lauren complained to Emily, who was already sick of reading the work emails that were still flowing in on a Friday night.

Emily smirked. "What's carbon paper?"

Lauren laughed, waving the question away.

Emily understood her mother's anxiety to get out of there. The dark energy of Rikers made Emily want to back away from the place with a crucifix held high, shouting, "Get ye back, Satan." And the cloying disinfectant smell made Emily uneasy, like it cloaked a secret. But Lauren was also about to break a thirty-year separation from her mother. Emily could only imagine how that felt.

The door buzzed. Lauren and Emily looked toward the noise.

Kathleen walked out, wearing wrinkled street clothes, the same ones she'd been wearing when she was arrested. She scanned the room to see who'd bailed her out. When her gaze fell on Emily and Lauren, her eyes glistened. Emily could see her trying to stiffen her face, but she swiped away a tear.

"Thank you," she said when she approached them.

Emily was pretty sure she was thanking them for more than getting her out of jail. This reunion with Lauren was a moment she must have imagined a million times.

"I've kept your money for collateral," Lauren said, drawing Kathleen back from making any assumptions about the state of their relationship.

Her statement had its desired effect. Kathleen's face retracted behind a neutral expression. Emily sunk into herself too. A part of her was so damn happy that Kathleen was her grandmother. The other part reminded her that she had a compulsive liar for a grandmother, which was no cause for celebration. Still, it hurt to glimpse Kathleen's pain at Lauren's greeting.

"The money was always there for a rainy day," Kathleen said. "I hope you have it someplace safe."

"I do."

Kathleen petted Rusty and gave him a scratch behind his ears. "Hey, little one."

"Come on," Lauren said, walking away.

Emily followed behind Kathleen with Rusty. He pranced alongside her, always seeming to see the bright side of every situation.

*   *   *

They took the bus back over the long bridge to the Queens mainland. They were the only ones on the bus this time. It rattled and creaked on the narrow roadway. Outside its windows, nighttime had overtaken the long summer dusk. Beyond the black water, Emily could see the distant lights of a LaGuardia runway.

"What's up with the name?" Lauren asked.

Kathleen was sitting between Lauren and Emily, the three of them on a sideways bench of seats near the back exit.

"Ah. My last name?" Kathleen said. "I changed it after I finished parole. When they began to digitalize criminal records and my conviction showed up on the first page of the Google results, I didn't want strangers perusing my background so easily. The police always have my fingerprints, but everyone in the world doesn't have to know my past. And I stopped using Kat years ago. I grew out of it." Kathleen turned to Emily. "I'm sorry I lied to you."

"You're Sophie?"

"Yes."

Emily felt the blood rising to her cheeks. "I was friends with an *imaginary* person. That is so humiliating."

"And for all that," Lauren piled on, "you put her in the cross hairs of a murder case."

Kathleen barked out an angry laugh, her eyes glistening. "You can't seriously believe that helping her get an interview for a City Hall job and renting her an affordable apartment was putting her in the cross hairs. That's what you want, Lauren? To make it all fit your narrative of the terrible mother you wrote off? So you can believe it was worth it that we missed over thirty years together, even though I was clean?"

"You call running a brothel *clean*? Give me a break."

Emily watched the two women, still stunned at the truth: her mother and her grandmother. She could see the resemblance. They even had the same quiver of their chin when angry. They were initially arguing about her, but they'd basically forgotten she was there.

"Do you know how hard it is to get a job when you have a felony conviction, especially back then? When I got out of prison, I hadn't worked in over eight years and my record said I murdered someone. I tried to get a job for months. Running a brothel was the best career path available to me."

Lauren blinked hard, processing that.

"Walk in my shoes, Lauren," Kathleen continued. "I know the ones you inherited from me gave you blisters. I couldn't be more sorry about that. Really. I worried about you every night in my cell for five years. The only reason I didn't kill myself after losing you and your father and ending up in jail was that I needed to find you. You were out there alone in the world, just a kid. I was terrified for you.

"When I came out and finally found you, you were safe. Not just safe—flourishing. That was such a relief. But you wanted nothing to do with me. I got that. You were justified in feeling that way. So I gave you your wish."

Lauren seemed to soften, her eyes tearing up. But when they left the bus and Kathleen and Lauren sat in the front seat of the car, Lauren didn't let up.

"Emily can stay the weekend in your rental. It's the dog's last weekend, but I want her to come home after that."

"No," Emily said from the back seat.

The two women turned back, as if just remembering her.

"I have a grandmother who—how can I put it?—took *inappropriate* steps to get to know me," Emily said. "She deceived me so I could have a nice apartment near her. And yes, I am highly disappointed that I didn't *earn* the City Hall interview." She took a deep breath. "So now I know I'm no better than Silver Spoon Max . . ."

Kathleen began to protest. Emily put up her hand to stop her.

"I'll stay the weekend with Kathleen. I'll decide after the weekend where Skye and I will live. I don't have to make that decision now. But Mom, *I* will be the one to decide."

CHAPTER

50

THEY RODE PAST cookie-cutter houses with penny-sized lawns toward the highway. Kathleen thought things over for a few minutes, ironically grateful for the awkward silence in the car. She felt deeply thankful to be out of jail, even though her problems and the prospect of prison still loomed large. She looked out the window. She considered how much she would tell Lauren and Emily, and why. She didn't want to be alone with the situation. She wanted their help and support. But she also wanted to salvage her reputation. She wanted Emily and Lauren to know she was telling the truth about her innocence. She wasn't naturally a liar.

She hadn't planned to sink to such depths of deception to get to know Emily. Friending her had seemed innocuous in the beginning. She'd never intended to do more than witness her granddaughter's life. She'd been impressed that Emily had finished graduate school and begun a challenging career while a single mother with a young baby. So Kathleen had ended up helping her here and there—that didn't make her a criminal. She'd left the old life behind a long time ago. She needed Lauren and Emily to know that. But Lauren still had a point.

"Emily, you are more than welcome to stay with me, but I may agree with your mother about finding someplace else . . . after the weekend."

"What?" Emily said with surprise.

"I had a visitor at the jail."

"Okay." Emily drew the word out, not getting the relevance.

"One of our neighbors, Antonia. She said her partner, Javier, saw someone going into the building right before the fire started."

"She told you but not the cops?" Lauren asked.

"Her partner is an undocumented immigrant. He won't go to the cops. But the surprising thing is that he was sure the man *was* a cop."

"That's quite an allegation," Lauren said skeptically. "She came all the way to Rikers to tell you that story?"

Kathleen was sure Lauren was being intentionally obnoxious.

"I imagine the man he saw could have been military or an ex-cop, too," Kathleen went on. "And it's only one of the strange things that's happened. Did you see what the newspaper said about Wayne today? The paper said he killed himself because his life was falling apart due to a divorce. That is ridiculous. Not the Wayne I knew. Take my word for it, that would be like Donald Trump killing himself over a divorce."

Emily laughed, a skittish sound, more nervous than amused.

Kathleen could tell Lauren was paying attention, even though she looked straight ahead as she drove. The set of Lauren's face reminded Kathleen of her vigilance as a child, when she'd seen shady characters coming to their apartment to buy drugs from Michael or to smoke, some staying for days to get high. More than anything, Kathleen yearned to hold and comfort her child, who was right in front of her but still a million miles away.

She forced her mind back to the present issues. She owed Emily and Lauren information. They had a right to weigh their risk for themselves.

"There's one thing Wayne and Sharon and I have in common," she said. "I didn't talk about it before, and Emily, I didn't tell you about knowing Wayne because of it. But I'll tell you this much: we all signed nondisclosure agreements with one of my clients. I think Sharon may have had the client's baby. He was married."

Lauren still focused her eyes on the road ahead of her. "How long ago was that?"

"Around twenty years."

Lauren asked, "Do you think Sharon or the lawyer was threatening to reveal it?"

Emily loosened her seat belt shoulder strap with her hand and leaned forward from the back seat. "Killing Sharon after two decades is like dropping a nuclear bomb to put out a forest fire."

"The solution would be way riskier than the original problem," Lauren agreed.

The car was silent for a moment.

"But still, all three of you have an NDA in common," Lauren continued slowly. "Two of you are dead. And you almost died in a fire that someone set on purpose."

"What are the odds of all that happening coincidentally to the three of you within two weeks?" Emily asked.

CHAPTER

51

THE MAN HUNG up the phone after a short talk with a member of his team. He swiveled around in his desk chair in the library of his Upper East Side triple-width townhouse, a mansion in disguise. The library was lined with bookshelves with built-in rolling ladders to reach its thousands of volumes, although he read on his iPad or phone like most people. He bounded to his feet, pacing on a hundred-thousand-dollar Persian rug, handwoven in shades of gold and brown.

Kathleen Harris had been bailed out. Emily Silverman had gotten her mother to do it, that much was clear. Emily had visited the home of a hacker. The hacker's electronic devices were impenetrable, which irked the man to no end. But today they'd found a photo on Emily's phone that some incompetent idiot hadn't noticed before. It was of Sharon Williams and her girl-toy.

He itched to add Emily to his project. It would be a fantastic doubleheader with Kathleen Harris. He imagined Emily tethered, him ripping her apart, stripping her to the bone before killing her. The way he liked to do it when he went on "safari."

The alpha men in his family all had the same craving. The trifecta: catch, torture, and kill. He could walk through the family estates in Charleston, South Carolina, or Rhinebeck, New York, and admire the portraits of his ancestors lining the entry halls. Some of their crimes had been passed down via whispered oral history, the older generations grooming the young ones with the stories. Other deeds he could only imagine, enjoyed imagining. Of course, no matter how heinous the actions, they weren't crimes, since no one was ever caught. In some cases, their feats were perfectly legal.

The family looked at this craving among its men as evolutionary. Like his predecessors, the man had started with the killing of wayward pets in childhood. One couldn't keep a pet alive on their estates if there was a boy heir growing up there. That had been a problem for centuries—if you cared enough about pets to call it a problem. Then came adolescence and young adulthood, when the family made donations to schools and police benevolent associations to bail the boys out as they trampled on rules and laws. Eventually, each young man learned to live within the social constraints of his times. The ability to do that came with maturity, and that was what the family gave its gifted boys: time for them to flourish and be free until their maturity caught up to their violent propensities.

They were a tight-knit and closemouthed dynasty, having protected their own for nine hundred years. Everyone recognized the bottom line: the males who possessed the riskiest traits were also the income producers, the ones with the outstanding minds for money and power. It was a package deal. But now, after Jackson's antics, the family was in unprecedented jeopardy. The earth had shifted beneath their feet.

The man felt an overwhelming need to punish and obliterate those who would help Jackson destroy the family. If there was one thing the man hated, it was people who posed a threat. Which brought him back to Emily Silverman. He was angrier each moment he thought of her. It would take every bit of his self-restraint to adhere to the family rule: when in the United States, do-it-yourself projects were strictly off-limits. The family made light of his concern, assuring him that Emily was nowhere near learning anything that could damage them. But even if she was only shadowboxing, it was the thought that counted, the principle of the thing, the lack of control. It made him hate, a hate beyond his ability to withstand. Once obsessive hate flowed inside him, it *required* expression. His self-control was already running on empty. How dare Emily Silverman oppose him?

He studied the photo of Sharon and her girlfriend, as he was sure Emily Silverman had done. He conjured the image of Sharon dying in the plastic-lined trunk of a car. He tried to calm himself with a fantasy of Sharon's dying moments. Had Sharon tried to call out her girlfriend's name after her larynx was severed and she was drowning in her own blood? He laughed at the thought of it.

He shuddered and stood straight, coming back to himself, smiling like a snake that had shed old, uncomfortable skin. First things first. Kathleen Harris. She had to go first, particularly now that she was out of jail. He had planning to do. He could circle back to the Emily Silverman issue afterward.

* * *

Kathleen savored her first sip of coffee while Emily showered and dressed. Skye was sitting on the floor near the table, leaning against Rusty after reluctantly eating breakfast in her chair rather than on the floor with him. Rusty seemed perfectly content with his new juvenile appendage. Skye had spent every waking moment with him since Friday night, when they'd stopped off after Rikers to pick her up from Hector's mother.

Kathleen only hoped that there was no risk for Emily and Skye in staying with her.

Emily didn't want to uproot Skye again after all the upheaval. Emily conceded that she'd been nervous. But she'd concluded that whatever was happening couldn't possibly include a conspiracy of roving arsonists following Kathleen from building to building.

Kathleen agreed. But she also knew that the mind had a way of finding equilibrium, minimizing any reality that fell too far outside its norm. Especially unpleasant reality. For Kathleen, the cuff on her ankle and the threat of a life in prison kept her acutely aware that nothing was normal.

And Kathleen had heard Emily speaking in harsh whispers by telephone with Hector. He was starting to worry about the risk. Kathleen couldn't blame him. Despite Kathleen's bliss at having her granddaughter and great-granddaughter under her roof, she planned to look into renting them a separate apartment. Nearby. She would never forgive herself if anything happened to Emily and Skye.

Kathleen sat at an angle to the round kitchen table. A wire ran from her ankle to an outlet in the wall.

Skye pointed. "What's that?"

Kathleen answered matter-of-factly, "I have a cuff on my ankle. It has to be charged every day."

Emily appeared in the doorway and looked at her with a disconcerted frown. "Yeesh."

"If it runs out of juice," Kathleen said to Emily, "the GPS stops and the nice people at the warrant squad come. I have to wear it twenty-four hours a day. It's waterproof."

"So stupid." Emily shook her head in disgust. "How long does it take to charge?"

"About a half hour." Kathleen lifted her I ♥ New York coffee mug, undoubtedly left by a previous Airbnb customer. "I come prepared with my coffee and iPad. And Skye has kept me company. I just need a positive attitude. Hopefully, the criminal case will be cleared up soon. I have an appointment with a new lawyer tomorrow."

Kathleen slipped her fingers between the cuff and the raw skin of her ankle, rubbing a chafed area. She didn't know whether to put lotion or powder on it. Unfortunately, she didn't think she'd get an answer by Googling, although she thought she'd give it a try while charging up.

"You're allowed to go there?" Emily asked. "The ankle bracelet won't go off if you leave the house?"

"My lawyer's office will be an approved destination. I can also walk around the neighborhood, go to the store, that sort of thing."

Emily poured a cup of coffee from the half-full pot.

"Skye, where's Rusty's ball? Can you take Rusty to look for it in the living room?"

"Rusty, come," Skye commanded happily, and scampered off with the dog.

Emily leaned against the counter. "I never expected this level of attachment."

Kathleen nodded. "How long until you get a new dog?"

"Just a few weeks. But that's the thing. Skye loves *this* dog. We'll get a new puppy, but I think I made a big mistake."

"Losing your home didn't help. You couldn't foresee that. You can't blame yourself."

"Rusty is getting new brother," Skye said matter-of-factly, coming into the room, obviously hearing part of the conversation. "Evie is having new brother too."

"That's right," Emily said, then spoke to Kathleen. "Evie is Skye's friend from day care."

Kathleen knew Emily hadn't figured out how to tell Skye that, unlike her little friend, the new dog would *replace* the old dog. Kathleen wished she had something wise to say to Emily, but she was coming up blank on grandmotherly wisdom.

52

Aₓ FTER EMILY AND Skye left for the day on Monday, Kathleen made her way to the State Office Building on 125ᵗʰ Street. She sat in a waiting room with bolted-down plastic chairs, like the waiting room on Rikers. A counter topped with bulletproof glass separated the probation officers from their charges, who waited for their designated appointment times. After twenty minutes, a receptionist called Kathleen's name, and Probation Officer Daniels appeared at a nicked metal door. She was middle aged, easily six feet tall, and wearing a man-tailored shirt. Rosacea patches bloomed on her cheeks.

Kathleen followed her down a cubicle aisle, and PO Daniels took a seat across the desk from her. "I've got to know all your regular destinations so I can preapprove you without the GPS reporting you AWOL."

Kathleen gave her lawyer's address, and the PO typed it into her computer. "I'll have to go back to my building, too, once the insurance company finishes its appraisal," Kathleen said. "I'll need to hire a general contractor and start work on repairing the building. I'd also like to go to a funeral home tomorrow on the Upper East Side."

"Okay. I'm sorry to hear that." PO Daniels studied Kathleen. "Somebody close?"

"No, no. Just an old friend." Kathleen didn't show how irritating it was to have this woman inquiring about personal matters. It was a dynamic familiar to Kathleen from her ten years on parole, an experience she'd hoped to never repeat.

"Where's the funeral home?"

Kathleen pulled out her phone and read the address off to her.

PO Daniels entered the information and faced Kathleen again. "Look, you can't go on a cruise to the Bahamas, but this should be mostly easy-peasy. You just need to keep me informed. Most people in pretrial supervision don't have ankle cuffs anymore, but you're charged with a violent felony. You're not eligible for the kinder, softer treatment."

"This is the second time I've been charged with a violent felony, and I've never done more than kill a mosquito."

PO Daniels leaned forward. "I get it, but don't do anything stupid. I don't want my kindness to look like weakness—to my boss, or the newspapers. Bottom line, don't embarrass me."

Kathleen forced an obedient smile. "I promise."

*   *   *

Two blocks from FBI headquarters, Carl spent hours at the U.S. attorney's office reviewing his testimony for the upcoming criminal trial of a guy he'd busted two years ago. Carl had been studying a lot, and today he'd gone over his testimony with the assistant U.S. attorney who was prosecuting the case. She wouldn't be allowed to ask leading questions in court, so he had to know the facts thoroughly. By the end of the session, he felt great. Sharp. Ready. Best of all, no sign of a slur to his words.

Afterward, he took a call from Emily while he walked across Foley Square toward the Federal Building. He stopped near the dry fountain at the center of the triangular "square," crisscrossed by Lafayette and Centre Streets.

"IT found an email that we think is from Jackson Mattingly," Emily said. "He was asking for tickets to the inauguration last year. He said he was interested in the mayor's views on the confidentiality of adoption records."

"Has Sullivan taken a stance on adoptee rights?" Carl asked, excited. Mattingly's question meant Carl had hit a bull's-eye about the kid not being the biological child of his parents.

"The mayor doesn't have an official position on it. Mattingly received a form reply. You know, 'Thank you for writing, thank you for your interest, we'll take a look at the issue.' Adoption confidentiality is an issue that's been gaining national attention. States are doing away with the right to anonymity for birth parents. But it hasn't been on the mayor's radar."

When Carl returned to his office, Rick and his "temporary" partner, Meredith, a young woman only a year out of the academy, were eating sandwiches and drinking coffee. Almond-complexioned and of Syrian descent, Meredith wore a short-sleeved polo shirt that revealed cut biceps. Carl yearned to get back in shape and had returned to the gym for light workouts. It was vital to exercise to the extent he could, and he'd regained much of his old energy level. But it embarrassed him that this young agent knew him only as the soft, diminished version of himself.

Carl sat at his desk, not knowing how he'd taken this hairpin turn into self-pity, especially after Emily's call. He hated self-pity in others and even more so in himself.

Meredith smiled broadly at him. "Carl. How's it going?"

She was always overly nice, treating him like Master Po, the blind elderly kung fu master in a TV series he'd watched reruns of during childhood summers in Puerto Rico. Carl was the elder stateman at Federal Plaza. Young agents allowed him to impart wisdom even though, deep down, they thought they knew better. Being disabled aged you in people's minds, even if you weren't all that disabled.

"I was onto something about the Mattingly adoption question," Carl said to Meredith and Rick. "He sent an email to Sullivan, asking about adoption confidentiality."

"That's amazing," Rick said. "From everything we've seen, adoption didn't happen to him, but he must have believed it."

Meredith agreed. "A delusion."

"There's an amazing amount of delusional people who write to the mayor, but Mattingly had at least some basis for wondering why he was different from his parents," Carl said. "And the purchases we've traced to him add up to far more than the Mattingly household income. There's a whole backstory we're missing in this case."

Meredith gave a closed-mouth smile, signaling grudging acknowledgment. "No one in the neighborhood thought he was doing anything to make money other than working as an orderly at the hospital after he graduated high school."

"So somebody funded him with the Bitcoin?" Rick asked.

"Since there's no indication that he was a Bitcoin wonder boy, yes, somebody. The techies are no closer to figuring out who. The Fifth Avenue search was a bust. There were some chemical traces there that indicate he received deliveries of items he used for making the bombs. But the mail-drop business doesn't keep records of when packages are delivered or who sends them. That's part of the draw of those places. Complete privacy. They don't want to know."

Carl sat down, wanting to take another look at the email Emily had sent over.

"It sucks that he didn't say anything, leave a note, something to explain his motive," Rick said. "It was bad enough that we never found out Stephen Paddock's motive in the Las Vegas shooting, but at least we knew where Paddock's money came from."

"There's a personal angle we're missing," Carl insisted. "And my gut tells me it relates to Mattingly's question to the mayor. I'm going to take a step back and walk through his bio again, birth to death. I think we're missing something important. Or someone."

CHAPTER

53

KATHLEEN WALKED INTO an opulent funeral home on Madison Avenue, her eyes needing to adjust after her sunny stroll across Central Park to get from the west to east side. She'd gotten lucky and found out from Legacy.com when and where the funeral services would be held.

Wayne lay in an open casket at the front of the large room. A few clusters of people were seated and standing. It was early yet. There were enough pews for hundreds to attend, and Kathleen suspected the place would fill up before the memorial service tonight. Wayne's widow, Linda, sat in the front pew, greeting visitors. Kathleen had seen her photo on her vacation rental website.

Kathleen ducked back out of the entryway and went to the ladies' room at the end of a gold-wallpapered hallway. She passed through a sitting room and entered a bathroom with muted lighting and marble floors, sinks, and walls. She used the facilities and returned to the restroom parlor area. Several teenagers lounged on a couch and chair on one end of the room. Kathleen didn't think any of them were Wayne's children. Their faces were too fresh and unworried. Their chatter quieted a notch when Kathleen entered.

On the opposite side of the room from the girls, old-fashioned mirrored vanities lined the wall, where women could clean up their makeup after a messy cry. Kathleen sat at a vanity, took a tissue from her purse, and dabbed at her eyes. She took out her phone and fiddled with it, opening random apps but not reading.

The girls quickly forgot she was there and resumed talking about boyfriends and gossip from the Hamptons, their summer interrupted by a return to the city for Wayne's funeral. Kathleen watched them in the mirror between glances down at her phone.

After a few moments, one said to the others in hushed tones, "My mother said the police found porn on his computer."

"Kiddy porn," a redhead said knowingly.

"Get the fuck out of here," said a short, pretty teenager with a five-hundred-dollar highlight job and bright-pink lipstick. "Uncle Wayne wasn't into little kids."

An older girl smirked. Taller, with a heart-shaped face. "You never know."

"If he liked little girls," the short, pretty one scoffed, "he would have tried something when we were little. He was always totally regular with me."

The tall one retorted, "Maybe he liked little boys."

In unison, all the other girls: "Oh."

Kathleen had heard enough. After a reasonable interval to make her exit appear unrelated to what she'd heard, she put her phone away and returned to the main room.

*   *   *

Wayne looked as if he'd died peacefully. Kathleen stood briefly in front of the casket, noting his shock of thick hair with graying sideburns. She felt detached from any emotion about his death. Theirs had been a purely business relationship, long ago, and their last encounter had been unpleasant. She hadn't wished him dead, but she wasn't mourning him.

She turned away and approached the pew where Linda sat with a man and a woman. Kathleen shook her hand. "I'm Kathleen Harris, a client of your husband's."

In her early fifties, Linda was Upper East Side emaciated, with a blond bob that accentuated cheekbones pressure-cooked with filler and Botox. "Thank you for coming," she replied.

"Of course. Wayne was a good man."

Not having much to say while Linda was surrounded by people, Kathleen sat in the pew behind her. Eventually, a lull in arriving visitors left a fallow space on the pew next to the widow. Kathleen slipped in beside her, speaking in soft but intense tones, her eyes focused on the casket as she spoke.

"I know this is a difficult time, but do you mind me saying . . . I'm finding the situation a little hard to swallow." Kathleen turned to Linda. "His death was very . . . sudden."

Linda took a closer look at Kathleen. "Were you one of his girlfriends?" She added, noting Kathleen's age, "Twenty years ago? We were married for twenty-five, you know."

"No. Not at all. I was a client. A friend. But do you believe that crap about porn?"

Kathleen knew she was being direct, even shocking, but her gut told her this was the way to break down the widow's wall. There was no reason Linda would talk about anything private with a stranger. Kathleen was counting on shock value.

As the woman assessed her, Kathleen tucked her legs farther under the bench, conscious of the bulky shackle at her ankle, her pants stretched unnaturally tight there.

"Who are you really?" Linda asked.

"Kathleen. You may have heard of me." She lowered her voice. "I'm having a similar problem. A hacker cleared out my account, supposedly from my computer, and I was accused of arson as a result. Suddenly, kiddy porn shows up on Wayne's computer. Frankly, I'd be very surprised if he were into kids. In the last two weeks, it's been like a plague on both our houses, if you know what I mean. And it all started with strange activity on our computers."

"Oh, I know who you are." Linda gave Kathleen a long look, then lowered her voice and said, "In the week before Wayne died, I received an email with photos. It wasn't exactly shocking that Wayne would engage in sex outside our marriage, but getting those pictures—photos of him with other women, adults—was the final straw. Then detectives stopped by. There was evidence that Wayne had visited a child porn site. They traced his IP address. The police didn't arrest him right away, but they impounded his computer, and after he died, they told me they found disgusting photos and videos . . . of children. They interviewed me to see if I knew anything about it."

"That's crazy."

"I agree. I told them he would never have done that. And between you and me, even if he did, he wouldn't leave photos on his hard drive. My husband was a lot of things, but stupid wasn't one of them. I'm one hundred percent certain he had nothing to do with that."

"And the overdose?"

"It had to be accidental. He was too narcissistic for suicide. He was sure everything would be straightened out in his favor, as usual. He would make sure of it. Our impending divorce barely fazed him. I moved out to our house in the Hamptons when I received the photos of him. But Wayne wasn't one to wallow in self-pity. By all accounts, he was already scoping out younger women who would look better on his elbow when making an entrance at Mar-a-Lago." She gave Kathleen a bitter smile. "He had a way of looking at the bright side of things."

Linda paused in thought before continuing. "I have no idea why I'm telling you this, but you probably know. Wayne never shied away from a good party. It wouldn't be a huge surprise if he got high. They said he had fentanyl in his system. Everyone knows taking heroin or cocaine nowadays is like playing Russian roulette. A fentanyl overdose can happen to anyone who takes drugs. But things have been so strange." Her eyes met Kathleen's questioningly. "His death had to be an accident, didn't it?"

C H A P T E R

54

EMILY HAD THE day off from work to attend Rusty's graduation, a date she'd requested weeks ago. She rode the Metro
North commuter train to Bedford, a mostly wealthy town in
Westchester County. It wasn't far from where her father and
Jessica had lived for the last few years before he died. Her mind
drifted back to those times as she watched the trees blur past the
train window.

Losses. Too many losses. Her father. The town where she'd
spent happy and sad times during her teen years. Now Rusty.

She shook her head. It wasn't only Skye who'd become overly
attached to him.

A van driver called out from the bottom of the steps that
led from the train platform to the parking lot, "Bedford State.
Bedford State." It was a regular routine, women and children
arriving by train from Manhattan to visit the prison. Emily had
disembarked with a group of mostly women with shopping bags
and strollers.

A van with *Puppies-in-Prison* etched on its side pulled up
behind the taxis taking the women. Emily and several others
walked over to their ride.

The prison waiting room was a sunnier, cleaner version of
the one on Rikers. Emily sat among the group of special visitors,
volunteers, veterans, and their families and what looked like a

local politician and his assistant. A corrections officer had told them that the Puppies-in-Prison staff would come soon to bring them to a separate wing, where the puppies and their inmate trainers lived.

"Hello." A woman with a high ponytail greeted all the visitors, raising her voice to be heard. "For those of you who've never met me in person, I'm Diana Tobias, assistant director of the program. It will be a half hour before we'll get you cleared through security to enter. Please be patient, and we'll be starting soon."

A man with puffy cheeks and an eye patch looked around, his facial muscles clenched. Emily decided to talk to him, thinking maybe he'd be Rusty's future owner and the conversation would take his mind off whatever was bothering him. As the last hurdle in their training, Rusty and his littermates had gone with a group of veterans to restaurants and malls. Then each dog had stayed overnight in a motel room with a veteran. That had been Rusty's final test before graduation. The dogs would leave with their new owners after the ceremony.

"Are you a volunteer or getting a puppy?" she asked him.

"Puppy," he said grimly.

"Lucky. I'm a volunteer." Emily put out her hand to shake, noticing his frown. She realized he probably didn't feel lucky to *need* a service dog. "All these dogs are amazing," she said, clarifying.

He shook her hand. "Nice to meet you."

"My foster dog is Rusty. Have you seen him?"

The man's face broke into a smile. "That's a great dog. He came with my group to lunch. I didn't take him overnight, but he's a sweetheart."

Emily's chest swelled with pride.

Diana approached. "Emily, could you please come with me? We're going to clear you first. Lucille wants to have a word with you."

"Oh, is something wrong?"

"No, no, everything's okay, but she needs to talk to you."

Emily put her backpack in a plastic container and onto a conveyor belt for X-rays. She walked through the metal detector, grabbed her backpack, and followed Diana down a hallway painted in glossy beige. They left the reception building and took a path that cut through a green lawn to a low building.

Lucille, the program director, was sitting in her office. She was tall and wiry, wearing pink plastic glasses. Emily took a seat and saw right away that it wasn't going to be good news.

"Emily, it's good to see you. I wanted to meet with you because we had an incident last night." She put up her hand to reassure her. "Rusty's fine. But when he was with the veteran he stayed with last night, they were in a hallway going to their room, and Rusty began barking wildly at a man passing in the hall. The vet became very upset." The director gave her a sad but judgmental look. "Rusty's behavior was exactly the opposite of what we want the veterans to experience with their service dogs."

"I can't understand it. Rusty never reacted that way to anyone. Ever."

"Remember the man with the fishing pole who upset him?"

"That was only one time, and he wasn't *that* bad."

"Well, this time it was bad." Lucille leaned forward across her desk. "Thank you for everything you've done with him. But we have to release Rusty from the program. We'll adopt him out to a good owner. He's just not cut out for this work, or maybe he had too many transitions. Two inmates trained him. Two different weekend volunteers. Sometimes there's nothing we can do to salvage a training that hasn't gone smoothly. You didn't do anything wrong. I hope you'll keep working with us."

Emily swallowed hard. "I can hardly believe it."

"Stay for the graduation and celebration. You'll get to say good-bye to Rusty."

* * *

An inmate with a fireplug physique was waiting for Emily outside Lucille's office. She wore a green uniform, and her hair was cut short and masculine. "They asked me to take you to the auditorium," she said.

Emily fell in beside her. "Thanks."

When they reached the path outside the low building, the inmate spoke. "Rusty's a good dog. I was surprised. I've been helping out, waiting for a chance to get a dog to train since I came back here. I thought Rusty was doing okay."

"It's still hard to believe," Emily said. "They're going to adopt him out."

"Yeah, they charge five thousand dollars to the new owner to make up for the costs to train him. Even the dogs that flunk out are better trained than ninety-nine-point-nine percent of dogs."

"I can't believe today will be my last time seeing Rusty, and it's not even for a good cause."

"Yeah, it's too bad."

Emily paused and put out her hand to introduce herself. "I'm Emily."

The inmate smiled, putting out her hand, seeming to appreciate the formality. "Angela."

Grasping her hand, Emily really looked at her, straight on; she looked past the green jail uniform. The woman's familiarity snapped into focus. Emily knew her. She'd seen her picture. "Angela?"

"Yeah, why?"

"Wait a second. Do you know someone named Sharon?"

Angela's eyes widened, but her voice went low and intense. "You know Sharon? Sharon Williams?"

CHAPTER

55

EMILY AND SKYE arrived at Kathleen's apartment after dark. Kathleen sensed that Emily was upset, but Emily didn't say anything right away. She left a restaurant takeout bag on the dining room table and took Skye to their room to get her ready for bed. The scent of curry seeped from the bag.

Skye ran out a few moments later in her pajamas and a plastic firefighter hat. "Good night, Kat-lee," she said, running in for a glorious hug.

When Emily returned to the living room a half hour later, Kathleen was pedaling on a stationary bike in a corner. Placid cats stared down at her from a Will Barnet print on the wall. CNN provided background noise to keep her company. The bike was one of the reasons she'd chosen this Airbnb. She enjoyed working out in the privacy of her home space. She pedaled with moderate effort, only mildly sweating.

Kathleen grabbed the remote control from a tray table next to her bike and muted the TV.

"You first," Emily said, sitting on the couch.

Kathleen stopped pedaling and told Emily what she'd learned at the funeral home. "I've been Googling for stories about Wayne's funeral. There hasn't been any follow-up on the first story."

"He was pretty well known," Emily said. "I looked into him myself while you were in jail. He appeared as cocounsel on dozens of cases. There were several newspaper quotes. But there wasn't much on his death and nothing about sex charges."

"Wealthy people hire publicists to keep things like overdoses and bad behavior out of the papers. If they're not celebrities, the stories disappear fast when the publicists give reporters plausible but false explanations. People worry about fake news, but they should worry more about the news they *don't* see.

"I once had a wealthy client who jumped out of a sixth-floor window on Fifty-Seventh Street after a weekend of chain-smoking crack. There was only one small story from the AP and it died—unlike my client, who fell on an awning. Lucky in life and the media. But it's crazy that they've been able to keep the child porn investigation out of the news."

"My turn," Emily said. "Equally crazy. It's Angela. She's in prison. Sharon's Angela."

"You saw her?" Kathleen came off the bike, shouting when the house-arrest cuff banged into the side of the bike. "*Ow!*" Pain rang out from her ankle, the cuff scraping her skin. She still wasn't used to accommodating the extra bulk.

Emily started to get up. "Are you okay? Your skin is irritated. It's really red."

Kathleen sat on the edge of the couch, slipping her fingers between the cuff and her skin. "It's blistering. They obviously don't design shackles with dry middle-age skin in mind."

"Or for exercise."

"I'm fine. Go on, tell me. Angela?"

Emily exhaled. "She's a puppy trainer. She knew Sharon was dead. At least I didn't have to tell her that. She sent one of her nephews to the building when Sharon stopped answering her calls. She said her nephew spoke to one of the maintenance men. Then she saw the news article—the one and only, like Wayne."

"No need to hire a publicist for that story to die," Kathleen said. "Did she have any idea why someone would kill Sharon? Any enemies or stalkers? Anything like that?"

"No. Angela said that, as far as she knew, Sharon had only one secret. She said Sharon was a cautious person but not really a fearful one, except when it came to that."

"What was it?"

"Sharon had a baby with a rich guy a long time ago, way before Angela met her. She put the baby up for adoption. He paid her a lot of money and convinced her it would be better for the baby. But Angela said she was always upset about it."

"So why was she afraid? Did Angela know about the nondisclosure agreement?"

"Yeah, but she thought Sharon was scared about more than that. Sharon wanted to know her son so badly that Angela had told her not to worry about the NDA. Angela told Sharon to try to find her son, at least to find out if he was okay. She told Sharon to put her name on the state birth registry, where adoptees can find their bio parents after they grow up. Even though the agreement said there would be a two-million-dollar penalty if she revealed anything, Angela said all Sharon's money was hidden anyway to avoid getting busted for tax evasion. Sharon rented her apartment and didn't own anything that could be taken away. So, Angela told her, and I quote, 'Fuck a nondisclosure agreement. Go find your fucking kid.'

"But Sharon told Angela that an adoption registry wouldn't list her or the baby. And, more than that, the father was powerful. She was afraid of something bad happening if she went back on her word."

Kathleen thought about that and shook her head with doubt. "I don't get it. I find it hard to believe she was worried about her safety. There's not enough reason for the father to kill her if that's the theory, and I just never got a killer vibe from him. I've always trusted my instincts about people."

"She *did* end up dead," Emily said. "And she ended up dead right after she contacted both you and Wayne, the only two people she knew who had a connection to Client 13. Maybe you need to rethink your take on him."

Kathleen said, "You're right about one thing: everyone who knew about her relationship with my client ended up in legal trouble and/or dead. Even Angela is in jail."

Emily frowned. "I don't think Angela is in that category. Angela said she's an addict and relapsed. She's been back in prison for at least six months, long before all the crazy stuff started. She violated her parole when she caught a DUI."

As they thought over the new information, Emily brought her takeout bag to the coffee table, the scent of curry strengthening. "There is one other thing. Angela said the adoption was weird. That's why the adoption registry wouldn't work."

"How so?"

"The father didn't want a paper trail. Back then, states were already talking about changing laws to make it easier for adopted kids to find their biological parents. The father trusted his nondisclosure agreements more than adoption laws. Sharon had the baby in a hospital under an alias with fake ID he gave her, and somebody paid cash for her hospital stay. There was never any official record that Sharon had a connection to the baby, no adoption papers or birth certificate with her name on them. She went in, had the baby, and handed him off to the father's people."

"A private adoption," Kathleen said. "Wayne would have been the attorney."

"No, that's not even it. There was no adoption at all. Angela thought Sharon was checked into the hospital with the new mother's name. The way Angela told it, the father's people found a couple who wanted a baby and had them move to a new town. They probably signed an NDA too. The baby's hospital record and original birth certificate would have their names as the parents. The biological father wouldn't have to worry about an adult child looking for him though an adoption registry. The parents never even knew the biological father's identity because it was all done through a third party. Sharon told Angela that the one thing she learned from the experience is that money will buy *anything*.

"But Angela said Sharon saved something from the hospital: the hospital bracelet she wore, and the baby's bracelet. Hospitals give the bracelets to the parents when they're checking out, a souvenir to take home after you have a baby. It was the one loose end the father didn't think of." Emily pulled her phone out from her backpack. "Angela couldn't remember the name of the baby, but she gave me her mother's address, where Angela lived before prison. Sharon used to stay there with her; the hospital bracelets are there. She said we could get them if we thought it would help us figure out what happened to Sharon. If Angela is right, the bracelets will tell the adoptive mother's name.

"Hector has Skye tomorrow night. We can go to Angela's mother's after I get off work. I want to find the adoptive family. They're the key to figuring out what's going on."

"Where is Angela's apartment?" Kathleen asked. "I have to get clearance to travel."

"East Harlem." Emily read on her phone. "Two-fifty East One Hundred and Seventeenth Street."

"I'll call Probation tomorrow to say I'm going to an NA meeting. There's one in East Harlem tomorrow night. POs love when their clients go to twelve-step meetings. We just have to go to a meeting after Angela's house so I can get a sign-in sheet signed."

"I'm good," Emily replied, dismissing the idea.

"It could be good for you to learn something about the disease that runs rampant in our family. Count your blessings you didn't inherit it." Kathleen felt a deep satisfaction at hearing herself say *our family*, even given the context. "But you can go home after Angela's house and I can go to the meeting alone."

"I'll think about it. Do you want curried chicken?" Emily asked as she walked to the kitchen for plates. "It's Jamaican from One Hundred and Twenty-Fifth Street."

"No, thanks. I ate already."

Emily returned and began serving herself.

"Now, tell me what else is wrong," Kathleen said. "You seemed upset when you came home, but you're clearly not upset about anything you've told me so far."

Emily exhaled, her sadness palpable. "Rusty flunked out. I'm sure it's my fault—from all the upheaval in my life."

CHAPTER

56

THE NEXT MORNING, the mayor's caravan made plodding progress through stop-and-go traffic on the Cross Bronx Expressway, heading for the funeral of the last subway-bombing victim. Rachel Ajiboye, the EMS worker. It had taken two weeks for Intergovernmental Affairs to get waivers and visas for the extended family to travel from Nigeria. They'd arrived in time to pull the plug. Ajiboye had already been brain-dead. Over the weeks since the bombing, the pain Emily felt for the victims had dulled to a low hum, but it sparked back to life as soon as the SUV pulled up a block away from the funeral home. Emily could viscerally *feel* the pain of Ajiboye's children. They were teenagers, just like Emily had been when her father died. She knew the disbelief, confusion, and loss they were feeling.

Martha spoke in a low tone to Emily as they left the car, double-timing to keep up with the mayor's long strides as he and his security detail led their group. "We're late. They probably held up the service for us. That's all we need today. The media never wants to hear about traffic unless they're blaming the mayor for it."

The street in front of the funeral home was barricaded. Beyond the barricades, uniformed city workers and members of the public packed the street, too many to fit inside for the service. Large black speakers had been strapped to light poles to bring audio to the overflow crowd. Firefighters and police stood in formation in the street directly in front of the funeral home entrance. Emily looked around with a start as she followed Mayor Sullivan and Martha toward the entrance. The firefighters and police were turning their backs on the mayor, a rolling about-face as he passed.

"Oh, holy fuck," muttered Marlo, cleanly shaved now and wearing flats and a black Hillary Clinton pantsuit.

Martha hissed, "I told him to cancel that damn fund raiser."

It had been a mistake for the mayor to go ahead with a fund raiser a mere week after the bombing. CNN, Fox, and MSNBC had talked about it then, and now they would resume talking about it. As Emily walked past the sea of uniformed men, each officer glaring at their group before turning, she felt as if she'd been punched in the solar plexus.

*   *   *

The bleak mood continued after they returned to City Hall. The mayor railed at Roger while they crossed City Hall plaza toward the building. In the press office, Martha power-walked while reading her iPhone, nearly banging into Emily's desk. "The *Post* already has an interview with Ajiboye's mother. They got her to say she was disappointed in the mayor for not suspending his campaign until her daughter was buried." Martha picked up a pad and pen from her desk and headed back toward the door. "I'll be in the Bullpen with the mayor."

Videos of the cops turning their backs on the mayor were going viral, only locally for now; #SULLIVAN was trending on Twitter, and Emily needed to work on getting counter-tweets out before it trended nationally. The campaign would be booking surrogates on cable news already to talk about the funeral.

Max turned from his computer. He hadn't gone to the funeral. "How could the mayor be held accountable for a two-week delay? He couldn't have suspended his campaign for that long. It's ridiculous after everything we did to get the mother a waiver. It's the State Department's fault."

"I know," Emily said, only half listening to him.

Max leaned on his desk, smiling at Emily. He wasn't getting the hint from her body language or minimal conversation. He seemed more interested in her every day. "So, what did you do yesterday, Em? We missed you."

Max calling her Em annoyed her, and the comment about her being missed made her shudder inside. They weren't that close, and his small talk felt inappropriate when everyone in the office was scrambling to do damage control. Plus, Hector called her Em. She didn't want to think about Hector. He'd been angry at her when they'd talked last. They'd argued after she mentioned her feeling that someone might be following her. She hadn't felt better until she'd convinced Hector not to worry and he'd stopped being angry, and she'd been disconcertingly upset about their argument afterward.

She'd been thinking about Hector more than she liked lately. It bothered her that her feelings for Hector had strengthened because she was under stress. That was so *typical*.

She sent a document to her printer with proposed tweets for Martha to look at.

"Em?" Max repeated.

Emily turned toward him and held up a hand. "The mayor's trending, and I need clearance for some tweets." Emily swiveled to her printer and grabbed the paper to bring to the Bullpen. Out of the corner of her eye, she glimpsed a tide of anger crossing Max's features.

She looked back at him. "I'm sorry. No offense, Max. I didn't mean to be curt." Max was always trying too hard with her, but that wasn't an excuse for meanness. There was no crime in him having a crush on her.

He waved her off. "It's nothing. You're busy."

CHAPTER

57

KATHLEEN STOPPED HALFWAY up the cement steps that connected the lower and upper portions of Washington Heights. Brick apartment buildings formed walls cradling the staircase. Kathleen couldn't travel far for groceries without the hassle of getting preapproval, but the cuff's GPS didn't count vertical distance, so she climbed to the grocery stores on 187th Street and Fort Washington Avenue. The first time she'd walked these stairs, she'd counted 130 cement steps in sets of about fifteen, with a landing between each set. She climbed slowly but surely now. She didn't mind—it was great exercise. She could reward herself with brunch in a street café once she arrived.

But she was winded now and had to rest. The ankle cuff under her pant leg was chafing her skin again. It was a hot day too. Sweat pasted her blouse to her skin. She would have worn a sundress or shorts on a day like today, but if she did, her ankle cuff would be visible. As it was, a close look would reveal the awkward thickness at her ankle. Luckily, few people looked closely at women her age. She appreciated her invisibility today.

Over the last few years, after she'd entirely abandoned her illegal lifestyle, she'd settled into a quiet, safe, anonymous life.

That had now been upended. When she'd met with her new lawyer, all he could say was that he was trying to get more information about the evidence that had led the district attorney to bring such serious charges against her. He didn't know enough to tell her anything other than the bad news about the lengthy prison term she faced. Still, despite her fear, Kathleen had a deep conviction that her current legal problem would eventually work itself out. She was innocent. She only hoped that meant something.

At least she had her health—the grateful refrain of a person on the downhill side of sixty-five. And tonight she would go with Emily to Angela's house. She looked forward to even the possibility of getting more answers.

She held her face up to the sun and resumed her climb. She might as well appreciate the summer day. And that she had her granddaughter and great-granddaughter in her life. And that she had the chance to have a relationship with her daughter. If having to fight a bogus criminal case was the price of admission for that, it would be worth it twice over.

She walked a few paces on the last flat landing between steps and continued upward, only a dozen more steps. It was quiet now, no one else climbing on the vertical street.

Almost to the top, Fort Washington Avenue became visible to her as her head came to sidewalk level. She smiled with the accomplishment, her thighs burning. She felt a breeze that traveled the two blocks from the cliffs overlooking the Hudson River. Just a few more steps upward.

Above, a lanky, curly-haired teenage boy ran past on the sidewalk. A red flying object drew her eyes, a Frisbee whizzing by in his direction. His hand flew up and he caught it.

A man paused at the top of the stairs. Sallow. Baseball cap. His eyes met hers momentarily.

Her eyes followed the sound of a group of teenage boys laughing above, behind the man. The teenagers were running on the sidewalk, following the first boy. A tall kid with an auburn Afro jumped to catch the returning Frisbee, reaching back in the air to grab the high pass.

He bumped into the man with the baseball cap.

"Sorry, sorry." The tall boy's words were drowned out by a loud pop.

A burning sensation seared Kathleen's head and snapped it sideways. Stars exploded. She grunted and fell, halfway onto the sidewalk, at the top of the stairs. Her elbow and shoulder cracked against the rough cement. A burst of pain. Wetness flowed down her face, into her eyes. Blood.

She heard a woman gasp, *"Oh my god!"*

She realized it was her.

Blackness.

58

Emily's phone rang inside her pocketbook. She'd missed the call by the time she pulled it out. Kathleen. She tried to call back, but it rang a couple of times and went to voice mail. Probably a pocket call.

Thea sat at her desk, working on an assignment Max had given her. Emily looked over at Max surfing the web. Emily could see the local news station's logo on his screen. Martha and Roger were in a huddle at her desk. Martha was waving around a poster that had mysteriously gone up on lampposts all over Tribeca. It featured what looked like a mug shot of the mayor and said, *WANTED: Mayor Derick Sullivan. Last seen running for president, not running the city.*

"The mayor's livid," Martha said. "What an effing day!"

Roger shrugged. "It's just the way things are in New York. It's a tough town for mayors."

"Hey, Emily." Max turned to her, excited. "Aren't you staying in Washington Heights?"

Emily pulled her attention from her eavesdropping. "Yeah." At least Max had called her by her proper name. Maybe she'd given him enough annoyed looks for him to get the message.

"There was a gangland hit in broad daylight." Max's lips parted into a smile. He was enjoying telling her a juicy piece of news. He lived for crap like that.

She would have preferred to ignore him, to get the message across that she wasn't impressed. But she *was* curious. She rolled her chair a couple of inches toward him. On his PC, Emily recognized the scene where the reporter stood, at 187th Street and Fort Washington Avenue. Behind the reporter, Emily could make out the sidewalk cafés of the Monkey Bar and Refried Beans, a Mexican restaurant.

"Just a short time ago, a woman was shot here in this quiet section of Upper Manhattan," the reporter said. "The police have released surveillance video of the shooting. We warn you that the video may be disturbing."

Emily had a bad feeling. Her jaw clenched. In the video, a man stood at the top of the 187th Street steps wearing a baseball cap that shadowed his face. A group of teenage boys were running by on the street above the stairs. One of them bumped him. The man was pointing a gun down at a small woman, her face blurred out. She was below him on the steps, and—

Emily gasped and stood, her chair rolling backward. "Kathleen!"

The others turned to look, and Martha moved toward her. Emily glanced back, hearing Roger take in a breath as he watched the auto-replay of the film snippet.

Emily watched the auto-replay loop. The shooter was pointing a handgun. The kid bumped into him. Kathleen's head jerked. Even with her face blurred, Emily knew it was her. Kathleen fell sideways and the shooter trotted down the stairs.

The reporter appeared again. "The woman was shot in the head. Her condition is as yet unknown."

Holding back tears, Emily grabbed her pocketbook from a desk drawer. "I've gotta go."

She felt a hand on her arm and turned to Martha. "What's the matter?" Martha asked.

Emily spoke softly. "That's my grandmother."

PART IV

CHAPTER

59

LAUREN MET UP with Emily in the surgical waiting room in New York Presbyterian Hospital on West 165th Street. They say in vinyl chairs with unforgiving chrome armrests. Rain careened down the waiting room windows. Fox News played on a television high on a wall in a corner of the large room. Lauren rubbed her temples.

A family group had gathered at the far side of the waiting room near windows that overlooked hospital buildings across Fort Washington Avenue, a view nearly obscured by the sheet of water outside the window. There were at least a dozen people in the family, children and adults of multiple generations. The adults appeared worried, but the children were happy to be with their siblings or cousins.

"She had you on all her forms," Emily said, drawing Lauren's attention back to her. "Health proxy. Power of attorney. HIPAA."

"You said she had a lot of friends."

Emily looked thoughtful. "She seemed to. But I guess she wanted you."

"I'm not sure I appreciate it. Who said I wanted responsibility for her?"

"*Mom.* We don't even know if she's okay."

Lauren fought back tears. The fact that she cared about her mother burned like bile. She'd built a great life for herself, one in which her mother had never existed. She'd been able to forget about her, the same way she'd nearly forgotten about her own drug problem after decades of not being around drugs. She'd thought she'd let go of her hatred for her mother years ago. She'd never actually forgiven her, but she'd settled into a neutral attitude, somewhere between hatred and not giving a damn. Indifference. And forgetting. That was where she'd ended up. But maybe indifference was just resentment waiting to be triggered. And that was exactly what had happened—she was so angry.

She'd also been stunned to learn that her mother's story was not what she'd perceived as a teenager, a perception she'd carried forward for decades. She'd never even considered that her memory of the things that had happened to her between the ages of ten and fifteen might not be the whole story. She hadn't entirely bought into the story Kathleen had told her and Emily, but there was enough truth in it that it called into question Lauren's entire idea of her own life history.

Lauren murmured to Emily, although she was still gazing across the room, "She's only been back in my life for a week, and look what a mess it's been."

"Not everything is her fault, Mom."

Lauren pondered that.

"What did Carl say when you told him?" Emily asked.

"He knows she was shot. I didn't tell him the theories about Client 13 or the attorney dying."

Emily's eyebrows raised. "Really?"

Lauren could see the treadmill picking up speed inside her daughter's brain. She locked eyes with Emily, wanting to convey her seriousness. "The last thing Carl needs is to be associated with some sort of criminal conspiracy involving my family. Getting off desk duty and putting his career back on track is his key motivator right now. I. Won't. Let. *Anything.* Complicate. That. Are we clear?"

Emily put up her hands. "I get it."

Lauren softened her tone. "Stress is terrible for MS. The trial drug is working. We can't let anything screw that up. You and I have to be on the same page about that."

"Okay." Emily took Lauren's hand. "I won't say anything either. We'll find out what's going on ourselves."

Before Lauren could tell Emily that this was not what she meant, Emily took out her phone. "Look at this." She opened her photo app and showed Lauren a picture of a list of code names and phone numbers.

"That from Kathleen's book."

"I stopped off at her safe-deposit box. The numbers are definitely encoded. I did reverse lookups of a bunch of the numbers already and didn't come up with anyone likely to be connected to Kathleen. But I doubt it's a sophisticated code, or she would have needed a computer to create it. Her using a physical phone book makes me think the entries were made before that kind of encoding app was publicly available. She probably shifted digits up or down in each phone number. I'm sure Tabu can break the code if I can't do it."

Lauren felt her blood speeding up, worried about Emily getting more involved. She knew how stubborn her daughter could be. "Jesus, Em. I doubt she'd be happy about you invading her privacy. And what are you planning to do? Call every man on the list and ask whether he killed Sharon or, better yet, tried to kill your grandmother?"

"Cute, Mom. No. It's just a backup plan. We may not need any of it . . . if she's okay."

Emily looked up toward the entrance to the waiting room. A tall doctor—at least six foot ten—approached them in blue surgical garb. His shoulders stooped as if he'd spent his entire life trying not to make people feel small.

"Ms. Davis?"

"Yes." Lauren rose.

"How is she?" Emily asked, also standing.

"She came through the surgery well. The bullet only grazed her scalp. It caused a concussion and required stitches. Scalp wounds bleed quite a bit, so I'm glad to say the injury looked far worse on the news video than it actually was. She did break her arm in the fall and tore her rotator cuff. The break required us to put in pins. We repaired her rotator cuff while we were in there. She has a fractured rib too, so she'll be sore for a while from that as well."

"Can we see her?" Emily asked.

"She's in recovery. It will be a couple of hours."

CHAPTER

60

H E REVELED IN the dark web's deepest places. Secret power. He thought about it as he walked through the wine cellar to the windowless room where he stored his collected weaponry in display cases and had an explosives workshop. Explosives were yet another interest he and Jackson shared. He rarely had a chance to use any of it, but on those occasions when he literally *needed* to blow off steam, he arranged foreign travel. His team picked up women who wouldn't be missed and cleaned up the mess behind him.

But the family had rules. New York City was off limits, except in extraordinary circumstances. So he'd gone a bit rogue. That would never be a complete surprise to his family. Going rogue was in his genes. And he had plenty of his own money to permit it.

He was furious that Kathleen Harris was still alive. She'd made it through surgery. She was a hardy bitch, as the ex-cop had called her. His mood had become increasingly black.

The job had been to kill her. If you wanted something done right, you had to do it yourself. The hitman had incredibly poor judgment; a poor excuse for a professional. You couldn't let the excitement of the kill make you take a bad shot. You had to know when to wait for a clean shot, even if it meant waiting an hour or another day. Foiled by a teenage Frisbee game.

Un-fucking-believable. The hitman wouldn't receive his second payment, but at least he was already safely out of the country, back to his homeland, posing no risk of apprehension for either of them.

Still, the man mulled over the failed hit, his belly scorching. He blamed his family for the outcome. The killer was nearly an amateur, not one of the normal mercenaries the family kept on retainer. The normal for-hires weren't available, or he wouldn't have had to turn to the dark web at all. The family had put a foot out to trip him. Had put a foot on his neck, more like it. He'd been told he was on his own if he continued down this path. He'd raged about it. But he didn't need them. Money could buy anything.

For now, Kathleen Harris was out of commission, which was a good thing. He had other fish to fry. Or, more aptly, bitch to fry. Then he'd get back to the whoremonger, if she ever became compos mentis again. Who knew with old people? Sometimes the simplest surgery could mean the end of their life as they'd known it, the shock and morphine taking their last marbles. Of course, she wasn't *that* old; he'd probably have to circle back to Kathleen later.

There was an upside, though. The dark-web booking of the old lady's hit had gone off without a hitch, a thrilling new tool in his arsenal. An enjoyable middle finger to the family. Even if the result hadn't been perfect, he'd found the whole process amusing: He placed the job anonymously on a dark-web site. The bidders named their price. It wasn't so different from a government RFP, the contract awarded to the lowest-bidding of the qualified contractors. Of course, it wasn't easy to determine who was qualified. Even with all the anonymity of the dark web, the bidders couldn't confess to their past successes to prove how qualified they were or provide references. No one was that stupid.

The customer made his deposit in the website's Bitcoin wallet with each transaction. It was as easy as paying on Venmo or PayPal.

But there were apparently limits, because there seemed to be a problem with his bid for the next hit. No one wanted the job. He thought he knew why. No one bid on jobs without doing some research first. They probably performed a quick background check on the victim. Kill an ex-madam/ex-con, okay. Criminals killed criminals all the time. But it wasn't easy getting away with killing a pretty, young, white City Hall staffer who didn't do drugs. Her death would be newsworthy. And it wouldn't be just one snarky tabloid headline.

Bottom line, the family wouldn't let him use their toy soldiers, and now he couldn't even find an independent contractor. Perhaps this should have been a sign for him to give up, but he enjoyed a challenge too much.

And Emily had to go. She was a loose end that needed to be cauterized. She was the only witness to Sharon's takedown. Emily and the old woman had been thick as running mates since then. If Kathleen Harris had told anyone her secrets, it was Emily Silverman. And now the man's hackers said Emily had new photographs on her phone. Lists of telephone numbers. It would be only a matter of time before she began reaching Kathleen's former customers, mucking up silt, narrowing things down. Although the story of Sharon's death was unlikely to unravel that way, Emily was tenacious. He could never go on with his life knowing there was anyone out there who could pull that thread. He'd mulled it over for a while and had now made up his mind: two people needed to be removed from the family's risk factors.

He exited the polished mahogany doors that fronted his townhouse, walking toward Central Park. The breeze carried jasmine. Fifth Avenue was wet and clean, guarded by pretentiously uniformed doormen with gold-braided hats. He didn't buy their disguise. He wore his own mild-mannered public persona as he strode down Fifth. He had the Clark Kent thing down to a fine art, his true self safely hidden after years of daily practice.

No one who saw him would ever guess that he was headed to the Street, to the darkest web, so dark there were no internet connections. A place where word of mouth was still the primary mode of communication. Even burner phones were barely trusted. He knew a guy, someone with connections. He got a charge at the thought. With all the world's technological advances, nothing surpassed the excitement of human contact of the darkest variety. So much so he wished he could risk doing the killing himself. But second best—death, fast and remote—would have to do.

CHAPTER

61

KATHLEEN WAS ANTSY to get out of the hospital. She'd asked the nurses twice since she'd woken up to their prodding and thermometers at dawn. Her shoulder throbbed from deep inside, and her head ached dully below the buffer of "happy pills" the nurse had given her. With her free hand, she felt the large bandage on her head. Her other arm was casted nearly to her underarm. Her shoulder was heavily bandaged too. She had no fever, and the doctor who'd made rounds had hinted that, although she'd have a bald spot for a while from where they'd needed to stitch up her scalp and she'd have lots of bruising, she'd be home recuperating in short order. It was hard to fathom how quickly hospitals released you nowadays, but she wasn't complaining. She only wished she were going home to her old apartment. She longed for it.

Thankfully, the cops had gone along with the doctor's demand that the ankle bracelet be removed. It was out of juice now, but no probation officer had arrived at her bedside to arrest her. Kathleen guessed they could read the newspapers and knew where she was. An orderly had brought a paper for her to see. She suspected his supervisors wouldn't have approved.

He grinned at her when he handed it to her as if he imagined everyone was happy for fifteen minutes of fame. The headline blared, Grandmob: Gangland Hit on Elderly Woman.

Sitting up in her partially raised bed, she shook her head. *Grandmob.* Someone was paid to think up shit like that. The idea of a mob connection had come out of thin air. She didn't appreciate the "elderly" remark either.

At the bottom it said, Sixty-Eight-Year-Old Woman Expected to Survive.

She was glad for that, at least. She was glad, too, for the paper's grainy screenshot of her attacker and a group picture of the teenagers who accidentally foiled the attack but no photo of her face. There were advantages to using a fake Facebook profile: at least the media had to work to find a photo of her. It wouldn't take long, though, given her recent mug shot. And then the press would really start digging. The next headline would probably call her "Grandmob Aronist."

She had asked the orderly and he'd told her there was no police presence outside her hospital room, so it didn't look like they were worried there would be another hit. Or maybe they didn't care. In the middle of that thought, the door opened. She lurched backward, her adrenaline skyrocketing, pain exploding in her shoulder at her sudden movement. "*Oooh.*"

Lauren entered the hospital room, looking around and half smiling politely. Kathleen's fear and pain settled. Her chest filled with an aching love for her only child. She could see Lauren as a baby just below the surface of her grown-woman face. The child she'd diapered and taught to walk and talked over everything with before their lives went to hell. Her heart keened with the pain of that loss, despite her new spark of hope for a future relationship. Lauren was claiming her enough to show up at the hospital.

"You're still an early riser?" Kathleen asked, hiding the fear she'd felt when the door opened. She didn't want Lauren to see her initial panic and decide she wasn't worth the risk of knowing. She remembered how vigilant Lauren had been as a child. She could only imagine what Lauren's watchfulness had morphed into now that she was an adult.

"Yes, up by dawn most days," Lauren said.

When Lauren was in elementary school, long before Kathleen began doing drugs, she would wake up before the alarm rang.

She would sit quietly at the kitchen table, dressed for school, her teeth brushed, her Princess Leia backpack beside her chair. Kathleen would make her lunch while Lauren ate breakfast. Lauren would pack her lunch box into her perfectly organized backpack, as if she intuited that her life was about to go to hell and she needed to have everything in order.

For the millionth time, Kathleen imagined how hard it must have been for Lauren when, one day, she realized her mother wouldn't be coming out to make her breakfast or lunch anymore. How lonely had it been for her in the mornings? How long had it taken Lauren to stop expecting Kathleen to do those regular things? Weeks? Months? Kathleen had no recollection of how Lauren had reacted, because she hadn't been mentally present in any meaningful way. The shame and guilt she felt about that washed over her in unbearable waves now that her daughter was standing in front of her.

"Emily didn't inherit the morning-person gene," Lauren said. "I guess you've noticed."

"She doesn't get enough sleep. But she's up in time for whatever she has to do. She's an impressive woman, your daughter. Perhaps it's best that she's not always ahead of the starter gun."

Lauren grimaced, then chuckled. "I'm proud of her."

"You did a great job with her—not that it's my place to say."

"Thank you." Lauren took a seat next to the bed. "Now that you're fully awake, I was wondering what happened with the police."

"I told them I don't know who it was or the motive, which is true. I doubt they believe me. They've got the organized crime unit on it. They think the shooting is connected to the arson. They probably think I owe money to loan sharks. I suspect they're running themselves ragged tracking down every known loan shark. My lawyer won't let me talk to them about the arson. I don't know anything about it anyway, so I'm not inclined to talk to them about it. We're discussing hiring a forensics expert to try to decipher what happened with my bank accounts."

"That sounds like a good plan."

"Lauren, is it possible for you to do one errand for me?"

"What is it?" Lauren's face folded in on itself. Suspicion. As if Kathleen were about to ask Lauren to cop drugs for her.

Kathleen's heart plummeted with disappointment at Lauren's reaction.

"You know how upset Emily is about Rusty," Kathleen said.

"Yes. Although I think it's the least of our problems right now."

"I called Puppies-in-Prison. I bought the dog for Emily this morning. They take credit cards. Can you believe they wanted five thousand dollars? I paid by phone, but someone needs to pick him up."

Lauren's eyes became tender. "Really? In the middle of all this?"

"Especially in the middle of all this. We don't know how *this* is going to turn out. And I had to buy Rusty before they put him up for adoption. I want it to be a surprise for Emily. She might balk about the money if the dog's not right in front of her already."

"Okay," Lauren said, seeming to warm to the idea, probably imagining how happy both Skye and Emily would be.

Kathleen handed Lauren a scrap of paper with the director's name and a phone number on it.

Lauren looked down at it. "I'll call them later."

They sat silently for a moment.

"There is one other thing I wanted to talk to you about while we're alone," Lauren said. "About Dad."

Kathleen braced herself, her emotions churning at the fraught discussion ahead.

Lauren took a deep breath. "Before he died, when he went to rehab, you had . . . men in. I figured out pretty quickly what was going on."

Kathleen nodded, not denying the ugly fact.

"Dad had issues, but at least he was loyal. You betrayed him and put me at risk, and he wasn't there to protect me. I hated you for that."

Kathleen forced herself to ask, afraid, "Did anything happen to you?"

Lauren shook her head. "Still, why did you do it? You stole the last vestige of family from me."

Kathleen took a breath. "I have no excuse. I loved your father, but I deeply resented him too. I don't want to diminish your memory of him, because he wasn't a bad man. He had an illness. He was sick; we both were. But I was so angry that he brought the addict lifestyle to our home and marriage. I take responsibility. I didn't have to try crack, and neither of us realized the addiction would take hold after only one time. But, after that, I wasn't in my right mind. When he went to rehab, he left me with no money, a raging addiction, nearly constant hallucinations, and I was very, very angry. Resentment and addiction are a combustible combination."

"I know that," Lauren said quietly.

"I am so, so sorry you lived through that, and for everything else that happened. I have never been able to forgive myself." Wiping away tears, afraid of what Lauren might say, Kathleen added, "I know I don't deserve it . . . I can't fully make up for it, but I hope you'll let me try."

The door flew open and Kathleen stiffened, Lauren's chair screeching as she stood in surprise.

62

H E FOUND HIS guy in East Harlem, better known as El Barrio until whites and Chinese took over much of it and forgot the old name. At East 116th Street, he entered a cuchifritos restaurant that kept up with the rising rents only because the restaurant owner had bought the entire building when East Harlem property was cheap. Thirty years later and the restaurant still served up fried and stewed Puerto Rican delicacies like pig ears in rich tomato sauce. It was surprisingly good stuff.

The air smelled thickly of tomato sauce, cilantro, and boiling grease. The fry cook, a hairnet covering his black hair and ponytail, looked up at the man when he walked in the door. Teardrop tattoos dripped from the fry cook's eye down his cheek—each one representing a murder. The tears condemned him to a life on the Street, if not prison. Stupid.

The fry cook raised an eyebrow when he saw the man. He chucked his forehead toward a door at the back of the narrow place, then leaned over to say something to the short, pudgy woman next to him, who took over the cooking.

The man followed the cook down an aisle that separated two rows of Formica tables, past wooden doors that said *Damas* and *Caballeros*, and out a screen door. In a cemented-over backyard area lined with garbage bins, the fry cook stopped and lit a cigarette.

The cook inhaled deep smoke and exhaled, signaling the man closer with the hand that held the cigarette. He murmured next to the man's ear, "Twenty thousand now, twenty thousand after."

"You need to make it a sexual assault. We need a motive. Just don't enter her or it will trace back to you. Make it an *attempted* sexual assault." He handed the fry cook a copy of Emily's LinkedIn profile page with her photo. "It should be fun. I wish I could do it myself."

The fry cook studied the photo. "Forty thousand now. Forty thousand after."

The man felt anger gathering like fast clouds during a Caribbean rainy season. He didn't like the guy trying to take charge of the deal. He didn't like being on the short end when it came to power. He didn't give a fuck how many people this guy had killed. His jaw quivered with outrage. "*What are you talking about?*"

The fry cook's lips were so close, the man could feel the heat of his breath. "White girl. Young. Pretty. She's not in the Life. That means more heat. And more money." He paused. "Deal or no deal?"

* * *

Emily backed noisily through the door to Kathleen's hospital room, her arms full of a flower-and-balloon arrangement. Hospital staff had put a DO NOT ENTER sign on the door and kept it closed at Lauren's request the night before, in case any reporters showed up. Relieved at seeing Kathleen bright eyed and talking to her mother, Emily grinned.

"You're awake!" She put down the flowers on the windowsill. "Do you remember us visiting yesterday?"

"It's hazy."

"I was worried." Emily kissed the older woman on the cheek. "Are you in pain?" she asked as she pulled up a chair on the side of the bed opposite her mother.

"Not so bad. They gave me a lot of pain meds last night. I was grateful for it, but I told them to cut the narcotics down today. I need all my senses about me." Kathleen shifted uncomfortably in the bed. "Even though it is a bit painful."

"We need to talk about next steps," Emily added gently. "Are you up to it?"

"Yes, okay," Kathleen said, although she sounded doubtful.

"Here's the deal." Emily sat at the edge of her chair. "We need to figure out how to keep you safe, we need to know who Client 13 is, and I have to go to Angela's house."

Emily's eyes felt gritty, but adrenaline and caffeine had beaten back the fatigue. She'd been up half the night trying to figure things out. Thankfully, she had figured one thing out: she needed to treat this insane situation like a work project. She had to take the reins and deal with it methodically, gather all the available information, and make a plan. You were either a leader or a victim at times like this.

"First off, I'm not looking to steamroll the team here." Emily ignored Lauren's raised eyebrows at the mention of a "team." "But I'm going to get the baby bracelets. It would have been better if you were with me, Kathleen, but it's not necessary. We can't wait to get the full story about the adoption of Sharon's baby. That's the first order of business. Once we put together an indisputable picture of the truth that we can provide to the cops, we'll be able to hand them a new suspect. They're not going to remove their claws from your neck until they have somebody else to grab. We have to get to the bottom of this story. Maybe they'll even try to protect you then."

Emily could see the openness in Kathleen's face, but Lauren was clearly skeptical.

Emily turned to her mother. "Until we can bring this to the cops through normal channels, we need to keep control of any evidence we gather that might exonerate Kathleen. She has to have an airtight explanation for everything going on, because the way I see it at this point, the cops will shoot down anything we say that pokes holes in their case against her. They have a sweet case with Kathleen as the defendant and will never willingly admit that was a mistake."

"Emily, can I say something?" Kathleen said.

Emily leaned back in her chair. "Sure."

"I don't know that I can allow you to take this risk on my behalf. I would never forgive myself if you or Skye became collateral damage."

"I agree," Lauren said.

"Hector has Skye tonight," Emily said, prepared for this objection. "Hector's mom can keep her for a couple more nights if needed. Skye had been doing fine with family. And nobody connected to the killer is going to know I'm asking questions. Why would they?"

Lauren began to object.

"Mom, you always said, 'If you don't stand for something, you'll fall for anything,' " Emily said. "And with Kathleen in the hospital, whoever the bad guys are will probably be lulled into thinking they've got nothing to worry about from her. It's good that Kathleen is off their radar for a bit. It will give me a chance to get ahead of this." Emily glanced at the closed door to the room, then back at Lauren and Kathleen. "We really need to hire a private security guard for that door, just in case. It's crazy that anyone can just walk in here."

Before Kathleen or Lauren could answer, the door opened. The tall doctor in surgical blues entered, a crowd of residents following.

"Good morning," he said with a jolly bedside manner. "Are you ready to go home?"

63

FREDDY WAS CHUNKY—"HEALTHY," his *abuela* called it, making it sound like a good thing when he knew there wasn't a damn thing good about it. Still, he had to love 'uela for always having a way of making him feel better about himself. And being fat *was* good for one thing: it made people underestimate him. He didn't stand out at all now, watching the apartment building where his target was staying.

He sat in a double-parked car on Bennett Avenue. Gnarly old trees canopied the block of six-story apartment buildings. He was barely worth noticing on a street where plenty of Dominicans lived. He sat in a line of double-parked cars, all of them except his waiting for alternate-side parking to end. Freddy wasn't the only driver sitting in his car, so his car didn't stand out. He felt cloaked in an invisibility blanket by his innocuous looks.

A wiry kid waited anxiously next to him in the passenger seat. Junior was six inches shorter than Freddy and had a baby face that made it hard for him to get into R-rated movies unless others from the gang went with him. It would be the kid's first kill. Freddy was the backup, because they couldn't chance Junior choking on his first gig. Cesar had already said they weren't going to try to make it look like an attempted rape. That was too much trouble, and it only gave cover to the client while making their gang look like animals. Cesar didn't want nobody thinking they couldn't get a girl without *taking* it. He said they'd get their money either way.

Freddy's eyes narrowed as he saw their target get out of a blue car that stopped in front of the building he was watching. The young woman looked around when she got out, at least a little wary.

"That's her," Freddy said.

Junior leaned on his door, pulling a nine-mil out of his jacket. He held it flush against his thigh, where he would hold it low until he was right next to her. The kid seemed ready, Freddy thought, and he was ready himself. His was the first car in the line of double-parked cars. He'd be out of there in an instant once the kid popped her, before her people even realized what had happened.

A woman in her late forties exited the driver's side. Dark hair, athletic body for a woman her age. He recognized her from 181st Street. She lived in an apartment over the Groom Team barbershop. *Oh, damn.* Puzzle pieces clicked in Freddy's head. He peered at the older and younger woman.

He clutched Junior's arm, getting a handful of jacket. "Wait a minute, wait a minute."

The kid looked back, his eyes jacked open with adrenaline. "What the fuck? She's gonna go in the building!"

"Wait." Freddy raised his voice, afraid Junior would escape his grip. If he thought Freddy was punking out, Junior would get the job done with or without his groom. This was his big break. Freddy pulled out a burner phone and speed-dialed the last call on it. The phone had been set up that way for quick, untraceable access.

"Yo," Cesar answered. Freddy could hear the roiling of a deep fryer in the background.

"I didn't realize who the woman was until I seen her in person, plus with her mother. She looks different all grown up now. But she's the girl who used to live on One Eighty-One. Hector's girl."

Freddy and Cesar had both gone to elementary school—kindergarten through sixth grade—with Hector. Hector wasn't one of them. He'd always played it straight, never juggled product, never joined the gang after it got organized when Freddy and Cesar were in prison. But they'd all grown up in the hood together. Hector was a geek, fo' sure, but that didn't mean he wasn't their friend. He would stop by to spend a few minutes at the corner with them if he saw them when he came out of the subway. He'd have a plate of food at Freddy's mother's house from time to time, and vice versa. Hector's mother and little sisters always welcomed Freddy in their home, although Freddy rarely went anymore. They never knew the worst things he'd done, but he stayed away. He didn't deserve to be welcome there. He kept the bad stuff from Hector too. Hector wouldn't want to know.

He had no idea whether Hector was still going out with the woman they were assigned to kill, but he knew Hector had loved her when they were in high school, and he was pretty sure they'd had a baby together. Freddy could never cross his friend that way, kill his baby's mother. He didn't think Cesar would either. He hoped.

"Cesar, yo, this shit is out of the question."

Freddy held tight to Junior's sleeve, making sure he didn't charge out and kill the woman while Freddy listened to what Cesar had to say.

64

KATHLEEN WAS WOBBLY when she walked from the car to the glass door of the apartment building. Emily knew Kathleen wouldn't let Emily help her too much, but Emily stayed close just in case. The doctor had said that by the time a person hit sixty-five, a good diet, healthy weight, and exercise could make a twenty-year difference in a person's biological age, and Kathleen was in great shape. Still, Emily worried that Kathleen's injuries had taken more out of her than they could see, the way a broken hip could age old people, making them timid and frail far beyond the physical damage.

Once upstairs, Emily settled Kathleen in the living room with pillows to prop her up. Lauren sat at the opposite end of the couch near Kathleen's feet.

"I agree with Emily," Lauren said. "You need to call a security company until we have a better handle on what's going on. You can't trust cops, fine. Understandable, under the circumstances. But you have to trust someone."

Emily observed her mother, the way she made it seem as if she were mostly worried about Emily's safety, since Emily had insisted on staying with Kathleen for now. But Emily was starting to think her mother's feelings were shifting, taking in the new reality of Kathleen, maybe *wanting* that reality. Emily thought Lauren's loss of her mother had been like an itch she couldn't scratch her whole adult life, an itch so deep she hadn't even known it was there until she got some relief from it.

Emily wondered if there wasn't a little bit of truth in that for herself. Kathleen had been a phantom limb for Emily too. She'd grown up without any extended family, no grandparents, no cousins. Since high school, Hector's family—cousins, grandparents, aunts—had become her extended family. But how long would that last if Hector became serious about another woman? It was surprising that he hadn't already.

Emily pushed away her own unruly train of thought, feeling an infusion of sadness at the idea of losing her connection to Hector's family . . . and to Hector too.

"I have a couple of guys that used to bounce for me in the old days," Kathleen said, her face sagging from exhaustion after the short trip from the hospital. "We took pride in being an all-female operation. It was empowering. Women in charge of their own sexuality. There was esteem in it for the women, especially the ones who'd shed pimps to work with me. But a large man in the picture was a good deterrent in case of a crazy john, and they kept pimps from making a move on my business."

Lauren began to leave the living room. "I'll get some tea." Emily thought her mother just wasn't up to waxing nostalgic about Kathleen's criminal heyday.

Kathleen spoke to Lauren's back. "I can call and see if they're still available for work. That's all I was saying."

Emily digested Kathleen's change. She wasn't used to seeing the self-assured woman so needy for acceptance. It was Lauren who did that to her. Emily wished she could talk some sense into her mother, but she was only now starting to internalize how deeply painful Lauren's loss of her mother had been when she was a kid. And heartbreaking for Kathleen too. Lauren and Kathleen both blamed Kathleen. It was a mess. Emily wished all the tension could dissolve already.

Emily spoke to Kathleen. "I'll bring your phone. You can call your guys. It's in your bag?"

The intercom buzzed, startling Emily as she retrieved Kathleen's pocketbook from a small wooden table in the foyer next to the front door. Emily pressed a button on the intercom on the wall over the table. "Who is it?"

"Hector."

Emily buzzed him in. Fear gripping her, she turned back to her mother. "Why is he here? Why didn't he call? Skye!"

"Skye's fine. She's with Hector's sister." Lauren calmed her quickly.

Emily frowned. "How do you know that?"

"Hector and I were talking earlier," Lauren said mildly.

Emily looked disapprovingly at her mother, who stood in the doorway to the kitchen. "Talking earlier? *You* invited my ex-boyfriend to my house? You can't possibly be matchmaking at a time like this."

"Me?" Lauren put her palm to her chest as if she'd never do a thing like that, even though Hector seemed to spend more time at Lauren's house than Emily did. Those two were definitely in cahoots.

"Is that Skye's father?" Kathleen asked from the living room. "It will be good to meet him."

Emily didn't know what to think about Hector coming here. She felt an unwelcome anticipation about seeing him, plus a bit of resentment. By the time Hector's knock sounded at the door, Emily was pissed at her mother for inviting him—but she was also happy.

Lauren came out of the kitchen to the foyer, both Lauren and Kathleen far more interested in the arrival of Emily's ex-boyfriend than she thought appropriate. "What's up with you guys?" she asked them.

"*Nada,*" Kathleen said. "I'm just interested in the famous Hector."

Kathleen and Lauren cracked up.

"Jesus, there are two of you now."

Emily looked out the peephole to see Hector. She opened the door and took in his smile. Then she lurched backward, an unexpected pressure on her leg. Wet. She looked down.

"Rusty! Rusty, oh my god!" She bent down to take the dog's face in her hands and hugged him. She spoke through laughter as he licked her. "What is he doing here?"

"Can I come in?" Hector kissed Emily on the cheek when she rose and edged past her to come inside without waiting for an answer. He handed Rusty's leash to Emily. "Thank your grandmother."

"Your grandmother bought him for you," Lauren said.

Emily closed the door and found herself dancing across the room to carefully hug Kathleen. "I can't believe it. Skye is going to go through the roof. Thank you!"

CHAPTER

65

THE MAN SAT in City Hall Park. A shady path lined with benches cut across the park between the backs of the nine-teenth-century City Hall and the Tweed Courthouse. His burner phone rang. The fry cook, Cesar. The name of a guy who was born to rule, or at least born to think he should rule. He'd ruled in prison—the most ridiculous concept, if the asshole would just think about it.

"Yo," Cesar said.

"Is it over?"

"Nah, man."

An Asian tourist family—a woman, two ponytailed pre-schoolers, and a grandmother—spotted a black squirrel and ran up to the bench where the man was. They excitedly offered nuts to the animal, and it posed for their photos.

"I've got your money," Cesar said. "You can have it back."

It took a moment to process what he was hearing. The man's spine thrummed with tense electricity. He didn't do well if a restaurant steak came to his table undercooked, or if a woman moved the wrong way when he was about to climax. This offside kick by Cesar could *not* be happening.

"You can come get your money," Cesar said. "The job is canceled."

The man snarled his answer. "There was no fucking cancelation clause in our contract."

"There is *always* a cancelation clause, my man. And if you give me the feeling you got a problem with that, I might cancel *your* ass. I ain't afraid of you."

"What?" The man's face turned red-hot. One of the little tourist girls turned from the squirrel and stared at him. He whisper-growled into the phone, "You trying to stick me up for more money?"

"You are one hardheaded motherfucker. No. It's the girl. We've seen her. She's off-limits. Her and her family. And look, I'm not trying to blow future business opportunities. It's not personal. But one more thing—stay the fuck out of my hood. Don't be sending nobody else in here to do it."

66

EMILY AND LAUREN drove past brownstones and storefronts, the trees feeble and sparse in this part of East Harlem. Lauren had agreed to go with her to Angela's. Emily was glad to have a second person. Two was better than one, for safety and to avoid missing important pieces of information. That's why cops and investigators always worked in pairs.

Kathleen had reached her bouncer friends and they'd agreed to help, but they wouldn't arrive until tonight. Hector had said he had no problem hanging out with Kathleen for a couple of hours until his sister needed to go to work and he had to get Skye. Emily had tried to object, but she'd been touched by his insistence.

Lauren parked in front of a relatively new brown-brick building that took up half the block. Emily knew it was probably a subsidized building for low- or moderate-income people. She'd attended several groundbreakings with the mayor for buildings like this one.

On the third floor, a young girl with dark eyes and a shy smile cracked open the black-metal apartment door. She turned sideways to speak inside: "Grandma, it's two ladies."

"Bring them in," a voice called. Emily smelled broiling meat when they walked inside the open-layout apartment, the kitchen to their right separated from the dining and living area by a breakfast bar. A large pot boiled on the stove, letting off starchy steam.

A heavyset woman with high cheekbones wiped her hands on a dishrag. "Excuse me, my hands are a bit wet. I'm Maria."

Lauren shook her hand, "My mother, Kathleen, was a friend of Sharon's . . . since Sharon's college days."

Maria's eyes hardened as if there'd been a bait and switch. "Angela said *Kathleen* was coming."

"I'm the one Angela met at Bedford," Emily said. "My grandmother just got out of the hospital today. She couldn't come."

"Oh, I'm sorry to hear that." Maria's eyes softened. "I hope it's nothing serious."

"She'll be okay. Thank you."

"Sharon talked about Kathleen," Maria said. "She was like a mother to her."

Emily looked toward Lauren, seeing a flicker of pain in her eyes and the lightest inhale. There was a whole minefield inside her mother. She didn't envy Kathleen if she wanted to navigate that.

Maria motioned them to follow her through the dining room area. A wooden table rested on an IKEA rug of deep-blue and beige squares that left a border of polished wood. In the living room area beyond, the girl who'd answered the door had resumed watching television on a couch next to large windows. Venetian blinds were three-quarters closed to keep out prying eyes from the building across the street. Beside the girl, a younger boy sat with his legs straight out in front of him on the couch.

"Sharon was a beautiful person," Maria said sadly. "She liked it here. She liked my cooking. And she liked being around people. It was better than her empty apartment. Sharon didn't talk about it much, but Angela told me Sharon's apartment was in the best neighborhood, in the lap of luxury. But she preferred a real home. I was happy to have her." Maria walked with them toward the apartment hallway, "Sharon didn't stop coming around after Angela went back upstate. She brought toys for the kids, my favorite pastries from Veniero's in the East Village, and fresh crabs from Citarela's, because she liked how I made them. I didn't need financial help, but she always tried to do something to cheer me up, with Angela gone."

Maria took in Emily, as if assessing her one more time. "Angela said you help raise dogs."

"Yes."

"That program has done so much for Angela. Unfortunately, drugs and alcohol are a powerful demon that dogs don't cure. Though you have to wonder whether things would have been better if she'd been able to get a job working with animals when she came out last time." Maria sighed sadly. "I told Angela I'd let you look around her room for things that might be Sharon's. Let me show you what's there."

They followed Maria down the hall, past several bedrooms, and entered a room with a queen-sized bed, blue walls, and lace curtains. There were a few karate trophies on a shelf and a trade school diploma on the wall.

"I'll leave you be." Maria turned back to them before she left. "Just one more thing. I need to say it. I don't believe what they're saying about how Sharon died. I knew she danced. I know that often goes with prostitution . . . even though it was never discussed with me. But Sharon was no fool. I'm glad she has someone asking questions on her behalf. What the newspaper said about her being killed turning tricks makes no sense to me. So, thank you."

"You're welcome," Emily said. "It's the right thing to do."

Maria turned and left.

"We have to look here." Emily picked up a corner of the mattress.

"Let me help," Lauren said, lifting the side of the mattress with Emily.

A plastic freezer bag lay on the box spring. They could see right away what it held, although the plastic was scratched and dull with age. Inside it, forlorn and lonely, was a tiny hospital bracelet laid flat next to a larger one. Lauren let go of her side of the mattress and pulled out the bag. Emily dropped the mattress and looked on as Lauren unzipped the bag. Lauren pulled out the baby bracelet first and laid it gently in the palm of her hand as if it were the baby itself.

Emily pulled the larger hospital band from the bag and read. "Elyse Mattingly. The mother." Her heart pounded. Her eyes met Lauren's.

"Oh my god," Lauren said. She murmured at the bracelet in her hand. "Baby Boy Mattingly."

Emily gave Lauren the bracelet and pulled her phone out. She Googled *Elyse Mattingly*, even though she already knew the answer. Her hands shook. The whole world would want to know that Sharon was Jackson Mattingly's real mother and that a rich person, probably a powerful person, was his father, a man who might be willing to do anything to keep it a secret, no matter whom he hurt . . . or killed.

Emily struggled for breath as the page loaded onto her phone. She read aloud, " 'Elyse Mattingly. Deceased mother of Jackson Mattingly.' "

"That's the motive," Lauren said, fear etched on her face. "Sharon, the mother. Wayne Carrier, the lawyer who drafted the nondisclosure agreements and maybe set up the whole adoption."

"And Kathleen," Emily said. "The most likely person that Sharon would have told, the person Sharon called after the bombing. Wayne Carrier must have told the father that Sharon called Kathleen that night. If Kathleen had died, everyone who could connect the dots would have been gone."

Lauren thought aloud, "And if anyone investigated, there would be a plausible explanation for their deaths—Kathleen was a criminal in debt, and Wayne Carrier was a pedophile who killed himself when he was caught. Who would look further?"

"Sharon, too," Emily said. "They dumped her body on North Beach to make it look like she was one of the prostitutes killed by a serial killer. The police have clearly grabbed that as an easy explanation. The killer was smart enough not to leave any evidence that would steer the police in any other direction.

"And Mom, what if me seeing the person Sharon went with makes me a threat too? A couple of times, I thought somebody might have been following me. I'm not sure, but . . ." Emily took the bag with the bracelets and put it in her backpack. "We have to call Carl. Sorry, Mom. Mattingly is his case, anyway."

"You're right. This changes everything."

67

THE MAN JUMPED up from his park bench, so absorbed in his rage that he paced mindlessly for a minute. Looking askance at him, the Asian mom ushered her daughters away, leaving the black squirrel on its hind legs, pissed, probably thinking, *Fucking tourists*.

Always a guy who tied up loose ends, the man called and said he wouldn't be back at work after lunch.

He made a second call. According to Kathleen Harris's GPS signal, she had left the hospital and was now back in her home-arrest cuff at the Airbnb. Emily had called out of work and picked up Kathleen from the hospital this morning. She was with Kathleen.

He'd never expected to get his own hands dirty. But it had become increasingly obvious that this matter called for micro-management, family rules notwithstanding. His entire family was at stake, even if some of them failed to comprehend the need for extraordinary measures. But beyond the logical reasons for his actions, his rage drove him. Rage and hatred. He could accept nothing less than complete control of the situation and obliteration of those who could threaten him. Joy swirled in with his rage at the prospect of personally doing something about it. He imagined Jackson had felt the same when he planted his bombs.

Fuck Cesar and his warning to stay out of his neighborhood. Cesar's delusions of grandeur were incredible. Money could buy anything. At the snap of a finger, he could exterminate Cesar's whole street crew without leaving a trace. He could even set it up to incriminate Cesar's rival gang. Hilarious. The city would be grateful. He added Cesar to his mental list of upcoming tasks in need of resolution.

First, the current situation though. Far from resolved. For now.

The man walked the path through City Hall Park toward Broadway, coming back into his calmly rational self with each breath. He'd be ready for action quickly, and he was only mildly concerned about being caught. He'd been bailed out plenty of times, and if everything went to shit, he was confident he'd be bailed out again. The downside risk of doing nothing was far greater than his concern about being caught. Charged up by the potential risks and rewards of his do-it-yourself project, he called his driver to come get him.

68

Emily sat beside Kathleen on the love seat catty-corner to the couch where Kathleen lay propped up with pillows. Hector sat down next to Emily. With Lauren looking on, Emily handed Kathleen the bracelets. "The baby's hospital bracelets."

Kathleen read the bracelets. "*No.*"

"Elyse Mattingly was the adoptive mother's name," Emily said. "The baby was Baby Boy Mattingly. Same birth date as Jackson Mattingly."

"That's a motive for killing anyone who knows about Mattingly's connection to the father," Lauren said.

Emily said to Kathleen, "That's why Sharon wanted to talk to you so badly the night of the subway bombing. She knew Jackson Mattingly was her child."

"It wouldn't have been vigilantes who killed her—nobody knew she was Mattingly's mother," Kathleen mused.

"Only the father knew. It had to be the father," Lauren said.

"No one would want to be outed as the father of a terrorist," Kathleen agreed.

"The father would know his NDA was meaningless if his son was a notorious mass murderer," Emily said. "It would be a huge temptation for anyone who knew about the illegal adoption to make money from that secret. A tabloid or book deal would probably pay as much as the two-million-dollar penalty for breaking the NDA."

"Plus TV appearances and reality shows," Hector said. "People will sacrifice a lot for fifteen minutes of fame."

"Wayne must have known," Kathleen said. "He would have drawn up NDAs for the adoptive parents. But I didn't know about the baby, so why me?"

"Wayne must have told the father that Sharon called you that night and that you were asking questions," Lauren said. "If the father is afraid of people following the bread crumbs to him, you would be a major bread crumb."

"If Client 13 is a psychopath," Emily added, "and the kind of guy who makes sure every angle is covered—like the kind of guy who would have his prostitutes sign NDAs—he'd probably want to get rid of you if you knew any piece of the story."

"Here's the problem with this narrative." Kathleen paused, thinking it through. "I never saw Client 13 like that. A control freak, maybe. Sexually neurotic, probably. But not a psychopath. I always prided myself on being able to read people. And I don't see it. I don't want to ruin the guy's life."

"Psychopaths can be the most charming people," Lauren said, "until they decide to kill you."

"It would certainly destroy his political career," Kathleen said thoughtfully. "He'd have a lot to lose."

Emily leaned over and took Kathleen's hand. "Political career?"

Kathleen looked around the room, meeting eyes with each of them. She breathed deeply, shifting herself on the couch, holding her bandaged shoulder to keep it from jerking. "Emily, Client 13 is the person who got you the interview at City Hall."

"The mayor?" Lauren asked. "That's why Mattingly went to the inauguration?"

"No, no. I don't know the mayor," Kathleen said. "Client 13 is Roger Merritt."

"What?" Emily stood. "No way. Roger? No."

Lauren and Kathleen spoke in tandem: "Why not?"

"I was at City Hall when the news came in about you getting shot." Emily paced a few steps, thinking. She turned to them. "Roger was there when the news station played the surveillance video and I said it was you. I noticed Roger's reaction. He was surprised. And upset. I could see it in his eyes. It was only a split second, but it stuck in my head, because it was strange that he seemed to care. I didn't think he knew you. But of course he did. Yes, he may be the father of a terrorist, but he didn't arrange for you to be shot. He had no idea."

"There has to be another explanation," Kathleen said.

"Carl hasn't called back," Emily said. "This is way more than we should be handling on our own for even another minute. I don't want to call my NYPD contacts."

"Carl needs to be the one to tell the FBI what we learned about Mattingly," Lauren said, "especially because we're involved."

"My calls keep going to voice mail," Emily said.

"He's in court today." Lauren gathered her pocketbook and water bottle. "He probably turned his phone off. I'm going to the courthouse. I know the name of the case he's testifying on. I can be down there and find him in forty-five minutes. That's the fastest way to get him."

"I'll walk you out," Hector said. "I need to get Skye. My sister has to go to work." Hector turned to Kathleen and added, "I feel bad about leaving you. Will you be all right until the bodyguards come?"

"Nothing will happen at home with Emily and Rusty here," Kathleen answered.

Remembering the apartment fire, Emily wasn't so sure of that. But Hector wasn't armed or much of a deterrence anyway. Emily reassured him, "The security guys will be here soon, and my mom will get to Carl in under an hour. I'm sure we'll be okay."

As Hector rose to leave, his phone vibrated on the coffee table, skittering toward the edge. Emily saw the name: *Freddy*. Hector tapped the phone to decline the call from his old friend and put it in the back pocket of his jeans. Emily figured he would catch up with Freddy when he was free, not in a roomful of people dealing with a crisis. She hadn't known he was still in contact with Freddy.

Before Hector left, he hugged Emily and said, "Call me if you need anything."

69

THE APARTMENT WAS quiet and tense after Hector and Lauren left. Emily looked at Kathleen and saw an uneasiness in her grandmother's eyes. She felt the same.

"I'd like to call Roger, but I'm not sure what I'd say," Kathleen said.

"I have your phone book."

"Don't remind me." Kathleen waved her away. "Anyway, I have his contact."

Emily had told Kathleen about taking the photos of her phone book. Kathleen hadn't been thrilled, but she'd only said, "What goes around, comes around," which Emily assumed related to Kathleen spying on her as Sophie.

"We can leave it up to the FBI now," Emily said.

"We won't have a choice," Kathleen agreed. "This is about to become a very different situation. Once people know Jackson Mattingly was Sharon's son and that she was murdered after the attack, the days of no one caring about her murder will be over. I imagine we'll have a houseful of FBI agents soon."

"I need to call in to work to say I'm not coming this afternoon. I feel guilty for not telling Martha about all this. The scandal could blow back on the mayor. But we don't know who's implicated, and I'm sure Carl wouldn't want me to talk to anyone, especially someone who works with Roger."

"Yes, be careful what you say."

"This is too big for Martha to do anything about anyway," Emily said, half to herself, as she located Martha's number in her contacts. "I hope she'll forgive me."

Martha picked up Emily's call. After greetings, she asked, "How's your grandmother?"

"She's out of the hospital." Emily looked over at Kathleen, smiling the way one did when talking about someone next to them. "Can you believe she's out already, after what we saw on the video? The doctor said she's lucky she was in such good health. Listen, I know I said I would come in to work this afternoon, but I don't think I can come until tomorrow."

"Okay, of course. Take whatever time you need." Martha paused. "It's weird, like something's going around. Roger and Max left with a family emergency too."

"That's a big coincidence. Both of them?"

"Don't tell me you don't know," Martha replied.

"Know what?"

"Max is Roger's nephew. Max called me. Then Roger left."

Emily felt as if the floor had been pulled from under her. *Max?* She could see Roger and Max in her mind's eye now. The general shape of their faces. The dimpled chins and stark cheekbones. They did have a family resemblance. And she remembered the flash of anger in Max's eyes the other day, the meanness to it. It had startled her, like seeing a whole other person living inside the guy she knew.

"But I thought a state senator got Max his job."

"That's his stepfather. He's small stuff compared to Roger. I think Max keeps quiet about Roger getting him the job, or people wouldn't take him seriously." Martha lowered her voice conspiratorially. "It must have been Roger who suggested that. I can't imagine Max wanting to keep it quiet . . . Anyway, I shouldn't be gossiping about a subordinate, but you know Max. I don't need to tell you."

No, Emily thought, frightened. *I do not know Max.*

Emily hung up, and memories coursed through her mind. Max was Roger's nephew. She'd told Max about Sharon, about seeing the man Sharon had gone with the night she died. Max had been interested in that, and so interested in Emily. She'd thought his interest was personal, sexual. And she still believed it was. That tension and his anger at her rejections were real.

But he'd also been the first one to see the video of Kathleen getting shot, as if he'd been waiting for it. Roger had been surprised. But not Max. She thought back to that moment; Roger had looked at Max. She'd noticed he'd looked upset but hadn't thought about how he'd looked at Max. She was pretty sure now that a communication had passed between them. She tried to dig in her memory: was it disapproval, anger? Roger had maintained a perfect poker face after that split second, but she was sure of it now: there was something freighted about his eye contact with Max.

Martha had joked with Emily once about Max wanting to be president of the United States someday. It had only been a half joke—he really *did* want to be president one day. That would never happen if Jackson was revealed to be Max's first cousin, and if his political patron, Roger, lost his power too.

70

Carl stepped down from the wooden witness stand, the defendant's eyes following him with a dagger glare. He knew he'd done well for the first few hours of testimony and reveled in his sense of accomplishment. The judge called for a fifteen-minute break before cross-examination. Carl wasn't looking forward to the grueling cross he expected from the defense counsel. He exited the courtroom through double mahogany doors.

"Carl."

He turned, surprised to see a slim figure walking toward him. It was Charlotte, the FBI techie on the Mattingly case. She wore smoky-blue eye shadow today and had a new buzz cut.

"Hey, Carl. How's it going?"

"Good. It went well in there. Are you testifying on a case today?"

"No, no. I wanted to talk to you. Your ASAC said your phone would be off."

Carl smiled with anticipation. "Don't tell me you had a break on the Bitcoin trace?"

"Unfortunately, no. I'm actually here about murder-for-hire sites."

"Oh, yeah, on the dark web," Carl said, mystified about why she'd want to talk to him about that. "Are any of those sites the real thing?"

"Not usually. The website owner takes an order for a hit. The person who orders the hit pays a sizable deposit. The website takes the money in Bitcoin. Most of the time, no hit happens. It's a con. The person ordering the hit doesn't even know who he paid. Can't exactly go to the police to complain. Easy money for a con artist."

"Rough camp for a would-be murderer."

"Sometimes the sites are real, though. Mostly mercenaries for hire. We've infiltrated one of the sites and came across something surprising."

For some reason, Carl found himself bracing for bad news.

"Someone has an interest in paying for a hit on someone you know," Charlotte revealed. "We found out she's related to your wife. Her name's Emily Silverman."

"*What?* That's impossible."

"Looking at her profile, we thought it was odd. She works at City Hall, assigned to the Mattingly case, but the public doesn't know about that, and it's not much of a reason for her to be targeted. There does seem to be a lot of smoke coming from her direction, though. Literally. Her building was recently the target of arson, and the arson suspect was the target of an attempted hit. Do you know anything about it? It's hard to believe it's unrelated."

*   *   *

Emily turned to Kathleen when she got off the phone with Martha. She said breathlessly, "Do you remember my coworker Max? The one who I told that I saw Sharon the night she died?"

"Yes. The gossipy one."

"He's Roger's nephew! I think he had Sharon killed and maybe Wayne, and maybe he tried to have you killed. He has a motive and enough money to wage a war."

"Roger's nephew." Kathleen thought for a moment. "He wasn't the person Sharon went with or you would've recognized him, and he didn't shoot me. So, he hired people?"

"Had to be," Emily said. "Max is from a billionaire family. Maybe he's a billionaire himself. Different rules apply. *Anything* can be bought. Right?"

"Sharon's baby disappeared at birth," Kathleen said. "No record of his adoption at all. It was as if he never existed. A family with that kind of power, money, and intention, it's no doubt they could and would hire killers. And they have a lot more on the line now than they did when the baby was born. You didn't tell Max where we're staying?"

"No, no. Thank god."

Emily's phone buzzed. Hector.

Emily answered. "Hector, you won't believe this."

Hector interrupted her. "Em, I just heard from Freddy. He called to warn me—someone put a hit on you. They tried to send Cesar's boys after you. They backed out when they saw it was you."

Emily's phone vibrated. She frowned, looking at it. "Hold on Hector, hold on. Carl's calling. I'm going to tell Carl."

CHAPTER

71

LAUREN PLANNED TO drop off her car before heading down-town by subway, the fastest mode of travel on a weekday. She drove up Cabrini Boulevard toward the entrance to the parking garage at the complex of buildings where she and Carl lived. As she drove, she thought about how she wasn't worried about just Emily anymore. She wavered between concern for Kathleen and flashes of fury that came over her without warning. She wondered whether Kathleen had struck on the truth. Maybe her rage did relate to the idea that, if she could forgive her mother now, she'd missed out on all those years with her for no reason.

Lauren's phone rang. She pulled the car over at the entryway to the garage and took out her phone. Two green circles were lighting up. Emily and Carl were both calling. Lauren took Carl's call first, relieved to be saved from the delay of going downtown to fill him in.

* * *

Max felt confident it wouldn't be a problem getting into the apartment building. He strode toward the building's outer door, double-timing it for a couple of yards to hold it open for an Orthodox woman wearing a wig and long skirt. No more than twenty-five-years old, she was pushing a stroller and trailed by several children. Max knew he was being filmed by building security cameras, ubiquitous in New York City. He reminded himself not to search the cameras out as he entered the building's vestibule, or he'd give a full view of his face. If he resisted the impulse to look, he felt comfortable that his oversize hat would minimize his risk of identification while also making him fit in well in the neighborhood.

The woman didn't seem to notice his lack of a beard, which an Orthodox man of his age would wear. She was too busy with her Pied Piper line of children. She didn't blink an eye when he followed her inside and through the inner locked door of the building.

She herded her kids down a hallway and up a couple of carpeted steps toward a first-floor apartment. He paused, the air conditioning raising goose bumps at the back of his neck. Not wanting to run into anyone in the elevator, he entered a hallway leading from the opposite side of the lobby. He found a staircase door and climbed four flights, two steps at a time.

He walked down the hallway, looking at the numbers on the apartment doors. He'd only been able to get the building address from the GPS attached to Kathleen's ankle. But having a hacker break into Kathleen's Airbnb account to get the exact apartment number had been as easy as paying a guy to take his SATs as a teenager. He smiled, his heart beating fiercely with anticipation as he approached the apartment at the end of the hall.

*   *   *

Lauren hung up with Carl, unable to obey his direction to stay calm and wait for the FBI to get there. He'd said he'd given the same instruction to Emily.

Lauren's car screeched as she pulled away from the curb and sped uptown on one-lane Cabrini Boulevard. She blew the stop sign on 187th Street, turning right. She honked at a slow car on the quaint block of one-story storefronts.

"Move it. *Move*," she shouted inside her closed car before pulling into the opposite traffic lane, no cars coming.

Timing an oncoming UPS truck that was still a half block away, Lauren ran a red light and made a sharp left onto Fort Washington Avenue. A block ahead, a school bus with its stop sign out was unloading kids, the cars lining up there, waiting. She couldn't get through. She swung the car to the curb in a no-parking zone next to the Chase bank, where her mother had been shot.

She pulled a lever under her dashboard to pop the trunk and shouldered her way out of the car door. A car almost hit her door. It swerved and honked as it passed, then stopped behind the cars waiting for the school bus to finish unloading kids.

Barely registering the near miss, Lauren ran to the back of her car and flipped up the trunk. She leaned in and pulled Carl's mini-safe toward her. She knew the combination to the box and how to use the gun. Carl had insisted she learn, just in case. She punched in the combination sloppily, her fingers trembling with surging blood pressure. It didn't open. She punched in the numbers again and heard the lock disengage. She opened the box and pulled out a shining black nine-millimeter Glock.

Her heart thrashing triple-time inside her chest, she flew down the steep 187th Street staircase, running so fast she barely touched each step. Skipping steps in her panic, she nearly tumbled halfway down. She grabbed the handrail, catching herself, and kept running. At the bottom, she sprinted full out toward the building where Kathleen and Emily were staying.

72

Emily hung up after trying to reach her mother without success. "Carl said to stay here and wait for him. He said we shouldn't move. It will just be a few minutes until agents get here."

Rusty jumped up from where he lay on the floor next to the couch. He ran to the front door and sat. He stared at the door, completely still. Emily had never seen him do that before.

Emily called to him, "Rusty."

His ears only twitched, as if he were acting on a command by sitting there. Emily frowned, unsettled. Rusty had never ignored her before.

"What's going on?" Kathleen asked.

A thought bloomed in Emily's mind. "Rusty?" she tried. The dog whined expectantly.

Emily thought back to a training video she'd seen. It was a Homeland Security video on explosives-detection dogs. The dogs walked an aisle of suitcases with their trainers. If there was even a trace of explosives in a suitcase, they'd sit down in front of it. If they sat down in front of the correct suitcase with explosive materials in it, they got a treat. That was it: smell explosives, sit down, wait for a treat. That was the entire science behind bomb-sniffing dogs.

"I think Rusty smells explosives," Emily hissed.

As if on cue, Rusty began growling, his hackles rising. He sensed a threat now. Enough of a threat to break his training.

"Let's go, let's go," Emily said, moving to help Kathleen up from the couch. "Rusty knows something. We're getting out of here, now! Whoever Max hired probably knows they can get both of us here. We can't wait for Carl."

Rusty was growling, backing up from the door now.

Kathleen grimaced in pain as Emily helped her up. "We can take the stairs to the basement and go out the back."

Rusty started barking at the door. He came back to stand in front of Emily, as if he were protecting her. He was whining toward the door again.

"I think we're too late for the stairs," Emily said.

"Call Carl!"

Emily looked at Rusty. "After. I think we need to go now."

Kathleen pointed to the living room window. "The fire escape."

Emily pulled the window open, no gate covering it. "What about Rusty?" Emily asked, her heart hammering inside her rib cage. "We can't leave him."

"Just help me get out the window. I can make it down the stairs myself," Kathleen said, taking Emily's hand. She grunted with pain and climbed out.

Grateful for every bit of deadlifting she'd done in the gym, Emily bent her knees and crouched low to pick up the seventy-pound dog. Rusty quieted now, calmly allowing himself to be moved. If he were any other dog, squirming and anxious, Emily didn't think she'd have been able to do it. But it seemed Rusty was finally satisfied he'd been heard. Emily staggered to the window and lowered herself to sit sideways on the sill, ready to swing her leg over. But Rusty scampered out of her arms and half jumped, half fell onto the fire escape grating. He righted himself and scrambled to his feet.

Emily scanned the living room before she left. "Where's my phone? Shit! Start down, Kathleen. I need to get my phone." She needed to stay in contact with Carl.

"No, come now!"

Ignoring Kathleen's objection, Emily ran a few steps back into the living room. She saw her phone on the dining room table and ran to grab it.

She heard a sound at the front door, a scrape. She paused, frozen. Someone was definitely there, and they weren't ringing the bell.

*   *   *

Max leaned his backpack against the door to Kathleen's apartment. It was ironic that he'd brought a bomb much like Jackson's, powerful enough to obliterate several apartments. He'd always had a thing for fire and explosives. Like cousin, like cousin. He grabbed the burner phone from his pocket that would trigger the explosives.

He felt a moment of great peace, knowing he would be rid of all the complications in his life in the next few seconds. He imagined Jackson had felt that way too—except Max had no intention of dying for the cause. He had big plans for his life, something Jackson had obviously lacked or hadn't cared enough about.

Max flipped open the cheap cell phone, ready to set the timer for forty seconds and double-time it to the stairs.

He heard a woman's voice shout behind him, "Drop it, motherfucker! I'll fucking kill you!"

Shit.

He glanced over his shoulder. A woman, red-faced, breathing hard. Gun out, pointed at him in a two-handed grip. Her rigid arms quivered slightly with adrenaline. Before he could fully analyze how he would handle the interruption, the stairwell door opened farther down the hall, behind her.

"FBI. Turn around. Hands up! Hands *up*! Put down your weapon!"

Max froze. *Jesus Christ.* Not looking at the cops, keeping his eyes on the apartment door with his back to them, Max heard them approach, the rustling of their clothes, weapons rising.

The woman shouted behind her at the voices, "I'm Lauren Cintron! My daughter is in there!" Her weapon clattered dully to the carpet, tossed away from her.

"Get on the ground, hands out."

Max didn't know whether they were talking to him or Lauren, probably both. His mind flipped through the options in an instant, his thinking preternaturally keen.

Go out like a boss with a bang? Ignite the explosives? No. He'd been saved by the family in the past. He didn't need to die here. If he surrendered now, he pictured house arrest in the Hamptons, awaiting trial for the explosives he possessed. The charges might even be watered down to harassment. If not, he could still escape. A private jet would whisk him away to an island paradise beyond the reach of extradition. The family owned several islands of the sort. He'd made a big tactical mistake. But he did not want to die. The family would take care of this.

He looked over his shoulder at the FBI agents now. Men and women were running the long hallway toward him, spit-shouting with guns pointed at him, "Hands up, hands up!"

Lauren was crawling backward, scrambling toward the line of cops.

Max raised his hands. Turned. He saw the barrels of their guns, then their faces. A familiar face was in the crowd of agents. A tall man with glasses. He met Max's gaze. Max felt a moment of relief, as if he were receiving a message from his family: everything would be all right. The tall agent was one of theirs.

A flash from the tall agent's gun. An earsplitting blast. Heat seared and ripped Max's belly. He jolted backward, flying off his feet, his back banging against the door. He looked in the direction of the tall agent.

One of the other agents, a Black man, yelled at the tall man, "What the fuck?"

Max couldn't hear it through his ringing ears, but he could see the agent's words leave his lips.

Max fell, realizing as he hit the floor that he wouldn't make it out of this hallway. Blood spurted from a gaping chasm in his torso. Pain surged through him in waves. But he still gripped the phone in his fist. They didn't know he was armed, didn't know his backpack was a bomb.

Go out like a boss. While he still had the chance, he pressed the call button with his thumb, bypassing the timer.

The backpack exploded, incinerating Max and blowing through the apartment door in a ball of roaring fire.

73

Lauren felt hands on her, helping her up. She heard muffled voices talking to her. She made her way silently downstairs, ears ringing, dizzy, confused, dimly aware of arms around her, guiding her. Her head and chest ached from the force of the explosion. She breathed in the smell of her own singed hair. The skin of her hands pulsed. Burned.

As the fog in her head dispersed ever so slightly, the noise in her head became louder: *Emily. Oh god. Emily!*

Carl's partner, Rick, was with her. They were walking through the lobby. He was talking to the other agents. "She's Carl Cintron's wife."

The agents knew Lauren's daughter and mother were the targets. An agent walked by holding a plastic bag with Lauren's gun.

Lauren's mind came into focus, the words bursting out of her. "*Emily.*" She grabbed Rick, sobbing. "Where is she?"

Sirens wailed in the distance, coming closer. Police cars. Ambulances. Fire trucks.

Rick tried to calm her. "Carl's on his way, Lauren. He'll be here in a minute."

"Oh no, oh no," she keened. Rick's response sounded like confirmation that Emily and Kathleen were dead. Her legs buckled. Rick and his new partner held her up and led her outside.

A blaring fire truck appeared, stopping in front of the building as Lauren and the two agents entered the fresh air. Firefighters jumped out. Unmarked police cars and SWAT trucks screeched to a halt, filling the block at angles. Their lights strobed the street packed with emergency personnel. Onlookers had begun to gather and mill around among the first responders, as no perimeter had yet been set up by the cops.

Smoke hovered over the top of the building. Lauren's vision was narrow and dark with dread and shock, and she panted with panic. Rick and his new partner each had an arm around her waist to keep her walking toward an ambulance, her hands held out in front of her, red and blistering.

On the sidewalk, cops ran by. They formed a line facing the milling crowd, shouting for onlookers to step back from the sidewalk, to let the firefighters work. The crowd backed up.

"You'll have to wait," a cop said to an Orthodox man who was trying to get around the barricade, calling out toward the building in frantic Yiddish.

Lauren pulled herself away from Rick and his partner. Her eyes blurred with tears, she turned 360 degrees, scanning the crowd for Emily and Kathleen. Tenants were streaming out the front door of the building, mostly mothers and children. One group ran to the Orthodox man, who embraced them and picked up a toddler. Emily and Kathleen weren't there.

"No, no, no." Lauren replayed the blast in her mind, the apartment door blown away, the fireball, the man's body consumed. Had that happened to Emily? Her cry came from deep in her belly: "*No.*"

"Come on, Lauren." Rick took her arm again, trying to steer her toward an ambulance attendant who was approaching them with a wheelchair.

Lauren was about to go with them when she saw, out of the corner of her eye, a shadow moving on the sidewalk. She froze. A dog. Her eyes focused on him, ten yards away. No leash. Covered with soot.

"Rusty! Rusty!" she called, her eyes searching around frantically. Moving toward him, Lauren shouted again, "Rusty!"

Rusty stopped. He turned back and took a few steps toward the side of the building, where an alley separated it from the brick wall of the next building. A group of EMS workers were waiting on the sidewalk there for clearance to go inside the building to retrieve any injured. Lauren ran to follow the dog.

A woman came around from behind the crowd of EMS workers. Lauren took in the sling on the woman's arm. Her head was bandaged. Kathleen. Rusty ran toward Kathleen but kept going, passing her. Emily emerged from the alley behind Kathleen. Rusty fell in beside Emily, and she put her hand on his head.

Kathleen, Emily, and Rusty, all three covered in soot, walked toward Lauren.

74

A WEEK AFTER THE explosion, Emily and Kathleen walked furtively, following Hector through the labyrinthine basement of Lauren's building. They passed a laundry room and reached a metal door under a red exit sign.

Hector opened the door and peered out. "All clear."

It was nighttime. They took dimly lit garden paths behind the apartment complex, scurrying from the cover of Lauren's building to the cover of the next. Emily glimpsed news vans still parked out front on Cabrini Boulevard. The reporters were waiting for a chance to see Emily. She'd been holed up, unable to go anywhere after the news had hit the internet about Max's motives for blowing up the Airbnb and trying to kill her and her grandmother. The media loved the story. It had trended on Twitter for days, under #LoveBomber.

Emily could barely believe it when she watched the FBI's New York director announce that Max, a young billionaire and member of a powerful family, had become dangerously obsessed with her. The director had told reporters, "Max Dawson also became fixated on the influence Emily Silverman's grandmother had on her. Dawson hired a foreign mercenary to set Kathleen and Emily's building on fire and made multiple attempts to assassinate them."

Kathleen's criminal case had been dismissed, although the police hadn't yet caught the actual arsonist or the shooter. The police said Max had been in contact with a Russian hacker, who they believed had drained Kathleen's bank accounts. Unfortunately, it was doubtful Kathleen would ever get her money back. She and Emily might never get their old life back either.

The case had been wrapped up with a neat bow. Within twenty-four hours of Max's death, his family had released a statement about him being off his bipolar meds. The family spoke to the police about his troubled past—harming pets and obsessing over girls who weren't interested in him. The family thought he'd improved after reaching adulthood, but he'd only become adept at covering up his conduct. They'd issued an apology to all those harmed and announced that they would compensate the injured, as well as Kathleen, the tenants of her building, and the Airbnb owner and two of his neighbors whose apartments had been destroyed. Thankfully, no one had suffered permanent injuries in the explosion.

Every time the media mentioned Max's family, they were described as "a well-known philanthropic family." The media treated them as Max's victims too—undoubtedly their PR team at work.

There had been no public report about a connection between Max and Sharon's or Wayne's death, or Max's connection to Jackson Mattingly, although Kathleen and Emily had both told the FBI what they'd learned. The hospital bracelets had been destroyed in the explosion.

Carl's car was double-parked on Cabrini Boulevard in an amber puddle of streetlight, a block south of Lauren's building. Carl was in the driver's seat and Lauren rode shotgun, her hands covered with bandages. She had second-degree burns that would heal. Her hair had burned on one side of her head too, so she'd gotten it cut short into what Emily playfully called a Jewfro.

Kathleen, Emily, and Hector piled into the back seat. Emily and Kathleen ducked down when they passed the gaggle of reporters gathered outside Lauren's apartment building on the one-way street. Lauren had signed a one-year lease for a new temporary apartment, having to use her name to avoid the landlord leaking that it was Kathleen and Emily who would be living there. They were headed there now, trying to keep the location a secret.

Hector had brought Skye to his mother earlier, keeping her away in case they failed in their attempt to get Emily and Kathleen out unnoticed. He would bring her and Rusty to the new apartment afterward. Hopefully, by the time Kathleen and Emily returned to Kathleen's building after the renovation, the media would have mostly forgotten about them.

"When will the FBI talk about Max's relationship to Jackson Mattingly?" Emily asked Carl, frustrated that the FBI had focused on Max's crush on her and ignored that he was probably a serial killer. Carl had been working overtime since the explosion, and she'd barely had a chance to see him. "They were first cousins."

"I don't know what the Bureau is looking at," Carl said. "There's a cone of silence around me, standard operating procedure when an agent has a personal connection to people involved in a case. I've got to believe they're still looking at it."

"There are threads on Reddit questioning why an FBI agent shot Max," Hector said. "They're saying Max had a secret that someone didn't want revealed."

"I'm sure there's a thread on Reddit for every police-involved shooting," Carl insisted. "Max was shot by accident by a hyperactive agent who got ahead of himself. Besides, with the hospital bracelets incinerated, there's no proof that Sharon was Jackson's mother. And even if there was, it wouldn't prove that Roger Merritt was his father."

"The FBI would need probable cause and a judge to sign a warrant to get a DNA test on Roger," Lauren added.

"A DNA test that showed Jackson and Max were first cousins would prove Max's real motive to hire someone to kill Sharon, Wayne, and us," Emily insisted. "The cops may not believe Wayne was murdered, but Sharon's murder is still unsolved."

"Maybe they checked, and Roger wasn't the father after all," Carl said. "Then the two wouldn't be cousins. I mean, no offense, but Sharon *was* a prostitute."

"I don't believe she was having sex with anyone but Roger during that time," Kathleen said. "Of course, nobody would pay attention to a madam's character reference for a prostitute."

Over the last several days, Kathleen and Carl had warmed up a lot toward each other. To Emily's relief, Kathleen's relationship with Lauren was beginning to thaw too. They'd barely argued during the time Kathleen and Emily had been holed up in Lauren and Carl's apartment.

Lauren looked back at Emily. "You told the FBI our theory about a motive. It's over. Just remember, you can't publicly accuse Roger of fathering Jackson Mattingly. He wasn't the one who tried to kill any of you, so there's no reason to push it. The legal fees from Roger's defamation suits would wipe us out."

"I agree with your mother on this one," Kathleen said. "Roger may have arranged a very coldhearted adoption, but it's not as if he sold the boy to a sex slavery ring. Jackson Mattingly was adopted by a perfectly normal family that wanted him. Roger doesn't deserve to be marked for life because of what Jackson or Max did, and Max is dead, so how important is it to tie Max to Sharon's death?"

Carl steered the car onto the Henry Hudson Parkway, which would bring them to their new apartment near Inwood Hill Park.

"Okay, I get it." Emily leaned into Hector, who put his arm around her shoulders. She covered his hand with hers. "I'm just glad it's over."

75

A MID A STATELY group of black-clad mourners, Roger walked
from the burial site toward a line of SUVs, limos, and luxury vans. It had been a quiet service attended by close family
who would mourn Max no matter what he'd done . . . or what
they'd done to him.

Their family had a history of men like Max. And Jackson.
And him. Even those in the family who lacked *the propensity* or
the gene, as they alternately called it, always knew the family's
power lay with those wily, ruthless ones: the income producers.
So the brothers, sisters, and cousins nailed up the storm shutters
and protected the gifted ones when they acted out.

Unless they couldn't.

Times had changed. Video cameras everywhere. DNA evidence. It wasn't so easy to cover things up when those with the
gene lost control. It was the job of each generation's gifted to
groom the next, but it was hugely challenging to rein in the
impulses of the young ones until they matured enough to strate-
gically control themselves. Especially in the modern age. In the
final analysis, no one person was more important than survival
of the family.

So, sadly, an errant shot by a trigger-happy FBI agent had
ended Max's life. Internet conspiracy theorists swarmed the story
like annoying gnats. But they'd come nowhere near the truth.

The family's own publicists had anonymously planted some of the most outrageous conspiracy theories on Reddit. Once Max was dead, Roger had only needed to make sure the FBI never ran Max's DNA profile through its database, which would have led them to his genetic relationship to Jackson. Since there had been no reason to run the DNA of a dead perpetrator whose motive was clear, it had taken Roger relatively minor effort to have his people inside the Bureau guide that portion of the investigation.

Roger strode down a grassy slope to the private road that wended through the cemetery. Drivers bustled out of their seats to open the passenger doors.

There hadn't been an extraordinary amount of mainstream speculation. The family lawyers, publicists, and well-placed allies had provided plausible explanations for Max's actions and swiftly spun and killed news stories as they arose. Solid planning was Roger's forte. Long before Jackson bombed the subway, Roger had obliterated any possible connection to the boy who sought to be part of the family. Roger's agents had paid the genetic relatives handsomely to take down their family trees from the various DNA websites and sign an NDA. Then accounts had been opened in the names of Roger's nephews and children using false DNA. He'd ensured that Jackson's DNA would never be linked in any meaningful way to the family.

Thankfully, Jackson had used a pseudonym and covered his online tracks for his own DNA searches, so no one Jackson had spoken with knew he was the Subway Bomber, or that he had any relation to the requests they received to take down their information. None of them had any idea that they could peddle that information.

Sharon had been a clean kill too. No one would question or find leads on her. Roger had used professionals. True professionals. He didn't make the kinds of mistakes Max made. Booking mercenaries on the internet? Giving a contract hit to a street gang? That was some sort of generational idiocy.

Roger's mistake had been confiding in Max about Jackson before the subway bombing. He'd had more of a bond with Max than with his legitimate children, who didn't have the gene. He'd recognized Max from the first time a pet went missing from the estate when Max was just a preschooler. The blood that traveled through Max's veins had traveled through the centuries, making their family the most feared inquisitors, land barons, and plantation owners. But Max had been arrogant, thinking he knew better than Roger when he was instructed to leave well enough alone after Sharon was killed. Wayne Carrier would never have exposed Roger, lest he be disbarred for his involvement with Jackson's illegal adoption. It wasn't just the NDA that bound Wayne. And Kathleen wouldn't have destroyed Roger even if she found out he'd fathered a terrorist with Sharon. Not unless she had hard evidence that Roger had killed Sharon. She would never have gotten that.

But Max had gone rogue, insisting on a scorched-earth approach. He'd thought Roger was too soft, over the hill. Max had deluded himself into believing that Roger needed his help, a young man's courage to handle the situation. Max was sure he needed to get rid of anyone who could threaten the family. But Max had gotten it wrong. Roger was smart, not soft.

Roger sighed as he entered a Rolls Royce to return to the family estate. His children, whiny and coddled by their mother, climbed into the back seat after him. With Max all but forgotten in the media, Roger looked out the window, relieved that he could return to his life. He looked forward to focusing on Sullivan's presidential campaign again. He'd lay low for a few days as a grieving uncle, but it was time to get back to work.

76

Before

J ACKSON LOOKED AROUND his kitchen. The sound of dawn birds floated in through a screened window. A crow screamed at an interloper, probably a hawk that dared sit on a branch of its tree. Jackson identified with that hawk. He was mightier and wilier, catching and killing, not feasting on leftovers like most people.

Jackson's duffel bag was packed, ready to go. He wouldn't leave a good-bye note for his mother, who would still be snuffling softly in sleep across the hall. She would get the point in a few hours. He set the timer for the explosives he'd reserved for her and his dad, then hefted the duffel bag onto his shoulder and headed out into the pink dawn.

He drove south for twenty minutes until he reached the Peekskill Starbucks. He stopped outside the store, pulled his laptop from the bag, and logged into the shop's Wi-Fi. He wanted no trace of his internet activities that might result in a premature release of information. He wanted everything to go according to *his* plan.

He logged into a site used to schedule tweets to be sent automatically. You could schedule tweets weeks in advance.

Jackson drafted a tweet and reread it to make sure there were no typos. No need to look like an idiot in his last bequest. He copied and scheduled it to go out as individual tweets directly to the *New York Times*, *New York Post*, and *Daily News*. He added the *Beacon Free Press*, mostly for the irony. Small-town boy makes it big.

In the tweet, he said simply, "I, Jackson Mattingly, am the son of Roger Merritt."

Jackson provided his XFactor username and password and a screenshot. He added a link to a clip of the audio of his only conversation with his father at the townhouse. It was the portion in which Roger all but admitted to being his father, the moment when Jackson almost thought Roger would claim him.

It was Roger who was the fool. He'd underestimated Jackson. And Roger would be sorely surprised when he learned that Jackson wasn't stupid enough to kill himself while leaving his asshole father unscathed. He would never give Roger that gift. He hated too deeply for that.

Jackson clicked into a blue calendar and selected a date two months in the future. That would give his father time to stew on how fucked up his life would be if Jackson's relationship to him ever came out. Roger's squirming anxiety from the first time he learned of Jackson's attack would turn into a long, razor-wire strangulation. All on Jackson's terms.

Jackson clicked SCHEDULE PUBLICATION.

He closed the laptop and breathed in. He felt a deep satisfaction that finally soothed the fury that had burned hot in his belly since the day he'd met his father. He drove south in the car that Roger's Bitcoin had bought. Jackson's only regret was that he wouldn't be around when dear old dad realized that Jackson had beaten him.

ACKNOWLEDGMENTS

To Crooked Lane—especially Katie McGuire, Melissa Rechter, Madeline Rathle, Rachel Keith, Rebecca Nelson and Jenny Chen—for helping to bring *Gone by Morning* to life.

To Writers House, particularly Susan Ginsburg and Catherine Bradshaw, for their undying support. I am deeply grateful.

To Dawn Walker and Sheila Stainback, who made sure I had the facts right about a press officer's life at City Hall. Any mistakes are my own.

To Ellen Weinstat and Katy Garrabrant, trusted first readers and much more.

To my Thursday writer friends for holding my hand during the roller coaster ride. A special thanks to Lawrence Block for his gentle prodding, guidance, and grimaces over the years.

To all my friends and fans who read, review, comment, share, and tell their friends about my books. It is a great pleasure to live in fictional worlds with you. I thank you for your support.

Finally, my heartfelt thanks to Kai, Shane, and Jerome Miller, my cheer squad and pandemic coworkers, for all your unconditional love, encouragement, and forbearance. I love you guys so much.

HOW YOU CAN HELP

To help previously incarcerated people regain stability and receive a second chance at life, please visit The Fortune Society at https://fortunesociety.org.

To support an end to violence against sex workers, please visit Sex Workers Outreach Project at https://SWOPUSA.org.